The Year of Second Chances

Also by Lara Avery

YA NOVELS

The Memory Book

A Million Miles Away

Anything But Ordinary

A Novel

The Year of Second Chances

Lara Avery

wm
WILLIAM MORROW
An Imprint of HarperCollins*Publishers*

This is a work of fiction. Names, characters, places, and incidents are products of the author's imagination or are used fictitiously and are not to be construed as real. Any resemblance to actual events, locales, organizations, or persons, living or dead, is entirely coincidental.

HarperCollins books may be purchased for educational, business, or sales promotional use. For information, please email the Special Markets Department at SPsales@harpercollins.com.

FIRST EDITION

Designed by Leah Carlson-Stanisic
Art by Pingebat/Shutterstock, Inc.

Library of Congress Cataloging-in-Publication Data has been applied for.

ISBN 978-0-06-327375-7

23 24 25 26 27 LBC 5 4 3 2 1

To Dane, my love

We know what we are, but know not what we may be.

—Ophelia, *Hamlet* Act IV, Scene 5,
William Shakespeare

Robin L, 33, Brokenridge

My little brother was waiting for me on my front porch, sun streaking behind him, turning the chipped white house and barn behind it pink and gold. I'd texted him my ritual plans, but his visit was a surprise. I should stop calling Theo my *little* brother. He's twenty-three. He's taller than me. But I can't help it: he'll always be a baby in my arms.

"Look who it is," I called from the driveway, loading a grocery bag into the crook of my arm.

He glanced up from his phone, curls framing his face. "I'm gonna help with the lasagna."

"You mean you're going to *eat* the lasagna?"

"Right."

It was a Friday, so I didn't feel too bad going home right at five. *Sorry*, I'd imagined telling anyone I met on my way out of the office. *Gotta go beat the shit out of some gluten.* Truth be told, I had kind of hoped to run into someone. Someone to ask me how to run a simple function in Excel so I could sit down for a minute and enjoy their little pops of satisfaction as I helped them solve their problems. But the carpeted alleyways between cubicles remained empty—people finishing meetings, people off to their cabins—and I rode the I-35 bumper to bumper, trapped in a time machine.

The secret to Gabe's lasagna was handmade pasta. Multiple varieties of cheese. Four kinds, if you have them, and I had them. Ripe tomatoes from the garden. None of these are secrets. Any Ina Garten fan will tell you the same. But my husband liked to wield his knowledge as if it were passed down to him on some ancient scroll—he loved to know how to do things, even things he did poorly, muttering memorized instructions to himself with a little satisfied smile, savoring the words *blanch the tomatoes and remove the peel* as if he were a newly ordained wizard uttering a spell.

Now, with his chicken scratch laid out on the kitchen island next to the ingredients, Theo and I followed the recipe carefully.

Tonight it would be a year, and everyone in Sisters in Grief had said they did a one-year ritual, and whatever my widow-support group said they were doing, I was also doing—or at least whatever things I had the energy to do since I'd joined, which were not that much. Mostly I talked and ate and drank with them at various widows' houses, appreciating that I never had to worry whether I was piling on too much as we commiserated about taking care of ill spouses, never having to fear that people would think I was too obsessed with my old life (I was), all of us braiding our old threads of memory, unraveling them, and weaving again, like a bunch of Penelopes forever waiting for their Odysseuses. I had also gone to my own counselor for a while, but I was deemed well-adjusted and decided to release myself. I'd been acquainted with grief a long time, anyway. Dad died when I was eighteen. And there had been that chilly morning near Easter a couple years ago when the doctor called to inform us that the tumor in my husband's liposarcoma had metastasized.

After, the prospect of death had chipped away at the next eighteen months, hollowing out our days. When it came, it was not the earth-shattering bomb it could have been—the world had already crumbled. My subsequent year without Gabe has been more like a medieval torture. Sometimes I'm in howling pain, being disemboweled, and sometimes I'm sitting in my cell—the tiny, creaky corner bedroom of an 1840s farmhouse—sweaty and alone, wondering how long the relief will last.

I slapped the dough on the counter so loud that Theo muttered, "Get it out, girl." Together we ran the gloopy blob through the rickety old pasta maker we'd inherited from my parents' restaurant, watching it flatten into a satisfying ribbon.

I'd almost gotten in a fender bender on the way home. Sometimes, for my own safety, I would have to turn up the volume on a Britney Spears song and belt along about the taste of somebody's lips, stretching my voice so high my throat began to hurt. It was always in the car when loneliness and helplessness would sneak up on me, my mind having nothing to latch on to as I drove the same old routes, no column of numbers to comb through, no budgetary puzzles to solve. Singing took everything buzzing and snapping in my brain and chest and forced it into words. That they weren't even my words, that they weren't even applicable to my situation, was the point. No memories to go along with the pink-tinted girl power, none of my story, none of my baggage. Sometimes the voices of pop stars were the only things that held me to the earth, those three-minute containers about nights out at the club keeping me from sliding off the plane of linear time into a thirty-car pileup.

I stirred sauce as Theo read me jokes from Twitter, watching the tomato-red bubbles glisten and pop.

Gabe had stepped away from the town's annual Easter Saturday parade to take the call from our doctor, I remember. It was unusual to get a call on a weekend, but the doctor had wanted to call us with the results of the biopsy immediately after she'd received them. Gabe had removed his ears—as the mayor and grand marshal, he had decided it was his duty to dress as a giant white bunny—and when the call was over, he looked at me, said, "That's that," and proceeded to lead a line of ribbon-twirled fire trucks, tulip-painted mail trucks, and little kids in their church finest looping around the town square. I'd tried not to cry as I watched him, the world's friendliest Grim Reaper, wondering how he could possibly celebrate spring as he marched toward the opposite. But that was Gabe.

Since then, every day, maybe even twice or three times a day, the air around my palms and chest would start to feel pressurized, as if a substance were being sucked out of it. I'd be dizzy for a few minutes, but in the space of a few heartbeats, coherence would return, and I'd still be standing. If Gabe were nearby, I'd hold on to him as if he would soon dissolve. Now, I had to pretend he was still there to hold on to, and that was how I was still waking up, still going to work, still leading meetings about changes in corporate tax code. I held on to routine. Objects. My mouse. My steering wheel. Somehow I was still here, and the one-year ritual should be something meaningful to commemorate Gabe, the other members of the Sisters in Grief had mentioned, something to show him, wherever he was, that I had not forgotten him. As if I could ever forget Gabe. As if anyone who knew him ever could.

I divided the fancy deli sausage I'd bought into chunks, handing each one to Theo to layer with the noodles and the cheese. Gabe used to weigh each tiny portion, insisting that it would be noticeable if the perfect ratio of sausage to sauce was off, even by a fraction of an ounce.

"Hang on," I told Theo, holding my hand over the dish.

"What?"

"Maybe we should put the portions on the scale. Gabe always weighed the sausage."

"Uh, no. I am not going to *pick* pieces of sausage out of this lasagna. No."

"But then we're not executing the recipe exactly as he would have wanted it."

"So? Gabe doesn't care."

"But . . ." I swallowed the swell of emotion rising in my throat. I tried to breathe as a small something inside me burst. A bit of nonsense and sadness I had not entertained in a while. The lasagna was a ritual, but it would not conjure him, I reminded a childish part of me inside. He wouldn't be coming back. Theo proceeded.

As I tore basil leaves to sprinkle on the top layer, my phone rang.

I ignored it. Could be a relative. Could be Gabe's parents, Juana and Jim, though we had made plans to speak on Sunday afternoon. Could even be some constituent or volunteer, who held my hand last year at the church, looking at me with silent, wet eyes, as if they knew me, as if Gabe belonged to them, too.

As the phone continued to ring, Theo glanced at me.

"I don't feel like it tonight."

He shrugged, looking back at his task. "I didn't say anything."

But it rang again. I opened my messages to find a frantic series of texts. Hey love are u home from work?? Accidentally left my keys inside the restaurant. Call when you can.

"Mom locked herself out," I told Theo, rolling my eyes, relieved it wasn't something more serious.

Theo erupted in laughter. "Classic. Put it on Speaker."

My mother's smoke-crackled voice resounded after the first ring. "Oh, my gosh," she said instead of a greeting.

"Did you check your apron?" I asked.

"Of course I checked my apron."

"What happened?"

"Well, geez, we were slow tonight, so Nance and I were relaxing at the bar . . ." Nancy Kelleher had been Mom's best friend since childhood. By day, a legal secretary at the courthouse. By night—or most nights, at least—she sat at the bar at the Green River, keeping Mom company while she manned the host stand.

"Focus, Mom." Theo said aloud what I was thinking.

"Is that Theo?"

"Hi, Mom."

"My baby boy! I didn't know you were in town. Don't you have classes?"

"It's the weekend," he said toward the phone by way of an explanation. Theo was working his way toward an anthropology degree. Slowly. He avoided my eyes. "Anyway."

"Yeah, so, I had gotten that new pinot noir that Bill and his wife, what's her name . . ."

"Carol," I muttered.

"Carol. So Bill and Carol had recommended this wine. You know, when they came up from the Cities. They said, 'Margie, you have to have proper wine, not this cheap stuff,' so I said, 'Sure' . . ."

I made a *get on with it* motion toward the phone. Theo, on the other hand, seemed to be thoroughly enjoying this. He would often get my mom talking and post it on social media—there were quite a few Margie stans among his college friends.

"Mom," I interrupted, "why are you locked out?"

"Oh! Yeah. Nance and I were having a sample of the wine, and we stepped out for a smoke, and I'm seeing now I forgot my keys inside."

"What do you mean, *a sample*?"

"Taste of the bottle. You know, to pair it with the right dish."

Theo snorted. "You sound like you had a big ol' taste, Ma."

"Once Nance and me get to talking, well, you know. I had her rolling silverware with me, and she was telling me about that bear they saw at their cabin in Four Oaks . . ."

Theo was right, Mom's speech was a bit wonky. It was a familiar sound to both of us. My mom's tipsy lilt was one of the sounds of our childhood, me a preteen, Theo in preschool, my parents stumbling in the foyer, whispering to each other as they tried not to wake us after they'd "closed up the restaurant" with their friends. Sometimes I couldn't get Theo back to bed, so we'd all sit at the kitchen table in the middle of the night, eating crackers slathered with peanut butter, the two of them red-faced and relaying to us the funny thing Nance had said, or the way Gus had fallen when they'd cleared the tables out for a dance floor. "So I must have turned the latch out of habit or something," Mom was saying.

"What about the back door?" I asked.

"That's always locked automatically, you know that."

"You didn't prop it open?"

"I didn't prop it, no. Or maybe Rick kicked out the prop, I don't know. But if you could get down here . . . It's getting chilly."

"Can you?" I whispered to Theo, making a driving motion.

"Jay drove me," he whispered back. *Sorry*, he added silently, doing a theatrical cringe.

A giant sigh I'd been holding escaped.

"Hello?" my mom called from the other end.

"Of course," I said to her. "We're on our way."

"Oh, you're my angels. Love you bunches."

"Bunches," Theo echoed. I hung up.

Theo poked at his phone, making a face. "Ugh, you're going to hate me, but I'm supposed to meet high school friends at the Red Lyon."

"Totally. I'll drop you at the bar after."

"Ugh, thank you. Sorry."

"Stop saying sorry." I scanned the spare keys near the back door. "So you and Jay are . . . ?"

"We're talking," he said as he typed a reply to his friends. "We're enjoying each other's company. Nothing serious."

I called something back to him, lost in a memory. It had been a while since I'd had a reason to look at the spare keys. They hung in two rows on a jagged section of wood, a rack I had made for Gabe for one of his birthdays.

"You find 'em?" Theo was standing at the counter, slipping on his shoes.

We had so many sets of keys—people seemed to trust us with their homes—we had to color-code them with electrical tape to keep them organized. Warm colors for my family, purples and blues for his, black for his bike locks. From the row, I nabbed a set of green. Green for the Green River Supper Club. "Geez." I gestured to the key rack. "I should get rid of some of these."

Theo looked uncomfortable. "Want to come out with me? Get your mind off . . ." Theo gestured vaguely to the key rack ". . . things?"

I touched my eyes to make sure nothing was coming out. Dry. "Nah. I'll be fine. I'm actually looking forward to a little downtime."

"What about the lasagna?"

We both looked at the meticulously layered pile of noodles and sausage and cheese on the center of the counter, ready for the oven. With Gabe, it would last two nights and a lunch, tops. Alone, it would feed me for weeks. "I'm gonna stick it in."

"Without preheating?" Theo raised his eyebrows. "Someone's feeling wild tonight."

"Woo-hoo," I droned. I lifted the pounds-heavy dish, turned on the oven, and set the timer on my watch.

When I straightened, Theo had a small, sad smile. He looked like our dad when he smiled like that. "You know I love you, Robbie."

I grabbed his shoulders and gave him a push out the door. "Love you, too, ding-dong."

The last traces of September sun were disappearing as Theo and I pulled up to the Green River Supper Club, the best restaurant in town, or so it claimed in fading cursive. It was the only restaurant in town, besides the McDonald's attached to the gas station near the highway. I suppose you could also count the pub food at the Red Lyon, but any resident of Brokenridge would recommend at least three beers before consuming their mozzarella sticks, otherwise you can taste the freezer burn.

Our dad and mom's place used to be somewhat fancy, a place to go for dates and birthdays and anniversaries, serving fresh-caught walleye or pork brats from the Sandersens' farm down the road. Dad set the menu and ran the business; Mom ran the front of house, and she was famous for it. Just as she could recite the worst gossip about her customers, she could also remember their grandkids' names, what teams they rooted for, the way they liked their steak. People came from miles away on a Saturday night because everyone knew that if you stuck around long enough after dinner service, Margie and Bart would tap a keg on the house, maybe set up a card game or clear the tables for dancing. The cops only ever came twice, my mom always likes to tell the story, once because Nils Gauer ran his snowmobile into the oak nearby, and the other because Sheriff Rundle himself was too smashed to drive home.

Tonight, the decorative iron bench under the green awning was empty of my mother. Cigarette butts overflowed from the concrete planter.

"Where is she?" I wondered.

Theo pointed to the side mirror.

We both turned in our seats. Mom was creeping around the back corner of the building, taking weird, light little steps, her hands up as if in a hostage situation. She was sixty-four, but she didn't look it from far away, her thick brown hair feathered like an '80s centerfold, her figure trim in her jeans and Vikings sweatshirt. A closer view revealed crags and sags from decades of laughter and menthols, and she'd never given up her blue eye shadow, no matter how much I pleaded. She held a single finger to her lips and motioned us to get out of the car. Theo and I followed directions, taking care to shut the doors quietly. My heart began to pound. Was it a robber? An animal? Bears did amble through here quite a bit.

"What the hell?" I whispered.

"Hush," my mom called over her shoulder.

Around the back we went, Theo recording on his phone, stifling laughter, me trying to figure out if this was, in fact, a little bit hilarious or purely annoying.

Near the dumpsters, Mom paused and pointed, her laughter escaping in snorts. It appeared Mom's friend Nance had fallen asleep sitting up against the brick wall. As a blanket, she had repurposed an industrial-size plastic bag of toilet-paper rolls.

Mom bent close to Nance's ear. "Nance!"

"Yuh," Nance almost shouted, straightening with urgency.

"The kids are here."

Nance blinked at both of us, then at my mom. "Holy smokes, Margie." She shoved the toilet-paper roll bag off her lap. "What the hell did you put in them drinks?"

"It ain't quality but quantity, Nance." Mom gave a thumbs-up to Theo.

Theo turned his phone on himself for his followers, putting on a fake happy cry. "God, I love my life."

As Mom helped wipe gravel from Nance's sizable ass, she glanced up at me for a moment, her laughter faltering a bit. I tried to push out a bit of laughter myself. "Here ya go," I said, holding the keys out to her.

Her expression remained curious as she straightened, eyes still on me. She took the keys and I looked away. I'd rather not have any emotional conversations next to a dumpster.

"Come on, Marge, I'm freezin'," Nance called at the restaurant's back door.

When my mother returned from locking up, Theo and I had gotten back in the car. She poked her head into the Volvo's window, her cheeks and nose pink from the chill or the wine or both.

"Look at my two babies," she said.

I nodded at her hand resting on the driver's window ledge. "Your cuticles look good, Ma."

"Oh! Thank you!" She looked at her nail beds appraisingly, but I could see that her eyes were still a bit unfocused.

Theo noticed, too. "You really hit the sauce tonight, huh, Margie?"

"Nah, just a long day is all." She straightened, dropping her keys on the ground.

"Get in," I told her. "Tell Nance to come, too."

"Pishposh." She let out a strained huff as she bent to retrieve her keys. "I'm fine. It was just a couple glasses."

Thankfully Theo backed me up, and Nance was certainly not going to say no to a ride, so stale wine and Clinique perfume were added to the list of smells taking over the Volvo. Mom requested the Tina Turner version of "Proud Mary" from what she called the *Booftooth*, and soon we were all singing, even my out-of-tune alto getting up there for the *woo-hoo-hoo* of the chorus. After we watched Nance wobble up her steps, accidentally kicking over her decorative Virgin Mary, I dropped Theo at the Red Lyon, and finally it was just me and my old mom, crawling down my childhood street at fifteen miles per hour so John Denver could serenade us before we got to the end of the block. The song faded, and I put the Volvo in Park.

"Gah, we have fun," my mom muttered. She hummed a few stray notes as she unfastened her seat belt. Her hand was on the door handle when she paused and turned. "You okay, hon?"

It hit me. She had forgotten. I thought Theo might have said something to her, but he didn't like talking about this stuff, either: his presence and the *I love you* had already meant a lot to me, and he knew that. Maybe I should just leave it. Gabe was *my* husband, anyway, not my mother's. I was a grown woman. I didn't need her to stroke my hair and sing me lullabies.

I looked at her square in the eyes. "It's a year today."

She clapped a hand to her mouth. "Oh, geez, Robbie. Oh, crap." She looked up at the car's ceiling, as if there was a calendar there. "I didn't know it was today."

I'd told her last week, actually, but I knew she had a lot on her mind. "The death certificate says 1:24 a.m. So I guess it's tomorrow, technically."

She put her hand on my wrist. "You want me to come stay with you?"

I smiled at the image of me waking up to her sitting next to my bed, snoring, as I often found her as a kid. "Nope, I'm good."

"Tell you what. We could go to the church. Have Father open it up, say a prayer."

"Gabe wasn't religious, you know that."

"Church is as good a place as any to have a sacred moment. That's where I go to think about your dad."

Something in me softened. Maybe I didn't realize how hurt I was that she had forgotten until now, until I felt like forgiving her. "I didn't know you did that for Dad."

"I light a candle for him." She smiled, cleared her throat. "It's nice."

"I think I'd rather have a sacred moment with just me and Gabe." In the silence, Mom looked ahead thoughtfully, nodded. "I made a lasagna," I added.

"What a great idea! Gabe made a damn good lasagna." She paused, then clapped her hands and recited: "Don't cry because it's over, smile that it happened."

That was a favorite Hallmark-worthy saying of hers, especially when talking about our father. "Did *you* do anything for the one-year? For Dad?"

Her eyes went back to the ceiling. "Oh, Lord. I still had Theo to think about."

"I know, but did you go to the plot or anything?"

"I'm sure I did," Mom said. "That time is all a blur, though, with the restaurant and everything."

My dad was buried where everyone was buried in town, in the cemetery next to Brokenridge Lake. Gabe wasn't, though. He was everywhere, in a sense. He'd asked that most of his ashes be scattered on one of his favorite bike trails.

"You know who helps me remember is Nance," Mom was saying. "Memory like a steel trap. Always there for a pint and a chat about old times. She's a good friend." She turned to me in the front seat. "And you're a good daughter. Don't know what I'd do without you." Her eyes had lost all of their wine-soaked amusement. She looked tired. "Are we still on for you taking a look at the books sometime next week?"

"You bet."

She paused again as she stepped out the door. "You call me if you need me. If you're feeling lonely."

Too late, I thought. And even if I did call, she wouldn't answer. She'd be out cold within ten minutes. "Sure will, Ma."

I watched her go. Even after she got inside, I stayed, waiting until the lights lit up the empty house, room by room.

After I removed the bubbling pan from the oven, I collapsed onto a stool at the counter and waited for the lasagna to cool. I brought the urn in from our bedroom to keep me company while I ate, but it was always hard to imagine it was Gabe in that simple, stainless steel, thermos-looking thing, at least what remained of him. I never knew there was a thing to a person besides a body until I had put my palms on Gabe's cheeks and looked from one eyeball to the other. And that's what they were: eyeballs. No longer eyes. I thought, oh, there *is* a thing that makes a person a person. *A soul*, if you want to call it that. Maybe it's just moisture or blood, but holding the cold cheeks, and the way the head is heavy in your hands, you don't really understand how the body is an object until you see it without the *thing* behind the eyes, and you realize that whatever it is that makes the body a person can slip out of its mouth with a breath, can be pulled out and vanished like a magician's scarf.

Sometimes I still ran my hand on the inside of his shoes and enjoyed the grooves left by his giant, floppy feet. I took apart every single board game in the house to find his pencil-scratched scores. Once, a paper towel I ran behind the bathroom faucets caught a couple of his stray beard hairs and I didn't throw it away for a week. That's what had gotten me about the key rack. Sometimes I needed these little hits of Gabe to get me through the day.

My god, the lasagna was good. The top had browned, and the inside was salty and spicy and smoky.

My phone dinged again. An email had come through. As I clicked on the banner, a shot of lightning ran from my scalp to my spine. Panic or excitement or both. Then disbelief.

The name in my inbox was Gabe's.

My biggest pet peeve . . .
Inefficiency.

"Read it aloud to me," Theo said. He was sitting at my kitchen island, focused on his iced coffee and a half-eaten breakfast burrito. Last night I'd stared at the message for god knows how long, my eyes darting over the words until my back hurt from sitting up, hunched over the screen.

I'd googled things like *how do you know if your phone has been hacked* and *how do you know if a gmail has been deleted*. I'd texted Theo, told him to come over as soon as he was awake, and I sat in my bed, my phone in my lap, waiting for answers.

"*Hi Robbie*," I read to Theo from my laptop screen, though I almost had it memorized by now. "*Before you freak out, it's really me. Your childhood dog's name was Pogo. Mine were Lucy and Freddy. What else . . . You secretly still watch Fraggle Rock! This is an old Gmail I used to sign up for free trials online so I hope you didn't find it and delete it. Okay, down to brass tacks: the other night you told me you'd never love anyone else.*" I stumbled as I read this part, just as I'd stumbled the first read-through, and every read-through after that. If he timed it correctly it would be a year, Gabe wrote—he must have set it up on his phone at the hospital. It was time to start moving on, the email said. He knew I wouldn't want to, so he was giving me a push: an online-dating profile with my name on it. I felt my cheeks flush as I rushed through the words. "*The app subscription lasts 12 months. Use it!*" I read aloud. "*Odds are you'll meet someone cool that you can enjoy for a while. Maybe forever. He won't be hotter than me—*" Theo snorted at that "*—but I don't like the thought of you being alone. If you won't do it for yourself, do it as a favor to me. Please!*" The message ended with a password to his email inbox, which he had used to create the app account.

"Let me look at it," Theo said, his mouth full of burrito.

"Clean your hands first."

Theo rolled his eyes and wiped his hands on his joggers. He reached for the laptop and began to study the screen, brow furrowed. After confirming that, yes, conceivably when Gabe knew it was time, he could have scheduled this message to be sent out a year in the future, and, no, neither my computer nor phone had any secret spyware some troll had installed, Theo was getting giddy.

"Wait—so he actually went through with the dating profile."

In Gabe's alternative inbox, I'd found two emailed promotions. *Welcome to Bubbl, Robin L!* the first one said. Then, *Take the next step toward true love, Robin L! Log in to make your profile visible!* "Yeah, but I haven't even looked at it."

Theo almost spit out his mouthful of iced coffee. "What? Why?"

"Because. I have no interest. No time." I ripped a paper towel and wiped up the drops from Theo's escaped coffee. "I wouldn't even know how to go on a date."

"All the more reason. You gotta get some practice for husband number two."

"Gross." I pulled out the leftover lasagna from the fridge, unfastened the lid, and took a fork to it. "God, it's even good cold."

"You're going to go against Gabe's, like, *last wish*?"

I looked up from my lasagna. "It's not like that."

"How is it not like that? Gabe clearly thought about this. He wanted this for you. He literally composed the email after a conversation with you about never loving anyone else."

I avoided Theo's eyes, focusing on the movements of my fork. "I guess."

That night—the night we talked about *after*—he'd been recovering from that day's round of chemo. He'd started to go from skinny with a beer belly to marathon-runner skinny. I'd started talking about our Thanksgiving plans, about maybe rewarding ourselves for a hard year, going somewhere nice, and he stopped me. He probably wouldn't be around for Thanksgiving, he'd said. That was a bullshit bad attitude, I'd replied. We argued until I went to bed.

Soon, his weakened immune system would be fighting another kidney infection at Fairview, which we'd taken great pains to avoid. Soon, he wouldn't be able to lift his arms to type anything. He saw how hard I could grip on to the reality I wanted. Now, he was trying to uncurl my fingers.

"I know life without him has to exist," I said to Theo. "But I'm just not there yet."

"Robin." Theo said it quietly. The pain that came with it was quiet, too. "Life without him is already here."

"Yeah, I know. But." I had no *but*. I was regretting telling Theo about the email. I should have just savored it, let it sit with all my other Gabe-soaked things. The key rack, the worn shoes, the handwriting, and now this message. This was the world I wanted. "I just feel like I'm not supposed to do this."

I put the top back on the lasagna and returned it to its proper place among all the other leftovers.

"What, move on too quickly?" Theo said from behind me. "You're worried what people will think?"

"In my heart, it feels wrong. Like a violation."

"A violation of who? Not of Gabe. Gabe is the one who wants you to do this."

"No, like . . ." I gestured to the heavens, feeling heat rise to my face. "Nature."

Theo took on a dramatic tone. "Like you're doomed by the gods to walk this earth in a burial shroud? You're not. You need—"

"Don't tell me what I need. I'm tired of people being up in my business about this, all right?"

Theo let out an exasperated sigh. "Fine."

It was a cheap card to play, but effective. Theo had seen how Gabe's death had been a public spectacle. A hometown boy, good-looking, progressive but still knew his way around his family's sugar-beet farm—he'd beat the incumbent mayor by a landslide, and he would have won again. Even before he was elected, we were the couple who hosted the dinners for everyone's visitors, whose guest bedroom people used when they got in fights with their partners, whose advice people sought when their cars weren't starting, their yard was dying. For Gabe, the hospital broke its own visiting-hour rules. Somehow it felt like we were rarely alone, which was all the more lonely.

"People just need to let me do things on my own time," I added, in Theo's silence.

Without looking up, Theo muttered, "If you do that, you'll be doing this forever."

"Doing what?"

"Tinkering around with all his old shit. Making his favorite noodle-based dishes."

"Stop." My voice was raised and clipped. He was joking, but I wasn't.

"You stop," he said. "Tell me I'm wrong."

I pointed to the laptop. "Are you in on this? Is that why you're pushing me?"

"No! Jesus!"

"Maybe you don't understand because you're young . . ."

Theo scoffed. "I'm an adult. I get it."

"I don't think you do. It's just not *physically* possible for me. He was like a part of my body. It's like an injury, like I'm limping everywhere, you know? I'm barely keeping myself upright. How am I supposed to flirt when I still *feel* him everywhere?"

"Hm . . . Here's an idea." Theo was looking at the ceiling sarcastically. "Every once in a while, get out of his ancestral home. Try that."

"That's mean." I dropped my tone. "How dare you."

"I mean, I'm sorry, but am I right or am I right?" His cheeks were red, but he didn't waver. "He took some of his precious time on this earth for this. If you don't at least *look* at it . . ."

"Fine," I snapped. "*You* do it."

"Seriously?"

"You look at it, and you can tell me if it's creepy, is it a huge fucking joke, if there are dick pics, whatever. Just tell me the whole deal." My mouth was suddenly dry.

"Are you sure?" Theo asked, but he was already turning the laptop toward him.

I was feeling it, what I had feared, this roller-coaster swoop of *No, not right, not yet*. This feeling of *unnatural*. "Do it," I told him, because the profile couldn't just sit there. Maybe once the mystery was gone, he would drop it, and I could delete the damn thing.

To distract myself from the nerves, I slipped into my gardening clogs and opened the back door.

"Where are you going?"

"I just need to—I need to weed." My stomach turned again.

Outside, wrens and warblers collected themselves for the journey south. I picked the last of the tomatoes and put them in an old Kemps gallon ice cream bin. Rain-faded vanilla from some distant Fourth of July. My clogs were splattered with memories, too: eggshell-blue paint for the soon-to-be-nursery of one of our friends. Gabe had pulled his back that day, and I'd tried to goat-carry him from the Volvo to our front door. We had collapsed on the lawn with laughter.

"Is this really what you want?" I said aloud to the cheeping yard.

A red-winged blackbird hopped onto the fence, looked at me, and flew away.

In Minneapolis, Gabe and I used to walk through the wealthy neighborhoods together and point out the houses we liked but could never afford. We ducked through alleyways to spy on people's gardens, admiring the pea shoots in their raised beds, measuring rhubarb stalks, making friends with protective dogs. When we were still dating, we would propose to each other as a joke. He'd present me with a clump of my hair he'd pulled from his drain: *Will you marry me? Marry me*, I'd say as Gabe let out a particularly heinous burp.

A couple of years after we'd graduated, we were on one of our walks, and Gabe was telling me about his parents' decision to leave Brokenridge for Milwaukee, to sell off the land his family had farmed since the 1800s. Technically it was Dakota Sioux land, anyway, Gabe had insisted. It wasn't theirs to sell. But as a temporary steward, did he want it? "Do we want it?" Gabe had paused, turned to me. My heart swelled simply to be asked. As we talked, we'd veered off the sidewalk and down the banks of the Mississippi, weaving through the leafless trees. The wide, lazy river had always been our refuge from the backfiring buses on University Avenue, the crowded sidewalks of the campus neighborhood where we lived, and that day in February the river was silent and frozen solid.

Gabe and I clutched mittened hands as we shuffled across the ice, heads on the swivel for any passerby who might report us, giddy with an edge of fear. We knew not to go too far out into the center where the current still moved, and when we'd gone as far as we could, I looked up at the giant old trees lining the sweeping banks, the lecture halls and museums and theaters on either side jutting above the treetops into the gray sky. It would be suffocating to go back home, I told Gabe, to be surrounded by people who'd known us since we were children, farmers and mechanics, many with big hearts but narrow minds. But my mother had begun struggling with the restaurant. Maybe if we were close by, I wouldn't worry about her being alone so much, wouldn't worry about Theo's safety as one of only a few openly gay people in town. Together we imagined Saturday nights eating sausage and sauerkraut, listening to people talk about where they were going ice fishing that weekend, building fires under the cloudless, frozen sky, the wood crackling in the quiet. Maybe we could do some good.

Gabe's pink-tipped fingers had pressed a simple gold band into the woven palm of my mitten.

"We should do it together, then," he said. "We can go back and grow something."

I had wept with happiness. Gabe wiped my tears before they could freeze.

Now, I plucked wayward grass from the soft soil surrounding the zucchini, added six gourds to the pile of tomatoes. We had recorded the growth of our little backyard garden meticulously, made decisions based on changing heat and rainfall patterns. This year it hadn't thrived without him. I tried to mimic what I'd seen him do, but I couldn't protect the waxy leaves from getting blanched by too much sun, couldn't prevent the heavy rainfall from uprooting the kale and the spinach altogether. I tried to imagine someone else kneeling beside me, someone who wasn't Gabe, and saw only a blank outline. Someone who might want me to do dumb things like go to professional sports games—overpriced, Gabe and I always agreed—or someone who wore too much cologne or tried to get me to listen to his podcasts. Someone who might want kids, and those kids would come out looking nothing like the kid I imagined, the kid with Gabe's eyes and hair. *Aren't you curious?* I heard a little voice in my head. Sure. Curious like you look over the ledge of a deep well and wonder what's at the bottom. Curious like you look up at the stars when you're camping in the north and get your breath taken away by the distant, colorless void.

I stomped through the still-dewy grass toward the back door. *Maybe someday*, I would tell Theo. Maybe next year, though the only thing on my calendar for next year was combing through Gabe's graphing notebooks, using whatever he'd jotted to return the garden to its former glory. The thought comforted me.

"You want zucchini bread?" I asked Theo, setting my bucket inside the back door.

"You *have* to read this," Theo said.

"I'm going to delete it." I kicked off my clogs.

"No, you're not." Theo sounded smug, but when I looked at him, he was smiling gently.

I sighed, braced myself, and leaned over his shoulder. The site page was navy blue and pale pink, with blocky font separated into squared-off sections, each with a bolded prompt and what was supposed to be my answer. A simple bubble logo shone in the upper left corner next to my name and photo.

Robin L, 33, Brokenridge

Describe yourself in five words or less . . .
Just let me do it.

A huff of a laugh escaped me. I could hear myself saying that exact refrain, *let me do it*, reaching for a tangle of cords over Gabe's shoulder as he fumbled with frustration, making the rounds to each colleague who had filled out their expenses incorrectly, sliding the restaurant's financial records toward myself as I sat across the desk from my mom.

Top three accomplishments . . .
Certified Best Birthday Gift-Giver Ever. Self-identified Sudoku champion.

"*Self-identified*. Psh."

Theo turned his head.

I pointed at the section I was reading. "I got on the leaderboard, like, three times on my app."

Zucchini bread won Best Baked Good at the Lee County Fair four years in a row—would have been five but someone couldn't resist eating it and it got disqualified . . .

"That was Gabe who ate it, right?" Theo said.

I nodded, smiling at the memory of finding him standing in the baked-goods tent, eating the loaf with his fingers, not a care in the world. "He thought the judging was already over."

Three things you wish you could change about the world . . .
Only three?

The smile on my face grew.

I'm looking for . . .
Handyman. Iron Chef. Green thumb.

"Of course," I muttered. He'd basically described himself. He wasn't wrong.

My eyes wandered back to the top of the profile, toward the photo. It had been a while since I'd seen it, but I recognized it from the lock screen on Gabe's phone. He'd taken it from his bike. He went out on long rides every day, but on weekends he would ride slow so I could come along on my secondhand Schwinn, him weaving easily as I pumped beside him. That day he had called my name. I'd turned, saw he was pointing his camera at me, and lifted my hands from the handlebars. My hair had blown back from my face, and I was beaming, a little surprised at my own skill. He'd caught me right as my gaze had locked on him, and you could tell by the look, the happiness in my eyes was about much more than the trick.

Do it as a favor to me, Gabe had said.

Theo watched as I clicked around to the profile's settings. *Make profile visible?*

My mouse hovered. Theo grabbed my shoulder excitedly, shaking it. I clicked. He cheered.

For you, I told Gabe in my head. *I'll do it for you.*

The dorkiest thing about me is . . .
My watch. But no one will be laughing during the apocalypse when I know what time it is.

That night I assembled a collection of sticky pads I'd gotten free from work and sat in Gabe's old home office with a fruity wine cooler my mom had left in my fridge. Theo and I had tinkered a bit with my online self—but for the most part, the Gabe-approved version of Robin was doing its job. Since making my profile active that morning, I'd received fourteen matches, each with their accompanying message. A pulsing animation of a bubble rested beside each name in the inbox. I began to read their profiles.

Damian R, 28, Minneapolis

My friends call me . . .
Naruto because I run funny lol.

I dream of . . .
Starting my own record label, shout-out to @mplshype on SoundCloud.

Next to Damian's name, I clicked on one of the animated insects, watching it light up and multiply, fluttering off the screen. I clicked over to the next greeting, reviewing the profile attached:

Hector F, 35, White Bear Lake

A typical day . . .
Working out, eating, work, working out, eating.

My secret is . . .
I'm an open book. Just ask.

I found myself pressing the bubble again, and again, until every message was highlighted, like a combination of an old Barbie computer game and a slot machine at the Red Lyon.

Hi, sweetie, wrote someone named Jens T. How are you? *Pretty good*, I said. His profile had a picture of him with a beautiful, chubby orange cat. *I like your cat*, I told him. That's Tito, he said. *Cute*, I replied and returned to the endless stream of profiles.

Devansh M, 38, Minneapolis

Favorite recipe . . .
My mom's daal or hot wings, depends on my mood.

At a wedding, I'll be the one . . .
Why don't you bring me as your plus-one and find out???

Another chime. To my message complimenting his cute cat, Jens had responded, You have a pussy you want to show me? He added an emoji with its tongue sticking out. I choked on a bite of lasagna. *Um, no*, I typed and deleted the message chain.

Your cute, said Damian R. His photos were different versions of the same, sleepy selfie. *You're pretty cute, too*, I responded, cautious now.

I refreshed the inbox. Another wave of messages.

Thomas R, 30, Saint Paul

Why I'm here . . .
Trying to find someone to fuck me before we all die.

Currently binge watching . . .
This app is a hellhole, I want to die, seriously kill me.

Thomas R, I wrote on a yellow note after reviewing his profile. *Deeply depressed*.

Your profile is funny, I responded to his initial greeting, hoping that his pleas to be killed were a cynical joke. I guess, said Thomas. So what did you today, he added, without punctuation. I began to respond, paused, and saw Thomas had already written, I would fuck you, for the record. Prolly wouldn't be able to keep it up though. I felt my eyes widen at the image he was conjuring. Sorry, Thomas added. I'm kinda drunk lol. I tried to shake off the thought with my own sugary gulp of wine cooler and deleted the message.

Damian had gotten back to me; he was very suspicious. He accused me of being a bot and a scammer. *I'm not, I'm real*, I tried to tell him, but he had blocked my account.

Good god, I texted Theo. What the hell did you get me into?

No response. It was a Saturday night—he was probably at the Red Lyon again. All the other friends I could contact for advice were those that Gabe and I shared. As much as I'd told Theo I was immune, I did care what people thought—if not for me, then for the sake of do-no-wrong Mayor Gabe. That's what he didn't really consider when he orchestrated this, not only how I would be perceived by his Brokenridge fan club but what it said about him, me being so eager to forget. What it said about our marriage. It was good, goddamn it.

The best.

A wave of anger bubbled up as I clicked through more profiles. Why was he making me do this?

Men in groups of men with suits. Men in the driver's seat of their cars. *Looking for a baddie with her own money. Just looking for my best friend*. I animated more bubbles. I threw sticky notes with names in the trash.

Their eyes all look so sad, I texted Theo.

Just pick one, he replied.

But I was afraid of poking the bears, afraid of being propositioned again. Was I a prude? To be fair, the closest I had ever been to dating was going to the Walmart parking lot at various Brokenridge boys' invitation, watching them do *Jackass*-inspired stunts in my periphery, pretending to ignore them.

Hi. Hey. Hey. What's up. Wyd. Are you real? Good evening.

Only one Bubbl message was more than one sentence. Colin Q: Who's got two thumbs and thinks you're cute? This guy!

What about this one? I screenshotted Colin Q's profile and sent it to Theo. In his featured picture, he was standing in front of a Christmas tree, arm around an older lady who was probably his grandmother, both of them wearing Santa hats.

Thank you, I wrote cautiously to Colin Q. I like your Santa hat. God, I hoped he wouldn't interpret that sexually. What if he was nice? What if I began to like him? This is how we would have to tell people we met—hunched over each other's photos and images of digital bubbles.

The night I fell in love with Gabe, it was the Friday before winter break our first year at the University of Minnesota. I had come back from a Nutrition final to a voice mail. My father had had his third heart attack. *Welp, kid, Daddy went to . . .* I remember my mother repeating in the recording, trying to finish the sentence *Daddy went to heaven*, and there was something so infantile in those words. I remember feeling sick at the thought of driving home, of having to comfort her. I had lost him, too, I kept thinking. I wanted to be a baby, too.

And yet by crying first, my mom had somehow beat me to it. Someone would have to be sober and calm in the coming weeks, for Theo's sake. But that would be tomorrow, I figured that night, so I'd drunk most of a fifth of Captain Morgan with my hallmates.

At some point I'd tried to wander home from a party. The windchill was probably in the single digits but all I felt was a warm, deep-end-of-the-swimming-pool feeling. Ahead of me, a tall figure in a dark coat crossed the street, ducking against the cold. He had seemed familiar, but in my drunken state, I couldn't believe it. This was who I encounter in the middle of the night, in the sprawling metro area of Minneapolis–Saint Paul: Gabe Carr.

I would call Gabe my high school sweetheart, but for the four years we were two locker blocks away, we barely exchanged a word. There are yearbook pictures of us from that time: Gabe, rail thin in dorky khakis, leather bracelet of a wannabe punk, holding the most unpunk thing imaginable—a voter-registration clipboard.

Me on the other end of the yearbook, front and center with the rest of the Future Business Leaders of America, short and compact like Mom, Scandinavian-pale arms sticking out of a supposedly professional sleeveless number I found on the clearance rack at Kohl's.

That night, he and I seemed to be the only two people moving through the campus. As he pulled out the keys to open the door to his dorm, I called to him, my cold-numbed lips barely able to form his name. "Gabe Carr."

He turned, squinted. He was wearing that same thin-lipped smirk he wore in the yearbook, a look I would eventually fall in love with. "Robin Lindstrom?"

"I was lost, so I followed you," I said, shivering. "You didn't see me?"

"I thought I saw someone, but I wasn't sure."

"You should be more careful," I said drunkenly.

His eyes darted back to the glowing entryway of the dorm. "You want to come in for a second?"

We'd sat on two love seats facing each other in the dorm's lobby, our coats still on, Gabe's headphones around his neck. His jaw had grown sharper, I remember noticing, and his face and lips had filled out to balance his jutting nose. His lankiness seemed to have more substance, too. There were veins in his hands I hadn't noticed before, shoulders that had spread underneath his wool coat. We began to talk, shallowly at first, and yet soon I found myself sharing things I hadn't told anyone else, how afraid I was that I wasn't smart enough to be there, that I was a hick.

He'd been feeling the same way, he told me, and he was starting to realize he'd been kind of an asshole to everyone he met this year, just to keep them from talking down to him. I was the first person from Brokenridge he'd run into, he said, and it was such a relief to be seen as his old self, his real self.

"And who is your real self?" I had asked. In the distance, we could hear more partygoers returning, laughing, making selections from the vending machines.

"I don't know what to call it," I remember Gabe saying, smiling as he lifted his thin hands lamely, color rising in his cheeks. "Why—what would you say?"

I should have expected the question, but I couldn't answer. He didn't know what to call his real self, and I didn't know, either. But right then, Gabe was the only person who could understand what the Dad-shaped hole would look like in our family, in our town, in me. Tears ran down my cheeks. Gabe's eyebrows knit together in confusion. After a silence, I told him.

"When?" he asked.

"Today," I said and wiped my nose.

Gabe stood up from his love seat. I remember bracing for panic or shame that I had revealed too much for a high school acquaintance but found none. He made his way around the coffee table that separated us and sat on the cushion next to mine. Then he lifted his arms, waiting. His face looked stiff and nervous, but he kept them raised. I leaned, and his arms landed around my shoulders. I circled mine around his waist. He smelled like wool and men's deodorant. We were still wearing our coats, I realized.

"I'm so sorry," he said, and I could hear the words through his chest. "I liked your dad. Everyone liked your dad."

In my teenage mind, that's when it began to feel like fate that he should be the one I followed home. I found that I liked his arms around me and mine curling around him, the way I could wrap them fully around his torso, how it felt to have his thin frame against my chest.

In the morning, I woke up when Gabe's giant metalhead roommate had walked in from the shower and found us spooning on top of the covers, still fully clothed. Over watery coffee and biscuits in the Union, I'd told Gabe I should probably get on the road, that I would have to return home that day to start planning for Dad's service, and maybe I'd see him around in Brokenridge over Christmas. I remember his brown eyes following me as I stood and refastened my coat. "I was going to go home, too," he said, his jaw tight as he set aside his nerves. "You want company for the drive?"

From that day on, Gabe and I would be inseparable, first as shadows that followed each other through our childhood houses over winter break—Gabe doing the dishes without being asked after the funeral reception, me walking his parents' German shepherds on lung-freezing January nights—and then as fixtures in each other's lives as we returned to school, my mother requesting I pass the phone to Gabe, Gabe's father asking what kind of meat I preferred for Easter, both as assumed plus-ones for various cousins' weddings. In an effort to find privacy, we would spend precious gas money driving to small campgrounds we scouted on the internet, finding new ways to bend in the back of my car to accommodate Gabe's height, marveling in the strange awakenings that arose from accidental touches, and when the accidental touches became purposeful, the new sounds arising from our throats, the new reasons to visit the drugstore.

My laptop speakers trilled. Colin Q had replied to my comment about his hat. My nana wears it better.

I clicked through Colin Q's other pictures. He had a pleasant, watery-blue gaze, and sandy-colored thinning hair. He seemed to be onstage a lot. Maybe he was an actor.

After that first year together, I knew I wanted Gabe's thin hips against mine every night of my life, his arms secure across my chest, his long hands playing with my hair. I wanted him as a constant, functioning part of me, breathing air into my lungs, jigsawing my every thought and feeling with his own. It seemed insane, to attach to someone so immediately with such force, such certainty. Even as young as I was, I knew it would make more sense to sort out my feelings when my mind was less clouded with grief. *But why wait*, I remember thinking. *Why delay?*

Would you like to go out on a date? I asked Colin Q.

Wow, Colin Q wrote. He began to type, then stopped.

I slammed the laptop closed.

As I rinsed my dishes, my heart beat against my chest too hard, as if it were scolding me. I picked up Gabe's *Far Side* coffee cup, which I'd been drinking out of every day since he went into hospice. Sometimes I still wrapped myself in his heavy coat. Sometimes I would put my thumb on the worn buttons of his old game controllers.

I pulled up the Bubbl app on my phone. A reply from Colin Q. I like your style! Meeting would be fun!

Great, I told Colin Q. As long as we met somewhere public. He agreed. Looking forward to it. The period at the end of the message seemed too formal, too final, so I added a smiling emoji. I got into bed.

After a minute, I scooted toward the space where Gabe had slept for ten years. Sometimes I imagined it still warm, as if he'd just gotten up to go to the bathroom. Tonight I paused before I reached his side and propped both pillows behind my head. It felt strange, to stretch my legs out in a V across the cool expanse of sheets. But I must have stayed long enough to fall asleep. I found myself waking up the next day there, in the center.

My secret . . .

Nice try.

My office is almost exactly the average size of a walk-in closet in a suburban house. A framed picture of Gabe and me from our wedding sits next to my monitor, along with my company mug full of highlighters and pens, and an old family photo from when Dad was alive. The place where I work, which towers above most buildings in Minneapolis's jagged blue skyline, has products in nine out of ten residences in the United States. To put it simply: we make chemicals. I work for the sticky division, including paper notes with sticky backs, and my job is essentially to make sure the sticky people get paid. And when everyone gets paid, I play Sudoku.

Whenever I opened the Bubbl app, which I had been doing more and more, I turned the wedding photo toward the wall, keeping Gabe's past self innocent of my indiscretions.

I was starting to recognize the flood of dopamine I got when I pressed the icon and found more messages—same as when I saw my initials on the leaderboard in my Sudoku app. *You waxed? You look like a tightass. I want to lick your feet.* Little fires they would set in my head, little fires I had to put out. It was becoming a game, and in the game I'd chosen, my avatar's job was to deploy insults I'd never be ballsy enough to use in real life. *Did I give you permission to talk about my anatomy?* I would type, adrenaline pumping as I ignored the chimes of my work inbox.

The problem was that many of the men found me telling them off just as titillating as if I had welcomed them into my bed. Others just blocked me.

There were nice men, too, who hugged dogs and asked me what I was up to, and I never knew what to say. Sitting at my desk? Heating up leftovers in the microwave? Watching teenagers run from psychos in masks on my TV? *Nothing interesting*, I'd tell them, and somehow I would always find myself drifting back toward the vulgar advances, eager for battle.

I'd almost forgotten about Colin Q until he sent me a message on Friday evening, asking—what else—what I was doing. I looked beyond the small screen of my phone to the large screen of my TV, which was playing the cursed carnival-ground scene of *Texas Chainsaw Massacre 2*.

Watching Leatherface be Leatherface, I responded to Colin Q's query.

When I had run out of reality shows, I had started filling dead air with all the old slashers and horror I used to watch when I was younger. I liked to look up how the wounds were carefully constructed from glue and strawberry syrup, how monsters were made from liquid latex and spirit gum. Now, I knew it was a little messed up, but there was something comforting about watching people scream and run from death when I couldn't. Their hurt would be over, for better or worse.

After a few minutes, Colin wrote, Texas Chainsaw?

Yep.

Confession, I had to google "Leatherface," he wrote.

That must have been an interesting set of results . . . Most people didn't like this one compared to the original, but this was some of Tom Savini's best special-effects work.

Are we still on for a date?

My stomach churned. A date. I'd pushed out the invitation last week like an inconvenient chore I'd wanted to get out of the way. I looked at Colin's pictures again. Since our last message, he had added another photo in what appeared to be his bathroom, looking at his own reflection with an exaggerated eyebrow cock. "Oh, Colin," I muttered to myself.

I can't, I typed, then erased it. I pulled up the profile Gabe had filled out, as I often did when the thrill wore off, when I felt overwhelmed by the stream of rectangled faces. I could picture my husband in the exact spot where I sat on the couch, sprawled next to a bowl of plain Chex, laughing to himself as he composed all my dating-profile answers on his gamer laptop with its clunky keyboard. I imagined snuggling up next to him, reading them over his shoulder, giggling together as he poked fun at me in ways only he could. Seeing myself through his eyes was making me fall in love with him all over again.

I'd made a commitment. To Gabe, if not to Colin Q. The guilt at not following through would be worse than the nerves. Probably.

Name the time and place, I typed and pressed Send.

That Saturday, I wandered through the aisles of Target before the date, loading my arms with amenities. Extra makeup in case I was feeling insecure about my lasagna-puffed face. Green tea to keep me from yawning after a long day of shopping at all the stores we didn't have in Brokenridge. It would soon be time to meet Colin Q at the restaurant he'd chosen, something with the word *Bowl* in the name, and I was beginning to panic.

What if he asked about my relationship history? What if my breath smelled like the Swedish meatballs I had eaten for lunch in the IKEA cafeteria? What if—and I had a feeling this was already happening—I sweat through my dress? Did I really care about any of this, and if I did care, did that mean I liked this person I barely knew? Did I want him to like me? Was I actually attractive, or was I just a woman on the internet? A passing glance at the mirrors in the clothing section of Target revealed someone I didn't recognize. The dress was navy, tailored, recycled from my early twenties, back when I thought I needed to look nice for work. Stomach full of Swedish meatballs pressing against tights I'd bought for some ancient Thanksgiving. My skin looked anemic, like one of those miserable women in Dutch medieval paintings. Maybe a visit to the candy aisle would help.

"Robin? Holy shit."

I turned. The giant shoulders of Gabe's best friend seemed to take up the entire oral care aisle. "Levi."

His neck-length brown hair was held back with an elastic headband, creating a curly halo around his face, and his meaty arms were almost completely covered in tattoos. I always thought he and his hound, Harpo, kind of resembled each other: both handsome if a bit jowly, both with big, sleepy eyes. We met in front of the toothpaste.

"I don't think I've seen you since . . ." At a loss for words, he threw up his hands, one of which held a lemon-lime Gatorade. "Fuck," he finished.

"The funeral, probably," I supplied.

"How are you?" he asked, leaning closer to me as if he were speaking softly, but his voice still held the same deep, nasal volume. Even louder, he added, "Wait, you don't live in Minneapolis now, do you?"

"No, no. Still out in Brokenridge."

"Still in—" A puzzled look accompanied his slight smile. He pointed behind him, as if Brokenridge were in the dairy department. "Still in the old farmhouse?"

"Our house. Yes." I pointed to his shirt, which was emblazoned with the logo of Palmer's, the bar where he worked. "You working today?"

"I was last night."

Now it was my turn to be confused. Palmer's was across the city, as was Levi's apartment, last I knew. "Did you move, or—?"

"No, I was—" He let out a gruff laugh, avoiding my eyes. "I was at a friend's."

"Ah," I said. I looked at him, unable to keep the *gotcha* out of my smile. "Another *friend*, eh?"

He pointed. "Don't judge."

"I wasn't!" I assured him, entirely unconvincing.

"You're silently judging me under the guise of politeness."

"I don't have a *guise*."

"Bullshit," he sang in a falsetto. "I know Minnesota-nice when I hear it."

"You're Minnesotan, too."

Levi scoffed. "I try not to be."

They were mostly younger than him, Levi's so-called *friends,* and they varied in size, appearance, vocation. Gabe used to come home from Levi's shows and tell me about the latest server or activist or dancer that Levi had declared The One, and we'd make bets about how long it would last before the woman started realizing the dreamy-eyed, giant teddy bear of a man who took her on trips to his family's cabin and fantasized about what they'd name their kids was the same Levi who prioritized NBA fantasy-league drafts over date night and ate lunch meat straight out of the package. It was the same every time. As the sheen faded, Levi knew he'd never be able to live up to the perfect-boyfriend image he'd built at the beginning, and he'd become evasive.

I tried to lower my level of upset down to nonsweating. "Sorry you thought my tone was judgmental."

"You can't even admit it."

"For god's sake. Sorry I judged, all right?"

"No, I'm sorry," he said, suddenly self-critical. "I actually have been seeing this person for a while. And why are we even talking about this? It's great to see you."

I kept my eyes on the toothpaste labels. "Welp, I have to get—" I gestured toward the cash registers with my full arms.

Levi didn't pick up the cue. Or he did and chose to ignore it. He popped open his Gatorade and wandered down the aisle, away from me. Over his shoulder, he called, "How's your mom?" He turned, waited.

To stay within earshot, I'd have to follow. "Fine."

"The restaurant's good?" he asked as we walked.

"Not great. Not terrible."

Levi nodded as he wiped his mouth after a large swallow. "Glad it's surviving, at least. Your brother graduated, right?"

This was a common misconception about Theo that I was having to correct more and more as he entered his mid-twenties. "Not yet. He's still got a few classes. How is the, uh . . . the band?"

Levi gave me a knowing smile. "You don't give a shit about band stuff."

I bristled. "That's not true."

"What's our name?"

I opened my mouth, but my mind was drawing a blank. Levi and his brothers had been in a regionally famous band since Levi was in high school—successful enough to allow him to pay his rent with only occasional stretches of bartending, at least. All I remember is Gabe coming home from afternoons of watching them supposedly practice, smelling like Hamm's, and speaking at an unnecessary volume. I sputtered, "Something about a pond?"

Levi guffawed, drawing startled stares from people near us in the aisles. "The Hidden Beaches. Don't know why I'm even bothering to tell you, because you're probably going to forget, but whatever."

"So sensitive," I muttered. Levi ignored me. The whole thing could have been avoided if he had just given me a generic *Pretty good* and moved on like a normal adult.

He was always doing this, poking at everyone with the truth, even when it was unnecessary. Gabe had once bought a shitty electric guitar in an attempt to join the band, and when I told him he was doing great and would probably get even better with lessons, Levi had simply said, "You suck, dude." They didn't speak for a month.

"Man, you *hated* us," Levi was saying. "You had to be dragged to our shows. This one time, I remember seeing your face in the crowd. You literally looked like you were in pain."

"It's just very loud."

"That's the point," he said, bumping me playfully with his shoulder. "It's rock 'n' roll. You get into it, you feel the energy." He bumped my shoulder again. "There it is." He was grinning, framing my face with his Gatorade-free hand. "There's the face. Such an expressive disgust. Truly have never seen anything like it."

I rolled my eyes.

"What are you listening to these days?" he asked. "Recaps of *Storage Wars*?"

"Nothing, really. But yes, I do still watch *Storage Wars*. Sorry I'm not cool like you."

He snorted. "Yeah, a thirty-three-year-old man buying butt medicine for his roommate, who happens to be a dog, so cool."

I had to laugh. I realized we'd moved from toothpaste to the pet section.

"Harpo misses Gabe, you know. For real."

At the mention of Gabe, we both became quiet.

Levi broke the silence. "I don't know if you knew this, but Gabe and I always used to meet halfway between Brokenridge and the Cities at this dog park in Lino Lakes. Whenever we go there now, Harpo always looks at me confused like, *Where's our friend?* He won't even run around without me reminding him that Gabe isn't coming."

Imagining the hound's confounded expression, I was surprised to find a lump in my throat. I swallowed it. "I didn't know you guys did that."

"God, I miss him. I keep trying to write songs for him, but I was always bad with lyrics. How do you pick words for all of those moments, you know? How do you take—what?—fourteen years of friendship and sum them up with a few lines? Whenever I'm trying to remember the big stuff, it never comes. It's always just random moments. I'll pick up my controller and start playing *Call of Duty* and I'm, like, waiting for Gabe's voice. Waiting for that 'Hey, dude.'" He took a deep, shaky breath. His eyes were a little wet, I noticed. "I always wrote about stupid shit so it never mattered, but now I'm, like, tearing my hair out as if Gabe is out there waiting for me to get it right."

"Well, if he were somewhere beyond, you know, looking down on us, I'm sure he'd love whatever you came up with. It was really good to see you, Levi—"

Levi stopped in his tracks. "And I think if *I* miss him, you must be . . . Jesus."

"It's hard." I kept moving, hoping he'd follow. We were approaching the self checkout. Levi's declarations were having an effect, burrowing into a tender place I didn't want to visit at the moment. My arm was cramped, and I needed to look at the time.

He didn't move. "So what about you?"

A shopper with a cart maneuvered around us. I moved out of the center of the aisle toward the sodas and magazines. "What about me, what?"

He held his arms out. "How has it been for you? The grief?"

A businesswoman excused herself as she reached behind me for the cooler, grabbing a Diet Coke. I sidestepped. "That's kind of personal."

"Oh." Levi looked confused, scratching his head with his half-empty Gatorade bottle. "Okay," he added, trying to collect himself. "I was just asking because I hoped we could, like . . . Never mind."

"I'm just not sure what to say." I could feel the eyes of people nearby. I felt the familiar panic of air being vacuumed from my lungs, the tingling in my fingertips. I lowered my voice. "I'm sorry, I just don't feel close to you that way. You and Gabe had your little thing going on, and I appreciate you sharing . . ."

"Our *little thing*? He was like my brother."

It was true, and Gabe had loved Levi, too. It wasn't as if I had hated the guy, but I didn't like him hovering over me now, trying to claim me, trying to pretend like we were the same. "I don't know what you want from me." Levi looked taken aback. Heat had risen to my neck. Now I knew I was sweating, and I didn't care. "I mean, what am I supposed to do, tell you about how I can't sleep, and how I can't get rid of any of his stuff? Is that what you want to hear? I haven't seen you in a year, Levi."

Levi stood still, blinking. "Understood."

I didn't move, either, trying to find normal breath and failing. His face had gotten a bit thinner since the funeral, I was noticing now, making the lines around his hazel eyes more pronounced. Levi had one of those gazes that bore into you, that made you feel as if he were inviting you to some spiritual acid trip of a place. When he was in a good mood, he was intoxicating to be around. But I had always been immune, always resisting his probing questions, his invitations to come along to dive bars. The two of them would get together every week, either in person or over gaming headsets, and I'd leave them to it.

Shame suddenly tumbled from my chest to my stomach. A shame I didn't want but knew was probably well-deserved. Levi wasn't the first person I'd shoved away like this, and he probably wouldn't be the last. What was wrong with me? "I should probably get going."

Levi pressed his lips together, held his breath, as if bracing himself for a leap into the deep end. "Listen, I do have something else. If you can stand my presence for two more seconds."

"Of course I can," I muttered, because unlike him, I could lie.

Levi had gotten an idea, he'd told me as we walked across the windblown parking lot. "It was the whole kickball team that was thinking this, actually . . ."

Every year Levi and Gabe had played for a recreational kickball team sponsored by Palmer's, and they were as serious as they were formidable, which was not very. The whole team had driven all the way up to Brokenridge for the funeral, wearing their neon-green kickball uniforms under formal jackets. I smiled at the thought. Had I sent any of them a card? I couldn't remember.

"We were thinking we could have a memorial game," Levi was saying. He drummed his fingers on a box of dewormer for Harpo, speaking with excitement now. "Maybe donate the proceeds to a cancer-related charity Gabe would have liked. I wish I had thought of it earlier, so we could have done it for the one-year anniversary, but hey, better late than never."

I paused unlocking my car door and looked at him. "So, is this you asking me to help out, or just telling me about it?"

"Whichever you want. You were always so great at putting stuff together. You are, I mean."

I tossed my items on the passenger seat. "For charity, you said? Which charity?"

"I don't know, I mean . . ." He swallowed. "If it's all right with you, I was thinking we could use any money we raise to help families dealing with cancer. Since you saw the toll it can take firsthand."

"Oh." I faltered. "Yeah. Totally." So many numb, grayscale days. I looked at Levi. "We both did."

Levi nodded, remembering. We were both silent, watching an old receipt catch in the wind and flutter up into the darkening sky.

"I don't know if I ever thanked you for that." I had a sudden memory of Levi picking Gabe up in his linebacker arms and carrying him to the bathroom, like a baby. Gabe was having trouble laughing without losing his breath. "So thank you."

"You did. You thanked me a million times."

"Oh. Good."

Levi rubbed his face with his hand. "Listen, if this is going to be too much—"

"No!" I took a breath. "No. I haven't really been out and about, so . . . Maybe it's good to get back to doing something for others."

"Good. Because a legacy of some kind . . . Something that helps people. That is peak Gabe, right?"

"I'm in, okay? I said I'm in."

"Great!" Levi said, looking genuinely relieved.

I finally glanced at my phone. Five minutes until I was supposed to meet Colin Q. Barely enough time to apply emergency deodorant. "Now I really have to go."

At this, Levi got a curious expression on his face. He took a step back, looking me up and down. "You're kind of fancy."

"Yeah." Considering we had almost made each other cry in a checkout line, there was no way I could tell him I was gussied up to meet Joe Random from the internet.

Levi pulled his eyes from me and cleared his throat, suddenly very formal. "Um, okay, then. Bye."

I watched him walk away. "Sorry I yelled at you in a Target, by the way," I called.

He paused in his path but didn't turn. Over his shoulder, he gave me a thumbs-up. "Super fun," he called back. "Let's do it again sometime."

At a wedding you'll find me . . .
Dancing to pop songs, scowling at all the other music selections, eating other people's desserts.

The sounds of Lake Street traffic and the burning smell rising from smokers along the sidewalk made me feel momentarily young, windswept by memories from my early twenties, going out on a Friday night during my first job. When I reached the address, I ignored my reflection in the tinted glass and yanked open the door to darkness and heavy objects crashing, rolling across wood in a dull thunder. *Bowl*, I remembered from Colin's message. So it was *that* kind of bowl.

A man rose at one of the tables, bulky, sweet-looking, hand up in a wave. My eyes adjusted. Beyond the dim front room scattered with tables, a series of lanes were bathed in blue and lavender light. Flashing animations of pins falling on the wall. Pitchers of beer. Cheering groups of friends. I returned the wave. There was no backing out now.

"Robin?" Colin grinned. He had very straight white teeth that didn't seem to fit with the scruff on his chin, the hiking-style tennis shoes, the wrinkled T-shirt under a button-down.

I looked down at my navy wool blend and wished I had some sort of cool jacket to tone down the nine-to-five look. "That's me," I said. I held my hand out.

He didn't notice the hand. "So you're an accountant?"

"Ten years and counting."

Colin laughed. I laughed because he did, then realized I had just made a joke. We sat.

I kept my hands under my thighs and ordered an IPA, hoping its bitterness would keep me from gulping it down. Colin ordered tots for the table and asked me how I was finding the app. *Infuriating*, I thought. *Humiliating*. "There are some nice guys," I said.

He straightened in his chair and took on an exaggerated, debonair tone. "Well, I'm absolutely thrilled to be counted among them." He dropped the act, adding. "Your profile is super funny."

Wherever Gabe was, he would be smug. I smiled, swallowed beer.

For him, Colin told me, it was so hard to find a woman who wasn't embittered or immediately defensive. "They talk to you as if you're some guy in a dark alley who's about to violate them. I'm like, *Hey, how was your day?* and she's like, *Fuck you!*" He shrugged. "Cue *Curb Your Enthusiasm* music." Now I was the one offering polite laughter. Colin brightened. "You like *Curb*?"

"I, uh . . ." I cleared my throat. "I know it, I just haven't seen it."

"Aw, man." He shook his head, his Crest-white smile fading. He looked somewhere in the middle distance. I was beginning to wonder if my lack of HBO had offended him in some way, but then he began to recount some of his favorite episodes of the show, which sounded to me like stories someone's grandmother would tell over the phone about her husband. I ate tots and offered occasional grunts of agreement.

"It's just so funny," he finally finished, waving his hand dismissively. "It's hard to explain."

"I'm sure it is."

Work was normal, I told him when he asked.

He hated his landscaping job, too, he told me. When I responded that I didn't exactly hate my job, Colin laughed as if I was being sarcastic and continued his diatribe against his profession, the backbreaking labor, the snobby people who on a whim made him dig up weeks of work and start over, mulch of all kinds. "I constantly have dirt under my fingernails," he told me, shaking his head. "But hey, not tonight," he said, clicking his tongue with a finger gun.

I finger-gunned back at him. He blushed.

"My real passion is improv," Colin was saying, leaning forward over his Michelob Ultra, eyebrows raised as if I should have some sort of reaction.

I was busy being self-conscious about the amount of grease-soaked napkins that had piled up in front of me. I tried to summon some knowledge. "Oh, like *Whose Line Is It Anyway?*"

Colin scoffed. "That's kind of a commercial bastardization of the form, but sure. We do long-form scenes. Someone in the audience suggests something, and then we build a whole world out of whatever they say. We basically write a play in real time."

"Sounds interesting." I sipped my half-drunk IPA and eyed the last tot.

"I don't know how interesting it is for the audience, but fuck them, right?"

"Um. Okay, sure."

"My group is kind of edgy," he explained. "We're called The Manly Men. It's a joke because we're totally the opposite. Look at me. I'm a blob." He forced a laugh.

As I laughed with him, he did the James Bond–style cocked-eyebrow thing, and my stomach turned, remembering the washed-out, smarmy look of the photo he'd recently posted. I guessed by *blob* he was referring to his general softness, which was fine with me, and probably would be fine with anyone. As long as he didn't do the eyebrow thing anymore, he would be cute. He sipped his beer. I sipped my own.

"I like *Storage Wars*," I said. And movies where ancient demons possess women named Cheryl, but I didn't mention that.

"Do you want to see some improv?" Colin asked.

The question didn't register right away. "Right now?" I finally said.

"Right *meow*." He pointed to an unseen corner, beyond the bowling alley. "They have a black box theater back there. There's a show that starts in a bit." He leaned across the table, doing the eyebrow-cock thing again. "That's secretly why I chose this place."

"Oh." My heart sank a tiny bit. "We're not bowling?" As we'd talked, I was slowly getting used to the idea. My dress was stiff but long enough to get a few good rolls.

Colin sighed. "Meh. I don't know. It's just hit the pins, over and over."

"True," I conceded. "That is how you bowl."

"I just get so bored . . . so." He finger-gunned again. "Improv?"

"Um, I may have to—" I pointed at my purse, which held my phone. "Let me see."

He stood, stretched. "You check, I pee."

"Sounds good."

He paused before he turned. "Hey."

"Yeah?"

He smiled down at me. "I'm having fun." His voice had dropped its jaunty quality, sounding lower, more genuine.

My heart began to beat. "Good," was all I could say.

While Colin was in the bathroom, I poked at my phone, though there was nothing there to check. It had been about forty-five minutes. For the dozenth time that evening, I had an urge to talk to my husband about the very thing I was supposed to be doing to move on from him, to excuse myself and call him and make this into a story we'd tell together, an inside joke about the time Robin had worn a horny secretary outfit to a bowling alley. *Use it!* Gabe had said. If I left now, that meant I couldn't even last an hour into my first experience of the app. And there were pleasant sensations to temper the weirdness—the sensations of being out and about, which I'd forgotten, the buzz of chatter, the smell of seasoned fried food. The IPA had left my head with a sparkly, cloudy feeling.

When Colin returned from the bathroom, I stood and held up my glass. "Are we allowed to bring our drinks into the theater?"

He lifted his fists, giving me a triumphant megawatt smile. "Yes! Huzzah!"

"Huzzah," I repeated.

In the black box, we sat in among a dozen rows of church-basement-style chairs. People stirred behind red velvet curtains dividing the room, and beyond the curtains the muffled crashes of bowling. I sipped on my recently replenished beer as Colin went around, greeting people in the audience he apparently knew. Sometimes he would point at me as he spoke to them, and I'd pretend not to notice, studying the uneven white polish on my nails as if it was a particularly interesting plaque at a museum. Soon, the lights dimmed and a hip-hop song from the '90s blared.

People in black T-shirts and jeans jogged up the outer aisles toward the curtain, whooping and clapping. Colin reclaimed his seat next to me.

"What's up, what's up, what's up?" a middle-aged man in Converse hollered at the crowd. He was flanked by two Colin-looking men, a skinny dude with glasses, and a woman with bottle-red hair. "We are Little Bang Theory, and welcome to the Bryant Lake Bowl & Theater!"

We cheered. The host began to explain the rules of the show, and the guy with glasses asked the audience for a word that would inspire their scenes.

"Telephone!" someone shouted from the back.

"Potato!" called someone else.

The actors began to mime the act of digging, speaking in Eastern European accents, performing a choppy, silly story about a journey to a witch to undo the curse over their potato harvest. More digging, more bad accents, a lot of rolling on the floor or climbing on prop chairs. I was starting to enjoy the small pause between lines where everyone's expectations were floating, watching the actors' faces when a line did not go where they thought it would, fumbling to catch hold of the twists and turns. I began to laugh out loud. The series of scenes ended with two peasants being slowly crushed by a giant potato, declaring their love for each other as they died. When the audience clapped and whooped, I joined.

"Okay, okay!" The bottle-red woman rubbed her hands together as she stepped forward. "It's going to get cold out there, right? And we're all looking for that special someone to keep us warm. It's almost cuffing season, y'all."

The audience tittered. I leaned over to Colin. "What's *cuffing season?*" I whispered.

"Cuff, like handcuff." He circled his hand on my wrist for a moment, then circled his own wrist. "Cuffed *together*." He gave me a joking, sickly-sweet smile, fluttering his eyelashes.

"Ah." Sensation lingered on the spot where he had touched me. I rubbed at it for a moment, as if trying to erase something.

The redhead shielded her eyes from the stage lights and surveyed the audience. "Raise your hand if you're married."

A few hands went up. Without thinking, I raised my own. Colin turned to look at me, surprise discernible in his expression even in the dark. I lowered my hand. "Oh, um . . ." Before I could gather an explanation, the woman onstage pointed toward the audience. Straight at me.

"Lady in the dress!" she called. "I saw that hand. Come on up here."

My heart leaped to my throat. I looked at Colin, then back toward the stage. "No, thank you."

The rest of the audience began to cheer encouragement. Under their shouts, I muttered to Colin. "I'm not actually married."

His brow scrunched. "Then, why did you raise your hand?"

I had forgotten. It was as simple as that, I supposed. "It's complicated," I said.

"Come on, lady in the blue dress!" The redhead was closer to us now, beckoning.

"Just do it for the show," Colin said, with an apologetic smile toward the actor. He put his hands on my arm, shoving slightly. "Go, go, go."

I stood and gulped the rest of my bitter beer, shaking off a slight, starry dizziness as the crowd applauded. They pulled a church-basement chair to center stage and guided me to sit. The hanging lights made me squint, warming my skin, transforming the audience into dark outlines.

"We call this *Scenes from a Marriage*," the redheaded woman told the crowd. A few people chuckled at the reference. "Here's how this is going to work. I'm going to ask—What's your name?"

"Robin," I said in a normal voice.

"Loud, so everyone can hear!"

"Robin!" I yelled.

The volume startled the woman, and she mimed covering her ears. The audience laughed. "Okay, Robin. Somewhere in the middle."

"How's this?" I called. The redhead gave me a thumbs-up. The heat of nerves briefly became a spark of pleasure. I was playing along correctly.

"So," the woman continued, "I'm going to ask Robin a few questions about her marriage, and we'll form a story based on what she says. Sound good?"

The performer looked at me. At the prospect of shouting about Gabe to all these people—Colin Q among them—my sweat glands made their presence known. I pictured Gabe in the audience, watching me with that smirk, his shoulders shaking with silent laughter. I tried to wet my dry mouth and nodded, giving a thumbs-up.

"How long have you been married?"

"I was married nine years," I recited.

"*Was?* You're not currently?"

"No."

The woman squinted toward the lights, trying to find Colin, and looked back at me, puzzled. "So that guy you were with is *not* your husband."

A couple folks in the audience gave a scandalized, escalating *Oooh!* One of the disheveled guys in the group stepped toward my chair and jerked his thumb in the crowd's direction. "That's frickin' Colin. I know that dude."

I tried to sound casual as I felt a nervous smile spread across my face. "Yeah, so Colin is not my husband, but yes, I came here with him."

The woman gasped, leaned close, and asked in a stage whisper, "Did Colin know you were married?"

I let out a choked laugh. "Nope. Sorry, Colin." I offered an exaggerated shrug toward his seat, prompting more sounds of delight and shock from the audience. "Ouch!" I heard Colin exclaim theatrically. "You go, girl!" someone shouted.

The redheaded woman wiggled her eyebrows. "So how does your husband feel about Colin, if you don't mind my asking?"

"Yeah, I'd certainly like to know." Colin had chimed in again.

"Shut up," someone called from the back corner. More laughter.

"Ha, well, he would probably think this was hilarious." I'd used the conditional, *would*. Could they tell? My pulse began to sound in my ears.

I felt the performance fall from my face, a heaviness taking its place. I knew this feeling, but I didn't know what to call it. A specific kind of dread for people who had bad news to share. "I don't know, though," I said in my normal voice.

"None of his business, right?" The woman smiled, lifting her hands, soliciting the audience's agreement. Her voice came from far away.

Deep inhale, a wind tunnel of my ears. Hands lifting off my knees, voice projecting toward the mountain range of anonymous heads. "He's dead."

A rush of air, which I realized was my own breath. The scale of the room shrunk back to its original state. The redheaded woman blinked mascara-caked lashes. "Your husband is . . ."

"He passed away." I had done it. I'd said it, and it felt . . . surprisingly good. Like I was setting down something heavy.

The redhead's eyes widened in horror. "I'm so sorry."

"Thank you. But really, it's okay." For whatever reason, I felt like sharing tonight. Maybe it was because no one knew me here. No one knew Mayor Gabe. I would finally get to talk about my marriage without a whole town's worth of people's expectations on top of it. I adjusted in my seat, trying to sit a little taller and made my smile reassuring. I was ready to keep playing.

"Uh, I don't think this works for the game, right?" The woman looked back at her stage companions, all of whom seemed as wide-eyed as her. She looked back at me and touched my shoulder for a moment, drawing her hand away. "Ergh." She looked out at the crowd, shielding her eyes again. "Sorry, folks! Just trying to be sensitive here."

"Let her leave," someone called out from the audience.

The redhead turned back to me. "How long has he—how long has it been?"

"A year. So, it's fine. You can ask me about . . . whatever."

"After a year it's allowed, I think," the guy with glasses said.

"What's allowed?" the redheaded woman asked.

The glasses guy looked uncomfortable. "I don't know. Stuff?"

"No! Hello!" The same audience member as before piped up again. "Just let the poor woman get off the stage."

"Oh, my god, come on. I'm not a *poor woman*," I said in the direction of the voice.

By the redheaded woman's expression, it was clear she didn't believe me, but she adopted a shaky smile and proceeded. "What is the most annoying thing about your husband?"

That was easy. "He took superlong showers."

"Long showers," the woman repeated. "Cool, cool, cool."

In the silence that followed, I thought I could hear one of the performers mutter behind me. "This is so fucking awkward, bro."

The woman pressed on. "What else?"

"Uh, let's see . . ." I thought for a moment. "Oh, here's another one. Every outing took three hours because Gabe had to stop and talk to everyone. You could never run a simple errand . . ."

Before I could finish, I could hear Colin Q adopting his finger-gun, stage-worthy voice. "Okay, that's it. Can we slow our roll? This woman is with me, and so I feel somewhat responsible."

"Colin," I said, half laughing, half sighing. "Please, chill."

He continued as if he hadn't heard me. "It's not funny to make fun of people's tragedies. I didn't know she was a widow, but this is clearly a touchy topic for people, and we as performers need to do better."

"They're not making fun of me or . . . my late husband, right?" I tried to find the eyes of as many people onstage as I could. None would hold my gaze. "They're making fun of marriage in general."

"Yeah, but using stories from your actual life," someone said behind me. I turned to look at the other Colin-looking guy, and he took a step back as if I had flipped him the bird.

"I have to agree," the middle-aged host said.

The guy with glasses gestured toward me. "She said she wanted to do it."

"She doesn't know what she's getting into, Cory." Colin again. I tried to make him out beyond the lights; he was standing, now. "You guys literally killed someone with a potato in the first sketch." He turned to me. "And here she is, like, sitting here, having experienced *actual* death . . ."

I smiled, rolled my eyes. "My husband didn't die of being rolled over by a potato."

Beyond the hot halo of lights, I could hear the laughter of a single person. The rest of the audience muttered. "Can we just get on with it?" someone asked. The redhead looked at me with strained eyes and clenched teeth. I couldn't tell if it was because she wanted to express her discomfort at my stubbornness or if she was in commiseration with me over the ridiculous proceedings. "What am I supposed to do here?" she asked everyone and no one.

The actors were frozen, stealing glances at each other.

The host stepped to center stage. "A year? It's too raw. It's just not appropriate. I'm sorry, lady. I'm not doing it."

The more polished Colin-looking guy called, "Give her a hand for her bravery, ladies and gents."

"For the love of god," I muttered. I stood from the chair and gave a sarcastic bow. My one sympathetic fan in the audience laughed again.

The applause was feeble as I made my way down the aisle, trying to appear dignified even as I couldn't see a few feet in front of me.

"Hey, wow, so sorry," Colin leaned close and whispered as I sat. I got a whiff of Michelob Ultra and powdery fabric softener. "Why didn't you tell me you were a widow?"

"What difference does it make?" I whispered back. The redheaded woman was seeking out another victim from the audience.

"I wouldn't have brought you to a frickin' comedy show for a date."

"What date is better?" I posed, not bothering to keep my voice down as the crowd cheered the next volunteer making his way to the stage. "Should we have gone to church?"

Colin chortled. "Can I say something? You're actually kind of funny."

"Gee, thanks," I replied, and the guy onstage began to talk about his husband's toenail-clipping habits. The audience was in stitches. When Colin turned his face back toward the stage, I picked up my purse, made myself as small as I could, and roamed along the wall until I found the exit.

My friends call me . . .

Robbie. Robin the Boy Wonder. What's-her-name-Bart-and-Margie's-eldest.

Six Bubbl messages from Colin Q had filtered in over the last seventy-two hours—Where did I go? Was I okay? Hope I was all right after the show. Did he do something wrong? He was just trying to be sensitive. I owed him an explanation—all of which remained unanswered while I worked during the day, and lay on the couch wearing Gabe's slippers, watching *The Thing*.

Wednesday evening, as I drove to my mom's house, an old feeling had emerged: the adolescent ache of being picked last. Here I was, trying to hobble back into society, playing nicely with Colin Q, listening to his rants, going to his stupid show, and when I'd tried to actually enjoy myself, I had been sidelined. Publicly finger-gunned and shooed away. Last night I had almost written back, *Sorry, can't talk, suffering slow death by potato*, but that would be rude. Less rude, most likely, than flat-out ignoring him, but I couldn't bring myself to open the app, couldn't bear the flashbacks of hot lights, pity claps.

"What did you bring?" Mom asked when I arrived, pointing at my bursting tote bag. Inside were a bulk stack of IKEA place mats I'd bought in Minneapolis for the restaurant and a Pyrex full of roasted broccoli.

"Just a few things." I followed her inside and set the bag and the Tupperware on the old kitchen table we'd had since I was a kid.

"You didn't have to bring anything. I told you I got a rotisserie chicken."

"But you always forget the vegetables."

"Bah." Mom waved a hand in front of her face as if she smelled something foul. "Boo, vegetables. No one needs vegetables."

She was only half kidding. Margie Lindstrom had always been considered the Cool Mom among my elementary-school friends because she didn't make us eat anything we didn't like, including anything leafy, green, or that came from the ground. Thankfully she still heeded Dad's advice that it wouldn't kill Green River to offer a salad or two.

I opened my mother's fridge and surveyed the contents: a six-pack of Mike's Hard Lemonade, string cheese, a pack of Colby, three Yoplait yogurts, a pack of butcher-fresh brats, and the aforementioned rotisserie chicken.

"You can put out the string cheese as an appetizer," Mom said, reaching around me to grab a Mike's Hard. "I'll be right back. I'm gonna check on how Rick's doing through dinner service and get a smoke."

My phone chimed: a Bubbl message had come through. "What do you want, Colin?" I muttered to myself. "Can't you tell I'm trying to get rid of you?"

But it wasn't Colin. The little circular avatar revealed someone in a Twins ball cap, sharp-jawed, eyes squinting as he smiled in a patch of sun.

Pole City Eagles >>> Brokenridge Bears, the first line of his message read.

Pole City was a neighboring town, a bit closer to the Cities, more of what they called a "bedroom community," with a Saturday-morning farmers market and a main street full of galleries and antiques. They were our better-funded rivals in high school, with nicer uniforms, a better gym. Curiosity almost got me to press the bubble, but I stopped myself. I wasn't emotionally ready to be serious about any of these guys. What was the point of playing with them?

And yet. His good looks were almost jarring. Were there hot scammer bots of straight women, too? Was he really a sad grandmother from Florida with too much time on her hands? I put the phone away.

As I finished setting the table, I was surprised to hear Theo's voice coming from the hall. He and my mom came into the kitchen as she offered him a sip of her Mike's Hard. "It's peach bellini," she was saying.

"Blech. Tastes like vitamins." Theo handed her back the bottle, his face twisting. He pulled out a pint of Smirnoff in a paper bag from his jacket. "Do we have any limes?"

"What are you doing here on a weeknight?" I had tried not to make it sound too accusatory, but judging by the look on his face, I had failed.

"What? I can't have dinner with my family? I spent the night at Jay's last night," he said, taking his own turn with the fridge. "Ugh, no limes. Okay, we can improvise . . ."

"Sounds fun." I put on a smile as I added a third plate and fork. "What's Jay up to?"

"Nothing."

"He's still working at the bank, right?"

"Still at the bank," Theo replied in a monotone, opening a can of Diet Coke he'd found in a corner of the fridge door.

"You shoulda brought him for dinner," Mom said as she sat down.

Theo smirked. "Have you seen his parents' house? Jay can buy his own dinner."

My mom bowed her head and muttered a Hail Mary. I stared at Theo as she prayed, trying to figure out what was different about him. His skin had red patches, just like mine did when I didn't get enough sleep. Dark circles under his eyes. I was always worrying about him, and I paid for it, literally. Loans covered his education, but I sent him bank transfers for his tiny apartment in Saint Paul, his utilities, his groceries. I didn't mind, I had the money to spare. Because Gabe's parents had gifted him our house, I had no mortgage, and I had been able to pay most of Gabe's medical bills thanks to good insurance from my job. *What?* Theo mouthed at me. *Nothing*, I mouthed back and smiled. He returned my smile with a clownish, exaggerated grin. I chuckled.

"Amen," my mom said, opening her eyes and looking lovingly back and forth at the two of us. "And thank you, God, for the opportunity to sit down to a meal with my babies."

Theo gestured to the rotisserie chicken in the middle of the table. "Are we supposed to, like, pull off pieces of meat with our hands or . . . ?"

"There's a knife," I said, nodding toward the serrated blade I'd put on the table.

Theo picked it up and examined it warily.

"All right, just give it." I stood and held out my hand. Theo thrust it blade first and thankfully I moved my palm in time to avoid a cut.

As I divided up the chicken, Mom told us about the latest gossip she'd heard at the restaurant. Peg Grossman's daughter got moved to an alternative high school in the Cities because she has some sort of eating problem. The Rundles' dog got out, got in a fight with a bobcat. Tammy and Burt Fink are sleeping in separate rooms. With each story, I could picture the people she was talking about, the people I had known all my life.

I dished myself more of the untouched broccoli. "How are classes, T?"

Theo was peeling a string off one of the cheese sticks. "Meh. I just have some scheduling stuff to figure out."

"Are you not liking Ancient Histories?" I asked. "I remember you weren't sure about that one."

"Yeah, so," Theo began, his voice dropping, "the issue is more that I'm not liking anthropology."

"In general?"

Theo sucked air through his teeth like, *yikes*. "Yeah. In general."

"Oh, shoot." My mom stifled a bellini-induced burp. "Sorry to hear that, honey."

I put down my fork. "So what does this mean?"

Theo was mixing another batch of Diet Coke and Smirnoff, stirring with his finger. "It means . . ." a tentative smile spread across his face ". . . I'm kind of looking at forensics."

My mom clapped her hands together. "Oh, like CSI?"

A burning mass rose from my chest to my throat. I didn't know if it was the chicken or the sudden rage. "You gotta be kidding me."

"I knew it." Theo looked pointedly at my mom. "Thank *you* for being supportive, Ma."

I put my face in my hands, seeing stars, smelling broccoli. "You have twelve credits left on your anthro degree, Theo," I muttered through my palms. "Four classes. One semester. Now you have to start all over."

"Not true. I still have my gen eds."

"Great." I smiled at him sarcastically. "Congratulations."

Theo matched my sarcasm. "Thank you so much!"

"Tell you what," I began, heat pulsing under my skin. "Can you go ahead and tell me when you plan on switching from forensics to frickin'... film studies? I'd like to put it on the calendar now."

"Robbie, come on," my mother said in a half-hearted attempt to referee.

Theo threw up his hands. "Sorry it's taking me a while to figure out what I like. Sorry I didn't immediately become an accountant."

"You don't have to be sorry. But you do need to tell me how much longer I'll be paying your rent. How about that?"

"Fuck it, I'll pay my own rent. I'll just quit school. Get a job."

"No," I said, almost involuntarily. For some reason, I thought of his carelessness with the knife, blade out.

"Then, what do you want me to do?"

The question was not just argumentative. There was part of him, I thought, that truly wanted to know. Under the exhaustion-tinted cheeks was the little boy who sat next to me at this very table in his footie pajamas, who needed me to be there for him in the middle of the night.

"I don't want this to be a fight," I said, my chest still burning.

"Me either," Theo said, indignant. "Like, I truly want to be a crime-scene tech. This is the thing I actually want to do. I promise."

That was what he had said about anthropology after watching a Discovery Channel documentary. I held my tongue.

In the silence, my mom whispered to Theo. "Can you grab me another Mike's, hon?"

"Happy to," Theo said, still looking at me as he reached for the fridge door.

I tried to slacken the grip of panic around my insides. "You always did like to collect stuff," I offered. "Remember your museums?"

"Aw, yes!" my mom cooed.

Theo nodded, smiling, and we began to reminisce. Theo liked to gather and label all the things he found outside. Buttons, feathers, snail shells, river-smoothed rocks.

He had been the kid that went around the neighborhood knocking on people's doors, asking to play with whatever child lived in the house regardless of age. By his senior year of high school, Theo was well-loved by teachers and students alike. He was voted Homecoming King. He went to class when he wanted, waltzing in and out of the house, grabbing food, avoiding work at the restaurant by citing his full social calendar and kissing Mom on the cheek. And we let him. He was coming back more and more weekends, apparently dating—or at least hooking up with—the only other gay kid in his graduating class, drinking for cheap or free at the Red Lyon because another friend of his worked behind the bar. Now, at the prospect of changing his major for the second time, his eyes were bright. "I'm excited."

"I hope this one works out for you, T. I really do." I lifted my water for a cheers.

"Nuh-unh," my mom said, putting her hand on my wrist. "Bad luck."

I chugged the water, and Theo poured some of the vodka and Diet into my emptied glass.

"To CSI!" Mom called out.

"To CSI," Theo and I echoed, and I swigged, gagging at the taste. Theo smacked his lips.

"Oh, and another thing to celebrate." Mom set her Mike's Hard bottle down with a clunk. "We just put out that new pinot at the restaurant, so cross your fingers that it sells. I bought four cases!"

"Four cases." The burning in my chest came back. I felt my jaw clench. "Mom."

"Uh-oh," Mom said, glancing at Theo, wiggling her eyebrows.

"Here she goes," Theo said, smiling and shaking his head.

"Here I go. Stating basic financial concerns."

"Honey, honey, please. I got a discount. And you've just got to try it to see what I mean. It's so good, Robbie."

"It doesn't matter, Mom. You don't have the wine sales to support four cases. Now you're over budget, and they're just going to sit there, collecting dust." I stood from my seat, my chair screeching on the tile.

"Oh, Lord, we've upset her again," Mom said.

"No, you haven't," I said. "I'm just . . ." I didn't have the energy for another clash. I was sick of being the bad guy. "Nothing. Never mind."

"It's going to be all right," my mom called from the other room.

"I sure hope so," I called back and took a seat in the makeshift office Mom had set up in the corner of the family room.

She had insisted on keeping the books on paper, and I had insisted on keeping them digitally, so we compromised with a classic bookkeeper's notebook filled with my mom's curly scrawl and a cheap laptop, where I entered the expenses and balanced them against the meager profit. As I waited for Excel to load, I heard the thump of the refrigerator close, the hiss of a new bottle opening. I turned my mom's first-generation flat-screen on to HGTV so I didn't have to listen to the two of them cackling.

We'd just have to cut costs somewhere else. Where, I had no idea. We had to pay Rick a living wage. We paid slightly higher prices for produce to support local farmers. Maybe we could close for breakfast or lunch. Save a few bucks a week on utilities. I opened my phone at a push notification from Bubbl: *Jake B's message is waiting. Are you going to respond?* Pole City vs. Brokenridge. Nostalgic thoughts of stadium lights and marching-band drums and shoe-polish messages written on cars drifted across the spreadsheet. I found myself smiling. I pressed the bubble next to his name and began to craft a response.

Earl the Eagle? Is that you? That was the name of their very purple, very Barney-looking mascot. I clicked over to his profile. *Jake B, 35, Pole City.*

Lol, Jake B wrote back. Busted.

I scrolled. *Weezer and old-school country only*, he had written under the *I'm listening to . . .* prompt and for *At a wedding, you'll find me . . .* he'd said *Cha-cha sliding with the best of them.* His photos seemed to all be outdoors, one giving a thumbs-up against a backdrop of mountains, another appeared to be a selfie with a surfboard, sunglasses perched on a head shaved bald with a hint of dark hair, the same color as the five-o'clock shadow on his face. His final written prompt made me do a double take: *I'm looking for . . . Something slow and steady.* Good things take time. Considering my previous relationship lasted over a decade, I had to agree with you there, Jake B.

So how long have you lived in BR? Jake wrote.

Almost all my life, I wrote back. You?

Same, he sent. Minus a brief stint at the U.

Same, I wrote. I commute to the Cities, though. D you work in PC or Mpls?

Mpls! Are we the same person?

I chuckled to myself and looked toward the kitchen where Theo and my mom were still sitting. Maybe, I typed, suddenly self-conscious. I glanced at the TV. Are you currently watching This Old House?

A bubble arose as Jake typed, then disappeared. I put my phone aside and tried to concentrate on the sheet of drywall being pummeled by a hammer, my heart beating. A ding from my phone. I scrambled.

I am now! Jake wrote.

And there it was in my belly, the promise of the app, almost like nausea, but lighter, sweeter, sparkling. Bubbles.

The most random thing I've done . . .
Ate peanut butter M&Ms while watching a mosh pit.

This time I was going to do it right. There would be no sweating, no impromptu trips to Target, no ancient businesswear, no finger-gunning, and by god, no mention of my late husband. I was going to keep it light and breezy. Over the week, Jake and I had found a few acquaintances in common, and it was also discovered that he worked in third-party risk at Target headquarters, just a few blocks away. Soon, we had moved from messaging via the Bubbl app to messaging by phone, sending each other pictures from our respective offices, trading anecdotes about the best little Vietnamese and North African spots in the skyway. Earlier that week, I had jokingly suggested we carpool, but he preferred to drive to a park and ride near the Mall of America and bike the Greenway. *Impressive*, I told him. *My husband used to* I had begun to type and stopped myself. No repeat of the Widow Humiliation Show. No Gabe. I deleted the text before I could send. Another message from Jake came through: Would I like to meet him at the Pole City Fall Fest on Sunday? I would. It had been years since I'd been to Fall Fest, I told him, and it had always been my dream to solve the infamous corn maze in under fifteen minutes. Odd and very specific dream, he replied, but okay. You're on.

Since then, I kept looking at the messages to confirm they were real.

I couldn't believe the words on the screen were mine, that my presence on the app was powerful enough to incite a positive response from a handsome stranger. The messages were like a glimpse into the life of someone else, and on Sunday, I would need to act like her, to look like her. No, not someone else. Like myself, better. On Friday, I texted Theo to see if he would go shopping with me.

No, he responded. You know I'm not that type of gay.

It was true. Neither of us had ever been the glitzy type, and our mom, with her grease-spotted apron and decades-old blue eye shadow, was hardly a model of grace and poise.

I'm not asking you because you're gay, I'm asking you because you're my friend, I responded. And I need help. I need a date look.

Aw <3, Theo wrote back. Idk, I just buy whatever is suggested to me on Instagram.

"With *my* money," I muttered to my phone.

I decided to text Marcy Reyes, a friend from Sisters in Grief. What's the name of your stylist again? I asked her, adding a haircut emoji for casual effect.

Mercedes, Marcy replied and sent me the woman's contact info, no questions asked. But DO NOT be late or criticize, Marcy followed up. She's a genius but she's very particular.

Jake hadn't mentioned a time I should meet him, I realized. Was I allowed to ask him about the time, or was that too eager? Should I text him again about some other aspect of the date, and simply hope he picked up on the fact that I was seeking information? Should I text him about something unrelated to the date, so as to display my nonchalance? I googled *what to text someone before a date*.

The advice was to keep it simple and lighthearted, to avoid heavy subjects or mundane questions. It was decided: I should not directly ask him about the time. Asking someone the time could be perceived as mundane.

I went with, I am looking forward to our date.

Same! he responded.

But I really wanted to know the time. I was not a spontaneous or laid-back person. The weather during that morning should be nice! I sent.

The idea was, if he had a time *other* than morning in mind, this would invite him to contradict me and propose the actual time. I congratulated myself on my cleverness.

Yep, supposed to be clear all day, he wrote. Then nothing.

I realized with a jolt: weather is the most mundane topic of all human conversation. It literally happens to everyone, every single moment of every day. I was ruining the date before it even began. I banged my head on my desk.

All afternoon, I jumped at every little ding, hoping Jake had replied, but it was just emails trickling in, then flooding. The accounting manager for the entire company had conducted another training on the new payroll system, and no one understood what was going on—except, apparently, for me. Soon, it was past six, and the clerks from soaps, cleaners, and even plastics were gathered in a conference room with their laptops while I ran an impromptu training, explaining and re-explaining the functions my manager had not understood enough to illustrate properly. After a hearty thanks and compliment session, I had a brief moment of satisfaction, only to realize that all of my efforts to help the others had caused my own tasks to pile up.

I returned to my office with a Pop-Tart from the vending machine and worked until my screen's glow felt like the only light in the building.

Still no word from Jake.

As the elevator slid down to the lobby, I combed through Gabe's email for a little comfort, as I had a million times before, wishing his matchmaking scheme came with a manual. That way I could read his vision for me and follow the steps, and I would know when I was doing it right. It would be like when I used to edit his speeches for Memorial Day and dedication events—I wasn't perfect at grammar, but I could understand him better than anyone, break down his big, wandering ideas and make them simple and efficient. He used to lean over the desk while I reviewed his drafts, breathing gently next to my ear as he read, occasionally absent-mindedly kissing me on the cheek.

When I reached the street, the wind cut across my cheeks. My phone dinged. It was Jake. What time works for you on Sunday?

The butterflies inside resurrected, though now they were beginning to feel bigger, more substantive. More like pterodactyls.

That Sunday, what was supposed to be an autumnal sun beat down on my heavily made-up face. I had woken up early—though, I hadn't really slept, half-due to nerves, half-due to the fact that I had propped myself up with pillows for fear of ruining what was admittedly an impeccable blowout I'd had from Mercedes the day before. By the time she was done, the strands around my face were arranged to make me look ten years younger. Marcy was right: she was a genius.

This morning, I had carefully risen from bed to follow a YouTube makeup tutorial, opting for a *natural* look, which, in my hands, turned into more of a *late-career Elizabeth Taylor* look. I'd always been a little heavy-handed and Halloweeny with makeup. Having risen early, I didn't account for the fact that I would have to eat without ruining said look, nor did I anticipate falling asleep on my couch midmorning during an episode of *90 Day Fiancé*, or having to slather on more makeup to fix the nap-induced smudges and gaps. Now, I stood in the unseasonable warmth between two hay bales in Pole City, waiting for Jake and breaking my promise to myself that I would not sweat.

This was Fall Fest, was it not? Fall in Minnesota, where one shivered against the creeping chill and tucked one's hands into sweaters, cupping mugs full of hot liquids. I had worn wool socks inside my boots and optimistically purchased a fitted flannel Oxford, tight corduroy pants, and a bomber jacket with a few extraneous zippers. As I scanned the crowd for Jake, jacket under my arm, beads of moisture pricked my scalp. It must have been seventy degrees.

I saw him before he saw me. He had stepped out of his gold Prius in the parking lot, wearing a ball cap, a T-shirt, and Docker-ish pants that hugged a taut, ropy frame that was just a couple of inches taller than me. He was smaller than many men I'd been attracted to, but he carried himself with ease. My eyes were drawn to the outline of his muscles under his shirt. Behind his Ray Ban–style sunglasses, he seemed to catch me staring. I waved, suddenly conscious of how heavy and floppy hands could be.

"Should have ridden my bike here," he said as he got closer, reaching his arms out and lifting his face toward the sun. "It's like June. I love it."

"Should have worn shades," I said, pointing to my face.

Without hesitating, he wrapped me in a warm hug, as if we were old friends reuniting. When he released, I realized I had forgotten to breathe.

Jake nodded toward the festivities, putting his hands on his thin hips. "This is my friend's land. Or rather, his family's. They rent it out to the city every year."

"Very cool," I said, and I meant it. Again, Gabe's name rose to my mouth, about to tell him about our own little patch of dirt, but I caught it before I could break my own rule.

"We used to camp here, like, every weekend. See that big tree?"

I shaded my eyes. Off in the distance, beyond the carnival games and Ferris wheel, an oak with gnarled branches and yellowing leaves rose over the rest of the tree line. "It's beautiful."

"Right?" Jake continued. "In the summers we'd just bring sleeping bags out here and build a fire and hang out all night. Have rock-throwing contests. Sometimes we still get out here on the weekends, but all my high school friends have kids now, so . . ."

"Mine, too," I told him, and we exchanged a look of kinship. Birth rates were declining across the world, but not in these hundred square miles. I could always entertain the idea of having children, but Gabe had never wanted them. He always used to tell me that he was called to public service, not fatherhood. The citizens were his kids.

As Jake and I walked side by side, exchanging more stories about the area, I snuck glances at him, enjoying the way his jaw cut a shadow across his winged shoulders, the way his nose sharpened under his frames. There was something so confident in his manner, the athletic bounce in his stride, his decision to shave his head—it was thinning, he'd told me, so he'd said screw it, he decided to get rid of it altogether. The bare skin of his scalp peeked out from under his baseball cap. I'd never been attracted to a man without hair before, but there weren't many men without hair who had a face like Jake's. On the hayride, I sat with my hip touching his, leaning against him as we hit the curves. Soon, we were making our way down the line of games, shooting bottles with air rifles and fishing for ducks. I dreaded to think what the sweat was doing to my YouTube tutorial creation, but I stopped caring after a while, sailing in giddiness, nostalgia. My limbs felt light, casting off the little balls during a "shooting hoops" game as if they were magnetically compelled into the net. I was having fun.

When the buzzer sounded, I grabbed a handful of napkins from the concession cart to wipe my face. Across the grounds, kids screeched with delight on the Ferris wheel. As I patted foundation off my skin, I could smell butter from the popcorn, cinnamon from the cider.

"Want to do the corn maze?" he called from a few feet away.

I pressed a napkin to my closed eyelids. "Give me a sec, hon," I replied.

All my nerves ignited before I knew why. I froze. Had he heard me? I lowered the napkin but couldn't bring myself to lift my eyes from the ground. My pulse pounded. Maybe I could pretend like it didn't happen. I had called him *hon*.

I risked a look. Jake had his head turned away from me, watching the Ferris wheel. The endorphins from the basketball game had helicoptered me into some other time, some other dimension where the man I used to call *honey* was still alive, still waiting for me to wipe sweat off my brow so we could complete the Pole City Fall Fest corn maze. My mind had not kept up with my senses, and my senses had fallen back into the past.

Jake, in the meantime, gave me a curious look, smiling. "Ready?" But it wasn't Gabe's smile. Of course it wasn't.

"Ready." I smiled back, relieved.

He seemed to have not heard, or if he had, maybe he just presumed the *hon* was commonplace. Maybe he thought I was like an old-timey waitress who called everyone *hon*. *Calm down*, I told myself. *Different man. Different hair. No parenthesis wrinkle near the mouth.* Jake was far from Gabe 2.0, and everything was fine. I was still following the rules. Except for the sweat.

As we breached the maze, I set the timer on my watch.

"She's serious," he said, his thin face cracking into a giant smile. "We're actually doing this."

"Oh, yeah, buddy. We're doing this." I had already gotten a few paces ahead of him—paces, I knew, that he would probably make up with his active stride.

We took a right. It was a pretty standard move, I told Jake, but this was supposed to be a pretty standard maze, as far as I remembered from the last time I was here, which meant that the path either followed a diagonal or some sort of circle.

But turning right had brought us to a dead end. "Oh, no!" I wailed.

Jake laughed and pointed back toward the beginning, to which we sailed as fast as my legs could go. Going left yielded better progress, bringing us into a series of uninterrupted zigzags. Time was ticking, but we might still beat the fifteen-minute mark.

"I have a feeling we're circling the center," I told Jake. "Maybe the end of the maze isn't actually the exit."

"Do you, like, do mazes in your spare time?"

"I've always been good at puzzles," I told him as we followed a narrow corn-flanked corridor. "I've always liked them."

"Oh, yeah? What else do you do for fun?"

"Um . . ." We'd reached a fork in the road. I was having trouble answering. Like all the *what are you up to* queries of all the nice guys before him, I didn't really have much of an answer. I watched a lot of TV and movies, I could say, but judging by all of his surfing and camping and biking, the number of *Scream* sequels I could quote probably wouldn't make a favorable impression. "Let's go right," I said, hoping he would drop the subject.

But my choice, once again, led us to an unyielding wall of corn. I tried to shrug it off as we backtracked. We were both silent as we made our way back to the fork. The other direction quickly led us to another fork, where I brought us right again.

Another dead end.

"I thought you said you were good at this," Jake said playfully, brushing his hand across the drooping green leaves.

For some reason this bothered me more than I would have liked. Not for any reason related to Jake: I knew he was joking. But something to do with me. Something to do with the fact that I couldn't answer his question about my idea of fun. My chest was tight, and there was a pricking in the corners of my eyes. Why was I getting emotional? Because of a stupid fucking maze? Come on. Though I had cried a lot over the past twelve months, I couldn't remember the last time I'd cried recently. I hadn't even let myself shed tears on the one-year anniversary. I pushed away these thoughts and looked at my watch. Thirteen minutes we'd been weaving. Two minutes to beat the record. I began to jog. My lungs and legs immediately protested, but I kept going.

"Slow down, turbo," Jake called, still walking behind me.

"We don't have much time!" I called over my shoulder.

Jake laughed. "Wow, hey, is there some sort of imminent threat I don't know about? Do we need to get to the center of this maze to dismantle a bomb or something?"

He had a point. I was being intense. For good reason, I thought, but I couldn't quite say what that reason was. I slowed. When he caught up to me, I pointed over his shoulder, trying to mask my disappointment. "You know what we should have done? Gone on the Ferris wheel to get a better look at the overall layout."

"What were we thinking?" Jake said, shaking his head, still chuckling.

After what felt like hours but was probably minutes, we finally found the center, a clearing of razed corn where more maze-solvers rested on a circle of hay bales. I had tried not to check my watch, but I couldn't help it: twenty-eight minutes. I collapsed on a bale, discarding my jacket, and gladly accepted Jake's offer to get us some refreshment from the small stand. My chest was still tight, but I chalked that up to being out of shape. Jake was still moving easily, naturally. He clearly belonged. *Good at puzzles*. I wanted to kick myself. Even if it was true, it was a very lame thing to be good at. Why couldn't I have an actual hobby? Like Rollerblading? No, that was probably even lamer.

I looked up from my lap. A short-haired, pinkish-skinned, middle-aged woman was walking toward me, sporting a Packers windbreaker.

"Mrs. Mayor herself! I thought that was you! Haven't seen you out and about." She stood above me, her eyes and smile a little too big, a little too bright.

"Hi, Tammy," I said, not bothering to correct the *Mrs. Mayor* designation, though it had always annoyed me. Mom and Theo always thought it was hilarious. I nodded toward the exit of the maze. "Are you enjoying the—"

"Did you see my Facebook post, by the way?" Tammy cut me off. "I tagged you."

"I must have missed it."

Tammy looked at me like I had cursed her mother. "It was a tribute to Gabe. I got all these old photos I dug from the campaign email inbox. There were five hundred likes. Maybe seventy comments. It was beautiful. But the whole time I was thinking, where is Robin? She's the one who should be liking this."

My chest continued to contract. I took a step away from Tammy, hoping this would free up some more oxygen. "I haven't been on Facebook for a while." For exactly that reason. It wasn't as if anyone was trying to get a hold of me for any present concerns. My wall was basically a digital altar.

"You check it out and let me know what you think. I think you'll enjoy it. Who's your friend?"

Jake had sidled next to me with a sweating bottle of water. I took the water, opened it, and gulped. "I'm Jake," he said as I chugged, offering his hand.

I should handle this, somehow, I was thinking. I needed to excuse Jake and me from this interaction so I could keep this date from imploding. The rule was No Gabe. Tammy was All Gabe. It's possible she even had nursed a crush on him. As I swallowed water, I saw her eyes move to Jake's left hand. She was putting things together.

She smiled up at him. "We were just talking about Robin's husband. Did you know Mayor Gabe?"

To his credit, Jake didn't miss a beat. "Oh, sure, yeah. He was on the news, right?"

"CNN," Tammy said, emphasizing each letter. "For his stoplight. A feature on small-town America." Gabe had fought the council tooth and nail to take federal grant money for a stoplight and crosswalk near the high school, Tammy explained to Jake. During his tenure, traffic accidents in Brokenridge had gone down sixty percent. With that publicity, he was able to secure even more federal grant money for Brokenridge's first food pantry. "The *Star Tribune* called him The Grantmaster," Tammy finished, beaming.

"So that's Robin's . . ." Jake turned to me, puzzled. "*Who* is he to you?"

I pressed my lips together in a resigned smile. "He was my husband."

"Oh," he said simply. He paused, the question forming.

I spared him of having to ask it. "He passed."

"Of cancer," Tammy added.

"About a year ago," I said to Jake. "A little over a year."

Jake put a warm hand on my shoulder briefly. "Oh, man. I'm so sorry."

"Feels like yesterday," Tammy said wistfully. "Brokenridge will never be the same, I'll tell you that much." She turned to Jake again. "He was an angel. You should have seen him at city council meetings. People would stand up and rail against this and that, and Gabe would just sit there and listen with this calm expression and respond to every concern. Heck, he'd have them volunteering by the end. He was so smart, but he didn't talk down to people. Like frickin' Mister Rogers. He had that little smile. You remember that smile." Tammy nudged me.

"I do." The tightness in my chest turned to heaviness.

"You should have seen the funeral," Tammy was saying to Jake. "Bagpipes. Color guard. Went on for freakin' three hours with all the people that wanted to speak. It was something to see."

"I bet it was." Jake glanced at me. His manner held no pity, though. No morbid curiosity or revulsion. I wished I knew what he was thinking.

Tammy tilted her head, somehow casual yet accusatory at the same time. "You know, we were wondering if you were going to do something this year for him."

The emotion from earlier was coming back. *Why?* I asked myself, trying to dim my panic. *Why couldn't you have done this literally any other time this week?* I took another step, trying to put further distance between Tammy and me. "I just did something at home."

"Do you want more water?" Jake asked.

"No," I said, grabbing his arm, though I was still parched, probably as pink-cheeked as Tammy. But now that the cat was out of the bag, I didn't want to weather her inquiry alone. And Jake's presence would dam the salt water building up behind my eyes. At least I hoped it would.

"Well, dang," Tammy said with a stiff smile. "Because me and Burt and a few people were wondering. I mean, private's good. Private's fine," Tammy assured me quickly. "But, you know. We wanted to celebrate him, too. And you and Gabe were always doing something. Pancake breakfasts and parades and whatnot. So I thought maybe you were going to do something we could all do together."

I sighed. "Yep. That is something we would do. Well—" I said, pointing to Jake as if he had somewhere to be.

Tammy was relentless. "I said to Burt, if she's doing something, I don't know what it is because I haven't heard anything. But I guess you gotta do what you gotta do." She looked at me with a little sad smile. There it was, the pity. With a good amount of something like resentment. Tammy would have done an event was what she was trying to say. Tammy would have been a better wife, a better member of the community.

The last line of defense was rage. I could turn the ill-timed panic and tears into rage, which at a small-town Midwestern event meant returning the passive-aggressive inquiry into Tammy's private life. It was automatic. "How *are* you and Burt, by the way?" I asked with mock concern. "Everything okay?"

Tammy stiffened. The pink in her cheeks went to red. "Everything's great," she said with a smile that didn't reach her eyes. "Why?"

"No reason!" I said, blinking innocently. "My mom was asking about you all."

Tammy's eyes narrowed. "Thank you for your concern."

Jake cleared his throat. I had momentarily forgotten he was there. The rage faltered. Everything faltered. Tammy's expression, which had slackened, suddenly reminded me of the way Levi had reacted in the checkout line at Target. Another outburst. Another victim.

"Sorry," I said, not sure if I was directing it at Tammy or Jake.

Tammy raised her eyebrows. "Sorry for what?"

The rage hadn't worked. A force trembled in my throat, my jaw. I struggled to keep my voice steady. "Sorry I didn't do a pancake breakfast for Gabe. Excuse me."

"Hey, hey. I didn't mean anything by it," I heard Tammy say as I walked away. "Oh, my word. I think I said something wrong."

"You're fine," I heard Jake reply. "Um, I should probably—"

My feet carried me through the maze without much thought for where I was going. The sun, lower in the sky now, cast a greenish-yellowish glow through the leaves. Sometimes I hit dead ends. Sometimes I didn't. I watched my boots fall on the patchwork patterns of shoe prints in the dirt, following the scent of popcorn, the occasional creak of metal from the Ferris wheel, the squeals of delighted kids. I stayed in motion; I kept the crying at bay.

When I reached the Volvo, I pulled out my keys and paused. I looked up. Jake was making his way toward me through the rows of cars.

"I'm really sorry," I said when he reached me. How many times had I apologized today? How many times this year? How many times in my life? *Sorry for what?* Tammy had said.

"That's understandable. I can't imagine losing someone—" Jake seemed to flinch but let out a little sigh, correcting himself. "Losing a spouse, I mean. That's a lot." He nodded toward the keys in my hand. "Are you headed home?"

"I don't know." For some reason, I didn't feel the relief I'd felt on my first date, when I'd broken the news of my widowhood. The ball of pain or sadness or whatever it was climbed back up my throat. I tried to head it off with a bitter laugh. "I am so bad at this."

Jake laughed a little, too. "What, dating?"

"Dating as a widow, I guess. This is my second time, and I was trying to make it perfect. Because I think you're cool." The words tumbled out quickly, before I could be too self-conscious. "So I was stressing about it all week. And meanwhile I'm the only one who knows how to work the new payroll system even though there are, like, a million of us in the department. So everyone's relying on me. And my mom needs me. And my brother needs me." I gestured back toward the corn maze, back toward Tammy. The tremor in my voice was back. "And now the town apparently fuckin' needs me, too. And I don't have a partner in any of this anymore."

Now that the sun was going down, Jake had finally lifted his shades from his face, and I could see his eyes. Same color. Not exactly the same shape, and the eyelashes weren't quite as long, but they were the same color brown as Gabe's. Warm and soft. "I think that means you need to focus on taking care of yourself," he said. "Right?"

That was it. The sobs came in silent shudders first, pushing through me, drilling down, shaking my shoulders. The tears followed, flowing hot. He had told me to take care of myself. It wasn't the most revolutionary statement—I had heard it before—but for some reason it was giving me the permission I hadn't yet given myself. Sure, I had wallowed, and sure, I knew how to avoid responsibility, but I didn't think this was the full expression of what anyone meant by *care*. In fact, I had no idea what it would look like to actually care for myself. The thought brought on more sobs, and I double-gasped as another wave hit. I felt Jake's hand on my shoulder, where it stayed as I sobbed, patting me awkwardly as if he were gently burping the world's largest baby. My face was now covered in salty liquid of various thicknesses. "I just want to watch shitty horror movies," I said when I could finally speak.

"We can watch horror movies," Jake said, sounding relieved that I was starting to resemble a functioning human again. "Just as friends, if that helps—"

"By myself," I countered and immediately hated myself for it. I sounded petulant, ungrateful. He was just trying to be nice.

Jake paused for a moment, keeping his voice light. "You can watch movies by yourself."

I straightened, hiccuping slightly as the waves of tears calmed to ripples. "I keep fucking this up." I caught a glance of my reflection in the Volvo's window. I looked like a melted clown. "Oh, dear Lord in heaven," I muttered. If I hadn't already pushed this man to the brink by calling him my dead husband's pet name, throwing a tantrum, and heaving snot into a puddle at his Tevas, my nightmare of a face would certainly be the kicker. I unlocked the driver's-side door. "I gotta go. Sorry about this. Have a good life."

"Oh! Like, right now? Okay."

I don't know why he was acting surprised. "Yeah, I'm out. I give up." It felt good to be honest. The tears were just as humiliating as—if not more than—the improvisers shooing me offstage, but they had a cleansing effect. I felt numb, oddly relaxed. Perfectly primed for a TV marathon. I got into my seat. "I'm obviously in no state to be hanging out with anyone. Let alone an eligible bachelor—" I paused to hiccup "—such as yourself."

"I respect that. Uh, all right, then." Jake tapped on my hood. "Do what you need to do."

"You seem really nice, Jake," I added. I swallowed. My voice was hoarse from crying. "Thanks for everything." I shut the door.

He moved out of the way, watching as I backed out. "See you, Robin," I heard him say.

"No, you won't," I said through the glass, though I knew he couldn't hear me.

Most people wouldn't guess that I . . .
Can quote Leprechaun in Space *word for word.*

After the Widow Humiliation Show, Part Two: The Blubbering, I admit I had regressed. I had gone directly from Fall Fest to the Whole Foods in a suburb near Pole City, piling macaroni and cheese from the hot bar into the largest container they had, spending an unspecified amount of time in the Kettle chips section. I took my stash of snacks home and made a batch of zucchini bread with chocolate chips. I tucked myself in Gabe's coat and slippers, still sporting Mercedes's blowout and what was left of my makeup, and sipped hot chocolate from his *Far Side* mug as multiple sequels of *Friday the 13th* began to blur together, as the mountain of food in my stomach congealed into one gloopy mass, which still hadn't quite left me a week later.

This was my life now, I told myself. I had a demanding job that I knew how to do well, I had been married, I had helped my husband get elected to public office—the second youngest mayor in Minnesota history, as Tammy's Facebook post had pointed out—and I had cared for him through cancer. Now, I didn't need anything else on top of all that. I did what I wanted, and what I wanted was to soak in the lukewarm pool of remaining days, and Gabe, bless him, was not here to suggest otherwise. I wasn't going back to Bubbl. No more rectangle men. No more tongue-lashings and blocked harassment. No more monologues. No more obsessing over word choice or outfits or hair. I would always be married to the man who lived in my mind, for better or worse. Lately I could picture his eyes soft with disappointment. *Sorry, love. You're stuck with me.*

This morning, Marcy had video-called me until I picked up. I hadn't RSVPed yet for Sisters in Grief, she informed me, and since I had missed the last one, she was worried I was hibernating again. It wasn't that I didn't want to go to the monthly meetings, I told her—in fact, I'd enjoyed them a lot—but putting on clothes that weren't stained and socializing with more than one person was a lot of work right now.

"You're going to want to be there for this one," Marcy had said, wiggling her eyebrows. "Wear pajamas if you have to. You have to see how real Pam is."

"Who?"

Pam was Pam Chomsky, a famous Chicago medium featured on *Oprah* in the '90s, often flown to LA for a so-called very famous client from the cast of *Friends*. According to another SIG member, Julie, the medium's ability to channel the dead was uncanny. The things that came out of her mouth could have only come from Julie's late partner, things like relatives' names, memories shared between the two of them, wisdom about Julie's career and what she should do next. Julie was bringing Pam Chomsky to Sisters in Grief at great expense because she wanted all the widows to experience it for themselves. And tonight, that would include me.

"What do you want?" Marcy asked as she greeted me with a cheek-kiss at the door. "Red? White?" She gave me a devilish look. "Tequila?"

"Red is great."

I watched her whisk around her stark-white kitchen in her chic wide-legged pants and bare feet, fetching a glass and a corkscrew, which she set in front of me alongside the bottle. "*Cin*," she said, lifting her own glass of white.

"Cheers," I said.

Marcy's Lake of the Isles neighborhood had still-green lawns and smooth streets, I'd noticed on the drive over. No gathering of dead leaves and McDonald's cups in the sewer grates. No trees, either. A sapling here and there in the front yards, naked and braced with vinyl, but no old souls like those that shaded the Colonials and Victorians of Brokenridge, wearing their histories in narrow doorways and crumbling carriage houses, rusted-out vans and El Caminos in front yards. Marcy's development seemed to want to erase all sense of the past. Wide garages for multiple cars, floodlights for every corner of the yard, stacks of rooms manufactured and duplicated. There had been parties in neighborhoods like these after Gabe had gotten national attention—before he had gotten sick—hosted by movers and shakers who wanted him to run for state office. Rooms full of huge personalities and egos and neuroses where I could just melt into the background and watch. Once, I had made the mistake of wearing black, and one of my elected representatives had handed me an empty glass and a used napkin. I had taken it to the kitchen without comment.

As Marcy busied herself getting ready for the group's arrival, I told her about the ritual beating of the dough and the stirring of the sauce, following Gabe's handwritten lasagna instructions. Marcy's one-year ritual had also been about food, she told me: she had made *taba ng talangka,* her favorite dish from childhood, the dish her late husband, Robert, had hired a Filipino chef to make the night he had proposed. I finished my glass as we talked, and Marcy became preoccupied with setting the ambience. Her poodle, Gerard, sniffed me with calculated assessment and went about his business.

Soon, I was wandering the house, squinting at the titles of all Marcy's legal books; she used to be in corporate law at the same company where Robert was a CFO, but after he'd died, she'd stopped working. I wished I could stop working.

The first to arrive was Julie, wide-hipped and silver-haired with a beautifully styled coif, wearing high-tops she refused to take off. "They're brand-new," she assured me in a flat, nasally California drawl. "Look." She lifted an old Saks shopping bag from her shoulder and set it on the counter. "I brought champagne, I brought sage," she said, her head tucked half in the bag. "I brought a picture of Darl." Darlene was

Julie's partner who had passed from breast cancer five years ago. Darl appeared to have been a thin, toothy woman with West Coast grace. I was touched by the frame, which looked old and well-loved in a battered, soft silver.

"I didn't know we were supposed to bring anything," I told Julie.

Julie put a finger on Darl's photographic forehead. "It's easier for Pam to channel when you have something of theirs. Consider pulling up a photo if you don't have anything with you."

"I'm getting cuff links!" Marcy called from somewhere in the house.

As more women arrived—only one of whom was willing to remove their shoes—I found a quiet corner near the piano to dig in my purse for something of Gabe's. Our house was full of his stuff. Surely something had found its way into my bag. But there were only credit cards, stray earrings, Chapsticks, mints from various lunch spots in the skyway. I refilled my wineglass. What did it matter, anyway? Beyond his little dating-profile stunt, Gabe wasn't here. If he were, he would have visited me long before I was playing ghost stories in a suburban mansion. Believe me, if I couldn't conjure him, no one would.

"I watch a lot of scary movies," I was telling a middle-aged, yoga-muscled woman named Audra, who I knew vaguely from past meetings. The canapés were out of the oven, and we were all gathered around a table in Marcy's bright white "breakfast nook" the size of a full dining room. By then, I was two glasses in. "I already know all the tricks, so it's comforting. I can predict what's gonna happen. It's nice."

"I'm a TV girl," Audra replied with a gravity I respected. "*Scandal*, *Homeland*, *This Is Us*. I can't get enough. My therapist calls it *numbing behavior*, but I don't care."

"What's numbing behavior?"

"Oh, you know." Audra lifted her glass of white wine. "Could be booze. For some people it's drugs, sex. Anything that prevents you from feeling the full breadth of your emotions."

This didn't sit right with me—in fact, it struck me as absurd. I laughed. "Yeah, but TV isn't a controlled substance. And I can still feel things while I watch TV. I cry all the time at *The Great British Baking Show*."

"Me, too. They're so nice to each other."

"And unlike alcohol, *Bake-Off* doesn't corrode your liver."

"Probably clogs your arteries, though," Audra said out of the side of her mouth.

We chuckled, and I noticed for the first time that Audra was still wearing two stacked rings on her left hand, one with a diamond. I still wore my ring, too—on a chain under my shirt.

Suddenly, a hush came over the women. Pam Chomsky had arrived. She was curvy and short, even shorter than me, and wore what appeared to be a sparkling rosary on her large drooping chest. Her thin hair stood up in curled wisps, giving the air of a mad scientist. That, and her blank stare, which she held as she paused in the kitchen doorway to survey the room.

"What can I get you, Pam?" Julie asked. "White? Red?"

"Gin, please," Pam said, with a possibly European curl in her speech, no change in her expression. "Botanical. With a twist of lemon."

Marcy sprung to life, calling over one of the caterers and relaying Pam Chomsky's order.

"Who is Barbara?" Pam called, her voice barely above a whisper. She looked at the walls as if they had animated, the rest of us following her gaze.

"She's starting already?" one of the women asked.

"Is there a Barbara here?" Pam repeated. "Called Babs?"

A stunned voice sounded. "I'm Barbara." Near the sink, a tall angular woman who I hadn't met yet was holding up her hand. "My hubby called me Babs. I can't believe it."

"He's here," Pam Chomsky said, her tone lighter now, almost conversational. "He says that you're doing a good job with the boys."

Gasps and utterances of *Oh, my god*. Across the room, Marcy did a quick sign of the cross and put her manicured hand on her mouth, shaking her head.

"That means a lot to me," Barbara said, smiling through the tears collecting in her eyes. "It's hard raising two boys alone, so thank you, hubs." She gave a little self-conscious laugh and looked vaguely toward the ceiling.

"Okay, there had to have been at least one Barbara," I muttered to Audra beside me. "And Babs is a very common nickname."

"I suppose," Audra replied, but she was twiddling her ring, looking as awestruck as the rest of the group.

We migrated to the formal dining room, which had been outfitted with enough white candles to be a fire hazard. It also appeared Julie had recently used her sage, casting the arched ceilings with a sweet, smoky haze. Marcy called for quiet. The Sisters in Grief placed their sacred objects in front of them: Marcy's cuff links, Julie's photograph. One woman had brought a comb. I slunk to the farthest chair from Pam, hoping to stay out of her line of sight, feeding Gerard pieces of shrimp under the table.

At the head, Pam took a sip of her gin and sat with her hands palms down on the tablecloth. She looked to her right, her eyebrows furrowing.

"I'm getting an *H*," she said. "Do we have an *H*? A Hank, or Henry?"

Henry was the grandfather of Kelly, it turned out, being relayed the profound and highly personalized message of *Think of me at the holidays.*

"The holidays were special to us," Kelly informed the group, dabbing her eyes with her napkin. "That's the only time I got to see him when I was a little girl."

It appeared that spouses were not the only people present. That, or Pam Chomsky had shot with an *H* name for a husband and landed on the board with a grandpa. The next few visitations were right on target. Audra, it seemed, had been twiddling with her ring because she had been remarried, and she sought the approval of her late husband for her new spouse. Julie's ghost, Darlene, referenced the Joni Mitchell song they danced to together after their civil-union ceremony in the '80s. Robert had also made an appearance, advising Marcy to go back to work and open her own law practice. "You bastard," Marcy had said, her lips trembling as she held his ashes near her throat. "You knew I wanted to. You knew I was getting bored."

I was just about to excuse myself when Norma, the oldest member of the group, called out, interrupting a long silence. "Excuse me, hello. Is there a Mike? It's getting late, and I need to go to bed soon."

Pam looked affronted. I had a hard time holding in my laughter.

"He's been moving things on my dresser. Ask him," Norma continued, gesturing to Pam. "Ask him if he moved my lotion."

"No Mikes," Pam said, annoyance at the edge of her voice. She sipped her gin.

"He's there." Norma blew her nose. "Probably hiding."

"If we could have quiet, please," Pam said. "Thank you." Now, her head was cocked to her left. "Gabriel," she said. "The politician. Gabriel."

A few of the women—including Marcy—shot me a significant look. *Go on*, she mouthed, her eyes wide.

I leaned forward to wave, giving the medium a small smile. "Nice Facebook research," I said under my breath. Tammy's recent post about Gabe had been publicly visible, after all.

Pam Chomsky kept her steady gaze on me. "He's here, but I can sense you're hesitant to speak to him. Is that right?"

Marcy's membership with the Minnesota bar had expired—that was public record, too. Julie had probably let slip about the Joni Mitchell song. "I'm just observing. Thanks, anyway."

Pam raised her thin, blond eyebrows. "He has a message for you, if you want it."

All the women at the table had turned to look at me, even Norma. This performance meant something to them. Marcy might even change her life because of it. They wanted to believe desperately, even if I didn't. I could play along.

"Sure." I sat forward and folded my hands on the table. "Do your worst."

"He says . . ." Pam began, pausing for dramatic effect, and the room held its breath ". . . *Keep going*."

My heart skipped a beat. From across the smoky room, I tried to examine Pam more closely, searching her gray-blue eyes for deceit. Her expression offered nothing, her stare remaining eerie and colorless, watching the space behind me. Still, *keep going* was a pretty generic phrase of encouragement. Lucky guess. "Is that all?" I asked.

"No. He's saying something about a path or a road. I see a field and a path. A maze? You turned the wrong direction."

Acute nausea took a hold of my stomach, a combination of fear and shock and, against my will, delight.

Now, she looked directly at me. For the first time all night, it seemed, the medium allowed herself a hint of amusement. "But he says not to worry. You'll find your way."

I did not stay to reflect and dissect after the medium finished her session, though I was tempted when cheesecake bites and coffee were served. Marcy saw me out, giving me a tight, long hug and several dessert samples on a foil-wrapped plate. Gerard sat at her feet, looking up at me hopefully.

"I'll bring your plate back," I promised as I zipped my coat.

"Of course. We can talk about what happened in there." Marcy leaned close, her look conspiratorial, her breath sweet with wine. "Did you see the look on Kat's face when you got a message and she didn't? And I think Audra might be having second thoughts about her new marriage."

I wondered if the other Sisters talked as much about Marcy as she talked about them. Maybe Pam Chomsky imitating the ghost of Robert was right: it was time for her to occupy her brilliant mind.

As I hit the highway, the medium's words returned, along with the image of her little smile, almost as if she relished my disturbance, victory over the resident skeptic. And now I had run away, afraid to let her see me shaken among all the other women, afraid that their reverent gushing and follow-up questions would rub off on me, setting me more off-kilter than I already was. I still didn't know if it was real, still couldn't quite let my heart take the lead from my head. But I did know what it was like to live in an empty, old farmhouse. What it was like to wake up in the middle of the night to creaks and bangs as the wood grew and shrunk, and wind with a vengeance, playing the columns of the porch like a fiddle. I knew the power of a lonely person's imagination, looking out into the country dark and wishing so desperately for another human presence, shadows begin to form. So I turned up a Carly Rae Jepsen song loud enough to drown out my thoughts.

When I reached home, my headlights swung across the old fir tree line and hit a figure sitting on my stoop. I jumped in my seat, slamming on the brakes. Then I squinted, recognizing the hulking form behind the raised hand, which shielded his eyes from the beams.

I opened my door and called out to him. "Levi? What the hell?"

"Hey, Robin. Sorry. I called, but you must have been driving."

I looked at my phone. Indeed, Levi had left me a voice mail and a few texts. "Oh. I had it on Silent. I was at a thing."

"Yeah, I stopped by the restaurant, thinking maybe you were there. And your mom said you'd be home pretty soon, so . . . Can you turn off your lights, please?"

"Whoops. Sorry." I turned off the engine and gathered my dessert, glancing at Levi as I passed him on the porch. "Want some cheesecake?"

"Uh . . . Normally I'd say yes, but I've been off the refined-sugar train recently." He patted his belly. "Christy has me eating healthier."

"Who's Christy?" I asked as I tossed my coat on the couch. Then I remembered: last time we spoke, he'd said something about "seeing this person for a while." This must have been her.

Christy was a massage therapist, Levi told me. She was a vegan, she wrote freelance articles for health magazines, she had him taking walks and practicing mindfulness. I tried not to smile as I felt my eyes involuntarily roll, digging into my cheesecake. "That's cool. So, to what do I owe the, uh—" I nodded toward the porch "—drop-in?"

"God, it's been forever since I was here," Levi said, ignoring my question. He was standing at a stretch of wall next to the TV, where Gabe had hung his Key to the City of Brokenridge. Levi ran his fingers across the brass. "He was so goofy about this. I mean, I know he worked hard, and it meant a lot for him to get recognized, but remember that day of the ceremony? He wouldn't even set it down. He was walking around, like—" Levi turned to me, his eyes pretend-wide, his voice high "—Here's my new toy, everybody!"

I laughed, my mouth full of cheesecake. I hadn't noticed then, but Levi was right. Gabe had held the plaque under his arm all day. "Yeah. Pretty cute. Okay, so you're off sugar. What about a . . ." I set my plate on the counter and scanned the fridge. "A diet something? Diet Dr. Pepper?"

"No. No, thank you."

"Water? Coffee? You want a weird herbal tea that Juana left here in 2013?"

"I'm good." He was pacing between the front door and the TV, picking up random objects from the bookshelves and wall hooks, examining them and setting them back down.

"At least sit."

"I'll sit," he said and pulled up a kitchen stool to the island.

I pulled up an adjacent stool. "What's the occasion?"

"Can't I just come here out of the goodness of my own heart?" he said, but he couldn't get through the question without breaking into an uncomfortable laugh.

I let out my own laugh. "Is this a guilt thing? Like, *I saw my best friend's poor, sad widow lose her shit at Target, and now I feel bad* type of thing?" I bit into another mini cheesecake. "Because that is not necessary. I'll have you know that I just came from a gathering of friends."

He shifted in his seat. "So you were out with *friends*, huh? Are you, like, dating?"

My face must have done something hilarious, because Levi burst out laughing.

"What?" I asked as his giant frame shook. "Why? I'm not—" I sputtered. "It's none of your business. And no, for the record. Not anymore. Why? Are you mad about it, or something?"

"No, it's good, it's good!" Levi said, assuring me as he recovered from the laughter. "I hope you are. I'm glad you are. If you are."

"What is it to you?"

"*What is it to you?*" he repeated in a mafioso accent. "I like this Robin."

"I swear to god, Levi. I have three more cheesecake bites and *Halloween: Resurrection* to get to. I am out of patience."

Levi sighed, staring at the floor.

I knew that look. The bad-news look. "What?" I demanded.

Levi threw up his arms. "I just don't know how to say it. Like, okay . . ." He rubbed his chin, his gaze back on the floor. "I got an email from Gabe."

The bite of cheesecake I was chewing froze in my throat. I swallowed it on instinct, coughs erupting as I struggled to find air. "What?"

"Are you okay?" Levi had darted up from his seat to stand near me, his hands hovering a few inches from my back, not sure what to do.

"I'm fine," I said, wheezing. I coughed again. "Wrong pipe. What did the email say?"

"A lot of stuff," Levi said. "But one of the things it said was that I should check up on you. I know, it's crazy," he added, watching my face. "But it's true."

"I believe you," I choked out, pounding my chest. So he must have received a timed email, too. The assurances that it was authentic. The pleas to move on, though I wasn't sure Gabe needed to tell Levi to find a new best friend. "And I don't need someone to check on me," I sputtered again, and a tingle in my throat sent me into more spasms.

"Clearly," Levi said, gesturing to my coughing fit. He fetched me a random coffee mug full of tap water and waited, watching me with those houndlike eyes.

I recovered. "So that's why you're standing in my kitchen at eleven o'clock on a Sunday night, asking me if I'm dating? You're checking up?"

A smile peeked through Levi's cautious expression. "Kind of. I asked about the dates because I saw you on Bubbl."

The brief shot of embarrassment at the thought of Levi coming across my profile was quickly shoved aside. "*You're* on Bubbl? I thought you and Christy were all, you know . . ." I made lewd gestures with my hands ". . . feeding each other vegetables."

"We are. I'm *not* on Bubbl. I saw *you* on Bubbl because . . ." Levi looked uncomfortable but seemed to recover. "There was a link to your profile in Gabe's letter."

"Excuse me?" *Come on*, I admonished my husband silently. *Isn't dating as a widow embarrassing enough? Now you have to bring in the peanut gallery?*

"Is it really you?" Levi asked, beginning to smile.

"Yes, it's me." I avoided his eyes. "Stop smiling like a dork. It's a favor. He sent me something, too."

Levi watched as I pulled up my email app and found my own special letter. I slid him my phone across the counter.

Levi skimmed. "Wow." He examined the screen closer. "Interesting," he muttered. He set the phone on the counter and slid it back. "So you decided to indulge the Gabemeister's request, but no longer?"

"So? What's your point?" I said, breaking into another cheesecake bite, chewing this one more carefully.

"I don't have a point. I—" Levi seemed to shore himself up. "Maybe I could help? I've been on Bubbl way too many times. I could probably relate to, uh, your struggles."

"Ha!" Now it was my turn to burst out laughing. "Hell no." I pointed to his front pocket, where I could see the outline of his own device. "Let me see yours."

"Hey, now. Buy me dinner first."

"Shut up. Your email from Gabe. I want to see what he said about me."

"It's personal."

I scoffed. "I showed you mine!"

"Yeah, um . . ." Levi looked away, clearing his throat. "You just have to trust me."

I stared at him, waiting for him to give in, but he just stared back, so I began to make us both a pot of weird herbal tea. I was too tired to worry about his sudden need for privacy. Maybe he just didn't want me to scroll through his inbox and see all the professional-wrestling newsletters he was subscribed to—according to Gabe, it was a lot. And now that Levi had finally told me why the hell he was here, I was feeling more at ease. Slightly less insane. I wasn't the only one being haunted. As I set a steaming mug smelling of grass and dirt in front of him, Levi cleared his throat again.

"So you want to meet up or something?" Levi put the tea to his lips. "Ow! Shit. That's hot."

"You have some sage wisdom about how to avoid fuckbois?"

Levi smiled knowingly. "You already know the term *fuckboi*—good."

I shrugged. "I guess it can't hurt. Theo is probably tired of me sending him screenshots."

"Whatever you want, dude. I think Gabe would at least want you to have fun with this. That's the least we can do to do right by that goofy tall drink of water over there." He pointed to the Key to the City hanging on the opposite wall.

"Cheers." I held up my mug and clinked it to Levi's. We sipped, cringing at the tea's vegetal taste. Then I had to smile. "Goofy," I repeated.

Gabe had been goofy. So naive in so many ways, but that's what made him lovable. And frustratingly effective. He never took into account anything, or anyone, in the way of what he wanted. What Tammy had mistaken for listening I knew was dreaming. I had a deep sense that I wouldn't be able to rest until I had done what he'd asked. Not that I believed he was a poltergeist of some kind, interfering, blowing on my neck, guiding my hand, no. He was an inextricable force in my world, and I was living in the wake. I had tried to float back to stasis, but the ripples kept coming, kept showing up on my doorstep. As they say, energy never dies. It has to go somewhere.

Levi took another pained sip. "Say, friend," he said, looking guiltily back and forth from me to the cup. "Do you have any sugar?"

I remain convinced that . . .
Nobody actually knows what the hell they're doing.

Midway through a Thursday afternoon meeting on PowerPoint protocol and email etiquette, Marcy texted me that she had *HUGE* news. I paused my progress through a Honey Bun, wiped my sticky hands on my pants. Inspired by Robert's posthumous encouragement, she typed, she was going to try and get her bar membership renewed and return to the legal profession. I wrote back with a protocol-breaking number of exclamation points.

So are you going to go into corporate law again? I texted. Or are you going to try something new?

Who knows??? I am open to the universe. I have another session scheduled with Pam, so we'll see . . .

To this, I rolled my eyes and typed, *You don't have to pay hundreds of dollars an hour to be open to the universe*, but I deleted it. Marcy sought her husband's advice via a vaguely European con artist claiming to speak to the dead; I did it via email with the help of a giant bartender-slash-punk bassist. To each their own. Levi and I had made plans tonight for what he was calling a Bubbl master class, and the thought made the Honey Bun spin in my stomach. There was no reason I couldn't back out, but I knew I wouldn't. Some sort of contract had been invisibly signed on

Sunday. Maybe because there was another person involved, holding me accountable. Maybe because I had exhausted the lineup of classic horror on all my streaming services, and the house was getting colder at night.

"Any other thoughts? Robin?" At the head of the conference table, my manager called to me. "You've been quiet." He rarely addressed me. Perhaps *quiet* was a sarcastic reference to the Honey-Bun wrapper that I had been crinkling for the last half hour.

"Right, yeah . . ." I shoved my phone under my thigh and squinted at the presentation screen, pretending to be critically engaged with Greeting and Closing: Best Practices.

"Nope!" I answered, giving him my best and biggest smile. "No thoughts at all."

I met Levi at the bar where he and his brothers would play that night, a holdout from the days when the Warehouse District actually housed wares. Inside a stack of bricks between converted condos, men in Vikings caps still drank beer and watched giant TVs playing SportsCenter. In a corner booth, Levi sat next to his guitar case in his usual dirty combat boots, a faded bluish-green flannel, and under it, a T-shirt featuring the cover of Frank Herbert's *Dune*.

The fries were soggy, the beer was acceptable, and the jukebox played country hits from the late '90s and early 2000s. Real *adult section of the skating rink* vibes, Levi and I agreed. What we could not agree on was the purpose of this so-called Bubbl master class. Levi kept triple-dipping fries and waxing on about the concept of second soulmates and how the human heart was meant to expand with age. "This is exciting, Robbie. You could fall in love again."

"There is no part of this that says I need to fall in love," I argued. When Levi tried to interrupt I held up a finger. "Gabe said I needed to *try it*, but he didn't say to what end."

Levi stretched his arms toward the mildewy ceiling in protest. "But getting crazy about someone is the fun part!"

"No way." I wiped ketchup from the corners of my mouth. "I will not be getting crazy. Any dates that occur from now on can come over to my house, and we will eat my food, and we will watch my choice of

TV—and only my choice. They stay completely silent and leave after an hour."

Levi burst out laughing. "That is not what Gabe had in mind."

I took another bite of burger. "Probably not."

"Come on, dude. You're supposed to have *fun* with this. Tell me. What's the most fun date you've ever been on?"

"Gabe and I didn't really do the whole courtship thing. You know that."

"Okay, what's the most fun thing you guys did together as a couple?" he asked.

I stared at a football game on a nearby TV, combing my memory. Winter sun on cold noses. Hands under the faucet, passing a brush back and forth to get the soil out from under our nails. Bruce Springsteen blasting as we folded town-hall flyers into thirds. I felt myself smile. "We went on walks and bike rides. We gardened. We went to town meetings."

"Town meetings. Kinky."

He was joking, but I was surprised to feel a little defensive. There was nothing about those years to joke about. Only to savor. I knew this, Levi knew this, and yet. "What are you asking, exactly?"

Levi shrugged. "I am trying to see what a fun date is for you. So you can actually get something out of this, you know? Like, really, truly, in your heart. What do you want out of this?"

"Ugh." I took a gulp of beer. What I wanted. Another version of the *what do you do in your spare time* question. I wanted a back rub the way only my husband could do it. I wanted to watch his forearms flex as he cut a freshly harvested melon into chunks. I wanted what I couldn't have. "I don't know. How am I supposed to know what I want? Like, do other people on Bubbl know these things?"

"Yes and no." Levi swallowed beer and paused his glass midair. After a moment, he set it down with a thunk. "Hang on. I've got an idea."

He slid out of his side of the booth and stood over me. I looked up at him.

"Scoot," he said.

As he shoved in next to me, my eyes were drawn to the frayed, stained cuffs of his shirt. "God, is that the same old flannel you've had forever?"

"This is not just a flannel. This is the best top layer a man can buy," Levi said. "This is an Arctic explorer's flannel. Built for ultimate cold-weather survival, this baby has three thermodynamic layers and five hidden pockets . . ." As he went on, the smell of it overwhelmed me, though not totally unpleasant—the same smell of the dorm rooms and apartments he and Gabe had shared throughout our college years, the smell of Harpo and Nag Champa incense and the New Orleans–style chicory coffee. I thought of lazy afternoons of dozing on the couch while the two of them played *Mario Kart,* the taste of late-night eggs and hot sauce, waking up on Gabe's mattress on the floor, noon sun across my face.

Levi brought my attention back to my phone, and I came out of my reverie.

"At least your profile is looking good," he said, scrolling through.

"That's all Gabe. He made my answers fun."

Levi looked at me intently, raising his eyebrows. "You like them, huh?"

"I mean, I wrote a few more myself, but I had fun seeing what he wrote." I shrugged. "He gets me."

Levi smiled wider, almost embarrassed. "Totally. Anyway. As far as what you're looking for. There are some . . ." he made a vague gesture, looking pensive ". . . *types*, if you will."

"Types?"

Together, we leaned over the small screen, and he took on the air of someone giving a TED Talk. Obviously there were differences in gender, Levi explained, but the Bubbl types and what they were looking for were generally the same. On the male-presenting side of things, he would adapt his knowledge and improvise as best he could.

We started with the Brosef Brandons, who only took pictures on golf courses, football tailgates, or at weddings, and probably had the emotional maturity of a fifteen-year-old. They wanted good-looking party girls who didn't want much in return. "So if you're not looking for anything too deep, they can be fun."

"I guess I'm not looking for *deep*, but I wouldn't describe myself as *party*," I said, holding up air quotes. Moments ago, for example, I had used the sleeve of my turtleneck as a napkin.

"Nor would I," said Levi. "Nor would I."

Then there were Sober Sams, who were not always sober but always had cats, used a lot of philosophy quotes, and could become as dependent on you as their substance of choice. "Very good in bed, though," Levi added. "Mm," he grunted quietly to himself, probably at some steamy memory of a Sober Samantha.

"Ew, okay, let's just establish right now the goal is *dates*," I reminded him, my face flushing. "Fun dates. And me not crying on fun dates," I added.

"Well, I can help you with two out of three of those goals," he murmured, swiping through profiles.

After my second beer, the fries started to taste all right, and Levi's assessments began to sound pretty convincing. I found myself wishing I'd brought my laptop so I could put together a spreadsheet of some kind.

"Beard, Carhartts, and fish," Levi was saying, finger-swiping through a man's blurry pictures. "Probably a Trad Chad." A Trad Chad was a hypermasculine man who was seeking a little wifey to cook his meals and bear his children. Levi had seen plenty of versions of the feminine side of this, women who mistook his generally large presence for someone who held a *caveman hunt, cavewoman cook* mentality. "Then she would realize I was more into getting takeout and watching the Timberwolves than, you know, procreating and starring in autumn-based photo shoots with her, so me and the Trad Tricias would part ways," Levi explained.

"But you still went out with the Trad Tricias?"

"Psh, hell yeah. I went out with everyone and anyone who caught my eye. I tried it all on for size."

"That makes no sense to me. Why would you waste your time?"

Levi scoffed. "Uh, sorry, not all of us get to fall in love on the first night like you and Gabe. Some of us have to work at it."

I had to smile at that.

Levi presented a picture of a goateed man in a T-shirt and vest, looking wan in front of a Miles Davis poster. "Have you read any David Foster Wallace? Do you know your Myers-Briggs type? If you match with this guy, you certainly will soon. This is a Poly Paul . . ."

Soon, I'd also learned to identify Nice Guy Nicks, Freelance Photographer Phils, and Emotionally Damaged Drakes. The types were kind of rude, Levi had admitted, and they flattened out real human beings into two-dimensional cartoons, but wasn't that the way the app had been built? Wasn't that the point of swiping people in and out of your life based on two square inches of photograph and a 150-character limit?

I liked the types, I told him. The types made it feel like a game again, like there was a set of fixed knowledge I could acquire and use to my advantage—unlike real life, where people were unpredictable and stubborn and mortal. Ah, yes, I said to myself, taking on the amused detachment of David Attenborough narrating a nature documentary, here was a Brosef Brandon, contorting in his khakis under a beer bong. There was a Freelance Photographer Phil, answering his prompts in nothing but flag emojis, and Poly Paul, inviting all Scorpio and Sagittarius placements to meet him and his wife for what he called *adult milkshakes*. Dodging these types, I'd like to think I was bobbing and weaving bad times. And I knew I didn't want a bad time. That was about all the progress I had made on the *what do you want* question.

Levi came back from setting up his amp and returned to his side of the booth, settling in and folding his hands across from me like a lawyer.

"So." I looked up at him from my phone. "Did you match with anyone?"

Bolstered by the pilsner and the blaring Garth Brooks, I'd pressed the bubble on several people that seemed to defy the types or were good-looking enough that the categories didn't matter. There were four or five immediate matches. I held up my phone, swallowing the tightness that had emerged in my throat. "A couple."

"Well?" Levi made a shooing motion.

My stomach swirled. "What, you mean—send a message? No. I'm waiting for them." That was the only way I could know if they really liked me. Once I realized this, it seemed absurd to say it aloud, so I kept my mouth shut.

Levi stared. "You've never sent a message first?"

I recalled only the flood of men's names, my finger sliding down the columns as I watched the bubbles burst. "I guess I never had to."

"Message first," Levi instructed. "Or hell, get off Bubbl and go on one of those apps where women *have* to message first. Sets the tone for the conversation you want. I always appreciated that."

I had started to tear up the damp cardboard coaster in front of my beer. "But what if the guy doesn't respond?"

"Then, fuck him."

"Okay. Right. Fuck him."

I returned to the phone, my eyes darting across names, faces, popping bubbles. I had thought my part of the game was over. Now I was expected to bring out something magical and witty on the spot? I'd never made the first move in my life. Unless you count calling Gabe's name in the courtyard outside the dorms as a move. Strange little hidden parts of me began to wriggle out of decades of stillness—the sensation of standing in the Brokenridge cafeteria at my first middle-school dance, Usher blasting, party lights pulsing, everyone waiting for the first brave soul to step out into the middle of the floor. I imagined holding out my chubby hand with its Bath and Body Works glitter lotion and messily painted fingernails to an anonymous torso in polyblend stripes.

I felt my heartbeat in my ears, Levi's eyes on me from across the booth. I scrolled. Smile after smile. Wanting. Open. Ready. I was none of those things. The only words that came to me were lines from cardboard Valentines. *Are you from Tennessee? Did it hurt when you fell from the sky?*

I put my phone down in a huff. "This is too hard."

"It's not. People do it every day. Someone in this very bar is doing it right now."

"I can't."

"You can. You just have to find something you like about them and say it. Or better yet, ask them a question." Levi put his warm, sweaty hands on my wrists, giving them a little shake. "What are you scared of?"

Being lost in the corn maze. The pressure of tears behind my eyes. The looks on people's faces. The cold hands and voices in the dark theater and the smell of foreign fabric softener. Gabe, sleeping on the couch because he's too weak to move to the bed. The past. The future.

"Everything."

Levi didn't move for a long moment except to furrow his brow. He took a breath, paused, and gestured for my phone. "Give it here."

I did. Gladly. I watched his finger move through the profiles, swiping and zooming in on pictures with the precision of a craftsman, not a care in the world.

"How did you do it, Levi?" I found myself asking him.

He glanced up from the screen. "How did I find Christy?"

"No, I mean—I'm happy for you, by the way." I gave him a smile. "But how did you do it before you found her? Like, you're a sensitive person . . ."

"Thank you."

"How did you keep getting out there after each, you know—" I made a tangling motion with my hands. I meant the dancers and activists and baristas and law students. The ones who always left him curled up on the couch like a giant boulder, weeping into cans of Hamm's and bags of chips, writing songs in a Takis-stained notebook.

A little smile from Levi. "All my failures?"

"Sure. What would you do if you were me?"

Levi sat back in the booth and cocked his head. "You want *my* approach? I mean, shit. It's all trial and error, I guess. It's not easy. You catch feelings. You break hearts. You might cry or get embarrassed again."

"I'm not going to cry again," I declared, half to him, half to myself.

"You might. I did sometimes. But I think it's way more fun that way. To go all in."

I leaned across the table. "But what does that mean, go all in? Like what do I *do*, in practical terms? Do I dress nicer? Do I hire a life coach or something?"

"You do exactly what you're doing right now."

"Eat bad fries at a sports bar?"

"You say *yes*." At my confused expression, he continued. "Instead of going home after work, you come to this random bar with your buddy." He pointed to himself. "Or you go get ice cream after the weird movie. Or when the hibachi guy asks who wants to catch a shrimp in their mouth, you raise your hand, open your mouth, and you say *Yes, gimme that shrimp*."

"I don't like shrimp." Seafood was, in fact, one of the only categories of food I didn't like.

"Metaphorical shrimp, then."

I considered him. "So, I say *yes*. Within reason."

"Within reason. Like one time, I followed this girl to something called a *sound bath*, where you just lie on the floor and a witchy lady bangs a gong. For, like, hours. It was surprisingly moving. That was *my* crying episode. Okay, now you try it." Levi had pulled up a profile and handed the phone to me. "Message first, and when the opportunity arises, say your *yes*. Then, when it's time to say *no*, say *no*. It's not a commitment, it's an adventure."

I took the phone. "*Mo A, 27, Minneapolis*," I read aloud.

His profile picture was taken in the dark, lighting up some sort of DJ setup. He was looking down at his turntables, headphones around his neck, one hand on a record, the other raised in the air. His full name, which I gathered from the Instagram handle connected to the account, was Mohammed Adan, and he appeared to have a big following around town, as well as a big family of Somali origin. *My catchphrase is . . . Dentist by day, DJ by night.*

I looked up at Levi. "He calls himself a *vibe curator*? What on earth is a *vibe curator*?"

"Hey, you pressed the bubble. He has good taste. And a nice smile."

It was true. In every photo—except for the one taken at his dental office, it appeared—he looked like he was having the time of his life. After several editorial rounds—my *Hi, Mohammed* became Levi's *Say you could mash up any two songs from Baltimore house, which two songs would you pick?* which morphed back into my *What's your DJ name?*—we had set the tone for a Robin-friendly interaction: thoughtful, practical, playful but not too flirty. Mo didn't respond right away, and judging by his log-in status, he hadn't been active for a while.

"That's a good sign," Levi assured me. "That means he's got other stuff going on."

As the basket of fries dwindled, Levi and I went back and forth over a few other matches. He kept picking experimental musicians. I kept picking men who didn't live in the United States and therefore could never conceivably go on a date. Finally, we landed on a fifty-one-year-old from Saint Paul with salt-and-pepper hair named Ted K. According to a prompt starting *Something you should know about me* . . . Ted was divorced with two kids. Kids who, it appeared, he took to a lot of natural-history museums. In one of them, I showed Levi, Ted was comparing the width of his own leg to a dinosaur leg. "Seems sweet. I like fossils and stuff."

"Meh." Levi ran his finger through the air. "You don't like kids."

"Yes, I do."

"Oh." Levi stared back, pleasantly surprised. "Gabe was just so . . ."

"Anti-natal? I know. For me, it was never a big deal." I held up another of Ted K's pictures in Levi's direction. "I like the lines on his face. They mean he smiles a lot."

"Aw. That's cute."

I decided to go with just that: a compliment about his eyes and his smile. This message I composed myself. If my nerves were fizzling and crackling before, now they were a full-on bonfire. Levi rubbed his palms together. "And now, we wait. My money's on Mo."

"I hope it's Ted," I said.

"Well, if it goes sour with either of them, you let me know. I'll kick some Bubbl fuckboi ass." Levi theatrically punched his fist into his palm.

I snorted. "You gonna do some WWE moves on them?"

He broke into a Hulk Hogan growl. "Hell yeah, brother."

The rest of the Berg clan began to arrive, drum kit and guitars in tow. The unlikely offspring of two gentle art professors, the Berg brothers were, like Levi, all over six feet and all extremely dramatic. One of Levi's brothers—I believe it was Ezra—soon joined our professional-wrestling conversation by setting down his guitar, grabbing Levi by the hair, and pretending to pound his brother's head into the table. I also shook hands with a very pensive-looking Eli, and Isaac wrapped me in a bear hug. All four Bergs implored me to stick around and hear their new songs.

My instinct was to politely decline, to go home and veg out, but I needed something to do besides check my inbox every three seconds. It wasn't as if I was eager to start up another Bubbl disaster, but these messages felt more significant. My first first-moves. Perhaps my success would be a sign that I could do this, that there wasn't something permanently wrong with me, that I wouldn't be stuck as a pitiable figure, forever shunned to the punch bowl in the middle-school dance of life.

I checked my phone again. Nothing.

The band finished getting their instruments tuned and levels set. I ordered water from the waitress and was directed to a LindySpring tank and a stack of Styrofoam cups.

My phone beeped. Mo.

My breath came quickly as I strode over to the stage, where Levi and Ezra were making farting noises into the microphone. I held up my screen. "Mo's DJ name is DJ Golddust. He says I can look him up on SoundCloud."

"All right, Robbie!" Levi held out his hand for a low five, and I hit it with a level of energy I hadn't accessed since I played organized sports. Levi shook out the sting.

Ezra leaned over to look at my phone. "Is that Bubbl?"

I nodded.

He pointed at my screen. "Did the guy ask you anything back? If he doesn't ask you any questions, he's a narcissist."

I looked back at Mo's pictures, as if I could discern signs of narcissism in a professional dentist headshot in aqua-blue scrubs. "How do you know?" I asked Ezra.

"If someone is talented *and* hot, odds are they're self-obsessed."

Isaac banged on his snare a few times. From the keyboards, Eli shushed him.

"Depends on how late in life they realized they were hot," Ezra went on. "The Aliyah Darby affair of 2017, for example. Did Levi ever tell you how he ended up in Miami?"

"Whatever happened to her little dog?" Eli asked, muttering into his mic. "I liked that dog." To punctuate his sentiment, he fiddled out the opening chords of "How Much Is That Doggie in the Window?" on his keys. Isaac joined in on the high hat.

Levi turned to his bandmates. "Stop! You guys are making Bubbl look bad for Robin."

"You mean we're making *you* look bad," Ezra said, plucking a long, piercing note. He looked at Levi quizzically. "Weren't you, like, three thousand dollars in debt by the time that relationship was over?"

Levi landed a very realistic WWE blow between Ezra's legs. Judging by the silent scream on Ezra's bearded face, Levi's brother might have been in actual pain.

Soon, the lights dimmed, the Hidden Beaches started to play, and a small crowd assembled on a makeshift dance floor. As the chords tore through the football highlights, I migrated to the bar, subtly plugging one ear as I checked Bubbl again.

A response from Ted. I pumped my fist in victory.

Your message made my day :), he wrote. Then, What is zucchini bread?

You've never had zucchini bread?! I wrote back and promptly wished there was an Undo button. Of course he'd never had it. He just asked what it was.

Nope! Should I have? Ted replied.

I responded that was a shame, and that if we ever met in person, I'd bring him some. That sounded nice, Ted replied, and I didn't know if it was the drinks, or the Berg brothers' charismatic dorkiness, or the hilarious facial expressions as the bar's regulars tried to discern the lyrics of "Fuck Me at the DMV," but I found myself nodding along to the Hidden Beaches' screechy invitations to *let me drive between your traffic cones*, even tapping my feet.

My phone buzzed again: Mo had sent another message. He was impressed by the Sudoku prowess I'd claimed in my profile and asked if I'd like to play against him in online chess. Mo had asked a question! He wasn't a narcissist! I had a funny urge to yell out to the brothers between songs. *Look!* I wanted to tell them, waving my phone. *I'm not a failure!*

In the worst-case scenario, which I felt it was my moral duty to entertain, Mo A could be another Colin Q, ushering me to the sidelines when he found out my tragic secret: *Give her a hand for her bravery.* But at least I knew now how to walk away, how to move on from that kind of simpering pity. I hated being called brave more than anything. *Brave* implied I had a choice in all of this. As if I had an option whether to lose my best friend or not, and death was the one I'd chosen. No. Given the choice, I would have stayed in my own cozy life as it was, thanks. Folding flyers, harvesting potatoes, dozing with my head on Gabe's lap.

But here I was, alone on a busted barstool on a Thursday night, listening to sad-man feelings fill up a neighborhood burger-and-beer joint. The reality was hard to swallow every day, and yet here I was, doing it. It wasn't brave, it just was.

I looked back at Mo's message. He would win every game, I knew that for sure, but maybe that was the point. Maybe I'd get better as I went along. As I watched the band of brothers prance and scream on-stage, Levi's advice echoed in my head. *You say* yes.

Sure, I told Mo, aka DJ Golddust. Online chess wasn't a sound bath or Miami or even a hibachi shrimp, but it was my version of *yes. Let's play.*

The last thing I read . . .
An email from a potato farmer.

Ted K stood up from our table in a sunny, bacon-scented South Minneapolis diner. It was a brisk Saturday morning before Halloween. I'd shoved the Volvo in a precarious parking space between two hybrids, jogging through the strollers and hypoallergenic dogs to be on time. Now, I took in the trace of extra pounds under his practical, sweat-wicking shirt, a smartwatch splattered with what appeared to be flecks of oil paint, and a neat haircut that refused to stay neat. "Edward Kim," he said, holding out his hand.

"Very formal," I said, smiling, still out of breath.

"In case you think I'm a serial killer," Ted said with a nervous laugh as we shook hands. "You have my full name now."

I laughed along with him. "And you have mine. Robin Lindstrom."

We ordered, and the server left to get our drinks. Me, coffee. Ted, black tea. "Feels like winter out there," Ted was saying.

It appeared we were going to follow unwritten Midwestern rules of talking about weather before anything else. "Hopefully we won't get any early snow," I said.

Ted agreed, comparing it to the timing of last year's snowfall, and we began to reminisce about the epic blizzard of 2015.

After the Jake B and Colin Q disasters, I had decided to reveal to Ted that I was a widow before we met in person. That way, if he couldn't handle it, I wouldn't be wasting either of our time. *It's nice to meet someone on here with as much baggage as me*, he'd joked on our chat. *Heck*, he'd gone on, *they might as well give me one of those neon signs for trucks that says* Wide Load of Issues, Do Not Pass. I'd laughed out loud in my office, reading that. When he'd said he had a free morning, I'd pounced on it. He began to straighten the condiments on his side of the table.

"Was the drive here okay?" Ted asked. Before I could answer, he went on. "I really appreciate it, by the way. You coming all the way here. I have to stay close to the city to pick up my girls from Terri later, and I'm never quite sure when they're going to get done with their—" he made a twirling gesture with his hands "—activities and such."

"Any excuse to hit IKEA." I wasn't going to buy anything, I told Ted, but I loved to wander in and out of the colorful fake rooms. "My late husband always said they made him anxious, but to me, they're like this immersive art exhibit of someone else's life. Someone organized, with more money and better taste."

Across from me, Ted looked gray and a bit sweaty. "Uh-huh," was all he could manage.

I cleared my throat, sipped my coffee. I hope he wasn't put off by me mentioning Gabe. He'd brought up Terri—who I assumed to be his ex-wife—so I thought we were in neutral territory. "Are you okay?" I asked, noticing how he gripped his tea for dear life.

He swallowed. "I'm fine."

He was not fine. And if he vomited, I, too, would probably vomit. "Are you going to be sick?"

"I think I just need to eat something." He picked up one of the menus and began to scan it, but I could tell he wasn't actually reading the text. In his hands, the menu shook. And judging by his weather-narration and denial of feeling bad, he would try and last the whole date pretending like everything was okay. I knew this because I could easily do the same—*had* done the same. He didn't want to be here. Maybe I could release him. Or at least release whatever was pulling on him so tightly.

"Hey," I said quietly. Ted looked up from the menu. "Guess what I brought?"

"What?" he asked, tense. His eyes darted to my hands, as if I were about to say *a knuckle sandwich* and bop him in the nose.

"Zucchini bread," I stage-whispered to him.

His face softened, remembering our messages. I saw a trace of that wonderful, full-faced smile he'd worn in his pictures. "Oh, yeah."

"We could have it as an appetizer. They probably have a No Outside Food policy, but a few bites can't hurt . . ." I lifted the foil-wrapped loaf out of my bag and put it on the table, opening one end of the foil, trying and failing to be sneaky. "Go on," I told Ted. "Take some."

Ted risked a glance over to our server, who appeared to be waiting for a new pot of coffee to brew. "But we don't have silverware," he said.

"Dig in," I told him, pushing it closer to his side. "It's all yours."

I watched him dig two fingers into the loaf and pull out a hefty chunk, laughing nervously as he popped it into his mouth. He closed his eyes, chewing. There was nothing in the world like watching someone enjoy what you've made. I decided to say that out loud. "It's like you feel the pleasure along with them, but double," I added. "Because you made it happen."

Ted agreed. "I get that every time I see one of our plays," he said. He was the development director for a small but prestigious independent theater, I'd learned. "Not that I have anything to do with the production," Ted was saying, now taking in more mouthfuls of bread. "But I get to be the one that applies for grants to make sure we stay open each year. The artistic director is pretty terrible at budgeting. Every year we have a surplus, they all look at me like I'm a wizard."

"*Are* you a wizard?" I asked. "You are legally required to tell me if you're a wizard."

Ted laughed hard enough to spray a mouthful of crumbs, attracting the attention of nearby tables. The zucchini bread, which was almost gone now, seemed to fortify him. Soon, he was telling me about his kids. "The girls are eleven and eight. They're great," he rhymed. "Ha." Their names were Franny and Zoey, literary-inspired names chosen by his ex-wife.

"Must be fun with a house full of daughters."

"Keeps me busy! And good to have sane people around to, you know, keep me from calling Terri, sobbing in the middle of the night . . ." He set down his mug of tea. "Crap. Sorry." He put a fist to his forehead. "That is not a first-date thing to say."

"It's all good." I'd been in his shoes, I told him. "It's not easy to get through these things without them popping up." *Them* being our exes.

Ted nodded. He understood. "See, but that's why you're the person who *least* needs to hear about my garbage. At least I get to *see* the person I'm grieving." He paused with a pained expression. "Eesh. Is that wrong to say?"

I leaned back in my seat. "Huh. That didn't even cross my mind."

"Really?"

"Really." Grieving Gabe was so consuming, so unlike anything I've ever felt, I didn't even think to compare it. I thought for a moment what that would be like to be able to see him but only from a distance. My heart did a twisted, complicated dance I'd never be able to understand here, eating breakfast with a stranger, but I tried to find the words. "Part of me thinks I would love to see him alive and happy even if I couldn't be with him, but . . ." I almost stopped here. I didn't know if what I was saying made any sense. But Ted was waiting, curious. "Being a widow, my love for him—our love for each other—gets to stay intact. I'm glad I don't have to wonder what went wrong." I glanced at him, hoping I didn't offend.

"Right, right, of course," Ted said, shaking his head.

"Just why, mostly. The *why* is what gets me. The *what* is easy. The *what* is *cancer*."

"I'm sorry," he said. We were silent for a moment. "If it makes you feel any better, I only know the *what*, too. Terri fell out of love. She's still here, but out of love with me. I don't know why."

"She probably doesn't, either," I offered.

"No, she does." Ted's laugh was bitter. "His name is Craig."

The server came by to refill my coffee, and Ted and I exchanged a conspiratorial look as her eyes landed on the crumb-covered foil. He told me about how holidays were as a single dad, about how strange it was that his girls had two holidays, doing all the same rituals and traditions with two different sets of people, as if they moved between two parallel universes. I told him about the bleakness of my last Christmas, watching *Jingle All the Way* on cable while Mom and Theo slept off their eggnog hangovers.

When our food arrived, Ted finally admitted why he had been feeling faint earlier. "This is my first date. I could barely eat or drink anything yesterday, I was so nervous."

I piled scrambled eggs on my toast. "I don't know if that's sweet or just a sign that you might need a therapist."

Ted lifted his knife and fork. "Can it be both?"

I smiled. "Sure."

"Terri and I are still seeing one," he told me as he cut his omelet into strips. "Same one we saw when we were married. Just to keep communication open. But the irony is . . ." he paused, egged fork aloft ". . . the more we explore our relationship after the fact, the more I see that my ex-wife is one of a kind. I mean, she was—she is—difficult. But she always knows what she wants. She keeps me on my toes."

Sounded familiar. And somehow, we had landed again on Terri. "It seems like you really loved her."

Ted nodded. "But if I'm going to have any sanity in my life, I need to move on." His watch lit up. "Speak of the devil," he said, his face transformed, fully alert. I glanced at the small screen. Terri. "Give me one second," he said, sliding out of his chair with his phone poised to his ear. "Hi!"

Over my Cowboy Breakfast, I glanced at Ted where he stood in the nook by the restroom, watching his expression turn from pleasantly surprised to confused. He nodded as he spoke, crisp, single movements, as if taking orders. *I need to move on*, he'd said. I laughed to myself and took a bite of bacon. *Good luck, buddy.*

A few minutes later, he returned, holding his phone with both hands like a priest with a sacred object. "Good news and bad news. Good news is Terri trusts me enough to take on some of her duties with the kids. That's a real big step for us." He was almost out of breath as he delivered this blessing.

"Good for you!" I poured more hot sauce onto my grits.

"The bad news is I have to go to a Trunk-or-Treat at my kids' school." Ted lifted his coat from his chair. "I'm so sorry."

I put down my fork. "Oh, right now?"

"Right now. Well, in about an hour." Panic started to creep across his face. "It turns out Terri volunteered me and forgot to tell me, I guess? And that means I don't have costumes ready for them, either. Crap. Shit."

I stood, too. "You were supposed to get their costumes?"

"Yeah, but I thought it was next weekend. They were going to be Thing 1 and Thing 2." Ted laughed as he said this, but he didn't seem amused so much as unsettled. "Oh, god, this is going to be a disaster."

"I imagine you could pull it together with a red T-shirt and a bit of white face paint," I told him as he signaled for the server. My brain couldn't help but spur into action, thinking about a tutorial I'd once seen for Grinch makeup. "Draw that big smiley mouth with a black pencil. A little blush for the cheeks and tip of the nose. No big deal."

"You know how to do makeup?" Ted asked.

"Barely. I just love learning how they do it in horror movies. I used to go all out for Halloween . . ." As we packed up our half-eaten meals, I jabbered on about the weird zombie-infected wounds or alien faces that I'd taught myself to apply through books I checked out from the library and, later, from YouTube videos. I'd never been creative, I told Ted, but I liked following the instructions, being methodical and precise until all the little steps turned into something big and otherworldly. "It's just kinda fun," I finished lamely.

"I wish I were the same," Ted told me. "My girls are going to look more like zombies than Dr. Seuss characters when I'm done with them."

Bills paid, we'd made our way outside where the brisk morning had turned into a windy, chilly afternoon. Beside me, Ted put on his gloves, moving from one foot to the other with cold or nerves or both. "Dang! I hate having to cut this short. I feel like we're going to be friends."

"Me, too." At the mention of friendship, I could admit I felt relieved. Ted also looked relieved. There was too much Terri for either of us to develop anything beyond pals, I was pretty sure.

Then he frowned, cocking his head at me. "You wouldn't want to come along to the Trunk-or-Treat, would you? Help with the costumes?"

I snorted. "Oh, man . . ." I started to shake my head, imagining the prospect. And yet. I didn't have any plans. It was not like I really *needed* to visit the little Swedish villages of IKEA kitchens and living rooms today. But I didn't need to randomly show up to an elementary-school parking lot with someone's middle-aged dad, either. No one needed that.

Ted seemed to read my mind. "Is that too crazy? Maybe it's against the rules. I don't know what I'm doing."

"Me neither, really." And there were no rules. Or rather, you had to make up your own. I opened my mouth to decline, but something stopped me. *Go all in*, Levi was telling me, somewhere. *Say* yes. "Sure."

"Really?" Ted asked, raising his fists in victory.

I couldn't believe what had just come out of my mouth. And yet, I was already following him. "Yeah, why not? Let's do it."

An hour later, Ted and I pulled into a school parking lot, Ted searching the rows of hatchbacks and minivans for Terri's SUV. When we finally parked, I sensed a few stares at Ted's vampire cape, half on, Target tags still dangling. And then there was me, still in my supposedly fancy date outfit in a parking lot full of superhero parents and their Minion children, not belonging to anyone. The crisp air and cloudy sky, the little Jedis and Elsas running around—all were bringing me back to Gabe's early mayor days when I'd meet him at the Halloween fundraiser at the health clinic, always a bit overdressed. Once he got elected, he had no longer wanted to transform into the sci-fi characters or nuclear monsters we'd donned in our twenties, hoping to project more of a clean-cut, family-friendly image among all the buttoned-up Brokenridgers. Eventually I, too, toned down my looks. My meticulously bloodied zombie brides became bug antennas or spider earrings. Today, I hadn't deigned to pick out a costume from the racks, either—offering the excuse that I was just the makeup artist—and now I was surprised to find a pang of regret.

A long-limbed, black-haired girl with braces glared from an SUV's back bumper.

"You're late, Dad," she said, glancing briefly at me. This, I could assume, was Ted's eleven-year-old, Franny.

"Sorry, peach," Ted said. "I was getting your costume. Where's your mom?"

Terri was somewhere inside the school, Franny informed us, taking Zoey to the restroom. "What did you bring?" she asked, her brow furrowing as she turned her attention to the Target bag, swiping it from Ted.

We'd managed to find a pallet of face paint, blue wigs, red T-shirts, and construction paper for the *1* and *2*, Ted explained to his eldest. When it looked like Zoey and Terri were returning from the restroom, I wandered between the rows of cars, trying to smile innocently at the costumed families I passed who waved or smiled at my unfamiliar face. *Just a friend!* I mentally projected. *What am I doing here, you ask? Not sure!*

Ted found me behind a neighboring pickup truck. "Share you are!" he said, vampire teeth muffling his speech. "Terri terk off and the girlsh are changing cloash."

When Franny and Zoey emerged from Ted's car, Zoey's hair hung in wild black strings under her blue wig, and Franny's red T-shirt was about three sizes too big.

"Oh, dear," Ted said, muffling a laugh. "You look like a pair of sad, off-duty clowns."

"Shut up, Dad!" Franny said, though more out of distress than hostility.

"We don't say *shut up*," Ted scolded lightly.

"Then, be quiet!" Franny said, tugging at her shirt.

I stepped in, my heart pounding. "Hey, it's all good. We can make you look like the characters, I promise."

Two pairs of dark eyes looked at me skeptically.

"Girlsh," Ted lisped, "this is my . . . coworker, Robin. Sheesh going to make you up to look like a Shing!" As they greeted me mechanically, Ted leaned over to mutter, "Sorry. It's jusht eashier than explaining we were on a date."

"No, that's perfect," I assured him back in a whisper. I turned to the girls with a winning smile. I held up the pallet. "Who wants to go first?"

Franny nudged Zoey forward.

I kneeled to Zoey's level, testing the white makeup on the back of my hand. As I gently tucked her stray hair into her wig, my nerves were fizzing, but there was excitement there, too. I hadn't gotten to play with makeup, let alone on someone else, since . . . god, I couldn't remember when.

"Your breath smells like coffee," Zoey said, matter-of-factly.

I scooted back, my face flushing. "Sorry."

She shrugged. "It's okay. My dad's does, too, sometimes," she said. I began to smear the white paint on her cheeks. "And my mom's," she added wearily. "And Craig's. And my teacher's."

"Adults are pretty stinky, huh?" I asked.

She let out a little laugh. "Yeah."

I glanced at Franny, who might have been holding in a smile as she helped her dad cut out white circles of construction paper, but I couldn't tell. When I was finished, Zoey looked like a pretty passable version of Thing 2, with the illusion of a protruding button nose on her slate-white face, rosy cheeks, and couple of cartoon lines that extended her smile. When I showed her what she looked like in the camera of my phone, she gasped with delight and, to my utter surprise, wrapped her little arms around my neck.

"I love it!" she screeched and began to run in circles on the pavement, pumpkin bucket trailing precariously off her elbow.

Ted dashed after her, trying to catch up. "Let me see, honey, let me see," he chanted, finally wrangling her long enough to get a good look. From bended knee, he, too, gasped and looked up at me. "You're good," he said. "You're *very* good."

Franny observed Zoey's face closely over her dad's shoulder. "Cool," she muttered. She straightened and said, almost a challenge, "Do me, too."

"Please," Ted corrected.

"Puh-lease," Franny said, rolling her eyes.

• • •

Fifteen minutes later, Ted had borrowed a few safety pins from a family of cave people to fasten the marker-drawn numbers to the girls' T-shirts, and the sisters had conceded to posing for a photo with their dad. As they stood and smiled, I watched Franny's expression fight between the glow of self-regard and self-consciousness. For one picture, Zoey asked Franny to hold her feet as she stood on her hands—a very Thing 2 thing to do, we all agreed.

"Want to trick-or-treat with us?" Zoey asked me when she was right side up again.

"I should probably go," I said, glancing apologetically at Ted. "I didn't bring a costume."

Ted waved his hand. "Of course. You have a life. Go. Girls, thank Robin for doing your makeup."

"Thank you, Mrs. Robin." Zoey hugged me around the waist.

I patted her blue head. "You're welcome."

Franny was busy being surrounded by a group of friends, who were all making a fuss over each other's costumes.

"Whoa!" exclaimed one of them dressed as Harley Quinn. She touched Franny's cheek. "How did you get your face to look like that?"

"My dad's friend," I heard Franny say.

"I like it, Mr. Kim!" the Harley Quinn called to Ted.

"Oh, I barely did anything," Ted said, but beside me, I sensed him straighten a bit with pride. "Franny, don't forget to tell Robin thank-you."

"Thanks!" Franny tossed in my direction. "Can I go?"

Ted nodded and called after her. "You look great, honey! Have fun!"

As she ran to catch up with her friends, Franny looked back at him. It was brief, but I saw a smile flit across her face and felt a matching one cross my own.

A random fact I think about . . .
Putting sugar on a cut will make it heal faster.

"Minneapolis, make some *NOISE*!" Mo yelled into the mic. He blasted air horn sounds to emphasize his point.

On cue, people whooped and lifted their arms under the hot, colorful lights blurred by a fog machine and Juul vapor. I made a feeble *Woo* and raised my hands tentatively alongside my neighbors, hoping I remembered to apply deodorant.

After a few rounds of online chess and lighthearted trash-talking—Mo: Nice bishop move, now I'm really gonna take u to church; Me: Do you hear trumpets? Because here comes the *queen*—I'd figured Mo and I were going to remain online game friends. After all, he was Levi's pick, not mine. But his replies came abundant, especially late into the evening, and soon our conversations became deeper, more personal. We'd talked about his hopes to open his own dentistry practice one day, and his love for vinyl, which he'd inherited from his dad, a radio DJ who had immigrated to Minnesota when he was about Mo's age.

My dad loved records, too, I wrote to him. Patsy Cline, Carl Perkins, Little Richard.

Little Richard was a pioneer, Mo agreed.

We should listen to music together sometime, I wrote. I added an *LOL* to tone down the seriousness of the invitation in case he wasn't prepared to take this offline.

But it seemed he was. Definitely :), he replied.

This morning, he took it one step further. Come out and see me spin tonite :). Attached to the message was a poster for an event. A date. So this could be more than chess.

The poster, however—which featured two women in sequins photoshopped over a low-resolution image of outer space—felt like the greatest test of my *Say yes* philosophy yet. I hadn't set foot in a club since before I was married. This also meant it was time to drop the w-bomb, which was dicey territory. At least three or four men had ghosted me since I'd started taking the widow-first approach. I was still getting used to the idea of rejection being a good thing.

Just a heads-up, I said to Mo after three drafts. I'm excited to see you tonight, but I'm going to have to move pretty slow on the whole relationship thing. I was married for nine years so I'm a bit rusty.

Mo had replied right away. Divorced?

I held my breath and typed. Cancer, I sent.

Mo had responded with condolences.

He had just gotten out of a three-year relationship with a girl he'd met in dentistry school. So I'm not looking for anything serious, he'd said.

Me neither, I'd replied. And then added, At least not right away.

I had a feeling he was on the same page. This afternoon he had sent me the link to buy tickets to his show, and I admit it had been thrilling to walk past the chattery, smoky line in a new dress tonight, giving my name at the door and watching the security man open the velvet rope.

From behind the DJ booth, Mo sent a wave in my direction. I lifted my cup in response, my VIP pink band glowing around my wrist. I was sipping something called a Golddust Gimlet, a drink so full of sugar and grain alcohol I could barely hold it in my mouth before my body started reacting to it as a foreign poison, but hell, it was necessary. As the night wore on, it seemed that Mo was either at the beginning of his DJ career or close to the end. Techno fell discordantly into some kind of metal, something Levi would like. Outkast bled into The Eagles, which switched suddenly to Lauryn Hill with a jerky, uneven tempo. At least he looked good up there, confidently turning knobs. I imagined what it would be like to be his girlfriend, dressed up like this every weekend, watching him from the wings. I sipped more Golddust and *leaned back* when prompted. The fabric of my new dress rode up my thighs as I danced, and I let it.

When another DJ took over, I spotted Mo weaving toward me in the crowd, pausing every few feet to speak to people. As he approached, I felt bold and warm.

"Glad you came," he called as he bobbed his head. He smelled like woodsy, leathery cologne. "This crowd is dope."

Before I could respond, Mo's friends soon began to circle him, all nodding politely as I moved out of the way for their handshakes and one-armed hugs. The women among them gave me lip-glossed smiles, carrying their bodies effortlessly. One of them handed him a celebratory shot. I waited for Mo to introduce me, which he seemed to be forgetting to do. They were wearing the same pink bracelets I was wearing, I noticed. So I wasn't the only VIP.

The headlining DJ put on driving, electronic sounds. Everyone was pressing closer together now, becoming less loving, more young, more restless.

"So how do you choose your songs?" I called to Mo, over what sounded like a synchronized *Star Wars* battle.

"What?" he called down to me.

"How—do—you—choose—" I began, but Mo shook his head, holding his hand up to his ear, laughing. He really did have a beautiful smile. And high cheekbones.

Soon, Mo's eyes were glazing, his smile getting more lopsided, his long arms continually landing on the shoulders of the glittery women, who kept shooting photos and videos in circles of light. I ducked out of their frames and checked my own phone. It was barely ten.

I think I might go, I tried mouthing to Mo.

He seemed to understand, and to my delight, it seemed like he might want to come with me. He exchanged a few words with his friends, and together we steered through the sea of elbows and polyester, away from the battering sounds. I took comfort in his hand at the small of my back.

But when I had paused to fish out my coat-check ticket, Mo had swerved away from the exit, taking a smaller side door out to a smokers' patio. I glanced back at the coat-check counter, which was unmanned. I could either wait or brave the cold. Out there it would be quiet, at least.

Mo was lighting up a cigarette. "Don't judge," he said as he exhaled, smiling.

"Interesting vice for a dentist," I said.

"I only have one after shows."

If I were being honest, I might have advised him to drop the cigarette and keep his day job, but what did I know about DJing? Maybe it was just a bad night. And I liked being out here with him, especially now that we could hear each other. My heart pounded.

He looked at my hands, which were trying to rub the thirty-five-degree cold out of my arms. "You cold?" he said.

"Yeah. Can I—" I gestured toward him. Watching the dancers move together, being near so many bodies, had made me feel the absence of touch on my own. Want touch, even.

"Sure," he said, looking pleasantly surprised.

I rested my cheek against his shoulder. The warmth underneath his jacket wasn't exactly a blanket, but it was nice. I was reminded of waiting for Gabe after some ribbon-cutting or council meeting, flashes of a distant July, the snapping *fwoof* of Roman candles, Gabe's tenor amplified down Brokenridge's old brick Main Street on a rare hot night. *And I'd like to thank my wife, Robin.* I'd felt so much pride, knowing it would be me he found at the end of the night. Those were the parts I looked forward to most, the moments after he had turned off his politician self and I was nestled against him. Gabe in his socks and slippers, an IPA in his hand, only having eyes for me.

I circled my arms around Mo's waist, tilting my head toward his. "I'd be really into kissing you right now."

Mo looked down at me with an awkward smile. "Oh, for real?"

At his refusal, I stepped back, loosening from his arms, my gut tight. "What?"

He looked confused. "I'm not—we're not—" He moved his hand between us. "It just doesn't seem like that's the vibe."

It dawned on me with quiet horror. *Come see me spin*, I remembered, but now with new significance. His friends inside, the women orbiting him. The lack of introduction. This was not a date. *Evacuate*, my thoughts seemed to chant, alarm bells cleaning. *I repeat, this is not a date.* "So you were on the app to . . ."

"Trying to spread the word about my shows, you know?" Mo said. "We both said we weren't looking for anything serious, so . . ."

I tried to smile. "Right. Of course. Sorry."

We stood for a moment in silence as he ground his cigarette in the ashtray. My insides seemed to burn and freeze at the same time. I was holding my breath for too long, I realized with a woozy dip in my vision, and the only thing that kept me from fainting was the sudden desire to bury myself under the pavement.

Mo cringed. "You okay, Robin L?"

At least he remembered my name. "Yep!"

He rubbed the back of his head. "You want to come back in?"

"Nope," I said, though I wanted to. I wanted to go back in, rewind time, and start the night over with the right expectations, cool and casual. But I couldn't do that. I could only stand here, pretending to look at a very important *something* on my phone.

"It was nice meeting you!" Mo called as he returned to his fans. "Tell your friends about the set, okay?"

I activated my frozen hands to give him a thumbs-up, trying to keep them steady as the cold penetrated my bones. It occurred to me that this was why Levi had pushed me to think about what I wanted from Bubbl. I wasn't looking for anything serious, no, but nor was I looking for a night in a foggy room where you had to stand for hours and shout to be heard, where your only purpose was to promote the career of a dentist-slash-amateur-DJ.

I began to walk.

The beat of the club still pounded in my tenderized eardrums as I wandered the rows of cars in the parking garage, aiming my key fob, listening for the *beep-boop* of the Volvo. No sounds. Nothing except for traffic and someone yelling on the street below. My feet were starting to get cold. My whole body was cold. Overwhelmed with embarrassment, I'd walked away without retrieving my coat. The plan now was to drive back toward the club, find a closer spot, grab the coat, get home, put on pajamas, and not move from the couch for twenty-four hours. But part one of this plan was hindered by the lack of Volvo. Maybe I'd parked elsewhere.

I kept replaying the meager attempt I'd made at kissing Mo, wondering if I needed to be so humiliated, if being rejected like this on a date was really that monumental or if I was just making too big a deal out of two mouths. When I had kissed Gabe for the first time, I hadn't thought about it at all. In his twin bed, I had moved my mouth along his neck and met his lips, as if it were a destination I'd expected to reach all along. I could see him in my mind's eye, raising his eyebrows. *I'm trying*, I told him. *You can't say I'm not trying.*

There was no Volvo in row D, either. No Volvos anywhere, that I could see.

A door slammed in the distance.

I turned to watch a gold hatchback reverse out of its spot. As it rolled in my direction, something in me sparked at the sight of the driver's bare head, his sharp jaw.

In what I could see of his face, there was the same slow recognition as he crept past. The brake lights shone. The Prius reversed.

The window rolled down. "Robin."

"Hi," I said, dumbstruck. It was Jake B. "What are you doing here?"

"Driving," he said drily. With a hint of amusement, he squinted at me, perhaps trying to piece together the situation. I noticed him glance at my bare arms, both of which I was rubbing with vigor.

"I'm lost," I explained. "I mean, I lost my car."

"You, uh . . ." Jake's eyes roamed his windshield for a second. "Want some help?"

"Oh, my god, yes, please." I got into his front seat, thanking him profusely, and we moved through the level C rows, eyes peeled for Volvos.

He was wearing a nice button-down, untucked from pressed pants. He had gone straight from work to a birthday party in Uptown, he told me, but now it was time to commute back to Pole City so he could get up for his winter-running club tomorrow morning.

"Winter-running club?" I repeated, as if it were a foreign language. "Wow."

"Yep," he said simply.

The silence was thick, but not tense. I was still in a state of disbelief. The sight of him wasn't entirely unreasonable—this garage happened to be within blocks of both of our workplaces, as I remembered—but that it was Jake, a man I'd put in some untouchable corner of my subconscious, made it all the more surreal. The last I'd seen him was almost two months ago, through a layer of tears.

"I was in a *club* tonight," I said, breaking the silence. "A dance club."

"The *clerb*, huh?" he said with a smile. "And you're going home? Don't you know the party doesn't start 'til midnight?"

He was razzing me. I didn't hate it. I threw up my hands, thinking of Mo's circle of social-media vapers and Red Bull drinkers. "Are we old?"

"Yes. We're the exact same old, if I remember correctly from when we—from before."

"Right." I swallowed. He glanced my way a couple of times with his deep brown eyes under sharp brows. "It's wild to run into you after all this time," I added.

"It's pretty wild to see *you*." His eyes darted to my bare legs, my purply arms returning to their normal color. "Can I ask you something?"

I nodded, wondering what it could be. Maybe he was thinking of that day, too. The unseasonable warmth. Calling to each other in the rustling green of the maze, before everything soured. Before I had soured.

"Where is your coat?"

I burst out laughing. I couldn't help it. Between the night's failed attempts at dancing and the awkwardness with Mo and the lost Volvo, this was too much.

"In the *clerb*," I answered.

He laughed, too. His smile wrinkled the corners of his eyes. "Do you wanna go get it?"

"No, no. I'll get it later. It's fine."

"You sure?" He looked at me with curiosity, but with a strange familiarity, too. He looked at me like we were sharing a joke. A laugh followed most things he said, I was noticing, some of them small, some of them big. With anyone else, this might have been obnoxious, but with Jake, it seemed to mean that he genuinely thought life was a little bit funny. As the recipient of one of life's cruelest jokes, I had to agree.

"You know what?" I slapped his dashboard.

"What?"

"Let's do it."

A half hour later, I was happily huddled in my coat in Jake's front seat. After our rescue mission, we had gotten gyros from a food cart, which I failed to devour without making a giant mess. Jake's car was very clean, I noticed, except for a patch of old mud streaked on the door, probably from some outdoor adventure. There was a pine-tree air freshener. A plastic holder for his phone. An insulated water bottle in his cupholder. This was an orderly place. Like the Volvo used to be, before I couldn't bring myself to do anything after work but turn on the TV, let alone clean; before I filled the floors with gas-station-burrito wrappers and Diet Coke bottles as I carted Gabe to and from appointments. I used to be a functional person, I wanted to tell Jake. There was a different version of me somewhere, who didn't forget where she put her car or abandon her coat or cry in parking lots.

We had discussed everything from our families—his parents had been divorced, he had a sister in Bemidji—to speculating about what happened to the Paul Bunyan theme park they'd tried to open on Highway 61 in the '90s. As we talked, I kept picking onions and lettuce off his floor and putting them in the foil wrapper to preserve the interior's cleanliness; he kept telling me not to worry about it.

Now, we were back in the parking garage, full of meat and on the hunt for the lost Volvo. Jake had assured me we would hit every garage in the Twin Cities metro area if that was what was necessary. Conscious of my onion breath, I couldn't stop thanking him.

"It's my pleasure," he said, after what might have been the fifth thank-you. "Really."

"No, it isn't," I said, as if we were still joking, but I wasn't. "You should be in bed but you felt sorry for me. I know I'm pathetic." I shrugged. "I embrace it."

"You're not." Jake's laugh this time had a touch of annoyance. "Do you know how bummed I was after our date didn't work out?"

"I didn't know that." I squeezed the foil wrapper in my hand. "I was bummed, too."

"You were?" He seemed surprised.

"Well, yeah. Of course."

"I thought maybe I had done something wrong or . . . I don't know." He glanced at me before taking the turn down row L. "I did notice your little Bubbl icon was still active after our date, so I was like, well, I guess I wasn't her type."

"Wait, what?" I was unable to keep the shock out of my voice. "I thought I ruined things with you. Because I freaked out."

"No way," Jake said. He cleared his throat. "I mean, yeah, you did freak out, but you didn't ruin anything."

"Damn," I said, keeping my gaze fixed out the passenger window. "You could have reached out."

Jake made a sound of exasperation. "I said see you later, and you said—and I quote—'No, you won't.'"

I buried my face in my hands. "Oh, my god," I said through my palms. "I didn't know you could hear me!"

Jake began to chuckle. "I heard you, all right."

"I'm so sorry."

"Don't even. It's no big deal."

"You're probably dating someone much cooler now."

He cleared his throat again. In my periphery, I saw his gaze flick in my direction. "Uh, nope."

"No cool, like, mountain-climber chick with amazing guns?"

"No—" Jake paused to laugh, almost embarrassed. "Not even close."

"Oh."

My breath caught in my throat. My fingertips tingled. I held them up to the heater vent, moving them back and forth in the warmth.

Suddenly, the Prius halted. Jake pointed. "Hang on, is that it?"

That was it, yes. My good old dirty Volvo, in B8. "I've already said thank-you, so I'll just say see you later." I found his eyes. "For real this time."

"You will?" He met mine, and he didn't look away.

I was still in his car, I realized after a time. Door half-open. Maybe I didn't want the evening to end. He had a string of tiny brown freckles across the bridge of his nose, I noticed. I felt almost tipsy, though I'd barely finished my Golddust drink. I ran my fingers across a *I Biked to Northfield* sticker on his dashboard. What would have happened if I hadn't run off that day? This was the same tiny voice that had leaned into Mo tonight, the same awakening thing that dreaded the stale, empty room waiting for me at home. The wind rattling the windows. The space heater clicking.

"Robin, um . . ." He swallowed.

"You want to drive back with me?" I found myself asking.

He furrowed his brow. "But I need to take my car—"

"No, I mean—I have an idea."

As we both safely reached the interstate, I pressed dial on the screen on my dashboard. We could keep each other company over the phone as we drove home, I'd proposed. Keep each other awake.

Maybe we could talk more about getting older, about what it was like to grow up in our little corner of Minnesota. After being closed for years, they were reopening the Brokenridge Holiday Market, I would tell him. The streets of downtown would be lit up again just like when we were kids, with sleigh rides and light displays and stalls selling handwoven sweaters. Everyone in the Lee County area would be getting the same clay ornaments in their stockings, sold by that one stall run by the long-haired family who might be in a cult. And there'd be hot, homemade mulled wine, making everyone's hands and breath smell like cinnamon and cloves. He would know exactly what I meant. The thought was comforting.

When the phone finally connected to my speakers, Jake picked up on the first ring. "What took you so long?" he asked.

My most irrational fear . . .

That not enough people buy Honey Buns from vending machines, and that they will stop making Honey Buns. Please buy Honey Buns. For me.

The sun was setting earlier now. Inside Levi's living room, he switched on a single brass lamp—he hated overhead lighting, I remembered—revealing the same old leather La-Z-Boy from when he and Gabe used to share this place, the same old antique coffee table, and in the corner, the '70s-installed radiator that appeared to still be working overtime. Levi had wanted to start making plans for next year's Gabe-themed cancer benefit—he might have to go on tour with the band this summer, he'd told me, and though we were approaching Christmas, next September would be here before we knew it. Tonight, I'd stopped by after work.

Levi was shoving aside a pile of throw pillows on the futon. Harpo ran to greet me, and I patted his head. I hadn't seen the hound since he was a puppy. I used to find white fur in clumps on Gabe's jeans.

I kicked off my boots and plopped down next to the box of memorabilia I'd brought. I bounced a little, feeling the cushioned material underneath with my fingertips. "You replaced the futon?" I called to Levi.

"Yeah, it was getting saggy," he called back from somewhere down the hall.

"Huh," I said to Harpo, scratching his ears.

Levi came back in gray sweatpants and a weather-inappropriate sleeveless T-shirt that revealed his tattooed arms, his hair twisted into a high bun. There was a laptop and photo album under one arm and in the other, a platter of hummus and carrots. *Carrots?* The throw pillows were new, too, I noted. So were the plants on the coffee table, replacing the usual game controllers and Altoids tins of weed. A candlelike scent overlaid the incense and coffee and wet dog I remembered from years ago. Levi, domesticated.

He sat on the floor, and we dipped carrots in the nothing-tasting gloop as I summarized my latest Bubbl adventures, my glamorous night as Mo's horny, elderly groupie, my on-the-fly creation of Thing 1 and Thing 2. "And you'll never believe this," I added, my insides tingling with pride and nerves. "Ted called me again and asked me if I wanted to try doing makeup for his theater's upcoming production of *Hamlet*."

"Wait, for real?" Levi asked through a full mouth of veg and dip. "Some guy you went on one date with is trying to volunteer you for community theater?"

I fiddled with a stray thread on Levi's photo album, feeling my cheeks flush. "He's not pawning it off. I took it on willingly." I looked up at him, feeling self-conscious. "You're the one who told me to say yes to things."

Levi's demeanor changed, now gentler, now somewhat impressed that it was a real thing. "No, no—you're right," he said. "That's amazing, Robin."

"I mean, I still have to sort of audition. But yeah, apparently the real makeup artist broke her leg, so they needed someone." On a real production. Because of Thing 1 and Thing 2. *Please*, Ted had begged. *We're a small operation. We can't find anyone who isn't already booked, and you're clearly talented.*

Levi was shuffling through the photo album. "And it's not like you don't have experience." He held up a picture.

I took the photo, feeling my mouth break into a grin at the image of the three of us, though we were barely recognizable as ourselves. A few years back, Gabe had realized how much I missed our old Halloween traditions, so we'd gone all out and entered a costume contest in downtown Minneapolis. I was Annie Wilkes from *Misery*, and Levi was Swamp Thing from *Swamp Thing 2* with green paint and putty all over his body, fake garlands from Michaels hanging off him, soaked with supposed bog water, all mustard dye and glitter.

But Gabe was the coup de grâce, my masterpiece: Pinhead from *Hellraiser*. A bloody grid I'd faux-carved with red and black pencil lined his face. Real nails stuck out of a skullcap which covered his thick, dark hair. It had taken me an hour to get it right, during which Levi entertained Gabe and me with his latest dating misadventures. We'd had Theo drop us off at the nearest light-rail station and taken the train in, I remembered, passengers gawking, asking me to take photos of the boys decked in my painstaking work. I didn't mind. At the venue, we were competing with blue *Avatar* characters and perfectly reconstructed ensembles from *Rocky Horror*. I never thought we'd win. But then, when all the other numbers had been called to the stage, they'd called Gabe's last. The applause hurt my ears. I'd always thought of that night as the purest luck—the light of the venue just so happened to fall on Gabe's pale visage perfectly, casting the nails I'd set in eerie shadow. I returned the photo to its proper place.

Levi was shaking his head, barking laughter that sprayed carrot all over the coffee table.

"I can't believe you're going to be a fancy theater person now because of a dating app. That's how you do Bubbl, y'all. Take note. I love it." He put on his WWE voice as he patted the mess with a paper towel. *"Can you smell . . . what the Robin . . . is cooking?"*

As Levi finished tidying, he answered my questions about Christy. Where she was from (Eau Claire), where she lived (Seward), whether they were serious (not yet; she traveled a lot). Regarding my own dating life—regarding Jake—I kept quiet. There wasn't anything to say, anyway. Not yet. We'd called each other again, twice on the sleepy-morning commute, waxing about dreams we'd had the previous night or deer we'd spotted on the side of the road. Our conversations were rambling and relaxing, like when I used to lie on the carpet listening to my dad's AM talk-radio shows. It felt too new to talk about, too undefined.

Meanwhile, Levi was dipping a three-carrot combo into the center of the bowl, taking a third of the hummus with him. "Now," he said. "Let's give the Gabemeister a proper show."

The funeral had been too formal and stuffy, Levi and I agreed, with the fire trucks and sheriff's cars leading the procession down the tree-lined road to the cemetery; the high school ROTC with their color-guard presentation; the bagpipes; the speeches from the senator Gabe had assisted in his twenties; the two former mayors of Brokenridge; the current mayor of Saint Paul or Minneapolis, I couldn't remember which—all of it recorded by the local news.

This new gathering—this fundraiser—would be more personal. This was for folks from the team and their families. For Levi's brothers. For friends. For me. We'd have a memorial kickball game, and Levi would finally share the song he'd written for Gabe, performed by the Hidden Beaches.

Tonight, I had two jobs: one, help Levi pick out photos to feature, and two, email a Save the Date to a long list of people we'd thought might want to attend and donate to the cause, whatever cancer-related cause we'd end up choosing.

Hi all, it's been a long year, I had written to start the email and left it in my drafts. That was it. I hadn't been able to go beyond that.

"Come on, shake," I said to Harpo, holding out my hand. Harpo looked at me blankly.

Levi held up two photos from my box: one of Gabe as a knob-kneed eight- or nine-year-old, posing with a baseball bat and a helmet on his too-big head, and the other as a laughing, dark-eyed baby at a Sears portrait studio. If Levi looked closer, he'd see my fingerprints.

"What do you think?" Levi asked. "This one to start? Or the baby one? Or both?"

"Both, sure. Whatever." I dangled a carrot in front of Harpo's nose. "Shake, Harpo!"

Levi reached across me to scratch Harpo's ears. "If he hasn't done it before, he's not going to do it now. Especially not for a carrot. Where are you going?"

"Maybe he'll be motivated by bacon or something." I had stood and wandered to the kitchen, where Levi had tried and failed to scrub a pan of what looked like crusted taco mix. There was the Levi I recognized, the Levi of our twenties who was always too busy running in and out of the apartment for shows or shifts or one-night stands. Now, our roles felt reversed. He was being the responsible one, putting all this together. And I was avoiding.

Harpo had come along with me, tail wagging. Through the little barlike window between the kitchen and living room, Levi noticed me standing at the stove, looking at the dirty pan. "I meant to get to that," he called.

"Sure." I opened the fridge, scanning the shelves crowded with condiments and take-out boxes. I held an expired carton of sour cream up to the opening. "You should throw this out."

"Get out of my fridge, please," he called from the living room.

I tossed it in the trash. "What can I eat in here? Like, real food? Hot food?"

"I'll make you something. Just get out of my business."

I ignored him.

It would come back minutes at a time, the funeral. I had read a Louise Glück poem Gabe and I both liked, at his request. I suppose he knew I couldn't get through my own words without losing it. I remember people I'd never talked to in my life coming up to me, asking me what time things were, and what they should bring for the luncheon, where should they put their condolence cards and flowers. I remember writing the schedule down for them on little scraps of paper because I kept misplacing my mock-up of the program. I remember I wore the same black dress for three days, spraying it with Febreze. No one noticed, or at least they pretended they didn't notice.

There was leftover taco meat in Levi's fridge. I could eat that. Suddenly I was nauseous.

Everyone had brought me food. Too much even for me, too much for the fridge to hold. Food sat out on the counters, spoiling. They had so many questions I couldn't answer. Was I going to leave Brokenridge? Was I going to live on the land all by myself? Was I going to sell it? Did I want people to come over and stay with me? Did I want to rent rooms for the extra income? Did I want to adopt an animal for company? What did I need? What was next? I didn't know anything. I always used to know things. We had been preparing what I'd do post death since the diagnosis, but without a *we*, what plans I'd made felt pointless. I'd pressed Decline on calls from college friends. Ignored the doorbell when neighbors came by, neighbors who Gabe and I had hosted for bonfires or potlucks. Maybe I had written them thank-you notes for the flowers and cards. Maybe I hadn't. Maybe they all thought I hated them. Maybe they all hated me.

Now, a stabbing fear arose, remembering how weak my connection to the outside world was then. Was still. Those months felt closer than I thought they were. A physical pain. I would still pull up message threads and find concerned rows of question marks, queries about whether I was okay, dead or alive, or if I'd gotten a new phone. Messages that were still unanswered, a year later. How to put into words a feeling between dead and alive. How to say *not dead, but the world feels like an illness* without sounding dramatic.

Soon, Levi had come in from the other room to stand behind me, gently pushing the fridge door closed. He pointed to the living room. "Are you going to help me or not?"

I sighed, following him, flopping again on the futon, and put my face in one of the throw pillows. I teed up an answer about being tired from work, but Levi and his sensitive bullshit detector would probably see right through it. I reached for the truth, mumbling through the pillow. "I haven't sent out the Save the Date yet."

"Oh," I heard Levi say through the fabric. "That's no problem. We can send it tonight."

I lifted my face from the pillow. "Do you really think it should be me?"

Levi looked confused. "Of course."

I couldn't help but laugh bitterly. I thought of Tammy, her thinly disguised disdain. "I don't know, man. I've been a hermit."

Levi was smiling, incredulous. "Nah. You're the exact person people want to hear from when it comes to Gabe. You guys became like . . ." He sputtered. "Like Amal and Clooney."

"Not anymore. You know all those names we put on that list?"

"Sure."

Levi had collected most of the names, and I'd added to them. That Arab sociology professor from the U that Gabe kept in touch with, Samman. Maureen, Gabe's angel-sweet, doe-eyed assistant at the mayor's office, who did things like call me to ask what kind of candy he liked so she could have a nice bowl for him whenever he was feeling stressed.

"I haven't seen or spoken to a single one," I continued. "Even when they tried to reach me. I straight-out dropped off the face of the earth. You'd have just as much luck hearing back from people. Maybe more." I looked at him, shrugging. Then I turned my eyes away before they could betray me. Before they could reveal how scared I was of this being true.

"Being a hermit after a death is allowed, Robin. Everyone knows that." He was too loud, maybe because he was uncomfortable. "I mean, that's what my therapist said. We're allowed to grieve however we need to."

"Yeah, my counselor said that, too."

"All your people are still out there. They'll show up. At least the real ones."

"Maybe. I certainly haven't been showing up for them." Harpo had come to stand against my leg, looking up at me with his sweet eyes. I rubbed his head. The radiator clinked. I was staring at my fingers running through Harpo's fur.

"Just because you and Gabe aren't making national news or hosting bonfires doesn't mean they're not . . ."

I let out a bitter laugh. "I told them to fuck off, and they did. End of story. I'm like this little goblin who only lets people into her cave if they bring her snacks."

"Hey, listen. If you still need to be a goblin, we don't have to do this. If it's too painful for you." Levi reached out his hand.

I tried to smile as I took it. "I think I've always been secretly that way. That's why Gabe knew this would happen. That's why he did all this Bubbl stuff. That's just what happens when you're in love. Everyone else falls away."

Levi shook his head. "Not necessarily."

"That's what happened to me." I looked down at our intertwined hands. "Are we shaking hands, or what?"

Levi laughed, sniffed a bit. "I don't know." We gave a few good shakes and let go.

I pointed at the plants on the coffee table. "Case in point. Lives merging. That's Christy's influence, I'm guessing."

He pretended to be offended. "Um, excuse me. That is all me."

"These?" I picked up one of the patterned pillows I had pressed onto my face.

Levi scoffed. "Yes. Men like to decorate, too."

"Fair enough," I said, grabbing another carrot. "Just remembering how you used to sleep on a pile of balled-up T-shirts."

"That was only because I left my pillow on tour. That pillow's still in Iowa somewhere." Levi *tsk*ed. "Poor baby."

"You should have gone on a rescue mission." I put on an Arnold Schwarzenegger accent and pretended to cock a carrot-gun. "Give me ze pillow and no vun gets hurt."

He snorted, pointing at me. "You're funny."

"I try," I said.

Eventually I abandoned my quest to get Harpo to lift his paw and helped Levi look through pictures of Gabe. I was tired, but after pushing out all the mixed-up loneliness, or at least starting to, I felt more clear-headed. I hadn't admitted these things to myself, before now. I hadn't had enough distance to know how to recognize what was happening, what I had done, where to begin.

As we slipped through Gabe's past, frame by frame, I found myself silently apologizing to the Gabe of each tableau: mugging for the camera in Rollerblades as a middle-schooler; in a tux at prom and awkwardly holding sequin-covered Hannah Harlow's waist; grinning and sweaty and hard-hatted for Habitat; college graduate. I was sorry that I was here with Levi and he wasn't. That I was still here, in his best friend's apartment, soon to sleep in his family's old home, in his town, his life. I hadn't done much with what I'd been given. I hadn't been living half of it. He had been right to push me.

After a couple hours, we'd put a few dozen photos in the discard pile and landed a few dozen good ones. But we still had to contend with more recent snaps and the enthusiastic footage of two 1980s parents with an only child and a camcorder. "Next time." Levi closed his laptop. "Now, I have a surprise."

"Is it Taco Bell?" My stomach had been growling.

"No. But maybe we can stop there on the way back."

I stood. "I'll drive!"

The lights powered on in a series of bangs, illuminating a bare field dusted with last night's snow. I was standing at home plate, tucked in my coat and scarf, watching Levi approach from beyond the dugout. We were in Chelsea Ballpark, abandoned for the season, but earlier this week he'd charmed the keys to the utility room out of a Parks and Rec employee.

Somehow Levi felt no need to hunch against the cold wind, strolling as nonchalant as can be, his massive shadow stretching under the lights.

"Behold," he called, arching his gloved hands. "The possible venue. I haven't reserved it yet, but—"

"Looks good," I called back to him. "Can we go now?"

"In a second. I just want you to picture it," he said as he got closer, his breath in clouds. His nose and cheeks, like mine, were pink, and his eyes were bright. He pointed. "We can set up a little stage at the pitcher's mound, for the band and for speeches. A projector for the slideshow."

"Whatever you want. I just want to get the hell out of this wind." I tucked my chin back into the scarf Juana had knit me.

"So it's official?" Levi asked, his gravelly voice almost breaking.

"Reserve it, yeah."

"You're not just saying that because you're cold?"

I did a cursory glance around the field to satisfy him, but then my eyes caught on the view of the skyline. There was only one field in this complex where the outline of Saint Paul was so clear. It was no Minneapolis, but it was lovely, and as Levi must have remembered, Gabe often pointed it out to the kickball team, always happy when they got to play here, even if they lost. The view was especially clear tonight, now that the nearby trees were bare.

"You done good, Levi," I said through my scarf. Then I untucked my chin to smile at him. "This is the one."

"Yeah?" He ambled over, kicking up a couple flurries with giant boots.

"Thanks for listening to me earlier, by the way."

"Anytime." Levi smiled back, quiet.

Suddenly, Levi blurted, "First one to the car gets Taco Bell."

"Wait, what?"

But Levi was already sprinting.

"Why can't we both have Taco Bell?" I called to his receding back. "Why does there need to be—oh, fuck it." I started running, too, a wayward laugh erupting out of me from nowhere, cold spiking my lungs.

Levi looked over his shoulder and laughed at the sight, my scarf flapping behind me like a makeshift cape.

"Shut up, you rat bastard!" I called, pumping my arms and feet as fast as they would go, which was not very fast. Eventually he slowed as we reached the edge of the parking lot.

"Whew! I'm out of shape," he said, huffing.

"You're out of luck," I said as I caught up, also panting. He tried to dash again, but I slapped the Volvo's hood just in time. I flexed my muscles in triumph.

Levi held open his arms, his face happier than most in defeat. "You got me, Lindstrom. Let's go get a chalupa."

I shook my head. "And you were going to eat hummus for dinner. Wow. Sad."

New year, new . . .

Menu at my mom's restaurant! Did you hear they're serving pierogis at the Green River now? Get 'em while you can.

On my way to the West Bank, my phone rang, though I was already on the line with Jake. "Can you hang on a second?" I asked him. "Someone's calling."

"I should probably go deice my driveway, anyway," Jake said on the other end. We exchanged a quick goodbye.

This morning we'd been playing license-plate bingo. We hadn't tried to meet yet—too many holiday obligations, and then he'd gone to a friend's house in Southern California for the New Year—but when we did happen to be on the road at the same time, I loved the thrill of spotting his car. I liked looking out my office window, imagining him in his own office just a few hundred yards away.

The new call still blinked on the screen in my dashboard. Ted. My nerves flared. I silenced it. A text came through at a stoplight.

Just want to make sure you're coming. See you at rehearsal!

By *rehearsal* Ted meant a read-through of *Hamlet* at the North Star Theater. After my initial giddiness about the prospect, I'd actually called him back a couple of times and tried to refuse. I was needed at the restaurant on weekends, I told him. And besides, any expertise I'd acquired over the years, I'd gotten from YouTube. What made him think I could prepare actual Shakespearean actors for an actual stage?

Not to mention I had plenty on my plate. I hadn't been this busy in I don't know how long—at least not for any good reason. Perhaps this was how it worked when you actually had things to do and people to see. People who weren't on-screen, running from monsters.

I was attending Sisters in Grief more regularly, and Levi and I had begun to reach out to a couple of Gabe's doctors, asking them which foundations they recommended we work with for the memorial-slash-fundraiser.

I was also trying to get the kinks out of the new point-of-sale system I'd installed at the restaurant so Mom didn't have to worry about keeping physical tabs on inventory and sales. So far, she'd been about as enthusiastic about the new system as she was about her smartphone or any other piece of technology released after 1980: the best she could do was an occasional amused interest, as if the very infrastructure of her business were a cute but useless animal that kept bothering her. I should have probably been at home right then, walking her through it.

And yet here I was in Minneapolis, turning down a quaint tree-lined street toward the small theater. I kept thinking of Gabe when they announced us as costume winners that night three years ago, winking at me behind his pins under the hot lights. He'd often said I should do something with my weird ability to make people into creatures, but I'd always thought he was joking. What would I do? We didn't live in Halloweentown. I was just good at coloring inside the lines, I'd told him. But the rush that night, the rush of completing a job well done, the power I'd felt at making fantasy a reality with my own hands—it was a feeling that I'd never been able to replicate since, no matter how many budgets I'd balanced.

Now, on the back seat behind me was a brand-new makeup case. Usually I'd just use old zipper clutches stuffed into a tote bag. Today, I would have multidirectional wheels. Heavy canvas with stainless-steel reinforcement. Removable compartments for my haphazard rainbow of colors in powder and lipstick. Slots for my time-stiffened brushes and sponges, my sculpting tools, my half-full bottle of fake blood, and a bruising wheel filled with purples, greens, and yellows. All now imperfectly preserved, but still functional. I hoped.

When I'd parked in front of the theater, I paused to consider the case. Was I really going to walk into this place like I was serious business? It would be more accurate to bring the scuffed, frayed tote bag. Keep their expectations low. But I went around to the back seat, anyway. I opened the new case and began to place my powder-streaked tools in the compartments, my heart beating hard and steady.

"I heard this is your first play," said the actor on whom I was smearing foundation. He had a coarse gray beard, and the pronounced vowels and consonants of a stage veteran.

"It might be," I answered, grateful that this time I had remembered mouthwash. "Depends on whether I can make you look sufficiently dead."

The test run the director had given me was to conjure the ghost of Hamlet's father. Behind us, the other players were going through their vocal warm-ups, oohing and aahing. "I'm sure you'll be marvelous," the actor said.

Across the seats, I glanced at the director, a large woman in a black tunic who had a cigarette-fried voice to top my mother's.

"If it helps, I'm nervous, too," the actor continued. "Imagine trying to fill Sir Laurence Olivier's shoes. Or Sir Patrick Stewart's."

I smiled as I applied a deeper purple to the corner of the actor's eyes. "That's the bald *Star Trek* guy, right?"

The actor let out a wry laugh. "He was one of the most prominent members of the Royal Shakespeare Company, but sure. We can call him *the bald* Star Trek *guy*."

"Right. Sorry." As I hollowed out the actor's jawline with purply gray, I tried to keep my hands from shaking.

I stepped back to look at what I'd done so far. My strategy was to start with Pinhead but without the pins: the same white creme with smoky lavender around the eyes, and then bluish lips, to give the ghost a frozen look—from my googling I'd been reminded that the play took place in Denmark. Might as well be winter, I had figured.

"Done?" the actor asked, shifting in his seat.

"Um . . ." I wasn't done, and by this time, the other actors had started running lines. I felt eyes on me. The director stood in the center of the small theater's auditorium seating, watching me as she chatted with Ted. "Just a bit longer," I told the actor.

At his silence—which was an annoyed silence, I was pretty sure—I swallowed my fear and set about sprinkling the powder on his beard, which, with a little water, would transform into glittering ice chunks.

Was I supposed to be done? I had wanted to make him look almost frostbitten, like one of the Arctic scientists from 1982's *The Thing*. I had watched ten or twelve different videos last night, combining and memorizing each step in meticulous detail, down to the different brushstrokes for different colors. I glanced over at the director again, who was looking at her watch. Ted had said it himself: they were a small theater, all they needed was someone last-minute. Now, I was stretching whatever last-minute good grace I'd earned into an hour. Maybe I shouldn't have worried about Denmark in winter. But in this state, he looked dead, but too solid, as if he'd walked directly from his grave to deliver his message. If I was going to do this, I had to do it the right way.

"Believe me," I muttered to the actor as I worked, "I know what it's like to be haunted, and if I were Hamlet and I saw you, I would assume I had eaten some bad cabbage and moved on with my life."

The actor burst out laughing, scattering some of the fine powder I was brushing on his beard. "Ted, who is this girl?" he called over to Ted and the director.

"I'm Robin," I said. I would have to redo a portion of his facial hair, but it was worth it.

"I'm Gregory," he said, still chuckling. "And you take your sweet time."

When I was finished, Gregory blinked in his chair, eyelids heavy with the silvery fake lashes I'd just glued on, and stood. The other actors turned to behold my work, on break from blocking the death of Claudius.

"How do I look?" Gregory called, fluttering his lashes again. "I feel like I'm back in my drag days."

The cast laughed—good-naturedly, but still. My stomach flipped.

"I mean that as a compliment," Gregory assured me as he stepped in front of the director.

Maybe I had overdone it. I watched the director regard him, arms crossed as she leaned close to his face. I found myself getting defensive. So the ghost's look was dramatic. So what? The best horror always toed the line between terrifying and absurd, at least that's how it was for me. The slowness of Jason's walk. Freddy Krueger's wit. The *Exorcist* girl clownishly spinning her head around. Even in my own life. Gabe's life. One week, he was next to me on the couch. The next, he was dead. It was nonsense, a parody of the way things were actually supposed to work. Maybe I didn't have it in me to create a realistic, sophisticated Shakespearean ghost because I had seen the reality, and I didn't care for it.

"Let's see it under the lights," the director rasped. "Kenzie?" she called, and a mousy person with a clipboard popped out from backstage. "Get the houselights, hon."

As the stage manager jogged back to the lighting booth, I began to pack up my case. I didn't want to see their reactions. *Whatever*, I thought. *I didn't ask to be here, anyway.* If they didn't like me, they could find someone else. It struck me that I never used to be like this. If this were a few years ago, I would have bent over backward to find out what the director wanted, what the show needed, to know I was essential, contributing. But grief had changed me. It felt good to stand by what I had done. I began to pack my makeup.

Ted was making his way toward me through the chairs. "Whoa," he said. "Robin, like really, *whoa*. I knew you could do it," he said with a touch of pride. "I had a feeling."

I smiled at Ted. "Thanks for the opportunity. It was fun."

Suddenly, the houselights went dark. I paused to look—I couldn't help myself. The stage lights clicked on, illuminating Gregory in the center. But he was no longer Gregory. The contours I'd drawn made his cheeks skeletal, his eyes like two black holes. The frost in his hair glittered in a crown. His blue lips began to form words, which he delivered in a hoarse growl. "I am thy father's spirit, doom'd for a certain term to walk the night . . . Revenge his foul and most unnatural murder . . ."

When his monologue was finished, a silent chill hung in the air. I didn't know if it was a good chill or a bad chill until Ted began to clap.

Gregory joined in, pointing his applause in my direction. A few of the actors did the same, talking among themselves as they stared at Gregory in a kind of terrified awe. He still looked inhuman, even in corduroys and cable knit, yet the earthly details I'd added—the ice in his hair, the touch of pink like burst blood vessels—inspired pity. I had done that. Something primal and proud and hungry bloomed inside me.

The director interrupted my reverie, pointing at me with a smirk. "You're hired. Now take that shit off him before I have nightmares."

A life goal of mine is . . .

To wave goodbye to someone from a train window, like in the movies.

In the car, Jake kept looking over at me as he tapped his hands to the beat of the radio. Service on our phones was getting spotty as we made our way north, so we listened to local stations, classic rock and jingles for furniture outlets. Deep green firs streaked past the window. Towns dotted the road with midcentury motor lodges and pine-sided bars and one-roomed churches, fading from view as quickly as they rose up. Above the rooftops, dawn was pink and lavender and blue-gray. We sipped steaming hazelnut coffee and milk from company travel mugs I'd fixed for us. Breakfast of hard-boiled eggs from the cooler. Now, we were quiet. Jake had turned his head from the road again.

"What?" I asked him.

"It's just so good to see you. It's cool we're finally doing this."

"What, ice fishing?"

Jake shrugged, tilting his head from side to side in a *maybe* gesture. "Sure."

Did he mean that *this* was more than ice fishing? Whenever we'd gotten close to the subject—the subject of *we*—one of us always seemed to back away, scared of disturbing the peace. I guess that's how we were together, we couldn't help it. We floated off into the jetsam of our rambling brains, or we were quiet for long stretches, only interrupting each other's solitude to share a point. Even now, trapped in a car with my nervous energy, he seemed just as at ease as he was when we were waxing poetic on I-35 about Baskin-Robbins flavors, or Jordan Peele, or the strange appeal of tiny houses. He was so easygoing, so pleasant, it was as if he was never uncomfortable, which made me want to be comfortable, too. But maybe that was the problem. What I loved about our interactions was also what kept them from ever coming down to earth, where I might have to address why it felt like seven sparklers were lit in my chest at once.

All week I'd felt like a teenager, bored in school, barely noticing the payroll and vendor contracts and bonus requests, staring out my office window in anticipation of closing time. He'd dropped the invitation on Wednesday, as casual as can be. *Wanna go with me? The deep freeze has hit the lake by now.*

Now, here we were, two feet from each other, and I wished I could just let things hang, like our airy conversations about nothing. But I wanted him to know more and more I had been picturing him as we spoke, that I could imagine us like this, as a couple, sharing sleepy insights over coffee, taking weekends up north.

Soon, a sign nailed to a mile-high tree pointed us to Lake Farway. The Prius turned and roamed deeper into the woods. In the stillness, the road crackled with rock and ice. Needled branches brushed the sides of the car. Jake began to get excited as we crawled closer to the water, reminiscing about past trips with his friends Diego and Smitty, about the fish they'd caught and hadn't caught, about how beautiful this area was in the summer, too, and that maybe I'd see it someday.

Would I see it someday? I thought but didn't say. Is that what he wanted?

Parked, we made our way down a thin, rocky path, toward the shoreline of smooth stones and snow-capped driftwood. When the trees broke, revealing the lake, I gasped at its stark beauty, squinting in the white glare. In the distance, two figures were putting up a small tent. Diego and Smitty spotted us, waving. To keep our balance on the vast, shimmering slate, we took each other's hands. I held Jake's tight. He squeezed back.

A couple hours later, the four of us sat on makeshift stools of overturned plastic buckets, our knees almost knocking around the hole augered into the ice. Whiskey had been poured into Coke cans. A tiny space heater pumped. Our poles were on the ground, lines unmoving. We had started with small talk, establishing that I was an accountant, that Diego was a consultant, that Smitty—a nickname for Abigail Schmidt—owned a tree-trimming business. Then the three of them had fallen into what almost sounded like another language, a shorthand of inside jokes and references.

They paused only to watch one of the poles move, though when Diego checked it, the bait had been nibbled, but the fish had escaped.

"Fair warning, I am kind of cursed," I joked.

"Uh-oh," Diego said as he hooked a new worm. "Is this why we're not getting bites?"

"Yeah, I was kind of wondering why you went out so far," I said, nodding out toward the ice. Before Theo was born, Dad used to take me out on Brokenridge Lake. He taught me how to tell how thick the ice was by sight and feel. How to grind a hand auger to make a hole. I was eager to share something I actually knew. "Usually you try to stay closer to the shallows in the morning for feeding, right?"

"*Stay closer to the shallows*, she says," Smitty said, turning to Diego. Diego snorted.

"Normally you would be right—" Jake began to say.

"Trust us," Smitty interrupted. "We know Lake Farway."

Jake had warned me that Diego and Smitty weren't going to be mean, but they were going to be wary. The three of them had grown up as neighbors, and with Jake being the youngest, they had always been protective. I steeled myself.

"So you two met how?" Smitty asked. She stared at me openly with her Baldwin-blue eyes, blond curls peeking out of a hunter's orange beanie.

"Don't pretend you don't know, Smits," Diego said. He was on the heavier side in a sporty green coat, with a full black beard and dark eyes that rested on me without pause. "We know you guys met online. Jake talks about you."

Smitty shrugged. "It's polite to let a couple tell their own story the way they see fit."

Jake and I glanced at each other. Hopefully my blush was hidden under the cold on my cheeks.

"Oh, we're not—we're not an official couple, or anything," I clarified as I smiled at both of them, my stomach in knots. Right for the jugular.

"And yet he invites you out to Lake Farway." Smitty raised her blond eyebrows and *tsk*ed. "That is not a taking-it-slow maneuver in this friend group, I have to say."

"Lay off," Jake said, laughing uncomfortably.

"Yeah." Diego kicked at Smitty's boot with his own, chuckling. "Stop policing."

"What?" Smitty continued. "Barbecue, sure. But dragging someone out to the middle of nowhere in subzero temperatures? And this is a very intimate venue, is it not?" Smitty lifted her gloved hands to acknowledge the vinyl walls.

"Ha, well . . ." I said stupidly. I couldn't bring myself to look at Jake. At anyone. Was I supposed to respond to that? What was I, a kid? Yes. In dating terms, yes.

After another hour, the lines had not moved. We'd eaten all the beef jerky and cheese I'd brought, gone through all the Coke cans. Outside, behind the thick clouds, the sun was getting higher. The fish wouldn't be feeding for much longer.

"All right, fine," Smitty said, tossing her rod to the ice. She looked at me with a reluctant smile. "Let's do it Robin's way."

I gave her a small smile back but was quick to start packing things into the cooler, not wanting her to think I was reveling in victory. Together, we deconstructed the tent, moving everything closer to shore. In what I thought was a good spot, Smitty began to chip away at the ice with the auger while Jake and I watched. Diego went to the car to procure more soda.

"Why did you say you were cursed?" Jake asked me after a moment.

"Oh, it was just something Gabe used to say whenever we went fishing."

"Ah." There was no Jake-like laugh. He dropped to his knees to take a turn at the auger.

Had I said something wrong? I'd been careful to keep Gabe out of his mind, out of mine. But even now, Gabe's voice wove in and out of my hearing. His boots had appeared next to mine on the frozen water, conjuring the Mississippi. Of course it wasn't really him. That's what I kept telling myself. But I'd begun to understand why Marcy liked consulting a woman who claimed to speak to the dead. Last night, as I dug through storage looking for fishing poles and gloves, Gabe seemed to be in the corners of every room, the corners of my vision. *Well? What's the verdict, hon?* When he didn't answer, I had goaded his ghost with an old six-pack of home-brewed beer I'd found in the garage. *This has gone bad*, I told the Gabe of my brain, daring him to appear. *I'm going to have to throw it out*. His handwriting was on the label of each bottle, always so precious to me, cramped and boyish. *Garobbie Beer*, he called it, a combination of our names. I'd stood at the sink and poured the sour yeast-smelling liquid down the drain, mourning the last workings of his hands as the liquid disappeared.

Wordlessly, I bent to take my own turn on the auger. I leaned hard into each spin, ice chips flying. Maybe Jake was sensing my split mind. Maybe we should have stayed commuter friends, or whatever we were to each other. Maybe pushing this IRL had been a bad idea.

Taking turns cranking, we formed another reasonably sized hole. The four of us settled back down on our buckets, and when I asked for the whiskey, Diego insisted on pouring.

"Strong," I said, wiping my twisting mouth.

"Welcome to ice fishing with us," Smitty said.

"Cheers," I said.

"To Robin," Jake said, lifting his can.

I couldn't tell what was in his expression, but I was happy to catch his eyes. "Don't cheers me yet," I said, smiling at him. "Not until we have fish."

"Eh, who cares. The fish isn't the point." He winked. I felt relief.

Soon, however, all four lines got tugs, bringing in flopping perch after perch, their splashes disrupting a game of blackjack that I had tried and failed not to win. Diego's and Smitty's cries of delight echoed across the ice. They held up their hands to me for high fives.

As morning stretched into afternoon, we rotated seats for our turn at being closer to the warmth of the space heater. We played Never Have I Ever and Diego lost, which, he reminded us, actually means he'd won at life. We found our preferred peeing spots on shore—mine was deeper into the bush, but I got to see a cardinal. Smitty passed around a Black & Mild, and I beat everyone at hearts, and we sang Queen to the empty tundra.

As we ended an off-tune rendition of "Another One Bites the Dust," Jake scooted closer on his overturned bucket and poked me with his elbow, eyes sparkling. "I'm glad you came."

If I were a braver soul, I would have kissed him right then.

As the sun set, we hit the road. The cooler was packed with ice and two perch. "I like your friends," I told Jake.

"And they like you."

"You think so?"

"They sure didn't sing with anyone else I've dated," Jake assured me.

My heart leaped. When it stayed up, I realized I was still holding something in. I remembered how quiet Jake had gotten as we'd drilled a new hole in the shallows. "Sorry if it was weird that I brought up Gabe."

"Aw, no," Jake said, shaking his head. "You can talk about him. It doesn't bother me."

"Nothing bothers you," I told him with a smile.

"That's not true."

"I just mean that when I talk about him, things seem heavy. And I like how light I feel with you . . . you know." I scrambled to make it sound more casual. "Hanging out. Sometimes when I talk about him, it opens a whole other can of worms."

"Nice fishing reference. But really," Jake said, his tone more serious, "try me."

I hesitated. Did he mean it? How much could I say without scaring him? Without becoming the same sad widow who'd sobbed in the parking lot when we first met? But he'd still come back after that, hadn't he? Maybe I could land for a moment. Maybe I could open up another part of myself.

"Well, I felt guilty going on this excursion, that's for one."

I thought of all the blankets and sweaters and stray socks I'd collected last night from every corner of the house—months and months of a sedentary life, and now I was leaving it behind without the one person who would have wanted me to. He would have been the one to dig into storage last night for the rods and snow pants, I told Jake. He would have been muttering to himself as he fiddled with his tackle box. He would have wanted me to get out.

"Even when he was alive," I said, "I would have probably stayed home if a friend had invited me to something like this. Or, like, gone and done whatever he was doing. He was my best friend, you know? I wanted to be around him all the time." I looked out the window. Cold climbed up the edges of the windows in spiky flowers of frost. "And now I feel guilty telling *you* this."

"I'm not jealous or anything," Jake said. "It's your past. It's part of you. I've got Roxana as part of me, too."

Roxana was the ex he'd split with a year or so ago, I'd learned through occasional references. They'd met while she was getting her biology PhD. The idea was that she would get a job and they'd get married, but they never made it past the postdoc before she went back to Europe.

"See, but I'm a little jealous of Roxana." I kept my tone light as I turned back to him, raising my eyebrows.

"Oh, are you?" Jake said.

"I am," I said, smiling. I leaned my head back on my headrest.

Good things take time. That was what Jake had written on his Bubbl profile, and the refrain moved through my head with the hum of the tires. The radio crackled in and out as the sun set over the highway. My eyelids got heavy.

When I woke, it was dark, and the peace I felt was strange. Usually I slept lightly and dreamed vividly—running up the side of a steep bank, grasping for roots; wandering a half-abandoned mall with too many levels and broken escalators—but here, next to Jake, I'd slept deeply. The kind of knocked-out where time jumped forward without me in tow. Something had shifted in the air. In me.

He cleared his throat. The car was slowing down now. "We're back in Brokenridge."

I smoothed my hair, my pulse beginning to wake now, too. "Wow," I said, fighting a yawn. "I guess I had too much fun."

A smile played across his mouth. "It was cute, though. Your little snores."

"Oh, thanks," I said, casual, though I found myself sitting up straighter. "We barely got to talk."

We hit a red light at the intersection before the courthouse, still glowing with Christmas lights.

I looked over at him. "I'm guessing you have to get back home."

"Do I?" Jake asked, his hands tightening on the steering wheel. "I mean, is that what you want?"

"I don't know," I said. The light turned green.

Across the street was the post office, and the Red Lyon, and the old Curl Up and Dye, where I had gotten my first haircut, my first updo for a school dance, where I'd gotten my hair done for my wedding. Behind us to the north was the Green River and my childhood home.

We ventured forward toward the south end of town, just a few minutes' drive to the farmhouse with the chipped white paint, and too soon we were making our slow way down the driveway toward the dark house. The car came to a stop, but I didn't make any moves to leave. I didn't even unbuckle my seat belt.

"Today was fun," he said.

"Yes," I said automatically, my insides jumping.

"What if I told you I didn't want it to end?" He said it slowly, in his pleasant, unflappable way, but his hands were still tight on the wheel.

I was still frozen in the front seat. My mind darted to and fro, trying to find an acceptable response, but I had no precedent for this. No template. All I knew was that I was ready to kiss him, here and now, but something would keep me in the car. Something about how still the farmhouse was in the dark, something I couldn't yet disturb. I could name it, I supposed: it was Gabe. He was there. He would always be there.

"I don't want it to end either, but . . ." I swallowed, nodded toward the house. "Not here. Not yet. Does that make sense?"

"No, no, I understand." He looked away, not stung, but the rejection showed on his face.

"But we could go somewhere else," I said quickly. The words were too simple, but I had a feeling we were speaking in code. I needed to find some way to communicate how much the day had meant to me, much more than my sleepiness and awkwardness about the house had implied. Sparklers ignited in my chest again.

He let out a breathy, nervous laugh. "Would you be ready for that? My place, I mean?"

A smile grew on my face. "I think so, yeah. I mean, definitely. Let's go to Pole City."

He turned the wheel of the Prius without a word, putting it in Reverse.

When we reached Jake's entryway, we scattered our snow gear on the floor. He led me upstairs, my hand in his. On his powder-clean bed, his mouth was warm and wanting, and his hands slipped up the back of my neck, through my hair. My skin felt ultrabare, almost chilly, but I was too busy watching his body to be self-conscious, his palms on my waist and thighs, marveling that such a thing was possible, that I was allowed to be so close to this new person. He had a barrel chest and a mole on his shoulder and those freckles I'd noticed on the bridge of his nose.

The novelty became pure sensation. From inside the waves of pleasure, I remembered how to ask for what I wanted when he touched me, to respond to the movements of his hands and his hips. My eyes began to close out of necessity, my breath catching and holding as my thoughts melted together.

After, as our breathing slowed, I waited to feel something bad, something akin to guilt, the way Gabe's absence sometimes came over me at home, like a chill or a fever. I waited for his voice in my head. I must have fallen asleep, waiting.

In the early morning—what I assumed was the early morning—something did come. A soft pressure like hands. I jolted, raising my head from the pillow, listening for the creak of feet on the farmhouse floorboards, looking for that dark shape I sometimes mistook for a presence, Gabe's coat hanging on the closet door. But it was a cat on my hip, kneading a foreign white bedspread.

Jake stirred beside me, yawning. "That's Tiger," he said, sleep in his voice.

"Hi, Tiger," I said through cracked eyelids, reaching out for her striped fur. I was not at home, I reminded myself. I was at Jake's, and Gabe was never here, would never come here, had never even known this place existed. But that was okay. Everything would be okay.

Jake lived in a row of townhomes on a hill. A balcony off the bedroom looked out over the farms and forest surrounding Pole City. I stood behind sliding glass doors while I drank French press coffee, taking it all in. Behind on the white walls, bicycles and skis and kayaks hung on racks, unadorned except for a few blown-up photos of family, post-mountain-climb pictures with friends.

That evening, we lay curled together on his giant gray couch, watching TV while the sun fell in Creamsicle-orange strips through his blinds. Between episodes of a detective show I was barely paying attention to, he asked me what I usually wore to work.

"Not this," I said. I was in his *10K for Pole City Kids!* T-shirt, underwear, and socks. "Why?" I asked, and in answer, he'd gently rolled me on my back.

Everything felt smooth. I suspect it was because we had been talking for so long, even the occasional awkwardness felt natural. We knew how to interpret each other's expressions and silence, how to give and receive, and how not to talk, lying together on the cushions in sweaty silence until one of our hands moved down the length of the other, until one of our mouths met skin, and we'd start all over again. Soon, it became too late to go back to Brokenridge.

On Monday, we carpooled into Minneapolis together, me in one of his sweaters, reluctant to leave the Prius in the drop-off lane until a bus blew its horn. On the commute home, we agreed we both should take time to breathe after our forty-eight-hour date.

"Until the next one, at least," Jake said and kissed me.

This year, I'm going to . . .

Finally learn the rest of the words to Journey's "Don't Stop Believin'."

Later that week, in the corner of my mom's living room, I played catch-up on the restaurant's books, receipt paper from the Green River's old-fashioned credit-card machine winding around my elbows like a ribbon. Usually this was a mindless task—even comforting, watching each sum click into place—but since I'd parted with Jake, I craved contact with him like I craved sweetness after a meal. I checked my phone for his name. Nothing yet. The house still smelled of the vanilla candles Mom had burned at Christmas, though February was just around the corner. The fake tree was still up, casting red and green light over the old plaid couch, the piano Theo used to play, the days-old snow piling up outside. I yanked my focus back to the screen. Lunch Sales: $1,857. Dinner Sales: $3,009. Liquor Sales: $986.

As I had predicted, the fancy wine Mom had invested in was not moving. Only two glasses purchased for the whole week, which meant an entire bottle had been opened and wasted for a few cents. I massaged my temples, fighting a headache.

Car doors slammed outside.

As Mom and Theo hobbled in the back door with a gust of cold, I met them in the kitchen. They had gone to get dinner, which from the looks of it, was two pizzas from the gas station and a six-pack of Hamm's.

"I'm never going outside again," Theo said.

"Oh pish," Mom protested. "Ain't bad for this time of year. How are the books looking, Robbie?"

"Not our best week," I said, the understatement of the year.

"Ah, well." Mom set the pizza on the counter. "We're always slow in winter."

The I-told-you-so rose in my throat, ready to rant about how liquor sales were below average, no thanks to the wasted pinot noir sitting on a shelf below the bar. But what was the point? I'd highlighted the numbers in red. That was about the best I could do. I swallowed my retort and put a slice of pizza in my mouth instead.

We sat around the kitchen table.

"There's just something about Casey's pizza," I said as I went for a second slice. "Is it the crust? Is it because it sits for hours under a food heater? God, I can't put my finger on it."

"It's not just good-for-a-gas-station good," Theo agreed. "It's, like, legitimately good."

"You know," Mom said, pointing at Theo, "this might work for the party."

"Mm," Theo said excitedly, patting his mouth with a napkin. "Good idea. Just use the restaurant as a space, and you don't have to worry about making food for all those people."

"What people?" I asked. "What party?"

Theo and Mom looked at each other. I felt a spike of annoyance in my chest. A bit of envy. The two of them were always close, even closer now that Theo was apparently coming back to Brokenridge every weekend.

"I've decided . . ." Mom sounded uncharacteristically formal ". . . I'm doing sixty-five!" She coughed and banged on her chest. "'Scuse me. And I'm doing it big."

My hackles rose, though I wasn't sure why yet. "Sixty-five as in your birthday sixty-five?"

Mom reached for the fridge and cracked open another beer. "Yepperoni. Sounds fun, huh? Kind of a half party, half St. Paddy's Day festival thing." They were going to invite the whole town, Mom and Theo informed me. They were going to block off the Green River parking lot and buy a couple of kegs. Theo was going to cover the cost of the beer, and Mom would be in charge of getting everything together for the band.

"The band?" I asked.

"Rick's band does Grateful Dead covers, but they said they could do some Bee Gees and Elton John, too," Mom answered, businesslike.

"Great," I said, sarcastic. "Thank goodness they do Bee Gees. I was worried about that."

"Don't be nasty, Robbie," Mom warned, pointing her half-eaten slice at me.

"I'm sorry, Mom, but if you're hosting a party at the restaurant that day, what's the plan for keeping all the parade business?" The Brokenridge St. Patrick's Day parade attracted people from all over the county. It was one of our busiest weekends of the year. They looked at me like I had just told them I was an extraterrestrial.

Theo let out a thoughtful *hm* and glanced at Mom. "What do you think, Ma?"

"Well, yeah. We might have to close, unfortunately," Mom said, a poor excuse for regret in her voice. "But it's worth it."

I scoffed. "Why can't you just have it on Monday, when we're already closed?"

Theo rolled his eyes. "People can't come out on a Monday."

"If you'd planned it enough in advance, they could."

"Well, we didn't, okay?" Theo said, testy. "It's out there now. There are already, like, a hundred attendees on the Facebook invite."

Mom opened the fridge and handed Theo another beer. My pulse rose. I took a deep breath, staring at the ceiling as I tried to pin down my racing thoughts. "You already invited people? So I'm the last to know, here?"

"You haven't been around!" Theo said, exasperated. "You've been too busy with dating. Not that I disapprove, but . . ."

"So you decided to throw a frat party for our sixty-five-year-old mother?" I could feel frustration bubbling up in my voice. All I could see were red Excel numbers. "We'll be playing catch-up for months, possibly all year."

"Theo, can you be a doll and get my slippers?" Mom said to Theo.

"What, are you just excusing him from the conversation?" I said as Theo stood. "Yeah, leave. Let the adults handle the money, and you enjoy your party."

He flipped me off as he left the room, eyes on his phone.

I turned back to Mom, shaking my head. "You are really going to close down."

"This is not the most profitable thing, I get it, I know." She lifted her shoulders. "But you know better than me that it's been a hard year, huh? We deserve a little fun. You only turn sixty-five once."

"No, you're right," I said and put on a smile. "I just thought you'd be retired by now. Get off your feet."

Mom waved a dismissive hand. "Nah. Sixty-five is still young. Just gotta drink a little less. Smoke less."

I would agree, of course, but I'd told her that before, and telling Mom to slow down only made her want to run farther away. Faster. So you learned to offer her water rather than ask her how many she'd had. To pick up Vicks whenever you were at the pharmacy. "Are you going to do it?" I asked tentatively. "Cut back, I mean?"

"Having a drink or two is part of my job. People come to the Green River to take a load off, and if I have a beer or two, I give 'em permission, you know? It's a social profession."

"Right," I said.

"You think I should cut down," she said. It wasn't a question, but she seemed to expect a reply.

"Might be fun to try something new?" I offered tentatively. "See if you like the clear head?"

"A clear head. That's hysterical," she said with a wheezy chuckle. "That's the point of the drink, hon. To clear your head."

"But you know it affects your health. You saw what it did to Dad—"

"Yes, Robbie, damn it," she snapped.

I leaned back in my chair as if I'd been slapped.

"Whew," she breathed. She raised her eyebrows. "Did not mean to curse."

"Sorry," I said automatically.

"How 'bout you live your own life, Robbie?" Her voice was tired, clipped.

"I'm trying," I said, my voice still feeling thin in my throat. I thought of all the new things I'd felt this weekend, waking up next to Jake, while Mom was waking up alone. Had woken up alone for years. She deserved to celebrate, I told myself. She deserved joy wherever she could find it.

"I'm not stupid. I know how to cut down when I need to cut down. And I've been in this business for years."

"I know."

"We're family. Let's be sweet to each other." She reached over and patted my cheek.

"Okay." We smiled at each other. Mom winked.

I felt a mixture of relief that the tension was gone and the same hopelessness I'd felt when I looked at the books earlier. Like I was fighting a windmill, here. Like no matter what I tried to say, it was always already done. The slump in business after Dad died was just temporary, Mom had assured me, and I had some idea how to fix these things—clean the grease trap, take better inventory so we weren't serving frozen food—but between the accounting job and helping Gabe, I could only do so much. And there were the supposed turnkey investments, the morale boosters. The portable Popsicle cart that now sat unused under a tarp near the dumpsters. The automatic paper-towel dispensers in the bathroom that stopped working three weeks after they arrived. The four cases of completely unnecessary pinot noir. And now, the party. Weekend to weekend, we had survived, but Mom was still working twelve-hour days.

Theo came back in, handing Mom her slippers. I wrapped the leftover pizza in aluminum foil: maybe Mom would want it later, when she noticed she'd barely eaten. The idea of her eating cold pizza alone in the kitchen, shuffling around in her slippers, was enough to make me want to reach for her. Hold her.

Before I left that night, I went back to the computer and turned the red numbers black.

If I could rule the world . . .

Mandatory naps. There would be no war if we could all take more naps.

"So fancy," I said as the appetizer arrived. Jake and I were at something called a *pop-up*, which I thought sounded delightful and sugary and popcorny, but it turned out to be an abandoned Chinese-takeout restaurant that had been temporarily transformed into a softly lit lounge with abstract art on the walls. This particular appetizer held what looked like a carefully constructed tower of raw vegetables in a puddle of olive oil.

"I know," Jake whispered back, amused. "Too fancy for us."

I was just happy to sit across from him, his usual T-shirt replaced with a button-down, his ball cap sitting beside his plate. We both seemed to be jittery with all the rituals of romance I'd forgotten: the pleasure of being picked up from work on a Friday evening, of kissing someone's cheek, of holding hands on the street. "What the hell is this?" I lifted a hard purple squiggle that might have been a carrot or a radish at some point. At my inquiry, people from nearby tables turned. "Am I too loud? Why is everyone talking really quietly?"

"Maybe they figured out that we're *spies*," Jake said in an intentionally loud voice, and we both laughed.

A chime sounded from the bell at the entrance—left over from when the place specialized in takeout, most likely—and I glanced over Jake's shoulder to see a familiar professional-wrestling-size form at the entrance, chatting with the hostess. "Oh, my god," I called, attracting more stares from the other patrons. "Levi, hey!"

Levi looked up and found me waving. His face broke into a grin. A tiny, svelte woman stepped in beside him, removing her fur-lined hood to reveal white-blond hair and wide-set blue eyes. The famous Christy.

"Do you know them?" Jake asked, turning to look.

"Yeah, this is my friend and his girlfr—the girl he's seeing, I guess? What a coincidence."

I laughed to myself. Levi had sent me a few texts over the weekend asking how Bubbl was going, so I'd sent him a couple back. Sorry, was on a date for like 3 days?? He's taking me to dinner again tomorrow at a pop-up in St Paul!!! I guess Levi showing up at the very pop-up I'd mentioned was viable, depending on how common such venues were in the greater Twin Cities area. Christy certainly looked like she fit in here.

"Well, well, well," Levi said, approaching our table. "Looks like we've got a few crudités going on."

"Crew de what?" I said. I followed Levi's attention to the nest of vegetables. "Oh. Yeah."

"You must be Jake," Levi said, holding out his hand. "I've heard so much about you, man." *So much* was a bit of an exaggeration. *Remember the guy from Pole City who I cried at in the parking lot of the corn maze?* I'd said in my text updates. That was about all Levi knew.

Jake returned Levi's handshake, a confused smile forming. "Oh, yeah?"

"Yeah, Levi helped me . . ." I started saying to Jake, swallowing a sip of water to stall, wondering how to put it exactly. *Helped me avoid fuckbois? Helped me find someone like you?*

"We've been putting together a little event," Levi finished. "And she mentioned you."

I looked up to lock eyes with Levi, grateful. Nice save. I turned to Christy, trying to sound chipper. "Hi, I'm Robin!"

"Robin, Christy," Levi said, suddenly very chipper himself. "Christy, Robin."

Christy turned her unblinking blue eyes to me. "Gabe's widow, right?"

"Uh, sure." A familiar wall of defensiveness formed, something that tended to happen when one of the most painful events of my life was tossed out by a stranger. My husband's name, so casually falling out of her mouth. After a year, I was still getting used to it.

Perhaps Christy could sense a chill. She put a hand on my shoulder. "Sorry. I'm awkward."

"Do you guys want to join us?" Jake asked. He looked at me. "Doesn't that sound fun?"

"Nah," I said and crunched on a bite of raw vegetables. "We should let them have their date."

"No, no, I think it would be fun." Levi looked down at Christy's upturned face. "Right, baby?"

I stared at my plate as I chewed, trying not to laugh. *Baby?* I'd never heard Levi use a term of endearment before, except when he called Harpo variations of *little baby dog*.

"If you guys don't mind," Christy said. From inside Levi's arm, she looked around at everyone, her angelic face contorted in a wince. "But I might need to keep my coat on. I'm still cold."

"Nope," Jake joked. "No coats allowed at the table."

The three of us laughed, though Christy looked taken aback for a second, as if this were actually the case. Finally, the joke seemed to register, and she laughed, too, a minute too late.

I got the server's attention to ask permission to add a couple more chairs. And perhaps they could bring us something with a little more substance than a vegetable tower. It might be a long night.

Once we had all warmed up to each other—though not literally, in Christy's case, as she was still in her coat—the impromptu double date was not as painful as I thought it would be. Jake and Levi were both so amiable, they seemed to become fast friends. It helped that Jake had heard of the Hidden Beaches.

"Yeah, dude, I hear you guys on The Current all the time," Jake was telling Levi over our artichoke flatbread. "Great shit, man."

"Aren't they so good?" Christy added emphatically, leaning across her untouched plate. "I've been trying to get them a write-up at *Pitchfork* or *Noisey*. I know some people."

"No, no," Levi said, wagging his finger. "No nepotism."

"No nepotism necessary!" Christy said. "You're going to blow up, anyway. It's like The Ramones meets the Jonas Brothers. Look at this guy." She waved a thin hand in Levi's direction. "He's a star. So sexy. I can't get enough."

Levi looked nice, this was true. He had put his long hair into a half-up, half-down situation, emphasizing a square shape to his face that was often hidden by greasy waves.

"He looks kind of like Thor in a dress shirt," Jake said, looking at me. "Doesn't he?"

"But Thor when he's depressed in that cabin in Norway," I added.

"Ha!" Levi almost spit out a swallow of water.

"No, babe . . ." Christy, with that pained expression again, reached across the table to comfort him.

Jake raised his eyebrows at me.

"What? He's laughing." Again, I felt too loud and out of place. "Any comparison to a Hemsworth is a compliment."

"It's fine," Levi said as his laughter died down. "Robin and I have known each other forever."

"Maybe I need to work on my date etiquette," I said.

"You need to work on your comedy act," Jake replied, playful. As Levi and Christy began to peruse the wine menu, he leaned close to me, putting one of the purple squiggly things in his mouth. "It's a radish, by the way. It's just cut weird."

"Good to know." Together, we snickered.

Christy began to tell us about her latest piece for *Bon Appétit*, an article that followed the life of an avocado from where it grew in Mexico to its time in the produce section of a grocery store. "Now it's with the fact-checkers. Fingers crossed it's out soon so I can get paid." She made an eyes-wide, tongue-out expression at Levi. "Freelance life, am I right?"

"So frickin' cool," Levi said, shaking his head, looking at her. "Such important work."

"It's kind of derivative of that *New Yorker* article about the price of beef, but you know." She shrugged in her coat. "I think it's important we keep reminding ourselves where our food comes from."

"Move out to where we live—" I nodded at Jake "—and you'll get a reminder every day."

"Yep," Jake agreed. "A manure-smelling reminder. Even worse when you ride your bike."

"You're one of those long-distance bikers, aren't you?" Levi narrowed his eyes with assessment at Jake. "Respect. I could never do that."

"Biking, hiking, running, camping. Nature clears the head, man." Jake gestured toward me. "Hopefully when the weather turns, I can get Robin out there."

Levi cringed, glancing at me. "Good luck. Robin's an indoor kid."

"Hey," I said, kicking him under the table. "I've camped." Just a few times, and mostly for private hook-up purposes with Gabe. But I *had* camped. I also resented Levi's label. If anything, he was the indoor kid. The city boy. The gamer. The man raised by professors who knew what *crudités* meant.

"I want to live out in the country," Christy was saying dreamily, pulling a piece of artichoke off her flatbread. "That would be my dream to one day have a little farmhouse . . ." She gave Levi a sappy look. "With goats and chickens and foxes and stuff? Wouldn't that be cute?"

"Yikes," I said. "You probably don't want foxes around if you have chickens. My husband and I used to have chickens, and it was like waking up to a Tarantino murder scene every day."

"Oh, man, I remember," Levi said, throwing his head back with a loud guffaw. "Gabe was obsessed with catching that fox. He used to call me, like, *I'm gonna get the bastard if it's the last thing I do.*"

I smiled, remembering. "We had to give the chickens to someone in a nearby town for their own safety. Get them out of the fox's territory. We even had to change their names," I joked. "The Chicken Protection Program."

Levi rolled his eyes. Christy offered a weak chuckle. Jake thought it was hilarious, which I decided was all that mattered, anyway. I looked over at him, taking in the pleasant roundness of his head under the hint of hair, his brown eyes catching the light from the candle. Here was a man who was kind, who was confident and relaxed enough to invite strangers to a fancy dinner, yet he could slip out into the wilderness at any moment and thrive. And he had laughed at my dumb jokes. I had held my own with his friends, and he was holding his own with mine. Or one of mine, at least. The jury was still out on Christy. She was a strange combination of one of the smartest people I'd ever met and somehow also one of the dopiest.

But as she rambled on about the scientific effects of meditating on the moon, Levi looking on, I could see the appeal. I felt an odd sense of pride in Levi. The Serial-Disappointer-and-Ghoster had snagged an impressive, mostly functional person. Not only that, he had held on to her. He had grown. I gave him an appreciative look across the table, nodding toward Christy, offering a thumbs-up.

In response, he put two rock 'n' roll fingers on his forehead, headbanging. *Hail Satan*, he mouthed. This was a common Levi gesture of general approval.

The bills came, and though I balked at the price of what was essentially a pile of vegetables and canned artichokes on cheesy bread, I insisted on paying my share.

"At least take the leftovers," Jake said as we walked out, offering me the take-out box.

"Nah, I prefer gas-station pizza," I said. When Christy laughed at that, I assured her that I was one hundred percent serious this time.

"She eats like a raccoon," Levi confirmed. "Hey, Robin—can I grab you for a second? To talk about memorial stuff?"

"I'll go get the Prius and pull around," Jake said.

"You don't have to—" I started.

"I don't mind at all." Jake kissed me on the cheek. I smiled after him.

Levi handed Christy his keys. When Levi and I were left alone, me stomping with cold, I noticed he was looking at me as if he were waiting for me to say something. "Well?"

I frowned at him. "What? I thought we were talking about the memorial."

"Nah, Robbie. Why do you think I came out to Saint Paul? I need the skinny on Jake."

So their arrival at the pop-up wasn't a coincidence. I gave him a little shove, which didn't move him a single inch. "You sneaky bastard."

Levi lifted his shoulders in an exaggerated shrug. "Christy wanted to go, anyway, so why not tonight? If we just happened to run into you, great. If not—"

"But you did. And what is there to report? He's great. You guys seemed to get along great."

"Sure, sure, but I get along with everybody. What's the deal with the two of you? Where's your head? Where's your heart?"

"My heart?" I scoffed. "Uh, same place it always was, I guess. And yeah, I super like him. We haven't put a label on it, though, if that's what you're asking."

"Good." Levi's voice was taking on an annoying, cautionary tone. "Keep playing the field. Make sure you're not putting all your eggs in one basket."

"You're the one who told me to go all in!"

"Yeah, go all in and get sloppy with a bunch of weirdos! Not go all in and talk about the frickin' future." He took on a deep, hollow tone, imitating his version of Jake's baritone. "*Robin and I are going camping when the weather gets better.* He's talking about *months* from now, and you guys have known each other for, like, three days. Like, slow down, turbo."

I shook my head, not sure if I was more amused or frustrated. "This coming from the man who basically proposes to girls the night you meet them. You're such a hypocrite."

"I know." He looked up at the sky, holding out his arms. "I know! But I feel protective of your wee little heart. I don't want him to be like me. Or, like, the twenty-five-year-old version of me."

"Nah, he's going to stick around." I kicked at a parking meter, avoiding his eyes. "We've been on the phone for, like, weeks. Since before Christmas." I looked up at Levi, unable to keep a smile off my face. "We talk to each other as we drive to work."

"Okay, that is so cute it's kind of annoying," Levi said, smiling back. "Why didn't you tell me?"

I shrugged. "I didn't know if it was going to be anything."

"But it is something, huh?" There was a sadness in Levi as he said it, probably the same sadness I'd been wrestling with as memories of my first love reared up at every turn, every new hand-hold, every little flame in my chest.

"I think so," I said, and I realized how much I wanted it to be true. Levi knew as much as anyone I couldn't live in those memories forever, that I needed a reason to grow like he was growing, to catch up with the passage of time. Behind him, I spotted the Prius's headlights, illuminating the first flurries of another new snow. "We'll see," I said. "We'll see."

Worst fad I ever took part in . . .
Really into Red Bull when it first got popular in college. Like let's-have-a-dorm-room-intervention into Red Bull.

St. Patrick's Day in Brokenridge is not so much a holiday as it is an airing-out, a . . . thawing of whatever has been stored up and frozen over the course of the winter. Emotions run high. Feuds escalate or come to a truce. Marriages begin and end. And all the while, the Brokenridge High School marching band plays on, usually a bit off beat and out of tune, lending the whole occasion the air of a circus gone wrong. Usually I'd be helping out at the restaurant all day, feeding giant green-clad families, cleaning ketchup and macaroni from the floors until around three, when the parade gets over and the crying drinkers take the place of the crying toddlers.

This morning, I'd left *Hamlet* rehearsal in time to get home and actually watch the parade for the first time since I was a kid. All the Irish families were out in full force, including our landlords the Sheas, waving their green and orange flags from their lawn chairs in front of the courthouse, where they were fighting a lawsuit with a rival, I'd heard. And there were the Kellehers, many of them dying out but their strongest members still thriving, including a young niece, who was currently playing flute in the marching band, and her proud aunt, our very own Nance. And, of course, the Byrnes, whose parade float was a giant papier-mâché leprechaun awash in soap suds, an ad for their car wash, which was rumored to be a money-laundering operation for organized crime out of Saint Paul.

Silly that I still knew all these rumors and stories, I thought as I watched the kids from the Pole City Hmong Cultural Center walk past and wave in their beaded traditional clothes. Why could I name random facts about the Byrnes when I'd forgotten half the things I'd needed to buy for Mom's party this afternoon? It felt like a lifetime had passed since I'd even seen these people, but somehow, I would always know their business. It wasn't as if I relished gossip in the way Mom did, but I always listened, always took note. As if I needed to know the outcome of the garden-shed border dispute between the Sheas and the Rundles, as if keeping tabs on that one Kelleher boy's arrest were essential to my survival. *Jamila Hassan: got into prestigious art school, dropped out because of anxiety issues. Hans Hinderman: tried to start a Quaker church, but nobody came.* But mine was not the only ledger of stories. They kept one on me, too.

The sound of the drums got deeper. Bagpipes whined and caterwauled, played by the same group of old men who'd played in Gabe's procession. What were they saying about me now, I wondered. Who was I around their kitchen tables if I wasn't Mrs. Mayor? All I knew was that I couldn't be the person I was at home, alone. A half of a person. A nothing person, who had ruined the garden, who had not had her shit together enough to throw a one-year anniversary, who spoke more to random people from a dating app than people who'd known her for years. So far, I'd tried to simply not exist anymore. The less of a life I had in Brokenridge, the less there was to scrutinize. Problem solved. That's what I was trying to tell Levi the other night. That's why, when I'd finally sent the email for Gabe's kickball memorial and the replies started coming in, I still had a lump in the pit of my stomach.

As the pipes faded and the VFW's clover-decked, flag-toting pickup brought up the rear of the line, I began to walk back to the Green River to start setting up. We'd gotten city permission to block off the street in front of the restaurant. The parade was already disrupting traffic, they figured, what's one more block. I'd rented space heaters for what was supposed to be a high of forty-five. Summer weather for most Minnesotans, but better safe than sorry.

Near the edge of town, an elderly woman had made her way across her yard, pausing at her open mailbox. I was about to remind her that the mail didn't come on holidays, but I knew this woman. She was a donor to Gabe's campaign. Construction money.

"Mrs. Mayor? Is that you?" the elderly woman called. "It's good to see you, dear." She gave me a once-over and added, "I barely recognized you."

I found I had nothing to say to that. Her words were a sharp reminder of how different I must have looked. In my haste to get everything together for the party—not to mention having to get up at the crack of dawn today to make up the actor who would play Ophelia—I had resorted to putting my unwashed tangles in a bun and throwing on a pilled green sweater. I supposed people were used to seeing me in straightened hair and the tailored skirt I always used to wear for Gabe's events, a skirt that no longer fit. *Thanks, lady. Exactly what I wanted to hear.*

"Happy St. Patrick's Day," I told her as I passed, feeling her eyes on my back.

I could practically hear her go inside and tell her husband, *You'll never guess who I just saw. The mayor's wife. Back out and about. I wonder why.*

Because I had to make sure Theo and Mom didn't burn down the restaurant this afternoon, that's why. And maybe I had to account for the new man in my life, maybe I wanted to. Maybe I wanted less Twin Cities dates at fancy pop-ups and less making out in alleys. Maybe that would mean more sidewalk stares or a scowl from the ladies' book club who met at the diner every Sunday morning. It meant a Valentine's Day date last month with Jake at the best restaurant in Pole City, served by a girl Theo went to high school with. That meant that Jake was coming today, to meet Mom and Theo for the first time, and Mrs. Construction Money and the Tammy Finks of the world were going to have to deal with it.

I wasn't hiding anymore. Because despite my best efforts, life went on.

• • •

Later that afternoon, the final notes of "Happy Birthday" hung in the air. To thunderous applause from a parking lot full of shades of green and raised green plastic Solo cups, Mom blew out two flaming *six* and *five* candles, and Rick and his band fell into a passable version of "Sugar Magnolia." I was looking for Jake.

My plan was to keep the introduction short and sweet. Best to experience Mom and Theo in small doses, anyway, I'd reasoned on the drive home from rehearsal. Too long, and Mom could get in one of her weepy moods, or Theo could lash out and say something rude. Either one could just as easily give the classic Minnesotan smile-and-cold-shoulder. I'd seen Mom do it with customers she didn't like.

People filtered around me with pizza and cake on plates, pausing at the table of old photos of Mom, occasionally fishing in their pockets for a five or a twenty. I'd had the idea to mark a giant punch bowl with *Birthday Blessings*, and though Mom had hated it—we didn't need charity, she spat—now, to my relief, it was stuffed with bills to the brim. At least she would be able to pay the mortgage.

Finally, I spotted Jake's forest-green ball cap at the far side of the parking lot. I began to weave through the partyers, noting a pair of cloverleafs bouncing around his shoulder, jutting out of a familiar brown-feathered mop.

There he was beside Mom, and Mom beside Nance, Mom gesticulating with her green cup in one hand and a menthol in the other. It appeared they'd been talking for a while. So much for short and sweet. My stomach turned.

"And she was toddling along, trailing poop all down the hallway, naked as a jaybird," Mom was saying, wheezing with laughter. "And she goes, as calm as could be, 'Mama, I need diaper change.'"

The poop story. Fantastic.

"There she is," Mom said as I approached. She looked back at Jake, pointing at me with her menthol. "See, Robbie always knew how to take care of herself. Like a little adult. But the trail of poop was too much. Bart and I were crying-laughing. Lord have mercy."

Jake grinned at me, chuckling, and put an arm around my waist, but I couldn't help but feel the drag of disappointment on my insides. By the sound of her words, it didn't appear like she was taking it easy, as we'd discussed. But it was her birthday, I reasoned. No use reminding her of moderation on her birthday. "I was looking for you," I told Jake.

"I was looking for you!" he said. "I got sidetracked by these two lovely ladies."

"Stop," Nance said, hitting Jake on the arm, her clover headband bouncing dangerously. "Gah, he's cute."

He was. Probably too cute for me, but there we were. I tugged at my sweater.

"Well, I'm glad we're all together," I said, swallowing. I glanced up at Jake, who nodded encouragingly, his brown eyes soft. "Mom, I wanted you to meet Jake because we've been spending more time together, and—"

"Well, yeah," Mom said, taking a drag of her menthol. "Duh."

"Okay," I said, laughing a bit, mostly to mask my discomfort. "It's kind of a big deal for me, so it means a lot that you're—"

"Ma!" I heard a familiar, tipsy yell from across the party. Heads turned, my heartfelt speech forgotten. "Margie!"

We all looked up to see Theo, followed by a group of staggering, laughing friends. He was holding what appeared to be a pint of whiskey in a paper bag.

My breath was coming in short bursts. I tried to inhale normally.

"Happy Birthday, Ma. Sorry we're late." Theo threw his arms around Mom with a lazy smile. His eyes were bloodshot against the kelly green of his sweatshirt. "Do you guys like the keg?" Theo looked around. "Is it working out okay?"

"We had to tap it without you . . ." I looked at my watch. "Oh, about three hours ago."

"The keg's perfect, honey," Mom chimed in before Theo could retort. "Thank you."

"Have you gotten any beer, by the way?" Jake asked me. "Or any pizza or anything?"

"No, no, Robin's fine," Theo assured Jake. "She's going to roam around micromanaging things, forgetting to eat, and then she'll get hangry and yell at someone."

"Thank you, Theo," I said sarcastically. I supposed if Mom wasn't going to make a big deal out of meeting the first man I'd brought around since my husband died, then neither would Theo. I ripped off the Band-Aid. "This is Jake, by the way."

"I'm Theo," he said to Jake, assessing him. "I like your hat. And your whole Patagonia zaddy thing going on." I scoffed, gave him a little slap on the arm. "What?" he said innocently. "I said I liked him. I'm happy for you guys."

"Thanks, man," Jake said, reaching out his hand for a handshake. Theo took it. "Robin told me so much about you."

"Did she tell you I'm a fuckup who spends all her money?" Theo asked.

"Oh, my god," I muttered, staring at my feet.

"Nah, man." Jake did not take the bait. His calm seemed to permeate the air. I looked up, and Jake was smiling at Theo. "You're just a wandering soul," Jake continued. "That's a good thing. I'm a bit of a wandering soul myself."

"Hell yeah." Theo pointed at Jake. "This is the energy I want in my life." He held out the whiskey. "Take a shot with me."

"You don't have to—" I put a protective hand on Jake's arm.

But Jake shrugged at Theo, glancing at me. "All right."

"Me, too!" Mom said. "Don't forget the birthday girl."

Jake tipped one back. He wasn't a big drinker, but perhaps he figured this was a shortcut to a Lindstrom endorsement. He wasn't wrong.

Soon, the sun began to sink behind the clouds, and people were zipping their coats and wrapping their arms around each other. Jake and my brother were passing around the bottle with Mom and Nance, and everyone was laughing at a joke Jake had made. The band played something fast, an old jazz standard they'd sped up and rockified. I nodded to the music, watching Jake and Theo try to replicate some sort of viral social-media dance. Not only had he made a good first impression, it seemed he was already sliding right into place in my family, charming everyone in his openhearted way. So it was all happening, all at once, without ceremony. Might as well go with it, I supposed. Maybe I didn't need to be so precious about this. So serious.

"Dance with me!" Jake called over the music.

The song was "Stayin' Alive." I said yes.

First round of drinks is on me if . . .

We can go home and watch movies soon after.

The next morning, I woke to the smell of food, to sounds coming from the kitchen.

In the doorway, I paused. Bacon sizzled. Jake was standing over a hot plate, poking the strips with a pair of tongs, sipping coffee. A podcast about running blared from his phone. He looked up at me and smiled. "Morning, hon."

In his hand was a mug. Gabe's *Far Side* mug. My mug, now. My lips to Gabe's lips every morning. "Sorry, what?" I said.

His smile went a bit crooked, confused. He lifted the mug. "Good morning?"

"Oh, yeah." I shook my head. "Good morning."

Jake glanced at me, concerned, but went back to flipping bacon.

"So . . ." he began as I shuffled around him, looking for another mug. "Last night had me thinking."

"Yeah?" The cup I'd chosen felt wrong in my hands, but I tried to ignore it. *Forget the goddamn mug.*

"What do we call each other?"

"Sorry?"

"Like . . ." He paused, and I could see a flush rise in his neck. "If I want to introduce you to *my* family, do I just say, this is Robin? Or are we . . ." he looped his tongs, gathering the words ". . . more than that?"

"Oh." At first—because we hadn't broached the subject of exclusivity—I'd kept my Bubbl active and half-heartedly started a few more chats with other men. But last week, we'd both deleted the app. We were exclusive, we'd agreed, but we hadn't discussed labels. "Um . . ."

"You don't have to answer now," Jake said, going back to his bacon. "Drink your coffee first. Or better yet, lend me a hand."

He wanted to know if I would be calling him my boyfriend. Or partner, or *something*. It wasn't unreasonable. Last night I was too exhausted to think about the significance of Jake beside me in my bed—our first night in the bed Gabe and I had shared—and now, scattered around us were more pans, a bowl full of whipped eggs, an open bag of bread, butter exposed in its dish. I began to tidy. Is that what having a boyfriend meant? If I said yes, did that give him free reign to touch my things, to cook in my kitchen, to make himself at home? My home.

"You okay, honey?" He glanced over again from his task.

I was being childish. Still, my coffee didn't taste right. "Yeah," I lied.

It occurred to me that if Jake became official, he wasn't a guest anymore. In Brokenridge, or here in my hibernation hole. My temple of snacks and pulp horror movies and memory tokens. It wasn't that I didn't know this would happen—if we were really serious about each other, it was only natural we'd spend time in each other's homes—it was the casualness with which it was now happening. The authority with which he was making his way around the island toward me.

"You hungover or something?" he asked. "I admit I'm feeling it pretty hard today . . ."

I tried not to flinch when he put his hand on my elbow, sliding his arms around my waist for a hug that was meant to be comforting. But if I said what was actually wrong, I would be dramatic. I didn't want to be that way. I didn't want friction. I shook my head. "It's nothing."

At my stiffness, he let go, his eyes examining me over a small frown. "Breakfast will be ready soon."

"Thank you." I tried to smile.

He made breakfast. The sweetness of the gesture was not lost on me, but it was drowning some place I couldn't see. *Honey.* The last time that word had been used here, it was Gabe's and mine. A long-forgotten stab of longing for his voice rose up in me, and I tried to stifle it. Jake was here, flesh and blood, and Gabe was not. I was moving on. I thought I was moving on. Until Jake drank from the *Far Side* mug again.

"Do you even *want* breakfast?" he asked slowly, swallowing his sip of coffee. "Or . . ."

"No, I do. Sorry." Without realizing it, I had wandered away from him, toward the back door. Jake's trainers were not on the mat, I noticed. They were somewhere else, where they weren't supposed to be. *Stop it*, I told myself. I slipped on a pair of shoes. "I just need some air."

I threw on my coat and stepped outside, watching the first rays of sun hit the frost in the garden. I didn't realize how sacred these drafty old walls had been to me until they were being treated like any other house. But I couldn't begrudge Jake for simply *existing* in my kitchen. Thriving, in fact. Bringing it to life. Wasn't this what I wanted? Who I wanted?

The yard would soon have to fight the woods behind our house, as it did every year. The kid who mowed the lawn for the neighborhood had grown up and moved on, and for a while the bluestem and bulrush were creeping up from the creek. I made a note to mow it back to evenness. It was always Gabe's job to barrel forward, mine to right whatever he knocked over. His job to build fires, plant heirlooms, helm parades, my job to stoke, to weed, to get the sweat stains out of his dress shirts. He never submitted or spoke any text before I had a go at it first, poking holes in his logic, imagining scenarios for which he could not account. Now, there were no scrawls on scrap paper to be found, laying out the next big plan. No yeasty home-brew experiments in the garage to critique. No socks and exercise bands left all over the floor to put in their proper place.

These jobs I used to have. Every day I kept finding new ways in which my universe was tilted, and I was always trying to tilt it back.

In the early days after the funeral, the counselor I'd spoken to had taught me how to slow my breathing. Four in. Hold seven. Out eight. Four in. Hold seven.

All our objects, all our things: no more would Gabe be the last person besides me to have touched them. They were no longer relics of our time together. Hold seven. Out eight.

I was always determined to be the best wife, the most patient, the most useful. I did the research, the treatment shopping, the doctor wheedling. I sent out emails to close friends and family with updates. I did this because I thought I would be rewarded for my diligence, and my reward would be my husband's full recovery—that was what I believed. Now, though I'd cried for him a hundred times, though I'd held his ashes in my hands, it seemed like this was the first time he felt really, truly gone. None of my good deeds had been worth anything, none of my rituals. He was still gone. The real world was encroaching, and Jake was the real world. The mug was just a mug.

That evening, I almost canceled on Levi, but we'd pledged to choose the cancer charity for Gabe's memorial, and these plans were as good a reason as any to get out of the house, to get away from the discomfort I was feeling in my own space. In my own skin.

I sat next to Harpo, scratching the dog's soft belly while we scrolled through the list on Levi's laptop.

The organization we liked best was local to Minneapolis, family owned and operated with an MO of being completely transparent about the services to which each donation was going. Together, Levi and I wrote a message informing them about our plans to sell tickets to the memorial kickball game in September, asking them how or if they'd like to be involved. This time, I had no hesitation pressing Send.

Levi decided to make us both Manhattans from a well-stocked vintage bar cart, another domestic touch he'd added to the living room. As we sipped, I told Levi about my stint as amateur *Hamlet* makeup artist. The director had liked my wintery version of Hamlet's father's ghost so much she had decided I would do the same hollow-eyed, ice-powder effect on everyone who had died during the play.

"It's like a walking metaphor of everyone in that castle being haunted," I told Levi, lifting my glass to my lips. "They're all going to come back during the final battle and just stand there among the living characters. So they want me to hang out backstage during the run and make everyone look creepy."

"Hell yeah, they do!" Levi did his rock 'n' roll devil horns. "You were always stupid good at that."

I smiled, feeling a flush rise to my cheeks. "It's nice to do something with my hands. I think I'm going to make Ophelia look like Dani from *Midsommar*. Just, like, drowning in flowers."

Levi raised his eyebrows. "That sounds genuinely disturbing."

"Thanks." I took another sip of my drink. "That's a real compliment coming from you."

"Are you going to keep doing it?" Levi burped a bit, putting his fingertips to his mouth in an oddly dainty gesture. "Makeup, I mean?"

I thought of the quiet contentment I felt dipping into my pallet, hovering my fingertips over my tools as I found the exact shape to execute each step, the click of satisfaction when a color matched the shade I had in my head. "Maybe."

"Then, I reserve you for Halloween next year," Levi said. "I want to be Hellboy. Calling it right now."

I snorted, feeling a bit loose from the cocktail. My second drink was almost empty. "I should probably go after this."

He leaned back into the cushion with a contented sigh, resting his glass on his belly. "Fair. But you're not leaving before you give me the gossip on Jake the Snake."

"Excuse me?" I looked at Levi, ready to push back on the nickname.

He shrugged. "Jake the Snake was one of the greatest pro wrestlers of all time. How are things?"

"Whatever. Yeah, um. Things are . . ." *Awesome*, I began to say, wanting to shut down this conversation until I could find a solution to the morning's anxieties, but I couldn't quite find the motivation for this particular white lie. Maybe I was tired. Maybe I was tipsy. Maybe I needed to get it off my chest. "Weird. I don't know. It's hard to explain."

"Uh-oh," Levi said, sitting up.

"No, nothing bad," I began. I told him about how Jake had started the boyfriend-girlfriend conversation and how I couldn't finish it. I told him how much it had bothered me to see Jake drinking out of

Gabe's favorite mug. The foreign sight of him in my kitchen, but somehow deeply familiar. Too familiar. He fit, but he didn't fit. "It's not Jake's fault. I'm just feeling kind of off about it," I admitted. It felt good to say it aloud. "Why do I feel so possessive of a cheap old cup? I feel like a kid throwing a tantrum."

"Nah," Levi said. "Tantrum away. I know that mug. That's *Gabe's* mug."

I leaned my head back and stared at the ceiling. "If he had just picked another cup, maybe I wouldn't be freaking out."

"I doubt it. I'm sure there'd be something else that set it off."

I shook my head. "There's always something."

"Ugh, I know," Levi said.

It seemed neither of us had to say much more than that. It was a relief to be immediately understood without having to explain. The apparition of Gabe's stubbly cheek against mine, as if he were leaning over the computer as I worked. A song blaring from the open door of a restaurant, conjuring Gabe thrashing joyfully next to me at one of Levi's shows. Every morning, seeing him out of the corner of my eye, reading one of the rare paper copies of the *Brokenridge Daily Beagle*, drinking out of the *Far Side* mug. Levi wouldn't know my loss exactly, but he was the closest to it. He would have his own versions of these sensations, I was sure of it.

"Did he ever get another guitar?" Levi asked, breaking the quiet. He leaned back, putting his hand behind his head. "I always kind of wondered after that time he tried to join the band."

I took a large gulp of my drink, feeling my throat burn with the alcohol. "Nope, just the one."

"Good."

My eyes rested on the muscles in Levi's upper arm swelling against the frayed cuff of his Slayer shirt. I looked away, trying to shake off the path on which my senses seemed to be taking me, taking note of all the wrong things. The shape of his lips in profile as he stared off into space. The movement of his glass resting on his belly as he breathed.

"I mean, I know you tried to take it easy on him, but he was . . ." Levi winced.

"He was shit at guitar," I said, fielding a burp.

"He was shit," Levi agreed, laughing, and I joined him.

A tension seemed to dissipate, as if we were laughing at more than what was said.

"Do you ever think about the fair?" Levi asked.

"Of course."

It was the last weekend of June, the week before Gabe was about to start chemo. To get his mind off it, the three of us piled into the Volvo to see one of Levi's friends' metal bands headline the Lee County Fair. I could close my eyes and still feel the wet heat of that afternoon, hear the cacophony of Top 40 hits blasting from the water slide, the smell of elotes and cotton candy, the braying of animals from the farm tent.

"I always think about it because he, like, really wanted us to remember it," Levi said, pausing to take a sip of his drink. "He kept insisting on taking pictures, remember? And he kept saying, *Remember this, guys. Best day of our lives.* And it *was* super fun, but it was also awkward because he was so . . ." Levi shifted beside me ". . . extreme. Am I wrong?"

"No, no. I remember it, too."

There was a wildness to his joy that day that neither of us had seen before. He was always upbeat, but he tended to keep it buttoned-up in public, always ready to get serious with a future constituent. But that day in June he was filling our hands with sticky, sweet funnel cakes and giant beers shaped like shoes, throwing his arms around the shoulders of strangers, insisting on putting me on his shoulders, somehow able to hoist up my solid, not-exactly-pixie-like body with some invisible source of strength. Up there above the small sea of people, it was hard not to get wild myself, even with all my anxiety and general curmudgeonliness. I'd clutched his raised hands for balance, whooping with joy. I'd bent to kiss his sweaty head, his soft, thick black hair warmed from the sun.

"He wanted us to get matching tattoos to commemorate," I recalled to Levi. "Like a skull and crossbones and the date, or something, right?"

"Exactly! Like it was his last day on earth. I was like, Chill, dude. You're young, you're healthy. You've got a great life, beautiful wife . . ." I felt my cheeks flush as Levi continued. "I was like, Don't worry. You're going to get through this. The chemo's gonna work . . ." Levi's voice faded.

And then the chemo hadn't worked. That was the next part of the story. The cancer had spread, so the chemo had had to get more aggressive, and the following June, he would be too tired to venture outside for that long. I stared at the bottom of my empty cocktail.

"He got really depressed after that." I could picture Gabe as I'd watched him in those weeks through the window above the sink, sitting in the backyard, his back to me, cross-legged on the grass, staring at the garden.

"Can't blame him." Levi let out a little bitter laugh. "That night, even. He got morose."

"Oh, my god," I said, putting a hand to my forehead. It was all coming back. "He put that ballad of yours on repeat on the way home. Remember? He was obsessed." I imitated what I recalled of Gabe's slurring entreaty from the back seat. "*Robbie, put on 'Bones,' okay, Robbie? One more time. Just one more time.* And finally you offered to play it for him live so I could have some frickin' peace. Thank you for that, by the way."

"Glad to help."

As Levi laughed again, a tear ran down his cheek, but I couldn't tell if it was from the mirth or the grief.

He lifted his shoulder to wipe his face, sniffing. "God, wouldn't it be great if we could do that this year? If he were still here. Maybe every year. The three of us at the county fair headliner concert. Could have been a tradition."

"That's what you two could do," I muttered to Levi. I thought back to Gabe's pink-tinted face in the clouds of secondhand smoke, writhing in ecstasy to each song, all of which sounded the same to me. "I'm sure you guys would have had even more fun if I hadn't been there putting in my earplugs, harassing you about sunscreen."

"No, no way. It wouldn't have been right without you. Gabe wanted you there. And I was so glad you came."

"Really?"

"Really. You always . . ." He smiled, looking suddenly shy. "Come on, you remember. I was always trying to get you to come to things."

I narrowed my eyes at him. "And I never understood why."

"I wanted you to relax."

"Because I was annoying?"

"No. Because I saw you fall in love with my best friend," Levi said. "And it seemed like you were only ever happy when he was happy. He was like this escape for you. Gabe and I used to talk about it."

"What do you mean?" I felt myself getting angry, but I wasn't sure if I was mad at the Levi in front of me now. More at the person then, who was apparently thinking all these things, talking about them with Gabe, never bothering to consult me. "Levi," I snapped when he was slow to answer.

He sighed. "We always kind of wondered what you were like before your dad died. Because it seemed like—" he glanced over at me, cautious "—don't get mad at me, but it seemed like you felt like you always had to be the adult. The responsible one. But that day at the fair—I don't know. You let loose a little bit more. It was like we were all equal."

A nervous knot formed in my throat, replacing the anger, though I wasn't sure why. I wanted to stay angry, but I couldn't. Perhaps because it was true. "Maybe I finally felt I could let loose because you stepped up."

"Then, I wish I had done that more often."

"Yeah, well . . ." Levi and I had been a team that day. When one needed a break, the other was ready to follow Gabe to the beer taps for a refill or cheer him on as he rode a mechanical bull or draw him away from some creepy stranger he'd befriended. We all got to lose ourselves in different ways. I felt Levi's eyes on me, thoughtful. "That day was different. Too much Gabe for one person."

"He succeeded in his quest, though," Levi said. "It really was the best."

I looked up at him and smiled. "The best."

Suddenly, Levi had this look I recognized but had never understood. It was as if we were in college again. Gabe could have been in the other room, could have just gotten up to fetch something. The way Levi used to stare was so open, so raw, it made me feel like the sight of me was being recorded, preserved to be savored later. I would have questioned his intentions, but I wasn't sure if he even knew what he was doing. He never said anything inappropriate, never did anything beyond look. He was doing it again now. He realized it just as I did, and he had to look away, almost confused by his own intensity.

I was confused, too. I might have been looking back.

Suddenly Harpo got up from his spot, leaping off to trot down the hall. I was conscious of the empty space the dog had left between us.

"Welp," I said, slapping my hands on my knees. "I should really get going."

"Yeah," Levi said. "It's late."

I stood.

Levi stood beside me. He opened his arms. "Uh, can we . . . ? Is that okay?"

"Of course it's okay," I said, a pleasant tingling rising on my skin as I reached around him, resting my head against his chest. "It's more than okay."

But as we hugged, I braced for something. It was nothing, I told myself. Levi and I had been close to each other hundreds of times, on birthdays or holidays or other gatherings, sharing hospital love seats. But I'd never considered his body beside mine, the heft and strength of it, the intentions behind the ways his limbs moved or didn't move, the thoughts that swirled under his curtain of hair.

After a few seconds, neither of us had let go, and the space between us was getting smaller. Small enough that I could feel his heartbeat. His middle rounded against my middle. The heaviness of his big arms around my shoulders, his hands and their slight pressure on my shoulder blades, the beginnings of my ribs.

He was looking down at me. I looked up at him. I could see little flecks of green and gold in his irises.

Finally, I pulled away from his gaze. "Thanks for the drink. I should get home."

He nodded, pulling open his apartment door, gesturing for me to lead the way.

"I'll be in touch soon," I said. "About the memorial."

"Sure," he said, his eyes searching mine.

• • •

As I started the car, my breath fogging, I couldn't ignore the pull of my own confusion. Why had I left like that? Because. Because of what? Because there was too much. Too much hug? Too much of him looking? Too much of me looking back? I could go on like that all night, I realized—beyond the night, into the morning, into territory I didn't want to roam.

There had been a moment.

The moment meant nothing.

The end.

But as the streets led me back to Brokenridge, answers started to replace the *nothing*. And the answers disturbed me. Not just because I had been finding an odd comfort in the presence of my husband's best friend. What I really didn't care to examine was why I needed to seek comfort in the first place. I'd practically run straight into Levi's arms from my own kitchen. From my own kitchen and the man standing in the center of it—a perfectly wonderful man, who wanted to be my boyfriend. Why was I afraid?

I shook my head, as if to shake off the thought, and sped into the night.

Two truths and a lie . . .

I've shaken hands with the governor of Minnesota.

I have a preternatural ability to know when everyone around me needs a snack.

I am legally a giant.

I returned home from Levi's to find an empty house and a text from Jake. Feeling back to about 95% after our epic brunch lol. Hope the charity thing went well. He'd left the kitchen relatively clean—though he'd used the wrong rag on the counters, and there were now shiny circles of grease visible under the lights. Gabe's mug, I noticed, was upside down on the drying rack.

Now on Monday morning, I was still haunted by the thoughts that had followed me home from Levi's: that somehow our happy, tipsy wade into memories meant that I wasn't ready for Jake. That at the first sign of permanence in the present, I'd run back to the past.

But the tasks of the week settled me. It was tax season at work, and spring-cleaning season at the Green River, and at night I practiced with my makeup to the peaceful hum of Jake's mountain-climbing documentaries. Maybe I had gotten spooked because we skipped a few steps, I thought. I had gone too quickly from *Storage Wars* and *Friday the 13th* marathons in my pajamas to playing house. But that's what one does in relationships in one's thirties—at least that's what the recoupled widows from Sisters in Grief told me. You fall into domestic routines. You go to bed together at nine. You make breakfast.

Soon, I put an extra toothbrush in Jake's bathroom and bought cat toys for Tiger. I relaxed into his steady breathing next to me in bed, into the pleasure of rubbing my hand over the prickle of his scalp as we held each other, the minty smell of Icy Hot he put on after a run, and into our commutes, where I was teaching him Britney Spears lyrics, anticipating the moment when he turned down the radio before he was about to ask me a nonsense question. My panic began to recede, replaced by the steady rhythm of life, the life we were building together. One night, as we were picking up takeout, I referred to him as my boyfriend without a second thought. We were both smiling the whole way home.

My Shakespeare-makeup debut was approaching rapidly, and before the dress rehearsal in April, I needed to be ready to quickly transform seven actors into ghosts—Polonius, Ophelia, Rosencrantz, Guildenstern, Laertes, Gertrude, and Claudius—all before Hamlet's death in the final act. I convinced Theo to volunteer to be my practice model. My quickest turnaround was ten minutes, but I knew I could do better.

At the restaurant, I put the pinot on special and made a chalkboard sign we could put out on the front sidewalk. Already we'd doubled wine sales, which I was tracking on my phone. In my journal, under *What's My Problem*, I wrote *I did not die, yet I lost life's breath*. It was a quote from a packet of worksheets passed around at Sisters in Grief, attributed to Dante Alighieri, a name I recognized from school associated with suffering and transformation. I underlined the words *I did not die*.

Last week, I began to get the frizz out of my hair. I moisturized my face. I dusted the baseboards and beat the rugs. I cleared the receipts and Diet Coke bottles from the back of the Volvo.

By the following Sunday, I'd found the only corner of my house that wasn't clean: the boxes of Gabe's old things. They needed to be taken to the church, I decided, where they had a rummage sale that found good homes for old things. Things even Gabe's parents hadn't wanted. Decades-old T-shirts whose holes in the armpits I'd repaired. Bicycle accessories I'd never use. A stray order of thousands of promotional pins we'd misplaced during the first campaign.

At the church, I fielded the volunteer ladies' questions as they dug for items to sell. They deemed the tools useful, the T-shirts rags. They were glad to see me looking better, they told me. How was my mother, they asked. They hadn't seen her at a service in a while. She was surviving, I told them, and they should stop by the supper club sometime. And who was that man they saw me with at the St. Patrick's Day party? He was a local boy, I informed the ladies with pride. They were delighted. They were impressed. They had received the Save the Date for Gabe's memorial fundraiser and couldn't wait to attend. They'd loved the pictures I'd chosen to feature in the message—especially the one of Gabe as a little baseball player. Levi had been the one to choose that one.

Levi. I hadn't talked to him much since the night at his apartment beyond a few texts about the memorial.

After a minute, I found myself going back inside the church and retrieving the shirts. I couldn't bear the thought of scissors slicing through Gabe's faded Nirvana happy face, the purple one from Brokenridge Spring Fling, the black-gray cotton with a Metallica logo. There were some things that needed to be preserved. I pressed my face into the fabric, searching, finding only the smell of a damp old house.

An hour later I was sweeping barn stalls when I heard Levi come up the drive, guitars and bass thumping even through the Honda's closed windows.

When he'd parked, he made his way across the side yard and paused to take in the sight of the barn, paint still bone-white and peeling, furniture and farm equipment under tarps and old blankets in hulking forms, towering behind me. His face looked heavier than I'd seen it in a while. His hair hung over his cheeks, bringing out the shadows under his eyes.

"What's all this?" he called.

"Just doing some cleaning," I called back. "Gabe never got around to getting rid of all his family's old stuff, so I figured I would . . ." I focused my eyes on the folded stack of T-shirts I'd rescued from the church. "Anyway, I thought you might want one or two of these."

Levi took the shirts without looking at me. As he sorted through them, the slightest intake of breath. Amusement or a sigh of nostalgia, I couldn't tell. "Not gonna fit."

"What about Nirvana?" I lifted up the black Nirvana shirt. It always hung baggy on Gabe. "Try it."

Levi looked at the shirt for a moment, stepped forward to take it from my hands, and peeled off his own fisherman's sweater. I turned my head from his bare chest and stomach, but his body was in my periphery, still winter pale, laced with colorful designs. When I looked back, he was pulling the clearly too-small shirt over his bulk. His wide, muscular stomach peeked out from the hem.

"Voilà," he said. "Fits like a glove."

I laughed. He smirked and pulled off the shirt, tossing it back to me. "Catch," he said and slid his head back into his sweater.

I refolded the Nirvana T and returned it to the stack. I'd texted him to come out because I wanted to be proactive, to make sure everything was normal. But now that he was here, there was still something in the air between us, something strange and unformed and stubborn. Levi probably sensed it, too. I closed my eyes and saw his iridescent irises close to mine. A pang of awkwardness. So he didn't want the shirt. Fine. That didn't mean anything, either.

I tried to smile gamely. "You want to help?" I threw a hand behind me. "There's lots to do back here."

"Sure." He strode past me, smelling like chicory coffee. I watched him maneuver through two long-rusted tractors toward a stack of old furniture. Soon, he had pulled back a tarp with a violent yank, revealing a dusty dresser. "I can dust this, I guess?"

"Sure," I echoed.

He picked up a rag and began to wipe it down. "So give me the update," he said.

"Just working on getting the house in order," I replied. "Keeping things going at the restaurant, messing with my *Hamlet* looks . . ."

Levi nodded, thoughtful, watching me. "And Jake?"

"All good there," I said, swallowing. I wasn't going to give anything beyond that. I didn't want to invite those unsettling feelings again.

Levi picked up the Nirvana shirt he had tossed aside earlier and smiled at me, traced with something like sadness. "All good. Okay. Great."

"Yep! Anyway," I said, "we can start moving forward with the charity, and I'm thinking Mom's restaurant can do the food. I'll just have to figure out how much we can spend to break even—"

Levi squinted at me, but he didn't poke or prod. For the first time since I'd known him, he seemed to be holding something back.

"What?"

"You're just gonna plow forward, huh?"

"What do you mean?"

He scoffed. "You're just gonna give away one of Gabe's favorite shirts like it's nothing. You're packing up like, *no big deal*. After everything we talked about."

"What, are you talking about the freak-out with the mug?" I attempted a casual laugh.

"The mug. The new boyfriend. All this . . ." Levi glanced behind me at the barn. At Gabe's parents' and grandparents' furniture. "Plus your family's restaurant. Your job. Your play. The memorial. It's a lot for any person. Let alone a person who's still in mourning."

"I'm not in mourning anymore," I said automatically, but even if I were, I resented that Levi brought it up. That was my business, not his. "Even if I was, my mom and I had to take care of everything when Dad died . . ."

Memories suddenly trickled from the dark corner where I'd sequestered them. Mom and I buying him the cheapest headstone because we knew he'd chide us for getting ripped off by the Burke Brothers Funeral Home. Trying not to cry as we dug through shirts that smelled like Dad's cigarettes, guessing what Theo might want someday, giving the rest to the church sale. Bringing life-insurance payout cash in an envelope to buy him a plaque on the bar at the VFW.

"I did it before, and I'll do it again," I told Levi. "Life has to move on."

"Yeah, I know," Levi said softly. "But the other night . . ." A catch in his voice. He continued, deliberate. "It seemed like you were still dealing with some stuff. Maybe we can put a pause on the memorial or something. It's okay to take a step back."

"No way," I said. I wasn't stepping back. Back to my cagey self, bitter and exhausted and alone. That was the opposite of what I wanted. "I see what you mean, but no," I repeated. I wiped my forehead with my wrist, giving him my friendliest I'm-over-it smile. "Jake and I are great. The Green River's gonna be fine. Memorial's going to be great. All good things. Onward and upward."

"Whatever you say, Lindstrom." Levi still looked skeptical, but he said no more as he helped me move a row of old sawhorses.

After a few minutes, a chime sounded from Levi's pocket. He paused and pulled out his phone. "Speaking of onward," he said, waving the device toward me.

In the dimness, a lanky brunette with olive skin and tattoos floated on his phone screen. I recognized the telltale navy/pink color scheme, the bubble graphic.

I leaned closer to his screen, confused. "You're back on Bubbl? What about Christy?"

"We broke up," Levi said, pocketing the phone with a shrug.

Now the dark shadows under his eyes made sense. He probably wasn't sleeping.

"Sorry to hear that," I told him, and I meant it. "I liked Christy."

"Me, too," he said after a moment. "I thought we had something. But I fucked it up, as usual." He picked back up the sawhorse he'd been transporting and plopped it in a corner. "So back to the drawing board, I guess."

I put my hand out for his phone. "Can I see?"

We leaned over the profile once again.

My most irrational fear . . . Zombies because I know my brain is tasty ;).

"What do you think?" Levi asked.

The girl's lines were pretty clever. My heart beat hard for some reason. "She seems cool."

"What should I say?"

I scoffed. "Why are you asking me?"

"You bagged a ten, Lindstrom. You're the Bubbl expert now."

"Very funny." I rolled my eyes, but I was smiling. "I don't know, tell her you prefer your brains medium-rare or something."

"See? I was too rusty to come up with something like that." He gave me a jaunty salute as he headed back toward the Honda. "Thanks for the shirt, by the way."

As he sped—way too fast—down the driveway, I went back to sweeping. The bristles made long streaks in the dust. In the corner where the sawhorses had been, the broom caught on a giant bug. I jumped.

Upon closer examination, it was long dead. Mummified. I added it to the nest of the dust.

Onward and upward.

Bet you you can't . . .

Guess how many Batman jokes I've heard about my name.

"Places!" The stage manager poked her head in the doorway.

Behind the North Star Theater stage, I was giving Gregory a layer of powder. A series of prop mirrors lined the long tables of the little room, many of them fitted with light bulbs so bright I broke a sweat. It was the second Saturday of our three-weekend run, and Gregory had been telling me about a Best Buy commercial he'd landed.

As I finished, he stood, surveying himself in an oval, gilded mirror once used for a production of *Snow White*. His pale, silvery tunic shone against his brown skin, now coated with a ghostly sheen.

"Sickening." He lifted his chin in a model pose. "You're doing this for me for the Oscars red carpet someday."

Two mirrors over, the actress playing Gertrude snorted.

"Gregory!" the stage manager hissed in the doorway with more urgency.

"Break a leg!" I called as he hurried off.

I began to set up all the palettes for the next series of ghostly transformations, and flowers for Ophelia—I'd found a way to make them look as if they were growing out of her skin. As Act II came to a close, I heard a familiar voice.

"Knock, knock."

I waved Ted in, soon followed by Zoey, darting across the room to touch a rack of costumes, and Franny, more reluctant, staying close to the door as if preparing for escape.

Ted grinned his nervous grin, swinging his arms. "These two want some Pixar, and I forgot my laptop upstairs, so I figured we'd swing by and say hello."

"Well, hello!" I was setting a small container of white creme at each mirror. I glanced at the laptop Franny was holding. "Why do you need your computer? Do you not have a TV, Ted?"

"Nope. Terri and I agreed. No TV." At Franny's glare, Ted's firmness seemed to waver. "It was more Terri's decision, but I . . . I see the merit."

"But you *do* watch TV . . ." I said to Ted. "Just on a laptop."

"On a crappy laptop," Franny muttered.

"We watch *movies* on my laptop," Ted corrected.

"Ted," I said, grabbing a handful of freshly cleaned sponges. "Just get a TV. Watch movies the way they're supposed to be watched. On a *big screen*."

"Well, excuse me, Martin Scorsese." Ted shrugged, glancing at Franny and me. "I just don't see the difference!"

I handed Zoey the sponges and directed her to place them next to each container of creme, which she did with enthusiasm. Franny began to argue her case—not for the preservation of cinema but because all her friends had TVs—and I was reminded suddenly of my own dad. Sneaking out of bed on the rare nights he and Mom weren't out partying after the restaurant closed down. Resting my head on his shoulder, clutching his arm in delighted fright as *The Shining* flickered, my fear dissipating with his belly laugh.

"The difference is in the details," I added when Franny's rant was over. "With a better screen, you can see the guts glistening in *Alien*. Or *It*. The rotten cracks in the clown's pancake makeup."

Zoey looked a bit disturbed but intrigued. Franny held up an entreating hand in my direction. "See?"

"Ho-kay," Ted said, rolling his eyes good-naturedly. "Not everyone needs their supernatural villains in disgusting detail."

"The beautiful things are more beautiful, too," I said, laughing. "I can't think of any right now, but you know. The fantasy." I slid over and elbowed Ted. "The romance."

"Ew," Franny said.

"Eeewww," Zoey repeated, looking at her sister for approval.

Just then, the large actor playing Polonius shuffled into the room in a doublet, wiping fake blood off his fingers with a wet wipe. We must already be deep into Act III—we had to get moving.

As the actor plopped into his chair and began to apply the face creme, he glanced at Franny, Zoey, and Ted, who were watching him with fascination. "'Sup," Zach said.

"Watch how we do Zachary's face," I told the rapt Kim family. "All the little details."

And as I moved in front of the actor, the rest of the room fell away. Everyone's skin in the cast was a different hue, requiring different shades of purple and blue, different types of fake frostbite depending on how long they'd been deceased and the method of their passing. Ophelia I would keep almost preserved, like wax, as if she'd stepped into the freezing river for a bath. The fake flowers grew out of her chest and neck, twisting and forming a crown in her hair, which I would coat with the same icy effect I'd given everyone else. That night, like most nights I'd spend at the theater, I would come home and collapse into bed—sometimes Jake's, sometimes my own—and sleep heavily, peacefully.

Now, I stepped away from the ghost of Polonius and assessed how Zach looked under the lights. One more touch of black for the tip of his nose.

"So creepy," Franny said behind me, shuddering a bit.

"So fun," Zoey said, picking up a brush with curiosity.

"Morbid," Ted said to me, shaking his head. "But amazing."

"Yeah, Robin's the GOAT," Zach muttered, breaking the spell of his appearance.

"We should get going," Ted said.

"Yeah, it's going to get crowded in here," I said. I nudged Franny and Zoey. "Hey, keep working on your dad about the TV. He'll come around. In fact, I wouldn't be doing all this . . ." I waved my hand across the makeup stations, toward Zachary ". . . if I didn't have a TV growing up."

"You're a bad influence," Ted said, but he was smiling.

Zoey carefully set the makeup brush she was holding back into its place, her face still struck with awe. "So *this* is your job?"

"Uh, no, I guess it's not," I said, taken aback, though it wasn't immediately clear why the question threw me off. In a way, it had become a sort of job. "I do it because I like it. I love it," I added.

"Can we stay and see this play?" Zoey asked her dad.

"No," Franny commanded. She was halfway out the door now.

"Sorry, sweetie," Ted said, steering her toward the exit. "This isn't for kids."

Zoey resisted, calling back to me, "Are you going to do another play, then?"

At this Ted, too, paused, raising his eyebrows at me as if to say, *Well, are you?*

I didn't know how to answer. It had started as a favor—never had I thought I'd be doing anything like this, even when I was having fun on Halloweens past. I loved it, this was true, but I knew what *another play* meant. It meant another commitment, more time taken away from Jake, from helping Mom at the Green River, from the things that were supposed to matter most.

"I don't know," I said, and before I could say anything else, Ted and the girls had to step aside for Ophelia. I couldn't think about the future right then, anyway. Act III was over, and the next phase of the play was about to begin.

We waved a hasty goodbye, I picked up my flowers, and I was lost to the world again.

Had it really only been six weeks since St. Patrick's Day weekend? It felt like a lifetime. Now, on a Monday in May, my phone buzzed in my pocket halfway through a presentation on equity in the corporate workplace . . . Some things hadn't changed, I supposed. The Honey Bun waiting for me in my office, for one. My boss glared from his seat. I glared back and silenced the phone.

The buzzing wasn't Marcy or Jake, I discovered later as I tore into my snack. It was a calendar alert. *Welcome Back Drinks with Manuel @ Wine Bar!*

Who the hell was Manuel, and why had I scheduled drinks with him?

Then, I remembered: Manuel was someone I'd chatted with on Bubbl before Jake and I decided to become exclusive. He was a short, stocky, handsome bodybuilder type, I recalled, with thick black hair and a cute gap in his front teeth. He was going out of the country for a few weeks, he'd told me then, but would I like to grab happy hour with him when he came back? Sure, I'd said, and apparently we'd even picked a date and location. At that point it had seemed so far away. After Jake and I had gone on our epic forty-eight-hour date, I'd been smitten, so the only reason I was still on Bubbl then was my flimsy promise to Gabe to use the app for a full year.

Now, my only problem was that I had no way to contact Manuel to cancel, unless I wanted to reactivate my profile. I couldn't do that. It felt too symbolic, like reactivating the old Robin. Besides, who knew if the chat I'd started with him would even still exist? Who knew if he would even remember me or the plans we'd made? Probably not.

But I found myself taking a turn toward Wine Bar after work, anyway. What if this guy did show up, waiting for me, wondering? I knew how it felt when people on Bubbl suddenly disappeared, and I imagined it would be ten times worse in person. I didn't want to do that to Manuel—he seemed lovely. And even without the possibility of actually dating, even if it wouldn't turn into clubbing with an Instagram-famous DJ or running through a corn maze or creating Thing 1 and Thing 2 on the fly, I had become fluent in *what the hell, why not*. Random calendar event with a world traveler? You say *yes*.

Manuel was sitting at the bar, looking up intently at a game of soccer playing on the TV above the bar. He had the sleeves rolled up on his crisp white shirt, which was tucked into a pair of well-fitting jeans. When I tapped his shoulder, he startled, almost knocking over his bottle of Michelob Ultra.

"Hi! Robin?"

"Manuel?"

"That's me. I didn't know if you would show up," he said as I scooted onto a stool next to him.

"Have I got a story for you," I replied.

"Oh, yeah?"

His smile was a bit shy—perhaps because of the gap in his teeth—but when I explained my situation, he laughed, and it spread across his face brilliantly. "Of course you'd nab a boyfriend while I was gone. You're a catch. Congratulations."

"Thank you." I smiled into my Sprite. His attention was warm and genuine, but no longer overtly flirty. He was good at this. I felt relaxed. "How was your trip?" I asked.

"Absolutely amazing." A friend of his had gotten married in Spain, he told me, so he'd used the opportunity to travel. He'd gone to Sagrada Familia and the Gaudi houses in Barcelona. He'd seen Louis XV's expansive Place de la Bourse and the Miroir d'eau in France. He stayed in cottages carved into hillsides and modernist glass condominiums that seemed to float above the skyline. "But my favorite was this Airbnb in San Sebastián," he said. "Giant windows with bay views. Built-in bookshelves. Ample patio. Greenery everywhere." He took a sip of his beer.

I'd been rapt, imagining every place he described. I'd never been to Europe. I'd never even been out of the country. "You must really love architecture," I said.

"What can I say? I'm in real estate." He took another sip. "And you? What do you do?"

"Oh, I just show up down the street and cut checks." I shrugged. "I don't love my job, but it's fine."

"You know what? That is fine. Our generation puts too much emphasis on finding our bliss or whatever. Sometimes you can show up. Go home. Have your fun after work."

"Yep. About to do some of my own traveling, in fact," I said with a little laugh.

"Oh, yeah?" Manuel wasn't acknowledging the sarcasm.

I blushed, realizing how pathetic my little joke actually was. "There's a setting on the treadmill at Anytime Fitness," I explained. Sometimes, when Jake couldn't go out and run in the bad weather, he would train for his next event indoors, and I would use his guest pass to run next to him—more like shuffle, more like galumph. Ragnar—the race for which we were supposedly training—sounded like a relay designed by Satan himself, I told Manuel. Every year, teams of masochists willingly traveled two hundred continuous miles on foot, each runner covering their segments in different shifts, camping for a night along the way.

This year, Jake's Saturday running-club team needed one more runner. My initial answer was no, twice over. Then, at one of Smitty's potlucks, they had surrounded me—Jake's good-natured friends with their wide-eyed encouragement and their healthy glow—and I'd said *yes*. A little exercise would do me good, I figured. When we first started, it was as torturous as I imagined, my feet made of lead, my body screaming with resistance. Then I started to realize that when I stopped thinking about how torturous it was, time melted away. "Anyway, my favorite part is the virtual trails," I finished. "Sometimes the treadmill takes you to downtown Seattle!"

Manuel nodded politely. "Ah, cool."

I gestured to his beer, which was now almost empty. "I should let you finish that and get back to Brokenridge." Better to get out now, before I made myself sound even more lame than I already was.

But he turned to me with curiosity. "Oh, you live in Brokenridge, huh?"

"I do, yeah."

"That's right. I remember now from your profile." He hesitated, looking at the soccer game for a moment, then back at me with a newly focused expression, though his demeanor was still friendly. "Can I ask, do you rent or own?"

"Own," I said. "Why?" What was he getting at?

He raised his dark eyebrows. "Brokenridge is about to be a big market. They've got that data-mining company building headquarters just down 35. Lots of new workers in your area."

"Interesting," I said, but just to appease him. It made sense that a Realtor would pay attention to that kind of thing, but it made no difference to me. I stood and held out my hand.

He stood with me and took it. His palms were soft and warm. "Hey. Thanks for not standing me up today. You're sweet."

"Happy to," I said. "Good luck out there!"

Before I reached the door to Wine Bar, it was Manuel's turn to tap me on the shoulder. "Before you go." His smile was shy again. He put a stiff, shiny card in my hand. His business card. He'd written his phone number in pen under his name and photo. *Manuel Arenas.* "If you ever think about selling."

"Ha! Right."

"I'm serious," he said. "You could get a great price. Quit your boring job for a while. Pack up. Go running around the Pacific Northwest for real."

I stared at the scrawled numbers. Sell the farmhouse? Then again, I was the last holdout. Everyone in Gabe's family was now scattered, back to Minneapolis, to Chicago, some of them on his mother's side even back to Guatemala. When the rest of the Carrs had sold off their plots, Gabe's parents had eventually given in, too, selling off parcel by parcel until they finally moved, leaving Gabe and me the last fertile acre. The last of the Carr-Morales land, where I now parked the Volvo and DVRed *Bride of Chucky*. But where would I go? There was no way. I tried to give Manuel back his card, but he refused to take it.

"Think about it," he said and went back to the bar.

The hallmark of a good relationship is . . .
An agreed time to leave for the airport.

A month later, I found myself back at the Lee County Fair, taking shelter from the afternoon sun in the animal tent. It was the first time I had been back since our pre-chemo trip with Gabe, and it was just as hot as it had been then, just as lively. It was almost as if the same gaggle of Red Oaks teenagers butted in line for funnel cake as they had that day three years ago, the same kid vomited popcorn in the trash can near the tiny but mighty Gravitron, the same Prince-themed seed art won first prize, though that was every year. The biggest difference, of course, was that Gabe was not here, and today, Levi was the manic one.

HELP, he'd texted. This chick on Bubbl wants to do a "group hang" instead of a date. Please come with and be in my "group." Please.

We don't refer to women as "chicks" . . . good god, what are you, the villain from an '80s teen movie?? I texted back. And I doubt your date means a woman friend. Take Ezra or Isaac.

No, she's young and very progressive!!! Levi had written back. There will be people of all genders there. My bros are all busy and you love the Lee County Fair! I can't be the lonely old man. PLEASE?

Let me check with Jake, I told him.

It had just so happened that Jake was at a family reunion in Bemidji this weekend. I had stayed home, citing my need to do a much-needed inventory sweep at the restaurant. But I could do inventory on Sunday, I'd figured, and when I told Jake about Levi's invitation, he had encouraged me to go. "Tell Levi I said hi," he'd replied. "And pick out some seed art for me!"

I couldn't tell if he was joking, but I didn't care. If Jake wanted seed art, I would get some damn seed art. Anything to feel the thrill I'd been feeling at the prospect of being more a part of his life, the prospect of our hazy morning runs—and the subsequent giant breakfast I insisted on making after—becoming a routine we'd built together.

Now, I lagged behind Levi, his date, and her friends, all of them holding giant Icees and taking photos of the big-eyed calves on their wobbly legs. I stopped at a sheep enclosure, bending to entice a lamb in my direction. Levi soon joined me, tugging the collar of his too-small, Gabe-inherited Nirvana shirt.

"That was meant to be a keepsake," I muttered beside him.

"It's my only clean Nirvana," he said, yanking at the shirt's hem near his belly. "Taylor likes Nirvana, so."

I nodded toward Levi's date. "Are you having fun?"

"I'd be having more fun if my friend would stop sulking in the back and join me."

"I'm trying not to be a third wheel!" I told him.

"There are many wheels," he said, gesturing to the two friends his date had brought. "You're making me into a unicycle."

"So what's her deal?" I asked, nodding toward the woman in question as we resumed our journey around the farm tent. She was tall and curvy, with the confidence and posture of a music-video dancer.

"We have mutual music friends," Levi said, wiping his brow again. "She does stuff with a loop pedal."

"And what number date is this?" I asked as she glimpsed back at us. "First, I'm guessing?"

"Technically third, but I can never tell because she always wants to do the group hangs," Levi said, putting up air quotes. "We text a lot, though. I love her texting."

A spike of envy, which surprised me. Probably because I was terrible at texting. "Why, what are her texts like?"

"A mixture of marijuana-fueled philosophical musings, and the rest . . ." Levi winced. "Well, that would not be appropriate to share."

"Gross."

"Don't be a prude. It's the twenty-first century." He nudged my shoulder. "Just because you and Gabe got together in the T9 era . . ."

"Call me a traditionalist, but I try to keep robots out of my sexual encounters."

"You're missing out. HotWifeCompanion3000 changed my life."

I snorted. "Stop."

Levi's date, I noticed, was looking back at us again.

"She does like you," I told him, nodding in their direction. "Or at least she wants your attention."

We had emerged from the cool red glow of the tent back out into the June sunshine. The three friends ahead of us headed toward the row of carnival games, gesturing for us to follow. We waved, still a few paces behind.

"But how do I translate that into an actual date?" Levi asked.

"You can't rush it," I muttered. "Just let her move at her own pace. She'll reward you for that."

"But what if she thinks I'm not into her?" Levi's head was on the swivel—it was hard not to be. Noises of every timbre and pitch rang out from the aisle of colorful booths. "I'm going to get her something. No, I'm going to write her a song." Next to a Go Fish booth, he stopped in front of the accompanying wall of plush toys, pointing to the top row. "She always sends me SpongeBob memes. I'm gonna get her one of those giant SpongeBobs."

"I seem to remember a similar strategy involving Goofy when you were trying to woo Olivia Gordie in college," I reminded him. "I'm going to tell you a secret about women."

"And what's that, woman?" Levi said, handing over bills to the carnival barker.

"They don't actually like oversize stuffed animals as much as men think they do." Together, we watched the man retrieve the SpongeBob with his giant stick.

Levi put the giant SpongeBob under his arm and turned to me. "But I'm an oversize stuffed animal, and they love me, so."

I rolled my eyes.

"Hey, Taylor!" he called, jogging ahead.

I walked faster to keep up with them, snapping a photo of the tableau for Jake with the caption *Levi is making moves*.

Jake texted back, Nothing more erotic than a sponge with pants.

We circled the fair again. While I chatted with one of Taylor's friends about their favorite *Doctor Who* episodes—not that I knew anything about such episodes, but they had a *Doctor Who* T-shirt on, and I knew from experience with Gabe and Levi that once you got a superfan talking, all they needed was an audience—Levi seemed to make headway with Taylor. She loved the SpongeBob, or at least it looked like she did, judging by the number of photos she took with it, and the two of them managed to break away for some alone time at the frozen-lemonade stand.

At one of the fair's biggest attractions, a towering three-story slide, Taylor handed her new SpongeBob to Levi for safekeeping, and she and her friends ascended the stairs at the back of the long line. At first, it seemed Levi and I were going to watch.

After a minute, however, Levi blew out a breath he'd been holding. "Screw it. I'm doing it."

"Have fun," I said. I knew I'd been trying new things lately, but carnival rides were where I drew the line.

"Are you sure you don't want to join us?" Levi asked me, wheedling. "Come on." He put on a deep movie-trailer voice. "Topple from the top of Saint Paul! Find your thrills and chills with this death-defying drop!"

"My health insurance doesn't cover thrills and chills." I pointed at SpongeBob. "Besides, someone has to watch over this guy."

"Your loss!" Levi said, handing me the giant plush.

"Bye," I said, making the sponge's gloved hand wave.

As Jake and I messaged back and forth about his family reunion—at least *he* liked my texting—I could spot Levi and Taylor slowly make their way to the peak of the six-laned slide. There, people were handed mats, which they hopped on headfirst, shooting toward the ground at speeds that shouldn't be allowed without a vehicle. Taylor and her friends took their mats and leaped like dolphins along the grooves of the slope, sliding to a graceful stop, where they collected themselves and moved from the bottom, windswept, looking up at the sliders to come. It was Levi's turn. He waved down to them and to me and took his mat.

When he propelled himself forward, however, the mat slipped out from under him. It could have happened to anyone—in the time that I had been observing the slide, it had happened to people of all sizes and ages—but it probably didn't help that Levi's Nirvana shirt had ridden up, exposing his skin to the plastic, turning his trip down the three stories into an extended, painful skid.

At the bottom of the slide, he stayed facedown, unmoving, and we all ran to see if he was all right.

His first sign of life, of course, was devil horns. He lifted his chin up from the ground to look at us all, embarrassment fighting through his joy. "Hail Satan," he said.

A half hour later, I'd accompanied Levi to get his friction burns treated at the first-aid tent, and we'd said goodbye to Taylor and her friends. Now, the afternoon was fading into evening. Levi had asked Taylor to dinner, he told me. Taylor had responded that she'd text Levi to hang out again. "Kiss on the cheek." Levi sighed as we walked back to the parking lot. "I'm gonna give up."

"Maybe a hangout is good," I offered. "It's only been a few months since Christy. Maybe you should take it slow."

"Nah. I go all in, remember?"

"But where has that gotten you?" I tried to dull the sharpness of that statement with a sympathetic look.

"I can't stand that look," he said, pointing at me. "Don't pity me."

"I'm not. I just . . ." I tried to find the right words so as not to add insult to injury. "It's almost like dating is this creative act for you. Like your songwriting. Epic trips to Cabo. Elaborate gifts. But getting to know someone doesn't have to be this grand gesture. Giant SpongeBobs are not sustainable."

"Yeah, that thing cost me fifty bucks," Levi muttered.

"Fifty dollars?" I scoffed. "No. Never again."

"But the people I go for, like Taylor, and the woman I kept going to Miami for . . ."

"There were *multiple* trips?" I asked, incredulous.

"That's what they expect," Levi went on. "They're beautiful. Everyone wants them. You gotta do something to stand out."

"I guess. But are you doing it for the game? Or for the love of your life?"

Levi looked over at me, huffing. "The love of my life. Of course."

"So you've got to be prepared for the love of your life not necessarily being beautiful. Sometimes they're just, like, profoundly annoying, or smelly, or get too drunk and want to listen to 'Bones' over and over." I smiled over at him.

By the looks of it, he, too, was remembering Gabe throwing his arms around us mere yards from this very spot, Levi goat-carrying him back to the car, where Gabe howled along to Levi's song.

"I guess what I'm trying to say," I continued, "is that when they're the love of your life, it doesn't really matter what you're doing. You don't have to go on adventure slides to enjoy things together. You made fun of me when we talked about this last year, but I really did love doing all those little boring things with Gabe. Going to meetings and weeding the garden."

Beside me, Levi nodded, the smile reappearing on his face, softer. "I know you did."

We stopped at the Volvo, looking up at the fair lighting up in the darkening sky.

"Life has been really sad recently," I said.

"I know," Levi said, putting a heavy hand on my shoulder. "The world is a really fucked-up, sad place."

I put my hand on his. "Any little trace of love is special. Maybe you don't want someone who can whisk you to Cabo." I looked up at him, patting his hand where it rested. "Maybe you just need someone you can do dishes with every day without wanting to murder them."

"Maybe I do," he said.

When I returned home later that night, the interior felt a bit stifling, retaining some of the day's humidity. The plans Gabe and I had made long ago to install central air had gone by the wayside when I'd started supporting Theo in college, and I hadn't bothered turning on the AC units. I kept the front door open and propped the back door open, too, letting the breeze slip through and clear out the old, stale air. I peeled off my cardigan—I always wore layers, just in case—and kicked off my boots. It was time to get out my summer clothes.

As I searched for them, buried under boxes in the corner of my closet, I found a brooch that had belonged to Gabe's mother. This happened once or twice a year, this accidental unearthing of Carr-Morales history. A piece of Gabe's homework on crumpled notebook paper, complete with an A and gold-star sticker folded at the edges. A button belonging to his grandad lodged in a crack in the baseboards. In Gabe's childhood room—what was now the office—taped outlines of his old Alice Cooper and Metallica posters were still visible. Once, Gabe had found a pair of his father's old sunglasses from the '70s on a workbench in the garage. When he grew out a mustache and put on the frames, he was the mirror image of his dad, gangly and big-lipped and sharp-nosed, except for the hair. He had his mother's dark, thick hair. I texted Juana a picture of the brooch, offering to send it to her in Milwaukee.

Hi, Robin. I don't remember that one. It's yours if you want it. —Juana, she replied.

Mine if I wanted it. That was how I'd come to inherit the house, too, which had still been under his parents' names when he died. What was the point of going through the hassle of putting my name on the deed? Gabe and I had figured. It wasn't as if we were going to get divorced. It wasn't as if one of us would die. We were invincible twenty-three-year-olds, and we knew everything. We had chased each other through the rooms, through the crumbling barn out back, and it was enough to stake our claim in random shouts. *This is our house*, we yelled to the yard, scattering the cardinals. *Our very own fucking house!*

I pocketed the brooch. In the other corner of the closet, more of his T-shirts I'd missed. So many shirts from so many events. University of Minnesota Political Science Alumni. Governor's Luncheon. United Way. Habitat for Humanity. St. Jude. Gabe would try his best to leave these events in a timely manner, knowing I was craving home. He'd hand me a stack of free cookies in a napkin, and I knew it was going to be a long night. So many hours he spent, listening to dreams and gripes, nodding and smiling, pledging a better future. A future he didn't get to see.

Suddenly, a crash. It seemed to come from the living room. I stood, my heart pounding, and strode out, braced for an intruder, an emergency. But the living room was as still as it always was, the couch painted in leafy shadows from the setting sun coming in through the open back door.

Then I saw it on the ground in the kitchen: the key rack. I walked over to pick it up, tracing the lacquered surface of the repurposed wood. It must have come loose from its nail. I gathered the keys that had scattered next to it on the floor, recalling the color-coding system I'd devised. But I hadn't touched them since last year, since Gabe had sent me the email that fateful night.

Add them to everything else collecting dust, I supposed. Key rack under my arm, I found myself wandering outside, to our garden.

Another spring had gone by where I had failed to tend it properly, contrary to what I'd pledged last year. Back then I had kept the weeds at bay, at least. Now, all the untended plants—weeds and vegetables alike—still dominated the beds with their colorless husks. I had cleared the occasional square foot once in a while, just as an afterthought as I talked on the phone with Jake, but I hadn't monitored it closely—too busy with the restaurant, too busy planning the benefit, running blindly through the countryside, chasing happiness. But when I bent to examine the zucchini, I found green tendrils feeling their way through the dead leaves. Green tomato stalks were reaching for their wires, soon to become vines. Asparagus poked through the mess like alert soldiers.

I pulled off a dangling green bean and bit into it, its earthy sweetness almost intoxicating. Somehow, I hadn't killed the garden. In fact, it had thrived without me. Maybe the rest of the house would do the same. I could try to make it my own, try to fold my new future into the rooms, but I had a feeling it would take me another lifetime. How could Jake ever be just Jake? How could I ever be just me? As long as I was here, I would walk the same old path, from the kitchen to the couch, from the couch to the bed, looking for Gabe.

I dug into my purse and found the stiff, shiny card next to some napkins. I entered Manuel's cell number into my phone and dialed. It was time.

A thought I recently had in the shower . . .
Early-career Britney Spears's vocal fry is harder to pull off than you think!

Something was digging into my back. Beside me, Jake snored lightly. Leagues above us, climbing ropes hung from the ceiling of an elementary-school gymnasium. I shifted on my mat, my sore hamstrings twinging with the effort. The hard substance pressing into my thirty-three-year-old posterior was the floor. The face of my watch glowed in the dim light. In a half hour, we were expected back outside, back in the van, back on the route again. Little did I know the night of camping described on the Ragnar website meant a few hours of scarfed protein bars and blankets on a gym floor. Little did I know that the race doesn't stop at sunset, so most participants run one leg in the dark. Mine was next. I needed sleep, but I was too nervous.

I always had trouble sleeping the night before I knew I had to run. I'd lie awake, listening to the gentle hoots or crackling of leaves, trying to let the chug of Jake's warm breath lull me back to slumber. Then, mornings before dawn, we'd lace up our shoes and hit the bricks.

Sometimes as I ran, my breath would rise in my chest for no reason and stay there, and anything I was thinking, the shallow, souped-up gasping of my lungs made it worse. Old feelings would shake loose—how I wished I was home when my dad died, how I should have taken a semester off to help Mom take care of Theo, how I should take it easier on her, how I should get her to stop smoking. *Pant. Pant.* Was Mom okay? *Pant. Pant.* Was Theo okay? *Pant. Pant.* My whole body hurt.

But wildflowers had started to appear along the road. Gabe would have known what they were called. I liked to pause and pull up the plant identifier, a long-unused app on my phone, and point it at the petals and buds. Anemone. Thimbleweed. Lady's slipper.

Smitty brought me back to the gym floor. "You awake, Robin?"

"Yeah," I whispered back.

Smitty turned on her side to face me, her blond curls in a frizzy nest on the top of her head. "I can't sleep, either. Mr. Protein Bar over here is farting up a storm." She pointed behind her, where Diego lay. We stifled our giggles. "Are you having fun?"

"I can't tell yet."

Smitty winced. "First leg's always the hardest. You'll find your rhythm for this one."

"Does running ever make you get into your head?" I asked.

She looked surprised. "The opposite. When I'm being grumpy, Mol tells me to go for a run." Molly was her partner, a tall, brusque X-ray tech with flaming hair and a scratchy voice. "That's why I'm so in shape," Smitty continued, rubbing her belly. "I'm grumpy all the time."

We tried to keep our laughs quiet.

Nearby, someone's watch started beeping. It appeared the noise was coming from Raj, one of Jake's running friends who I'd met once or twice. He sat up and started rolling up his sleeping bag. I swallowed an acidy taste. "Uh-oh."

Smitty sat up, too, rubbing her hands together, giving me a look. "Here we go!"

On my other side, Jake turned over, yawning. "How'd you sleep?"

"I didn't."

"You ready for this?"

"No," I said and gave him a weak smile. But together we rolled our mats under our arms and walked out into the night.

The exchange point was in the middle of a patch of trees down the road from the elementary school, marked by a bright inflatable arch. The runner who preceded me—I believed her name was Justine—had gone eleven and a half miles in the same deep, dark farmland I was about to venture into, and then she would take her place in the van and it would be her turn to sleep.

Runners from other teams had started to line up under the arch, shaking their limbs and stretching. I joined them, doing my breathing exercises, trying to determine if my intestines were just knotting themselves out of nerves or if I really was going to lose my bowels. Jake stood by my side, massaging my shoulders, muttering encouragement and advice. The rest of our teammates surrounded me, too, some of whose names I remembered, some of whom I had only met and cheered for last night. Only nine miles, people kept saying. Only nine miles, I kept repeating, as if I believed it. I could barely hear them over the sound of my heartbeat. The distance from Brokenridge Lake to the edge of Pole City. Double the distance I'd ever run without stopping. For one portion—the final portion—the van would be riding alongside the path, cheering me on until it was my turn to hand off the baton.

For most of it, I'd be alone. To run an insane distance in the middle of a city, in the broad daylight was one thing. This would be something else entirely. My route was supposed to be pretty flat, according to the topography map: a two-lane road sandwiched between a cornfield and a series of old mounds people used to use for skiing when the snowfall was higher. The nearest farmhouse was across the tree line, over the mounds. The nearest light source would be the moon. This would be country dark.

Jake stood in front of me, adjusting the headlamp on my forehead, switching it on and off to find the correct setting. I watched the circle of light flicker on the black-green forest floor. "What if I collapse in the middle of nowhere?"

He put a warm hand on my back. "You're not going to collapse. You can just walk."

"What if an animal comes bounding out of the cornfield, hungry and vicious?"

He laughed. "Come on, you grew up in the sticks. You know what to do."

I lifted my arms, making myself as big as I could, and made a bear-adjacent noise.

"No, no, no." Jake joked. "You play dead."

"That won't be hard."

The more likely danger out of all of these, I knew, was getting attacked by my own panicked thoughts, but I didn't mention that. I looked down at the number on my shirt and made sure the safety pins were secure.

The team had started to mutter excitedly, scattering to the sidelines. I stood in the painted box and nodded at Jake, who gave me a thumbs-up, and put my headphones in. "Toxic" by Britney Spears lit up my ears. Justine was coming down the path. I prepared to run.

By the time we'd reached the two-lane road, everyone had passed me, leaving me alone with the plop of my shoes on the packed dirt, the circle of light bouncing in front of me, illuminating the trail markers along the path. In one ear—I'd taken one earbud out for safety—Mandy Moore sang about candy. In the other, crickets chirped. The night air was cool and still. The moon hung in a crescent over the soft mounds in the distance.

A shadow darted past the moon in my periphery. I flinched but kept going. Probably an owl diving for field mice.

Gabe and I had told each other we loved each other for the first time on a night like this. Lying in his back seat at a campground outside of Owatonna. We were sweaty and mostly naked, a blanket we'd swiped from one of our dorm rooms wound around our young bodies haphazardly, our chatter coming in lazy bursts, that kind of postcoital bliss that knocks you flat on your back and makes everything funny. His shin bones were so long, I remembered. I traced them with my own feet. His feet were long, too. And his femurs and torso and skinny arms beside mine.

In my open ear, there was a rustling in the corn. At this time of year, the stalks were only shin-high, so whatever was moving could hardly be a threat. But still. I paused my music and took out the other earbud, holding them both in my fist.

Nothing.

I couldn't remember who said "I love you" first. Was it me or was it him? It didn't matter, because the other person had said it right back. We were already sharing a mind, a soul. I remembered the words were like cool drops of rain on my flushed and sweaty forehead. Startling but welcome, refreshing in the most primal, animal way.

Someone was nearby.

No, that was wrong. It must just be paranoia, wind.

But the noises didn't quite match a breeze, they sounded intentional. Like there was a consciousness behind them. Was it me or was it someone? Or something? It was no one.

I slowed, as slow as I could go without walking.

It had been so quiet when he died, so ordinary. We'd just been at the hospital to finish dialysis a week earlier, so we knew it was probably his kidneys. He'd gotten in the bed himself, his thinness painful to look at, but he'd still had the strength to joke with the nurse that it had been way too long since he'd seen her. I had packed an overnight bag for both of us. Underwear, toothbrushes, deodorant. His Twins stocking cap in case his head got cold. His favorite sugar-free ginger candies, which claimed to settle his stomach, but we could never tell if they worked. Crossword and *The Autobiography of Malcolm X* for him, Sudoku for me. We knew the drill.

Then his heart had become arrhythmic that evening—stopping and starting again. We'd both been dozing when the alarms sounded, the bag full of our things sitting on my lap. The night-shift nurse came in quickly, but he had already gone into arrest. As movement on the monitor spiked in and out, I remember absent-mindedly digging around in the bag for something he could use, something to make him more comfortable, as if ginger candy could usher him into death. But, of course, there was nothing. Just *I love you, I love you, I love you*, whispered over and over. My hand in his, his parents on Speaker from Milwaukee. I remember hating that fucking useless bag on my lap. The shiny zippers. The merry little graphic pattern on the side. The delusion of it.

On the dark road, I shook my head, trying to clear it, watching the circle of light swing back and forth. My mouth was dry, and my movements were sluggish. It wasn't good for me to be immersed in my own thoughts this long. That's why I still used the TV. Even now, even as the new Robin had taken to writing in my journal or assembling tomorrow's lunch, I still needed the white noise to keep my brain from lumbering into these gray, sad places where it would get trapped. Where I would get trapped. I put my headphones back in, pushing Play on Mariah Carey's "Fantasy."

That August night, the night he predicted he wouldn't be alive for Thanksgiving, I had slammed the bedroom door on him, on his voice, which I knew wasn't going to carry. A few months before that, I had started dawdling at the entrance to our house, savoring the seconds alone before I had to go inside, where I would have to keep both our heads above water. Where Gabe would lie unmoving on the couch, and I would have to tell him what appointments we had that week, or quiz him about his side effects, or gently suggest he take his shower now, while he was still awake, and he would look at me like I was the one slowly killing him instead of the one who was trying to save his life.

My hands tingled. I shook them out by my sides.

Here I was again, making myself the victim. Let it not be forgotten I'd bought the second TV for the bedroom long before the cancer, or at least before we knew. That way, he could play his games with Levi, and I wouldn't be disturbing him, I'd justified. But really, I'd just wanted a wall between us, to be in a different world for a while. A world where my only concerns were whether the amateur bakers would get their cupcakes baked on time. A world where I wasn't Mrs. Mayor, where I wasn't the Best Wife Ever, where I didn't have to love him so much, where he wasn't at the center of every moment of my life.

My lungs burned. I could feel my blood in my fingers, at the tips of my ears. *Pant. Pant.* Little did I know I would spend my days alone, clutching for it, that center. *Pant. Pant.* At least once a day I would tell myself I'd give anything to go back there. *Pant. Pant.* I'd throw out the TV. *Pant.* I wouldn't get so annoyed when people called me Mrs. Mayor.

"Agh!"

I wasn't watching the ground. My toes caught on a crack, and suddenly I was yanked downward by my own momentum, catching myself on my hands just in time before my chin hit the dirt. My knees stung with the impact. Little sharp rocks spiked my belly and breasts, the heels of my palms. As I rose to sitting, I could see the number pinned to my chest was ripped.

"Goddamn it," I said to no one. I repeated it, louder, hoping it would have some kind of effect. Nothing. Not even an echo.

This would be a fine time to stop. No one would blame me for walking the rest of the way. In fact, no one would blame me if I stayed right here and called in the little golf cart they sent for people who'd been injured. *What seems to be the problem?* the medic would ask. *I've hurt myself*, I would respond and hold up my hands. Bruised knees and bloody scratches were easier to explain than what was roiling inside me.

I found myself looking over my shoulder, my ears perking. The leaves nearby had rustled again. The hairs on my arms stood. I stayed perfectly still, holding my breath.

From out of the new corn, a large cat padded softly into the road. Bobcat or lynx, I couldn't tell. The cat paused, taking me in with its glowing gold eyes. I gazed back, transfixed. What it made of me—my crumpled, despairing shape, wailing nonsense curse words in its territory—I would never know. It cocked its head forward, breaking our shared stasis, and moved on.

When I could no longer hear the cat in the field, I stood, brushing my clothes. Something about it had made me want to finish what I'd started. Its complete indifference to my plight, whatever reasons I'd invented to stay where I was. Those were petty human things. Out here, I was just a creature. To survive, I'd have to keep my senses focused on what was ahead. I'd have to break the stillness.

One step. Two steps. Three, four, five, and we were running. Toward the moon, though it seemed to get farther away. Fainter. Bushes took the place of crop rows. Something howled, far away. I howled faintly back. There was honeysuckle on the breeze.

Gabe's arms around me in a twin dorm bed, my knees pressed against the wall. A powder puff blotted with foundation in my fist. *CNN*. His cheek near my cheek. Stray campaign pins in corners, under chairs, getting stuck in the vacuum. *I'm not going to be around for Thanksgiving.*

Bubbles popping on the courthouse steps. Tumbling on the wet grass, green stains and blue paint from someone else's nursery. The ears of the bunny costume. *I know you told me you'd never love anyone else.* Sobbing in the shower. *And who is your real self?* The ring on a chain that slapped my chest with each step. You are now free to kiss the bride. The bride. You are now free. Ashes along the bike trail. Bagpipes. The *Far Side* mug. Holding his cheeks in my hands. *I love you.* Following his skinny form through the city. The gold ring on my palm, my feet planted on the frozen river, the city rising around me. *I love you, too.* His brown eyes, losing light. *You want company for the drive?* The city in the rearview mirror. Mrs. Mayor. Mrs. Mayor. Mrs. Mayor.

"Robin!" A honk. "You're doing it, Robin!"

I looked to my left and saw an impossible sight—the faces and clapping hands of people I knew, Diego and Smitty, beaming from the open door of the van, which had slowed to a crawl to keep up with my snail's pace.

And there was Jake, his smile so big his eyes were barely visible, reaching for me.

Tears were steaming down my face. The packed dirt had turned to pavement, and a dull heat traveled up my shins to my knees, to my hips, but somehow the fire had not destroyed the legs. My legs. They were moving, and my arms were moving, and my heart was pumping, my belly heaving, and my eyes were open to the road ahead. I had no idea how many miles had gone by, but the sky was turning from dark purple to robin's-egg blue. A hint of sun spread out on the horizon.

"Hi," I pushed out between breaths, my mouth lifting in what I hoped was a smile. My brain felt like baby food. My brain was my body, and my body was my brain, which was a single-cell organism, somehow floating in the primordial soup of existence. "I didn't stop," I told them, panting. "I fell, but I didn't stop."

"Here," Jake said, and a water bottle suddenly appeared by my side.

I grabbed it and sprayed it into my mouth. The water was like what I imagined silvery mercury would taste like, sweet and cold and metallic. As I drank, I thought of the cat. Had I imagined it? With the change in light—the sound of voices, full sentences returning—all those dark thoughts felt far away. I flopped the bottle back toward the trundling van, to Jake's waiting hands.

"You want some goo?" he asked.

There was a special gellike edible substance for runners Jake liked to deploy on his longer runs. Supposedly it was nutritious, but I'd always been wary—it looked like Tide Pods, I'd told him once. But now was no time for nitpicking. I needed all the fuel I could get, even if it was too close to detergent for comfort.

"Goo me," I said and held out my hand.

As I glanced over, I could see Jake rip the little package with his teeth, while Smitty and Diego looked on. Behind them, trees rolled past. The van was blasting "I Won't Back Down" by Tom Petty. As Jake frantically passed me the Tide-Pod-that-wasn't-a-Tide-Pod, I was struck by the incredible beauty and strangeness of this little tableau. I couldn't believe this was my life. And yet it was. Maybe it was the lack of blood to the head, or maybe it was the pink sunrise painting the trees and wildflowers gold, but as I choked down the cloying Jell-O-like substance, I was overcome by a sense of euphoric gratitude.

"This is disgusting," I called to my team as I squeezed the last of the space toothpaste. "I love it."

The goo went to work. The burning ache in my limbs became more like a dull throb. According to Jake, I had about three miles to go. I was going to finish; I could feel it. Compared to what I'd traveled already, three miles was nothing. I had come so far.

Dating me is like . . .

You tell me. I could use the feedback.

Franny and Zoey ran past me out the door of the Green River, each holding a kids' menu place mat they'd refashioned into a paper airplane, Franny's phone held aloft. They were going to have some kind of airplane-throwing contest, Theo told me, following them with his own device.

"Make sure you recycle the paper when you're done!" I called after them.

It was my birthday, but no one needed to know that. The cast and crew of *Hamlet* were gathered to celebrate something better: our own little Shakespeare show featured in the annual "Best Of" issue of the local Twin Cities paper, beating out all the big-budget musicals and experimental plays. "*Hamlet* Guided by the North Star" ran today, along with the bolded summary of the article: "A small nonprofit theater struggled to fill seats. Now, their visual reinterpretation of a timeless classic has put them back on the map." The special-effects makeup, specifically, had been cited as a triumph. *Mesmerizing*, the reviewer had called it. *Eerie, uncanny*. Hamlet *does elevated horror.*

I'd been restocking napkins when Ted had called this morning, practically shouting into the phone, commanding me to look at the article, to come down to Minneapolis because the director had brought the whole staff into their little offices in Minneapolis to break the good news. They wanted to have a celebration, they said, and I was invited. A celebration, huh? I'd said to Ted. I couldn't leave the restaurant today, but I knew a place where they could get the best brats and potato salad this side of the Mississippi.

Now Jake had acquired a frame for the piece and put it up over one of our longer tables, alongside the colorful "Best Of" cover. A few minutes ago, he had disappeared. Gone on some mysterious errand, Mom informed me, wiggling her eyebrows.

Marcy was here today, too, mostly for birthday purposes. Since she'd arrived, however, she seemed less interested in joining in the celebration than eyeing a certain nonprofit-fundraiser-slash-single-father.

Ted was pretending not to notice. He kept laughing too loudly at everything, running his fingers through his hair as he looked over to where she sat in her summery jumpsuit.

"One Fanta, coming right up," Mom was saying to a little girl at the register, who I believe was the daughter of the man who played Claudius. "You like the color orange?"

The little girl nodded.

"Me, too," Mom said. "Nice and bright, like your shirt."

The girl beamed. I smiled, too, watching Mom chat as she fetched the soda. As the actor pulled out his wallet, Mom put her reading glasses on her nose, squinting at the screen that had been installed as part of the new point-of-sale system.

"Let's see," I heard her mutter as she took a sip from her travel mug. "Drinks, drinks, drinks. Used to be I could just type out the price, take the money, bing bang bong, we're done. Now, I got all these dang buttons . . ."

Just then, the airplane-fliers returned from their quest, dinging the bell at the entrance, sweaty and chattering. Theo came over to show me a video he'd taken of the girls' paper-plane flights on his phone. But all I could hear was Mom's voice. "Don't worry about it," she was saying. "On the house." She gestured toward the point-of-sale device. "Can't figure this thing out, anyway."

Suddenly I wondered how often Mom had put things on the house since we'd installed the new system. I was tracking a few gaps in sales and inventory, but I had chalked it up to an adjustment period as she figured things out. I certainly didn't consider the possibility of orders not being entered altogether. I did now, though.

I started toward the register.

Theo looked up from his phone. "Don't."

"No, I'm just curious how often she's giving stuff away . . ."

"I know," he said, shaking his head. "I know. But now is not the time. Go be with your cast. I'll show her how to do it."

"She knows how to do it. I've seen her do it. She just doesn't want to because she's probably frickin' drunk." I pushed past his warning arm.

He followed me.

"I noticed you're still having trouble with the system," I said to Mom, gesturing toward the register as cheerfully as I could manage. "Do you want me to show you where the Fantas are? Remember, they're under Specials?"

"Well, they should be on the permanent menu," Mom said. She took another sip out of her gas-station travel mug. I recognized the way her words ran together. I could probably guess what was in that mug. "People love Fanta."

"See, and that's why you need to *use* the *point-of-sale* system . . ." I started, my smile fading with my frustration. "If we don't keep track of Fanta sales, I won't know how much people love the Fantas. I need *numbers*. Accurate numbers—"

Theo put his arm around Mom, steering her away. "Here, Mom. Let's figure this out."

Before I could protest further, I turned to behold the stern face of the director, her arms crossed over her usual black tunic. Ted sidled up beside her, sipping iced tea.

"Hello," I said. "Hi, Ted."

The director glanced at the register and then at Mom. "Are we busy?" she asked.

"Not busy at all," Mom said and winked at me. "Robbie shouldn't be running around, anyway. It's her birthday."

"Happy Birthday," the director said flatly.

"Thank you. So how about that article?" I said.

"I wanted to talk to you about your career." The director nodded toward Ted. "Ted tells me you're not going to pursue another show."

"I told him I didn't know," I corrected, though I didn't know why the distinction was important. Looking back, the *I don't know* was meant to be a polite version of a refusal. As my eyes roamed toward the cash register, I decided to clarify. "Unfortunately, I can't spare the time."

But Ted had started to shake his head with conviction. "Robin, that would be a tragedy."

"Frankly," said the director, "I'd tell Ted to hire you for *Newsies* if it wasn't putting my other girl out of a job."

"What's *Newsies*?" I asked.

The director ignored me. "Listen, I don't just dole out praise," she said, leaning closer. "So when I say you've got something special, you should listen to me."

I felt my face flush. "Okay."

"Okay?" she said.

"Yeah." I swallowed, but I didn't know what, exactly, I was affirming. I respected her opinion, of course, but I felt like with one little word, I was signing a contract I wasn't prepared to sign.

"What's *Newsies*?" the director muttered as she walked away, rolling her eyes.

Ted turned to me with a conspiratorial look. "What did I tell you? Even *Elaine* thinks you should do something with this."

"No, I get it," I said. "And I'm very thankful. Message received."

"One more thing," he said, lifting a finger. "And I'll back off. I know you're gonna say no, but I think you should say yes."

I sighed. More *yes*es. Hadn't there been enough *yes*es? Wasn't all this—the theater friends, the new hobby, house on the market, cute boyfriend off running a cute errand—the culmination of *yes*es? How much more could there be? But my curiosity was getting the better of me. "Say yes to what?"

"There's this makeup-effects program. Out in Portland."

"You're trying to get rid of me?" I asked, teasing him.

"A former actor of ours works there," Ted continued. "Apparently most of the graduates go on to TV and movies. I sent her some *Hamlet* photos, and she said you should apply."

"Me in *movies*?" I looked intently at Ted to make sure I'd heard him correctly. I almost laughed. "In Portland? Get out of here."

"Hey, you helped me out, *multiple* times. And it meant a lot to me. Now I'm trying to help you."

Across the room, we watched Gregory teach Franny and Zoey a hand-clap game. For a moment, I allowed myself to consider it. Not because I was going to do it, but I admit I had enjoyed the director's approval, had puttered around all day with the "Best Of" reviewer's words floating pleasantly in my head. *Eerie. Uncanny.* It was fun to imagine. I could see a movie set at sunrise. Long nights working, strategizing with storyboards and sketches. A trailer full of colors and tools. The first glimpse of my creation on-screen, inspiring in someone the same shivery wonder I'd had myself as a girl.

"So what's this program called, anyway?" I asked Ted, trying to be casual.

"Ha!" Beside me, Ted slapped the table. "You're thinking about it, aren't you?"

"I am," I admitted. "But that doesn't mean anything." Just because I was flattered didn't mean I could spontaneously set things in motion. Not a giant move like this, anyway. "You can't just peer-pressure me into turning my life upside down."

"Sorry." Ted didn't look sorry.

"Send me the link," I said. "And that's the end of it."

To make sure of that, I pointed to where Zoey and Franny were now seated across from Zachary aka Polonius, all three giggling and hunched over a small bowl we'd set out with the Parker House rolls. "I think Zachary just tricked your daughters that butter is ice cream."

"What?" Ted whipped around and started toward the far corner of the restaurant. "Oh, god. Zoey, don't eat that!"

Soon, I started to gather dirty dishes. Cast and crew stopped over to say their goodbyes. After I assured them I'd be in the audience for *Newsies,* whatever that was, I slipped into the back with a full bus tub.

As I rinsed plates of leftover food and loaded them into the industrial dishwasher, the director's words were having a strange, inflated effect on my insides. The feeling was jarring, unfamiliar. A sort of pride that doesn't get easily dismissed with modesty, a pride that takes residence. *Something special*, the director had said. I'd never been special—I hated how corny that sounded, but it was true. Like any good Midwestern woman, I knew how to work hard, how to bounce back, how to keep my head down. But special I was not. Not until now. Suddenly I felt a pair of strong arms wrap around my waist.

"There's the birthday girl," Jake said.

I started at first, got my bearings, and turned around to kiss him. "Guess what?"

"What?" He nuzzled his face in my neck.

"I just got told I should apply for a special-effects makeup program in Portland, Oregon. Like, movie makeup."

"Movie makeup?" Jake repeated, unburying himself from my neck. "I mean, I guess I'm not surprised. You're talented enough."

"There's no way I could do it, though, right?" I continued. "People are just being nice because of the article."

Jake leaned back from our embrace for a moment, looking at me square in the eyes. "You could totally do it. You'd kill it."

"Yeah?"

"Absolutely. I mean, I'd be sad if you left because . . ." He swallowed, seeming suddenly nervous. "I like what we have, and I'd like to see where it goes. Selfishly. But . . . you know. I support you."

"Thank you. That means so much to me . . ." Tears filled my eyes, but I wasn't sure why. They must have been good tears. Overwhelmed tears. I kept them at bay. Through my anxiety about my family, my obsessive tinkering with weird makeup in his bathroom, my random fits of grief, he had been there, joking and waxing poetic and lacing up his running shoes.

"I think about it, too," I continued. "Our future, I mean."

"Well, hey," he said, stroking my hair. "Maybe we should talk about it. See if we can actually do this thing. I'm ready to start thinking about this stuff." He looked at me with a tentative grin. "Are you?"

It wasn't as if I'd never thought about it—moving in together, sitting on Jake's balcony, Tiger in my lap—but whenever I started to consider it seriously, I stopped myself. *One thing at a time*, I'd said and tried to stay in the present. But the present was here, right in front of me, making me an offer.

"I think I'm ready, too," I said.

"Yeah?"

"Yes."

He moved closer again, and soon we were against the industrial sink, his breath mingling with mine as he found my eyes. His hand moved from my arm to my waist, tracing my hip.

He raised his eyebrows, nodding toward the supply closet.

I let out a surprised laugh, and Jake hushed me, laughing himself.

With the closet door shut behind us, our mouths met, tongues flicking against each other, then pressing. We found ourselves descending to the cold floor, where he pulled me on top of his hips, lifting my shirt, moving his mouth across my bare skin. Unable to wait, we moved frantically to pull fabric aside until he was filling me, my knees rocking on the concrete as I gripped the wire shelves on either side for balance. Our breaths soon filled the tiny space. The need to be quiet—the remaining restaurant patrons were only fifteen or twenty feet away—seemed to heighten every sensation, every motion. When I had to cry out, I did it in the crook of Jake's shoulder and neck, every muscle in my body contracting against him, my toes, my thighs, my nails burying in the warmth of his back.

After, we scrambled up, breathing in tandem, smoothing each other's clothes.

Right as I opened the closet door, his hot breath tickled my ear. "God, I love you," I heard him say, almost a sigh.

I paused. "Did you just say what I think you said?"

"Yes." I could hear the smile in his voice.

"Really?"

But before he could answer, voices rang from out front.

"Happy Birthday to you . . ."

We emerged from the dishwashing area to investigate, my shirt still soaked with patches of water. There were Mom and Theo, holding a sheet cake, their faces aglow with as many lit candles as could fit. Next to them, Marcy, Ted, and Ted's daughters—Ted was adding an unnecessary operatic trill to his notes, I noticed. The cake looked homemade in the best way, heavy with little mountains of frosting. *HBD Robbie,* Jake had spelled out in passable cursive.

So this was Jake's errand. My heart melted.

I could love him. I really could. Somewhere between my belly and my heart, where the butterflies had settled, there was room for a new type of feeling to grow, a feeling that carried me across these thresholds, that loosened my grip finger by finger.

At the register, Mom was looking up from the screen, taking off her reading glasses. As she joined the others, I could hear her crackling voice, see her lift her bony arms above her feathered hair, pretending to conduct the choir.

Theo darted over to turn off the lights.

We met at a table in the center of the room, the candles sparking and crackling. "I better blow this out before we burn the whole place down, huh?"

The group tittered.

"Make a wish first!" Franny said.

"Nah," I said, looking around at the assembled faces. I smiled at Jake, who winked back. "I've got everything tonight."

My Love Language is . . .

Chores. Clean with me, you have my attention. Clean for me, you have my heart.

What would I do with all these old towels? Was it strange to still use towels that you'd shared with your dead husband? My only solution was to sell them all, to bury my face in them once more, as if time and washings hadn't stripped them of the past and put them on a card table for fifty cents.

In order to stage the house properly without our things inside, Manuel had asked that I try to be out by the beginning of next week, and since I was already spending so much time at Jake's, we decided I'd move into his place for a little while—a sort of trial run for the real thing.

All week I swam in memories as I dragged Gabe's parents' headboards and side tables and dining-room chairs out to the garage, agonizing over the price of an heirloom, double- and triple-texting Juana to make sure she didn't want anything else. *No*, she'd told me. *We've got our hands full*. As the garage filled and aching muscles replaced the ache of nostalgia, I started to understand what she meant.

Today, the sticker prices were as low as I could make them without giving it all away. Soon enough, word got out, and the whole town showed up to pick over the contents of decades of Carr-Morales-Lindstrom accumulation.

The gardening tools went to Barb Rundle, who had just won a civil suit against the Sheas for more property.

Board games to Peg Grossman, whose daughter was home for the summer from alternative high school and wanted to host her new friends.

Jamila Hassan was going to make an art piece out of all the old rugs.

My best customer was Tammy Fink, who had not only walked away with a dresser, three mirrors, and four barstools, but all of Gabe's old T-shirts, which she said she would find some use for. I was afraid to ask what use that was—maybe one of those quilts that would sew them all together—but that was none of my business.

Where was I going? they asked. Just down the road in Pole City, staying with my boyfriend until I figured out a more permanent plan. Would I still be helping at the restaurant? Yes, of course. It was satisfying to have answers, and all who asked seemed satisfied in return, handing over their quarters and bills for all our bits and bobs.

The sale wound down around midday; the smell of rain-to-be was heavy in the August air. Now, as I began to bring the tables of remaining items inside, Levi's Honda wound down the driveway, as promised. I found myself smiling at the sight. I had been on guard all day, following the many unspoken rules of Brokenridge small talk, and it would be nice to see a friend. We'd been texting about memorial planning, but also about our lives, too. About his latest adventures with Bubbl, how the Hidden Beaches were about to record their next album. About my impending move to Jake's, my slow and rocky transition from slasher-watching, snack-eating goblin to miles-running, cat-doting, live-in girlfriend.

"Where is it?" Levi asked as he got out of his car, scanning the open garage with mild panic. "You didn't sell it, did you?"

He was referring to Gabe's barely used guitar, which I had promised him as part of the move. Not like he needed another guitar. "Of course I didn't sell it. I told you it's yours, and that means it's yours."

"I kept thinking on the way here that you'd give it to some scrappy neighborhood punk."

"I am giving it to a scrappy neighborhood punk," I said, motioning toward him. He was in his usual pair of cutoffs and a sleeveless T, this one splattered with a skull logo. His hair was slicked back into a bun with what looked like sweat.

"Ha." He picked up one of Theo's old Lego sets from a card table. "Looks like you got pretty cleaned out."

"Not bad. We'll see if folks come back tomorrow."

Levi was swinging his leg over the seat of my old Schwinn. When he placed his feet on the pedals, his knees were almost as high as the handlebars. "Beauty."

"It's a bit small for you," I called, crossing over to him. "But it's yours for five bucks."

"You cannot sell this, Robin," Levi said and began to ride in circles on the gravel.

I turned, following his path. "Jake says it's not going to last. Probably going to get a road bike, anyway."

"This should be your road bike," Levi said.

"It's old and squeaky."

"But it's yours. Your transpo. Your trusty steed."

"Not since Gabe was alive. Stop." I reached out to block his path, and he braked, inches from my foot. "You're making me dizzy."

He twisted his palms on the handlebars, his chest lifting slightly with the effort he'd just expended. The wet appearance of his hair was not sweat, I realized, but a recent shower. His soap or shampoo had a peppery, sweet-leather scent.

"What did you decide about Portland?" he asked.

I'd told Levi about the program, about how when I'd explored the link, I'd seen the odds and the price and immediately balked. "I told you, even if the restaurant were doing well enough for me to leave, hundreds of people apply for, like, twenty spots. God only knows if I'd make it past the first round. And now that I'm getting serious with Jake, I don't want to test things by moving halfway across the country . . . It's not worth it."

He threw up his arms. "You're not even going to try?"

"All right, let's say I did. Would I even like it over there?"

"Who cares? It's just a stepping-stone to Hollywood." Levi dinged the bell on the bicycle. "That's showbiz, baby."

"A stepping-stone where I have to pay rent." I reached over to ring the bell, myself, a couple of times. "At least the bike would come in handy. I wouldn't be able to afford my car."

"You'll be with smart people, doing what you love," Levi said. "Everything else is going to fall into place."

"You make it sound so easy."

"What?"

"Dropping everything and going. The professional musician, waltzing around, following his heart or dreams or whatever . . ."

"Uh, it's not that easy," Levi assured me. "While you and Gabe were here in Brokenridge playing house, I was standing at the door of the 331 every weekend, working my ass off. And I had to try a lot of things before I knew what fit. It was exhausting." Levi squinted at me, assessing. "But I don't think you're going to have to do that."

"Do what?"

"Figure out who you are. I feel like you came out of the womb fully Robin, one hundred percent."

"Ha!" I was smiling, but this was the first time it wasn't a joke. The first time since my birthday I was thinking about the program as an actual possibility, rather than dismissing the opportunity as if it were from a different life.

"Just listen to your inner voice." Levi poked his own belly, tracing a swirling fingertip up to his head.

"I don't have one."

"Sure, you do," Levi answered. "For instance, my inner voice sounds like Will Ferrell's impression of Harry Caray." Clutching the handlebars, Levi tucked his chin, imitating the comedian in a nasal, sports-announcer shout. *"Levi! Harry Caray here! Don't try to play pop music, just play what you want! You don't have enough sex appeal for Top 40, Levi!"*

As we laughed, I found myself wistful. "God, I miss being younger."

"Why?"

"I never had to think about what I wanted," I said, using air quotes. "Something needed to be done, I did it."

He smiled briefly at that. Then he was thoughtful, nodding at the farmhouse. "Remind me, why did you guys move back here?"

"Me and Gabe?" I nodded behind me. "The house. And I figured it would be good for my family."

"Even though you had a job in the city?"

"So?"

"So you did it out of obligation."

"Yeah, and?" I was pretty sure where Levi was going with this line of questioning, and I didn't care for it. "Why did we stay in Brokenridge? Why do I pay my brother's bills? Why do I stay at my job? Because my family needs me. Because we needed the health insurance. Sorry Gabe got cancer and I couldn't roam around, finding myself," I added, sarcastic.

Levi shook his head. "I'm not saying it's his fault or anyone's fault. I never said that."

"You're saying I'm a boring square who just goes along with what everyone else wants from me."

"No way, dude. No one would ever think that about you. I'm just saying, you've got this talent, this opportunity to start over, and what are you going to do with it?" He pointed down the driveway. "Move a couple miles down the road to Pole City and do the same shit you've always done?"

"God, you *really* want me to do this makeup thing." I kicked at Levi's bike tire.

"Doesn't have to be the makeup thing," Levi said, shrugging. "I just want more for you. Something that's all yours."

"I was under the impression that my entire *life* was mine." I kicked at the bike's tire again, this time harder.

Levi wobbled a bit but kept his balance. "It is," he said simply.

I had just come to terms with the fact that what I *actually* wanted—for Gabe to come back—wasn't going to happen. I had just begun to start something new. Why did Levi always have to do this, prodding at me in the most sensitive of places?

"Then, stay out of it," I said. "Okay?"

"Fair enough." Levi nodded, pretended to rev the handles of my bike like a motorcycle. "As long as you're happy."

"I am."

Levi looked up at me. I was getting used to the electricity behind his looks these days. I didn't look away.

"I suppose it wouldn't hurt to keep the bike," I added, smiling at him. "If you're not going to take it."

He smiled back. "Good," Levi said, ringing the bell. "Because I feel like a clown on a tricycle when I ride it."

"Or you could give it to your latest Bubbl date. Cheaper than a SpongeBob."

"Nah," Levi said, wiping a patch of dirt from the frame. "I think my dramatic wooing days are over."

"I'm glad to hear that," I said.

"Oh, yeah?"

I didn't know what exactly I was about to say, but it felt right to say something, especially after our conversation the other day. My pulse rose. "Like I said, you don't have to sweep someone off their feet. You can just be yourself. Loud, way too sensitive, sweaty—there are people out there that go for that kind of thing."

"Like who?"

"People." I straddled the front wheel, putting my hands on the handlebars next to his, rolling his bulk across the driveway. "Or, who knows?" I said, pushing forward with all my strength. Levi was pedaling backward, laughing. "Maybe you need some time of your own, too."

I leaned forward for one final shove. Our faces were inches from one another.

He didn't move away. "Maybe I do," he said.

"Hey." Jake's voice sounded behind me.

The Prius must have pulled up silently. I felt a stab of guilt as I let go of the bike, though I didn't know why.

"Hey!" As Levi caught his balance, I made my way toward Jake. We exchanged a quick kiss.

Jake's eyes darted toward Levi, who swung his foot over the bike and back on the ground, straightening to his full height, the bike beside him. "Hey, man," Levi called.

"Hey," Jake said, nodding.

The three of us made polite small talk as I retrieved Gabe's—now Levi's—guitar.

As Jake and I drove away, I turned to look out the rear windshield at

Levi carefully maneuvering my old bike back to the garage, which he had volunteered to shut. I was still absorbing everything he had said. What Levi had expressed seemed to put into words a feeling I hadn't acknowledged in a long time, perhaps ever. A feeling that had settled and calcified somewhere, deep and unknowable and unmoving. But now it was unsettled. Unburied. I wanted peace and quiet to let it all land, to make sense of it.

"I think I'm going to stay back today," I said to Jake as we took a turn toward Pole City.

Jake's face tightened with concern. "You're not coming to the lake?"

"I just need some alone time," I said, giving Jake a reassuring pat on the shoulder. "That okay?"

"Okay. Bummer. Is everything all right?"

"I'm just tired," I said. "Don't worry."

"Oh, I'm not worried," he said, as lighthearted as always, but I couldn't help but notice that we were quiet for the rest of the drive.

The secret to getting to know me is . . .
Trying to beat me at Monopoly.

"This is a love song," Levi muttered into the mic, strands of his wavy hair falling into his face. Behind him, the sun had just dipped behind the jagged skyline of Saint Paul, hitting cotton-candy clouds that had threatened rain all day. But the prospect of a storm had passed, and with it the last of my stress. Despite the nightmares of lightning delays and running out of food that had woken me—and by proxy, Jake—every few hours last night, the memorial had gone off without a hitch. The kickball game had concluded in a tie after a few nail-biting innings, and now the Hidden Beaches were almost done with their set.

Levi strummed and sang the first lines in his melodious growl.

Can you feel everything waiting for us?
It's the start of our big win.
I know it'll all fall in place,
when we jump into love again . . .

Cheers thundered from the outfield.

I was traversing the fence line, changed out of my dusty kick-ball uniform into an airy floral skirt and comfy sneakers. The skirt had pockets—useful for carrying spare duct tape in case one of the blown-up photos of Gabe we'd put up around the field lost its grip and fell; extra pens, in case any were misplaced from the table where folks were handwriting their messages and memories on a giant banner; and wristbands for anyone who wanted to join us but couldn't pay. The last attendance count was around two hundred and fifty, but the money count was higher—those who could afford it had gone beyond the fifteen-dollar ticket price, likely surpassing our fundraising goals. The representatives from the charity were thrilled.

Keep the lights on real bright,
fill the place with all our cheer.
Fill the closet door with our pencil marks
while we shrink each year . . .

Levi was singing from the stage in an uncharacteristically waltzy tune, and I found my head bobbing along.

Theo was on the first base line with a group of friends, filming each other dip and drop athletically to Levi's song. In the center was Mom, who was apparently taking a break from her shift at the concession stand to do some kind of Baby Boomer mix of *Saturday Night Fever* disco and the Twist, no gas-station mug in sight. Maybe I didn't have to worry about them so much. Theo was having to retake chemistry this semester, he'd told me, but he'd got a few more of his other required courses out of the way over the past few months. As long as he stuck with it, I didn't care how long it took. And Mom looked happy.

In the outfield, Jake danced with Diego's daughter on his shoulders. I smiled, watching them. The band dropped into what sounded like the chorus.

Any day you'll see what we can be,
so I'll keep hanging 'round.
Gotta love with everything we got,
this time around,
this time around . . .

The smell of smoky meat drifted my way, making my stomach grumble. I'd barely eaten all day, too preoccupied with getting the posters from the printer, picking up massive orders of brats and potatoes from the Green River's suppliers, helping Levi and Mo get the sound system set up—last week I'd gotten the idea to DM Mo on Instagram, asking if DJ Golddust was available for a last-minute gig warming up for a punk band; he'd risen to the challenge with a mix of glam rock and Little Richard. Now, I spotted him having his secret cigarette behind the dugout, probably swiping through Bubbl.

At the concession stand, I could see Rick passing out brat after brat, punctuated by the occasional cardboard boat filled with spiced potato wedges.

I sighed.

Mom was supposed to be the one distributing food and drinks while Rick manned the grill. I'd also given her stacks of coupons for a free glass of pinot with the purchase of a meal: hopefully the free advertising would gain us some new customers.

Looking toward the first base line again, I searched for Mom among Theo and his friends, but she was no longer there.

At the concession window, I bypassed the line with a few polite *excuse mes* to a couple of Gabe's U of M classmates and reached Rick. "Where is she?"

Rick shrugged, busy sticking a charred brat into a bun for a Kelleher boy. "She and Nance went for a smoke break, I think."

"I just saw her with Theo. She didn't come back?"

Rick shrugged again.

"I'll try to get her back here."

"It's fine," he said, patting his brow with his wrist.

It's fine was, of course, Midwestern for *I'm mad but won't say anything about it and resent you for decades to come.* I left the stand with my eyes peeled for a cloud of smoke, my ears open for a cackle.

This time around, we don't sweat the little things.
This time around, I'll let you hear me sing . . .

Levi's song had slowed down, and he strummed what appeared to be final notes.

Any day you'll see what we can be,
so I'll keep hanging 'round.
Gotta love with everything we got,
this time around.

As the crowd cheered, he scanned the audience. He was looking for me, I realized. I lifted a hand, and he waved back, pick still between his finger and thumb. No time to find Mom now. And it was her restaurant, not mine, I reminded myself. Now, I had my own responsibilities, which sent my heart skipping.

"For our last song," Levi said into the mic, his voice echoing across the field, "we have a very special guest. Please welcome my amazing co-organizer, wife of the late, great Gabe . . . and my dear friend." Levi smiled and winked. "Robin Lindstrom."

I grinned back at him, taking his hand as I climbed onto the riser.

"Hi," I said, startled for a moment by the volume of my voice carrying over the sea of people. I heard light laughter. I spotted the mayor's assistant and waved. "Hi, Maureen." She offered a little wave in return. "Hi, Ted. Hi, Marce." The two of them looked at each other and blushed. They had come together tonight, and now they were standing a chaste distance apart, Franny and Zoey between them. Next to them was Gabe's favorite professor from the University of Minnesota. "Dr. Samman, hello. Thank you all so much for being here. All of us together from so many parts of Gabe's life, can you believe that?" A delicate round of applause broke out, gaining volume as I encouraged them, clapping myself. Levi played a celebratory lick on his guitar. "My husband, as you know, was a total nerd for democracy." More laughter. "So to pay him tribute, for this final song we thought we'd do something collectively. If you have the program that was passed to you, bring it out."

Levi and I had come up with this idea two nights ago, when we were finalizing the program over a batch of late-night snacks. On the back,

I told the crowd, they'd find lyrics that the Hidden Beaches' very own Levi Berg had written just for this event.

"He was Gabe's best friend," I continued, looking at Levi. Under the glow of the ballpark lights, his smile was close-lipped and trembling, as if it could barely hold everything that was inside him. "And he really is the best," I finished. "So just pick up the melody whenever you get it. Levi will guide you. Take it away, Levi."

As I left the stage, Levi said quietly into the mic behind me, "This song took me way too long to write. I probably didn't say it enough when he was alive, but it's never too late to say what you gotta say." Then, louder, up to the heavens, "I love you, man."

Only a few brave souls joined the band right away, following the words on their programs like churchgoers with their hymnals. The verses conjured their friendship with a depth I had only witnessed from afar—reflective chats over their gaming headsets, metal-listening sessions that seemed to bend the rules of time and space, roughhousing with each other on a disc golf course like hyper little kids. As he sang, I stared at the slideshow running behind him. Gabe from all angles, near and far. Politician Gabe, Rollerblades Gabe, husband Gabe. Like I used to do when he spoke to crowds like this, I closed my eyes and savored the parts of him only I knew. Gabe on the couch that night in August, living and dying. Instead of going to the other room, in my mind I stayed. I nestled on the cushions beside his skinny body and made him look at me, drinking in the sight of his eyes, lively and loving me, scheming the years to come. The years for me. *Thank you, hon.* I could feel him, his gangly arms around my waist, his chin on my shoulder. His fingers sliding between mine. *Thank you, thank you.*

At the chorus, the band dropped out, and Levi stepped to the edge of the stage, cuing everyone to sing.

But you're not gone.

The voices rose together, disparate in tempo and out of tune and achingly beautiful.

No, you're not gone,
you're not gone,
you're not gone,
until we say so.

You can go now, I told him in my brain as the chorus crescendoed around me. *I'm going to find something of my own. I'm going to be all right.*

His hand slipped out of mine. The wind breathed on my neck. The light left his eyes. I was alone, and he'd never come back. I was alone.

"Robin?" Jake rested a hand on my arm. I hadn't realized my eyes were closed, my head hung. I looked up. Theo was next to him, his face alight with panic. "It's your mom."

The hospital had called me first, but I'd had my phone on Silent. In the crowded waiting room at Fairview, Jake, Theo, and I found a clump of seats, Theo shaking with silent sobs. *She's still alive*, I kept saying as I stroked his back, but I wasn't sure if I was saying it aloud or just whispering to myself, a protective spell.

It all started when Mom noticed we needed more potatoes. She was going to the nearest grocery store, she'd told Theo, but she had ridden in Rick's truck to the fundraiser, so she didn't have her car. Instead, Theo had handed over his set of spare keys to mine. Witnesses told the state patrol that she had lost control on an exit ramp and run into a concrete guardrail. Fortunately, she had slowed significantly before she veered, or else she wouldn't be alive. The Volvo's hood had been crushed.

She was waking up somewhere down the hall, where they were testing for a possible traumatic brain injury. We could see her once she had come out of the MRI, the receptionist had informed us, but we should be prepared for the results to take hours, for the possibility of things getting worse before they got better.

Now, my whole body was pulsing, my skirt in clumps in my fists as I sat staring at nothing, poised for action though there was nothing we could do. It was familiar to me, the smell of stale air and hand sanitizer, the quiet sniffles and mutters that would play on a loop around us for hours. I knew I wouldn't be able to cry until everything was all right, but I didn't know when that would be. Perhaps never.

"It's my fault," Theo was saying beside me through his tears. "I shouldn't have given her the keys."

My stomach knotted. A suspicion that had hovered in the back of my mind now made itself known. "Did she have her travel cup with her?" I asked Theo.

Theo shrugged. "Probably. I don't remember."

I noticed Jake was watching us both, curious. He didn't know, I realized. Jake couldn't have known what I meant because I hadn't told him. But now wasn't the time to clue him in, either. I didn't want to get into Mom's troubled history, into all the stories that had brought us here. I wanted to speak the shorthand of our family without having to explain.

"Can you give us a minute?" I asked Jake.

He was taken aback for a moment, but the expression left as quickly as it had appeared. He stood. "Anybody need anything?"

Theo shook his head.

"No. Thanks." I gave him a small smile.

When Jake had disappeared, I scooted my chair closer to Theo's. "Hey, T. Be honest with me. Was she drinking?"

Theo gathered himself for a moment and sniffed. "We had a few beers together. She seemed a bit tipsy, but not out of control."

I held my tongue as my insides began to burn with anger, but I wasn't sure where the anger was coming from, where exactly it should land. At Theo, next to me, making excuses. At Mom for being so casual with her life. At the poison that seemed to have such a hold on her. At the stupid gas-station travel mug, which likely still held her booze at this very moment, sitting in one of the cupholders behind a pile of twisted metal that could have left us both orphans. All I could do was loosen my grip from my dress, put my hand on his curly head.

"Theo."

He turned his head to look at me.

"Were you drinking, too? When you gave her the keys?"

He considered me for a moment, his jaw working as tears still fell down his face. "Nothing huge. Just a few with friends. Nothing out of the ordinary."

"Right." I had suspected as much, but I didn't know why I'd had such an urge to confirm it. Knowing the full details of the situation wouldn't make either of us less miserable. But a small part of me wondered if things would be different if he had been more responsible. If he hadn't been so loose.

Theo took a shaky breath. "Are you judging me?"

I balked. "No, no. I was just trying to understand . . ." My voice faded, my face flushing with the white lie. "I just want you to promise me that you'll be more careful. I know you're scared right now, and I'm scared, too, but if she gets through this . . ."

"Don't say *if*," Theo said, anger joining the fear in his voice. "Like, *please*, Robin. For once. Don't think the worst."

"I'm not. I just want to make sure this doesn't happen again—"

"We're not doing this." He stood. "I shouldn't have given her the keys. I know that. I'm a piece of shit, all right?"

I reached for his hand, regret churning alongside the frustration. "You're not a piece of shit."

He pushed my hand away and began to pull up something on his phone. "I can't sit here while you silently judge me."

"You can't leave."

"Watch me."

And suddenly, he was walking away, and I didn't know what to say to stop him. Right out the hospital doors. I considered running after him, but I was frozen inside my own cyclone of feelings. And if I went, who would be left to speak to the doctors? To make all the hard decisions? No one.

So here I was again. Holding down the fort while he got to storm off and distract himself from his own guilt. My anger rose up again, biting.

An hour passed with no news. No Theo. Soon, Jake returned with a couple of coffees—he, too, more silent and stiffer than usual. Every time the automatic doors whooshed open, I looked up. Stranger after stranger. Finally, Nance appeared, clutching her rosary, her red-gray curls frayed by stress and humidity. And after Nance, in walked Levi. I hadn't known he was coming.

I rose from my chair and fell into his arms.

"Is she okay?" he asked.

"We don't know yet," I muttered into his chest.

I didn't know why I was finding his embrace so soothing—maybe I was just overtired—but I stayed in Levi's arms for a long time, squeezing back as hard as I could.

"Yikes, go easy," he said, unlocking my hands, glancing at Jake.

"Have you seen my brother?" I asked Levi.

"No," Levi said. "Why? Did he leave or something?"

"Maybe he's just getting some air . . ." Jake said tentatively.

"He's not," I snapped. "We fought."

"Sorry," Jake said, raising his hands. "You didn't tell me."

At the shock and confusion in Jake's expression, I took a deep breath. "I'm going to go take a look outside."

"Can I come?" Jake asked.

"Sure," I said. I tried to smile at him, turning to take his hand. "I'd like that."

Outside, the night was quiet and cool. We walked down a path along the parking lot in silence. Either his phone was turned off or he had blocked me. "Theo?" I called.

After my third call with no reply, Jake said gently, "Even if he is out here, I don't think he's going to answer you."

"You don't know that," I said, letting go of his hand.

I paused under one of the young trees next to the path. Jake stopped, too, his arms folded, his eyes on his shoes.

"Are you going to tell me what happened between you two at some point?" he asked.

I thought I could detect bitterness in his voice. I knew I should probably wonder why, but the anger and worry inside of me was drowning out everything else. "It's just Theo being Theo. I'll explain someday. It's just all messed up right now."

Jake nodded. "Okay, then."

"Should we go back?"

"If you want."

And yet, within the panic, something was telling me to pause here, to investigate. Something was wrong. "Are *you* okay?" I asked.

"Yep," he said, flashing me a brief smile, which didn't quell my doubts.

"Okay." I couldn't take him at his word. "Are you sure?"

"What?" he said, tension edging his voice. "I'm fine."

"You don't seem fine," I said. I'd also been so-called fine a million times over the past two years. What I had really meant was that I was in pain, but I was going to bear it anyway, because I couldn't stand the shame of not knowing how to make it go away. It would never really go away. "I'm beginning to think that word has lost its meaning."

Jake let out a humorless laugh. "It's just that . . ." He sighed. "You want me here, right?"

"Yes, of course," I answered, tentative. I wasn't sure where he was going with this, and I wasn't in the mood for guessing. "Why?"

"I'm just not so sure anymore."

"What? What did I do?"

"Nothing," Jake said, shaking his head. "Nothing. But, like, we were on this path, we were talking about the future, and you're staying at my house . . ." He tossed up his hands. "And now you won't tell me what the hell is happening. It's like you're in the middle of a disaster, and I want to rescue you, but you won't answer me when I call out." Jake swallowed, like he was fighting nerves as he kept my gaze. "So this is me. Calling out. *Hey. Hello.*"

"Well, thank you." I felt my guard drop an inch and smiled. I couldn't help it. "I don't need a rescue, but I do want you here. I'm glad you're here."

"But . . ." he prompted, indicating that I should fill in the blank.

Now I was beset with my own nerves. "I want to tell you everything. I do."

"But . . ." Jake repeated.

I remembered the fresh anger at Mom that had rolled over me in the waiting room, the anger I'd seen reflected back at me in Theo's eyes. "I guess there's stuff that's coming up that not even I knew about."

"See? This is good," Jake said, his own small smile growing. "This is what we need. You letting me in."

Still, I felt resistance. The same hard center I'd run into when he'd tried to be nice by taking over my kitchen. "But it's not your mess to clean up. It's mine. And it's not over."

"That's the point of a serious, long-term relationship, Robin," Jake said with that mirthless laugh again. "Sharing life stuff. Family stuff."

"Obviously I know that," I said, my own disdain now palpable.

"And you do let people in," he added. "Just not me."

The sharpness of his voice gave me pause. "What do you mean?"

Jake was quiet, considering. "You don't want me to get into this."

"Get into what?" My heart pounded. "Go on. Tell me."

He sighed. "Has anything ever happened between you and Levi?"

My mouth fell open. My stomach dropped, though my mind was blank. "What?"

"There's just something *off* about him and you. Even that first time we met him at that pop-up, remember? He was always looking at you . . ."

Was he joking? He wasn't. "I'm so confused."

"*You're* confused?" Jake asked, sarcastic. "Imagine being your boyfriend. The sheer number of texts between you two. Then this last month before the memorial, you leave early, you come home late."

"Because we're busy!" I said, incredulous.

"No. Because you're into each other. That other day I pulled up after the garage sale? You were practically about to make out."

Heat rushed to my face. I thought of that day, of Levi's face close to mine, the smell of him, the playful shove I'd given him as he rode my bike. "We're *friends*."

"Whatever . . ." Jake put his face in his hands. "Never mind. You two are close. You have to admit that."

"He's known me forever."

"I know. Just forget it. I was just trying to make a point."

"Sure. You want to be part of my family drama. Welcome."

"I wanted to be close to you," Jake snipped. "Sue me."

"Want*ed*?" I emphasized the past tense.

At that, he just looked at me, perhaps unsure of how to answer. Perhaps I had just answered myself.

I felt sick. Weary. At capacity. Soon, I knew, I would feel nothing, and I didn't want to feel nothing. I didn't want to lose him. "God, I wish we weren't doing this right now."

"I know," he said. "I'm sorry." In the light coming from the hospital, he looked genuine. He hesitated, rubbing his hand across his scalp, and seemed to steel himself. "But you can't blame me for speaking up. Something changed between us."

"It doesn't have to."

He gave me a sad smile. "I think it does, actually."

I felt my insides seize up. Jake turned and walked away. This time, I didn't follow him. I stayed for a moment, alone, watching his back.

Gabe had left me standing outside of a hospital, too. Two years ago, now. *I shouldn't have let him go*, I thought to myself. Utter nonsense. I didn't have a choice in the matter, of course. But something chided me. One of my inner voices, perhaps. *You could have done better, and it wouldn't be this way. You could have clung harder.* A breeze snaked down the row of branches lining the parking lot, shivering the leaves. *Take me with you*, I said to Gabe. To no one.

The one thing I want to know about you is . . .
Your acceptable average decibel level.

The next morning, I woke up stiff, curled in a ball, my knees and back aching. Mom lay asleep in her hospital bed. Her slack mouth might have been a scary sight for anyone who didn't know that she always slept that way, so I leaned over her and tried to close it gently so she wouldn't wake up thirsty. Her jaw remained stubbornly open. The good news was that she had been concussed, but not contused. No bleeding in the brain—thank goodness. But even so, her wrist, hip, and leg were shattered at the point of impact. Her limbs now hung suspended from her sleeping body, wrapped in white.

It was the best possible outcome, I supposed, considering what could have happened to a person inside a smashed-up car. We were just glad she would recover. It was hard to celebrate fully, considering I hadn't seen Theo since last night, not to mention that in the wake of the accident, my second chance at love was disappearing, almost gone altogether.

It was a miracle that I had even slept, spending hour after hour staring into the dim room, turning over Jake's accusations, revisiting every moment in the last few months, trying to see what he saw. Jake didn't understand my full history with Levi, I kept telling myself. He had mistaken the unnatural closeness that happens when you grieve someone together for falling in love. All of this I wished I could tell him—if only he would answer my texts with anything beyond *I need some space*, which he'd sent around midnight last night. Then, *Hope your mom's okay.*

"Morning," Nance said behind me.

She had spent the night in a chair, too. I didn't think she would last, but apparently she'd come prepared. She had tucked herself under what looked like a handmade quilt and had a neck pillow around her shoulders, a blindfold now pushed to her forehead, where her curls wilted.

"Want gum?" she asked, extending a package of Trident. "Sugar-free. Like brushing your teeth."

I took a piece. "That's sweet, Nance," I said. "Sweet of you to stay."

"Oh, pish posh," Nance said, stuffing her gum back in her purse. "My BFF's in trouble. This is just what you do."

Voices in the hall. The squeak of the door. I looked up, expecting Jake or Theo, though I hadn't heard from either. Hoping.

Levi, armed with two bursting bags, strode past the blue room divider and into our little corner.

"Hey!" I said, probably too loud. My eyes went to the pack of water poking out of his bag. My mouth was suddenly dry. Why was I nervous?

"Hey." Levi followed my gaze and tossed me a water. "How is she?"

I chugged. "Sleepy," I answered him between gulps.

"There's my favorite!" Nance called, unapologetically flirtatious.

"Long time no see, Nance," Levi said.

Nance and Levi had sprung into action together last night at the memorial, managing the cleanup and break-down. The whole field was now clear, food wrapped and equipment stored, and with Nance's help, Levi had even managed to pick up a change of clothes for Mom and, from the looks of it, provisions. Now, wearing a clean white T-shirt, his brown hair trimmed to the shoulder, he was a vision—and not just because he was holding snacks.

"But really, she's good, considering," I continued. "About to go into surgery. They just have to wait for the swelling to go down."

"Tough break, Marge," Levi said, pulling the blanket gently over her uncovered foot. He set down his bounty on a nearby table. "Man, I remember her dance moves at your reception. She's gonna have to train herself back up."

I let out a small laugh. "She'll be back to disco shape in no time."

We all watched my mother for a moment, still unstirring, her hair in a poofy halo around her sleeping head.

I sighed. "God, this shouldn't be happening."

"Eh, shit happens," Nance said. "This isn't the first scrape Marge has been in. Won't be the last." She folded her blanket, setting her neck pillow neatly on top. "Well, I'm gonna go home and get my own clothes," she said. She lifted a plastic drugstore bag. "There's some treats in here. If she wakes up tell her I'll be back in a jiff."

When Nance was gone, I peeked inside. Nicotine patches, chewing tobacco, and three or four airplane-size bottles of vodka. Oh, and gum. Sugar-free. On one of the bottles, a handwritten note was taped: *Put these with those little cans of tomato juice they give you and you got yourself a Bloody. xo, Nance.*

"Jesus Christ," I said under my breath.

"What is it?" Levi asked.

I held up the vodka with the note taped to it long enough for Levi to read and tossed the lot of it in the trash. Except for the gum.

Levi snorted and collapsed into Nance's chair. "Damn. With friends like these . . ."

"Who needs friends?" I finished, catching his eye as I popped another piece of gum in my mouth.

"Maybe it was supposed to be a joke," Levi offered.

"Well, it's not funny. They took her blood the night of the accident. She's going to get charged with a DWI."

"Oh, my god." Levi sat up in his chair. "I'm so sorry."

"It is what it is," I said, echoing something my dad used to say. "Not looking forward to relaying the news to Theo, I'll tell you that much."

Levi looked around, as if noticing Theo's absence for the first time. "Where is he? He never came back?"

I shrugged. "He isn't taking this very well, Mom being mortal. Maybe he can sense this is the end of an era."

"End of what era?"

The era of pretending twelve packs of Hamm's didn't disappear every night between the two of them. Both of us looking the other way while Mom sampled the product behind the bar. Theo filming Mom's loopy rants for social-media clout.

"Mom's partying days, I guess," I said, putting air quotes around the euphemism.

"You think she has a problem?"

No one had ever asked me that before. No one, not even me, had ever explicitly referred to Mom's drinking as a problem. I was hesitating, searching for the same resistance I'd found when I'd tried to open up to Jake. Levi's gaze was thoughtful, patient, not demanding of an answer. I trusted him, I realized. Not to judge. And to tell me the truth, always, even if my own relationship with that particular concept was dubious. I pointed to Mom, knocked out in bed. "Don't you think this is proof enough?"

"It's not for me to say." Levi held up his hands. "But I support you if you do. I've seen a lot of that in my time in the service industry. Just let me know how I can help."

"Thank you," I said and felt the first small pocket of relief in twelve hours. "I appreciate it more than you know." Then it slipped out. "You're basically all I have right now."

"What do you mean? You and Jake . . ."

I shrugged. "Unclear. He isn't speaking to me."

Levi grimaced. "Why? What's going on?"

I kept my eyes on the hospital tile. "Partly you."

He laughed, incredulous. "Me? What did I do?"

I shook my head. "It's so ridiculous. He actually thinks . . ." I pretended to be interested in a granola bar I'd dug out of one of Levi's tote bags. My heart began to beat harder. "He thinks we have a thing for each other."

"You and me?"

I glanced up at him and nodded.

"Damn." He didn't speak for a moment, running his hands through his hair. When he did speak, his voice was low, quiet. "And what do you think of that?"

"I guess I see why he would go there," I said, slowly. "We are friends. And we've been spending a lot of time together. But I don't think that's the only thing. It's more about him feeling like I wasn't letting him in. Since he can't do anything about that, he found a different target." I gestured lamely in Levi's direction. "But he's way off base, obviously," I added.

"Well, shit." Levi looked conflicted. "What are you going to do?"

"I have no idea," I said.

"Huh," he said and propelled himself off his hospital chair. I watched him as he began to move around the room, picking up the remote for the TV, smelling a clump of flowers Nance had brought for Mom, staring out the window, as if he needed to distract himself, or as if the answer were among the parked cars below.

"Actually," I began. A thought had arrived.

"Please." Levi gestured, magnanimous.

"I do want to show Jake he has a place in my life. But I can only convince him of so much . . ." I wasn't sure if it would work. I wasn't even sure of how I would end the next sentence. "Would you . . . would you be willing to talk to him, make it clear that there's really nothing between us?"

Levi turned from the window. "I don't know if I can do that."

My stomach flipped. I felt my brow furrow. "Why?"

"Can't you guess?"

"No." My mouth was dry again.

"Robin." Levi's smile was weary, but tender. He took a step toward me.

"What's that look?" I tried to swallow, failed.

"I can't convince Jake of anything. Because the truth is . . . I do have a thing for you. One thousand percent, I have a thing for you."

My first instinct was to smack him, but I'd never hit anyone in my life, and I wasn't going to start now, especially not in front of my ailing mother.

Instead, I said, "You do?"

"I do. And it feels . . ." He looked at his feet and then back at me. "Really fucking good to say it."

My second instinct was to run. As fast and as far away as my stiff joints would carry me. "And what about how I feel?"

He looked panicked. "How *do* you feel?"

"I'm not sure what to call it, but the words that come to mind are *what the fuck*."

He ran his hands through his hair again. "Fuck. Okay. That makes sense."

Jake had been right. I couldn't believe it. My brain was still struggling to keep up. For a *year*, I'd been naively lying on Levi's futon, petting his dog, running around with him in the Cities, having a grand old time. Meanwhile he'd been keeping this huge secret, this part of himself hidden from me. "So you've been harboring . . . feelings."

"I tried not to." His voice became low and gravelly, like it did when he was getting emotional. "I didn't want to feel this way. I didn't want anything to happen, Robin. Truly."

Levi. Looking at me like that. I had to look away. "Maybe you're confused."

"I am, but not about this." He let out a small laugh of disbelief. "It was just this door that always stayed open in the back of my mind."

"Always?" My heart pounded. "How long has this been going on?"

He scratched his forehead, calculating. "Uh, since I met you and you fell in love with my best friend. Ha," he added weakly.

The hospital-room air seemed to press on my ears, my skin. I didn't think my body could take another shock. And yet the words came, without my command. *"In first year?"*

Levi nodded slowly, his eyes glazing. "I remember the exact day. I remember the morning. You got out of Gabe's twin bed, still in your winter coat, and you were all bleary-eyed and beautiful, and you looked like you had the world on your shoulders, and all I wanted was to lift it off for you."

I tried to remember where Levi was that day, a day I had revisited so many times, but only within the little snow globe of Gabe's bed, Gabe's arms. "We met each other for, like, two seconds, Levi."

"We had breakfast," Levi corrected.

"I can't believe you remember that." But now I could, too. I could picture young Levi, tattoo-less with his waves in a messy shag, the majority of his bulk still baby fat. While Gabe and I picked at our biscuits, making eyes at each other, he had been scarfing down his food, spilling bits on his Black Sabbath T-shirt, headphones blaring.

"But you were listening to your music," I argued, as if I could reverse this madness by pointing out continuity errors.

"Yeah, but I was super curious about you," Levi went on. "Gabe came back, and you guys were dating, and I grilled him about you. Grilled him," Levi repeated. "He actually got kind of pissy. Thought I was going to make a move."

Suddenly, I bristled. *Gabe.* What would he think of this? Our perfect little trio, now not so simple. Levi looking at me from onstage while Gabe and I cheered him on at his shows. Levi watching us as we jogged down the courthouse steps at our wedding, trailed by bubbles. Levi and I racing to the car, Levi and I laughing over hummus and carrots, Levi and I grinning at each other onstage last night at the benefit. All of it was twisted now, distorted. Bile rose in my throat. It occurred to me that everything he had done for me this year—was doing for me now—he might have been angling for something else. The thought churned my stomach.

"Are you okay?" he asked, watching me.

My eyes landed on the faded permanent-marker checklist he'd written on his hand, the bags he'd brought, the change of clothes for Mom. "So when you asked me to *help* with the memorial . . ." I looked up at him, holding up air quotes ". . . and you *helped* me with the dating app . . ."

"We were just helping each other, that's it," he rushed to assure me. "I was really trying hard with the profile, too. For Gabe. I tried to sort of channel him, when I was writing those things about you . . ."

My ears began to ring. I held up my hands. "Wait, stop. You mean Bubbl? The—the prompts?"

"Yeah." Levi cringed. "Those weren't Gabe. Those were me."

"He didn't—*you* wrote those? You wrote the—?"

"Yeah," Levi said, taking a deep, shaky breath. "The letter was his, but I set up Bubbl. Gabe gave me a million photographs to choose from.

I probably wasn't supposed to write that much, but I was kind of on a roll . . ." He let out a nervous laugh.

My breath was caught in my chest. "Why didn't you tell me?"

"Gabe asked me not to," Levi said. "I was going to tell you the other day at the garage sale, but you didn't seem to . . . I decided to cut my losses."

The floor began to turn. All those nights I'd pored over the profile to lose myself in Gabe's words, I was actually losing myself in Levi. Levi? I supposed it made a kind of twisted sense, now that I knew how he felt. How he'd always felt. "They were so . . ." I said faintly, almost to myself. "They were accurate."

"I did my best," Levi said with a bit of pride. "I didn't know if you'd use them, but I wanted to make you laugh."

I tried to keep my voice steady as nausea rose again in my throat. "Did Gabe know?"

"Know what?"

"How you *felt*, Levi!" I yelled. Mom stirred in her bed. I lowered my voice as I continued. "How would he feel about you taking on this little project if he knew how much you wanted to bone his wife?"

I saw a flush rise above the collar of his T-shirt. "God, Robin, no. And I don't want to *bone* you. I mean—" he coughed a little "—I am, like, attracted to you, but I wasn't trying to undermine . . . I'm still trying to make sense of it myself."

The smell of the hospital, the taste of it, was snaking through my nose and mouth. I remembered holding Gabe's hand in a room like this, trying to find the familiar weight, feeling too many bones. Levi had been there from time to time. Levi had rested a hand on my back. Tears rose in my eyes. "And what about while he was *dying*?"

Levi looked as disgusted as I felt. "Good god. *No*."

I wanted to wash off the memory of him sitting with me as we watched Gabe sleep those gray afternoons, the feeling of his comforting touch. "I know what it's like to love someone. You can't just turn those things off."

"*No*," he repeated. Levi looked as if he was about to cry, too. "I shouldn't have said anything. I would never . . . Gabe was like my brother. You know that."

"How am I supposed to believe you?"

"You have to trust me. I just felt things, sometimes, when I looked at you. Nothing more." If it wasn't for the bass in his voice, the breadth of his presence, he would sound like a boy with a crush.

I couldn't look at him anymore. "Just go."

He turned to leave. I kept my eyes on Mom, but I could sense he was still here, hesitating.

"The door," he said.

"What?"

"Being in love with you. I told you it was like a door cracked open. It swung closed when Gabe was sick, and now it fell open again." I heard him take a breath. "That's the only way I can say it."

I said nothing. His footsteps faded down the hall.

Soon after he'd left, Mom stirred again, turning her head slightly, her mouth still open. I brought her cup and straw to her lips in case she wanted to drink, but she didn't open her eyes. Selfishly I wished she would. I wished she would wake up well and whole, not just for her own sake but for mine. I wished she was here to tell me everything was going to be okay. To hold me, so I didn't have to hold myself.

The door to the room, I noticed, Levi had left propped. I got up to shove it shut.

I know the best spot in town for . . .

Pizza. It also happens to have the cheapest gas prices in town!

That afternoon, Jake and I had arranged—in a series of brisk texts—that I would take a cab to his place to retrieve my things while he was at work. Once I'd picked out my clothes from his drawers and retrieved my toothbrush, there wouldn't be too many more traces of me left to erase. We'd talked about framing a photo of us next to all his others on the wall, but we'd never gotten around to it. Was this really the end? I found I couldn't let it go, perhaps because I couldn't grasp what had happened in the first place. I made sure to give Tiger one more scratch under the chin, in case it was the last, and as I left my key under the mat, I swallowed a lump in my throat. I knew I would have to reckon with Jake at some point—I had learned too much about how long it took to say goodbye, if this really was goodbye. But I had to put Mom first.

Now, I was jogging through battering rain in the hospital parking lot, my change of clothes rendered useless, my overnight bag getting soaked in my arms.

Since I'd told Levi to leave that morning, I'd composed a hundred messages, ninety-nine percent of them angry. The remaining drafts were just a long line of question marks. But I wasn't sure I wanted to know the answers. I was afraid of more betrayal, of encouraging him any more than I already had, of replacing the vision I'd cherished of Gabe and me, our lives perfect and boring and wrapped up in each other, Levi on the periphery. That was what I knew. Now I knew so little. The only certain thing was that I was closer than ever to losing Levi as a friend. I may have already lost him. No, more like he had lost me.

As I approached Mom's hospital room, I heard familiar voices. Nance, Mom, and—with a hint of relief—Theo. But when I reached the doorway, I paused. My eyes went straight to three plastic cups on Mom's food tray, filled almost to the brim with red liquid. Tomato juice. And the small bottle Theo was tucking into his pocket appeared suspiciously like one of Nance's treats I'd thrown away.

"Come on in, Warden," Nance called. Nance and Mom had taken to calling me Warden since I'd prevented Nance from wheeling Mom out for a smoke.

But I stayed at the threshold, dripping. "What is that?"

"What does it look like?" Theo asked.

"Are you drinking?" I asked. I strode toward them, dropping my bag, picking up the cup in front of Mom. The smell of vodka stung my nostrils. "You have got to be fucking *kidding* me. She is in the hospital. She is on *pain medication*. You cannot mix that with alcohol."

"Oh, psh," Mom said from her pillow. "It's basically aspirin."

Theo and Nance exchanged a glance, giggling. I took the cup from Mom's tray and looked around for somewhere to pour it out.

Mom made a sound of protest. "What, you think I'm gonna drive, Robbie? Where am I gonna go?" She gestured for the cup. "Come on. Relax."

"Don't you dare," I told her, my pulse pounding in my chest, my ears.

She huffed, taken aback at my tone like I was a teenager, sassing her. "Don't I dare what?"

"Did you tell them who came by earlier?" I spat, searching for the call button in Mom's sheets. "Does Theo know?"

Mom sighed and looked at Theo. "They got me. DWI. As if I ain't already punished enough."

"Boo," Theo said, sipping his Bloody Mary.

"Eh, who hasn't gotten a DWI?" Nance muttered, waving a casual hand.

"Most people. Most people do not drink and drive," I found myself saying, half to them, half to myself. "Maybe I should just let you get another one and go to frickin' jail. Maybe that's what needs to happen."

Theo rolled his eyes. "So dramatic."

"That goes for you, too!" I said, feeling my voice crack as it rose in volume. "You're feeding her Bloodies *two hours* after a police officer just dropped off a ticket. This should be a goddamn wake-up call. For all of us."

"This generation," Nance muttered.

Mom scoffed. "Don't I know it, Nance. Everything's so black-and-white."

"Am I crazy?" I looked at the three of them, my hands holding my throbbing temples. I began to count on my fingers. "Misdemeanor. Concussion. Car destroyed. Clearly alcohol is a problem, and we are making it worse. You two most of all."

"Geez Louise, we're hardly closing down the bar here, Robbie. It's one drink."

Nance let out a chuckle. "If giving your friend a pick-me-up is a crime, lock me up."

I tried to speak slowly through my frustration. "I'm just saying booze is the last thing she needs right now. The opposite."

"What, you want to cart Mom off to rehab for one DWI?" Theo asked, looking skeptical. "You'd have to bring along half the town of frickin' Brokenridge, then."

Nance snorted. "Hell, they should just turn the Red Lyon into a Betty Ford." She stood and stretched, looking around for her purse.

"I didn't say rehab," I said, but I should have. I began to get angrier. At myself, at them, at everyone. I pointed at Theo's cup. "Just get that shit out of here."

Theo looked at Mom. "What do you say, Mom? You want us to get out of your hair?"

"I'm gonna use the ladies'," Nance muttered on her way past me. "Too much ruckus for me."

"But you come right back," Mom called to Nance as she left the room. "None of us are going anywhere, and neither are the drinks. You took mine away, okay, Robbie? Happy? Let them be. They're not doing any harm."

"They shouldn't be drinking around you. I'm going to call the nurse in here . . ." I finally found the call button and held it up. "And they'll agree with me. They might even kick you both out."

"You can't just barge in here telling everyone what to do," Mom said, trying to sit up. She winced in pain.

"Robin . . ." Theo tried a gentle approach. "Why don't we stop talking about kicking people out and focus on making Mom feel better?"

"Theo, you're not dumb." I lifted the cup in my hand, spilling a bit of tomato juice. "You know this is bad. We can't just have a party and let her walk out of here with a bandage on her head like, *Oopsie daisy, had a bad night out!*"

"But that's exactly what happened!" Mom cried. "For chrissakes!"

"It's not just one night," I said to Mom. "It's not just one drink. You *know* that."

"Excuse me." Theo's voice was stiff with anger. "Do not shame her. I know you expect everyone to be perfect like you—" I tried to contradict this, but Theo went on, talking over me "—but people are allowed to make mistakes. This could have happened to any of us."

"But it didn't," I said. "Because we know our limits. Mom doesn't."

"Mom is an adult," Theo snapped.

"You know Robbie just likes to run things," Mom said to Theo. "That's what she does at the restaurant, too—"

"The restaurant has nothing to do with this!" Rage roiled in my gut, in my throat, behind my eyes. "Mom, you ran drunk into a wall on the highway. You could have killed yourself, you could have killed someone else. You should be worried about what's going to happen next. Maybe it will be a bad liver! Maybe it will be a heart attack, like Dad! Maybe—" I stopped to catch my breath, but I found I couldn't finish.

The two of them stared, shocked.

Mom was the first to turn her head away, as if she couldn't bear to look at me. "Leave your dad out of this."

Theo was still considering me. Something passed between us, the silent understanding we used to share more often. For a moment, I thought he was finally hearing me, that he was seeing what I was seeing.

But he sighed, instead. "I don't think you should be here right now, Robin. Mom needs to be around good energy. She needs people who love and support her. For who she is," he added, taking Mom's hand. "Not who you want her to be. Okay?"

It was the two of them against the world, as always. There was my family, and there was me.

"I do love her, T." I felt my voice shake, with anger or hurt, I wasn't sure which. "I love her as much as you do. That's why I have to tell her the truth."

"Oh, fuck off," Theo said, exasperated.

"Language," Mom said.

It was this, this dismissal, that sent me over the edge. After a lifetime of protecting him, entertaining him, caring for him like my own child, I couldn't believe who I was becoming in my brother's eyes. An annoying inconvenience. A villain. Fine. If he wanted to leave me alone in this, he could fend for himself, too.

"Okay, then," I said, my voice lifting over my pulse. "I'll fuck off." I pointed to the phone in Theo's hand. "We'll start with the phone. Find a way to pay your own bill."

Theo still glared coldly. But a slight panic rose behind his blue eyes. "That's not what I meant, Robin," he said.

I couldn't believe what I had just said—what I was daring to do—but I couldn't stand the hypocrisy. The entitlement. "I think I'm gonna go ahead and stop your rent payments for the semester, too."

"Come on, Robin." He stood. His defiance had been replaced by pure fear. By hurt. "You're really going to do this now?"

"Why not now?" I said, though in truth I knew it was a horrible time. My hurt felt bigger than anything else in that moment, bigger than my sympathy, which had finally run dry. "I don't want to enable an enabler."

"Excuse me?"

"You want to let Mom die, fine," I said. "You're not going to do it on my dime."

"But what am I supposed to do?" Theo asked me.

"You can stay with Jay or Mom, I guess," I said. All I'd ever wanted to do was help, but my help wasn't wanted. So I didn't really have much use in Theo's life, did I? That was what the anger was telling me. The anger was loud, and I needed something to hold on to, to tell me what to do. I listened. "Figure something out. It only makes sense, right? I let Mom handle her shit, and I let you handle yours."

I realized I was still holding Mom's half-spilled drink in my hand. I threw it in the trash, hoping this time it would stay there. My phone was vibrating in my pocket. Grateful for a distraction, I began to walk out of the room. Where, I didn't know.

"Robin!" Mom called. "You can't just leave him out to dry!"

"What is wrong with you?" I heard Theo ask me.

I paused at the door. "You should be asking yourselves that."

I was determined not to look back at them as I turned down the hall, Theo's face falling in my periphery. I didn't want to see how young and scared he looked. I had to stay mad, to take a heated pleasure at my small victory, because any alternative would break me. At the end of the day, I was in the right. Sure, Theo didn't like my controlling, judgmental hovering—unless, of course, it benefitted him.

But any other time I'd thought about cutting Theo off—or confronting Mom about her drinking—I had wanted to be cool and collected, to have a plan, to be certain. Instead, I'd screamed my head off so loud they couldn't understand what I'd said. Refused to understand. Now, there was only uncertainty everywhere I turned. An invisible fog that crept out of the dark rooms along the corridor, blanketing my thoughts, disorienting me. And all the while, I couldn't shake the image of Mom. Mom, frail and alone in her hospital bed. Mom's tiny hands with the dishwashing wrinkles and the perfect cuticles. And now, the only person here who could help me save her I had just pushed away. Maybe for good.

The missed call was Manuel Arenas, my Bubbl date turned Realtor. This was a surprise. According to the timeline he'd given me, they had only just finished renovations. I hoped nothing had gone wrong.

Outside, under an awning, I slowed my racing heart to the sound of the rain and called him back.

"Hi there," Manuel picked up in his pleasantly smooth voice. "I have good news."

"Thank god," I said. I could use some of that.

An hour later, I rode along the driveway in Manuel's Jeep, Manuel in his usual crisp dress shirt and pressed pants, me in my still-damp clothes. We could have exchanged the paperwork remotely, Manuel had said on the way over, but he figured I'd want to say goodbye.

But as we pulled up to the house, it seemed that whatever I could say goodbye to might have already left. It was almost unrecognizable. The farmhouse's faded, chipped white paint had transformed into bluish gray with white trim. New glittering rocks composed the gravel driveway. The front door was now coral. Porch rocking chairs in chartreuse.

Inside, Gabe's maroon walls had become a quiet sea blue. Track lighting along the ceilings. A bowl of lemons on the kitchen island.

Out back, they'd added a row of firs to the tree line, a living fence that perfumed the air with pine. The barn had been razed, and on the new dirt, they'd added more raised beds and cleaned up the old ones of weeds, attached a rope swing to one of the drooping oak branches, planted colorful patches of wildflowers.

"What do you think?" Manuel asked as we stood side by side, watching the dwindling rain sprinkle the kitchen window.

"I'm speechless," I said.

"The new owners feel the same way. Two ladies from Grand Marais who just adopted their first child."

"There's going to be a kid in here?" For some reason, I had tears in my eyes at the thought.

Manuel put his hand on my shoulder. "I'm sure they're going to be really happy."

I looked back out at the yard. "I'm sure they are."

"So I have the final purchase agreement here when you're ready," Manuel said behind me, laying out the paperwork on the counter. "I believe I mentioned this in the car, but we're looking at five thousand over asking, all cash, which is really pretty generous."

"No, that's great," I said, turning to join him, wiping my tears. "I don't know why I'm getting so emotional."

"I think I do," Manuel said, his dark eyes sympathetic over his gap-toothed smile. "I google all my clients," he added with an apologetic wince. "And my dates."

I had to laugh, which I immediately regretted, since the action seemed to let loose a bevy of snot. Manuel handed me a tissue from a nearby box. I'd never thought to put tissues around the house. Gabe and I had always just used toilet paper.

"So you know this is the former home of everyone's favorite mayor," I said, blowing my nose.

"And his widow, apparently a badass makeup artist," Manuel said, his eyebrows raised, impressed.

"Ha!" I weathered a pang of bittersweetness at the mention of my hobby. Even through everything else going on, I had missed it. My colors, my tools, my fake blood. "Thanks."

"So," he said, straightening one of the neat, crisp sheets in the row of documents. "You'll just sign everywhere you see a sticky tab."

"Ah, yes. The Assorted Color *Sign Here* Flag Set. I'm familiar."

I picked up the pen. But as I poised it over the first dotted line, I couldn't bring myself to put tip to paper.

Another wave had suddenly reared up but seemed to hold at the crest, choking me. For some reason I was thinking of those December mornings my first year of college after Dad died. I remembered watching Mom as she put on eye shadow before going in to the restaurant. It had been mere days, but she was going back. Was she sure? I had asked. Was she sure she shouldn't take some time off? *Oh, I'll be all right,* Mom had said, brushing blue across her eyelids. Aqua blue. Sea blue. That's around when she had started carrying the travel mug with her everywhere.

Maybe I had been too harsh. Maybe I shouldn't have brought up my dad. I'd never spoken to my mother like that before, or to Theo. To anyone, for that matter. Perhaps that was why Gabe and I had said some of the worst things we'd ever said toward the end. There was something about a loved one fighting for their life that made you want to cut to the core of things, no matter what bombs you dropped along the way.

"Everything okay?" Manuel asked, watching me.

"Yeah, yeah. Sorry," I pushed out, my tears returning as I signed next to the sticky note. Another lie. Every day the same white lie, like breathing. *I'm fine*. "I'm okay."

But I wasn't okay. Nobody had ever taught me how to say it. Only how to bear it and move on.

A gentle hand on my back. Somehow I had let go of the pen.

Somehow I was on the floor, where Gabe had liked to slide around in his socks like a kid. Where I'd sat among the spoiling funeral food that couldn't fit in the fridge.

I had thought the raw slap of grief still only hurt at certain times of day, certain angles of light, only if I let it. I thought I had put that time away, turning up the TV volume so I couldn't hear it echoing in my head. Not true. The river of lonely days I had almost drowned in was still inside me. I was still swimming.

Manuel bent, and soon he was fully sitting next to me, cross-legged, our backs against the cabinets of the island.

"You're going to ruin your beautiful pants," I said between stuttering sobs.

"Don't worry about the pants," he said.

We sat there like that for some time as the crying wracked me.

"I'm sorry," I said again to Manuel when my breath had mellowed.

"Nothing to be sorry about," he said, frowning thoughtfully as he found the words. "Your first house with your late husband. It's a huge thing. I can tell the couple we need more time."

"No, I'm going to sign," I told him. "I had a really hard day, and then signing this got me thinking—I have nowhere to go."

The reality of this hit me in the gut. I was family-less. Boyfriend-less. Purposeless. I couldn't go back to Jake's. After today, I didn't want to go back to my mom's, where Theo was likely going to stay. A week ago, I would've asked Levi if I could crash on his couch, but now our whole history was twisted, alien. I had no one.

The thought of it would set off another wave of tears if I let it. But

I didn't want to cry. I just wanted to sit here for a moment more on the floor. With my Realtor, a kind, sane person who barely knew me.

"You'd mentioned you were staying with your boyfriend?" Manuel said, sounding concerned.

I shook my head. "Not anymore."

Manuel straightened briefly, returning after a moment with the tissue box. "Well, like I said, you've got five thousand over asking."

"What do you mean?"

"Moving money. Play-around money. Go exploring." He smiled. "I'm kind of envious, actually."

"Envious?" I snorted. I lifted my hands, clutching crumpled tissue, drawing his attention to the fact that I was wearing sweats covered in snot, sitting on a kitchen floor that now no longer belonged to me. "Why the hell would you be envious?"

"Because you're about to have an adventure," he said easily, lightly. Much more easily and lightly than I would have if I were talking to a deranged woman, gathering her used Kleenexes into a pile.

"Manuel, I have no car. No partner. No family. In the last week, I have screwed up things with everyone—almost everyone—important to me. This is not an adventure I want to be on."

"Then, what adventure *do* you want to go on?" he said, hoisting himself up to standing to dispose of the tissues. "Go on that one, instead."

"I can't," I said, folding my knees into my chest. "My mom—"

"She'll get better," he said.

"No, but she's got substance issues, so I need to get her into some sort of program," I explained, resting my head on my knees. "And her restaurant has been closed for a while now, so we're not going to be in a good spot. Probably going to have to look into some loans. My brother's struggling, too. He doesn't know what he wants to do in life, and I'm trying to help him while he figures it out, but I went about it all the wrong way, and I'm worried I've made everything worse."

My words trailed off into the dark, muffled space between my knees. At the list of my obligations, I felt a headache coming on. The crying, I'm sure, hadn't helped.

"Ah," I could hear Manuel say as he moved around me. "You're a glue guy."

I looked up from my sweats-lined cave. "A glue who?"

He had found a glass somewhere—probably stored in a cabinet for show, because it definitely wasn't mine—and now he had his hand under the flow of tap water, waiting for the right temperature. "A glue guy," he went on. "Or *gal* or *lady* or *person*. Whatever. In soccer—"

"Just a heads-up, I know nothing about soccer."

"You should change that."

"You're sports-shaming me?" I cocked my head. "Is this why you're still single?"

Manuel rolled his eyes at the joke. "A glue player is talented, but they don't necessarily get all of the goals and assists and accolades. You don't see them light up the stats sheet, but they're super influential on the field. They're givers, important to the team's chemistry."

"Sounds made-up," I said. "Sounds like an excuse for not scoring points."

Manuel handed me the glass of water. "It's not made-up. I could name seven glue players right now. Lindsey Horan, Lyon FC. Richard Dixon, here in the US—"

"All right, all right. So you're saying I'm a glue person. Which means what, outside of soccer?" I began to gulp as much water down as I could.

"It means that your thing is making sure everyone else does their thing."

I went to the sink and poured myself another glass. "I think I see what you're saying. Like, my family are the superstars, but I'm the one running around on the field, kicking them the ball?"

"Bingo," Manuel said. "But a glue player can also score in a clutch. And you're not letting yourself score—"

"Whoa, whoa, whoa." I put up a hand as I swallowed my latest gulp of water. "I have had plenty of my own wins," I explained to Manuel. "I actually had a pretty great year."

Manuel squinted at me, a skeptical smile rising on his face. "You have? May I remind you that you were just weeping in a ball on the floor?"

I was about to argue, but I found I couldn't go back to that kind of white lie.

"I mean, does it matter, though?" I said aloud. I thought of Nance's refrain: *That's just what you do.* "Isn't that what family is for? Taking care of each other? How am I supposed to focus on my own—my own *goals* when they need my help?"

Manuel sighed, his smile wary. "This is none of my business . . ." he said, hedging.

"No, please," I said. "Tell me."

"If your mom's in the hospital—because of some sort of substance-related thing, you said?" He paused for a moment, in case I didn't want to go there. I motioned for him to continue. "And your relationship is on the rocks, and your brother's not doing well, either . . ."

He paused, took a breath, measuring the moment. Trying, it seemed, to be sensitive. It sounded so different, everything terrible collected like that. Connected. But I think I was beginning to see his point.

"You're saying that whatever I'm doing isn't working."

It hit me like a ton of bricks. All of my careful planning. My hours spent at Mom's side. My money in Theo's bank account. My new system for the restaurant. I thought I had it figured out, and it was only a matter of them seeing things my way. But my way had us lost. Broken.

"But how do I help them?" I asked Manuel, desperate. "What other way is there?"

"I don't really know," Manuel said, his face scrunched in concentration as he removed a spot from the counter. "It's probably going to be a learning process. But I know that if you live your life for other people, in the end there will be nothing left of you. Trust me."

"Why, did something like this happen to you?"

"It happened to my family." He let up on the smudge for a second, retrieving a Kleenex before returning to it with greater vigor. "My sister is a glue player, too. I mean, she would probably hate to hear me call her that, but let's just say the lesson she had to learn was that love should connect you to people, not chain you to them." He smiled to himself with satisfaction at the newly clean spot and looked up at me. "If you need a therapist, my family and I had a really good one."

"Ha. We're not there yet, but hopefully someday." I found his eyes, grateful. "Thank you for sharing that. Really."

He gave a courteous nod and put a hand next to the paperwork. "So. What do we think? Do you still need some time?"

I took a deep breath, picked up the pen, and began to sign away the house, thinking about what he'd said about love. About chains.

With each signature, my limbs felt less heavy. Their lightness would take some getting used to.

"Thank you again, for everything," I said to Manuel, who was locking up the front door. I opened my arms. "Can I hug you?"

"Please do."

"Oh, god," I muttered, my chin on his shoulder.

"What?"

We broke apart. "What the hell am I going to do now?"

At first Manuel shrugged good-naturedly, but as we reached the Jeep, he found an answer. "You know what? If I were you, I'd probably drop everything and go to Chandigarh, India. The pinnacle of a progressive city. Practically the mold for midcentury modern style. But that's just me."

I thought of what I would drop everything to do. I thought of a brightly lit row of mirrors and every color from the muddiest brown to alien green to the bloodiest red. I thought of monsters.

As we watched the house disappear behind the line of trees on the winding driveway, I rolled down the window to smell the pines one last time. I had to find a new way to love my people here. To love myself. And unless I wanted to permanently damage my spine on shoved-together hospital chairs, I had to find a new place to sleep tonight.

My unusual skills include . . .

Deceptive amounts of upper-body strength. Tying my hair into a knot. Hiding in group photographs.

The next morning, I checked out of my hotel, greeted the nurses at the reception desk, and crept back into Mom's hospital room. My head felt clear, if a little raw. Like the world had lost a layer. Here, the blinds were drawn and the lights were off, dimming the sunny skies outside.

"Who is that?" Mom muttered.

I was about to answer her when I saw a curly-headed form stretched out on one of the chairs next to her bed. "It's Robin," Theo said.

"Hey," I whispered to Theo. "Can we talk?"

"You don't have to whisper," he said in his normal voice. "We're both awake. She just had a headache."

I sat in the second chair, looking back and forth at the two of them. Where could I begin? I had so much to say, so much about the last few years—about our lives—that seemed to shape-shift under this new way of thinking, under this broad, unruly definition of love. And I loved them so much, I realized. That was all I felt, all I wanted to feel. Connections, not chains.

"So what have you been up to?" I threw out to Theo.

"A lot," he said simply. Then he sighed and went on. "I'm, like, destroyed right now."

My heart began to beat with a mix of annoyance and concern, though I wasn't surprised. "Are you okay?"

He sat forward in his chair, putting his head in his hands. I could hear his voice break as he said, "I'm not."

"Me neither," I said, my own voice trembling. The waterworks were on full blast today. But let them come, I thought. I felt steady enough to be the soft one. I didn't have to be strong. I could show him that I was ready to be his big sister again, and nothing more. Not his life coach. Not his bank. Not his playmaker. "Theo, I just want to say—"

"No," he said, lifting his face to look at me. "You're always the first one to say sorry, and that's not what this is, okay?"

"Okay," I said.

In the gray light of the room, he looked frustrated, but it didn't seem to be aimed at me. He looked tired but composed.

"Mom, you can hear this, too," Theo said.

"Sure, sweets," Mom said from her spot on the bed, a slight wheeze in her words. She might have been falling back asleep.

"After we fought the other night," Theo began, gaining some composure, "I texted Jay to pick me up and he said he would, but he didn't come for hours, and I was just, like, standing there under a fucking streetlight in the middle of the night, waiting. And I was so pissed at myself for running away. For not going back inside. For not being able to handle this. But, like, you didn't come get me, either—"

"I looked for you," I interrupted.

"No, that's not what I'm saying." He put his hand on Mom's duvet. "It's good that you didn't find me. But I wanted you to. I expected you to. Because, like, that's your job. You're the one who saves me. You're the one who apologizes. You're the one who pays, who picks up after my mistakes . . . And I'm realizing I'm pissed at you for that."

We were all quiet then, though I could tell he had more to say. It would take all my patience to not try and say it for him. I wouldn't do it, though. Not today.

"But I realized I was also so pissed at you for throwing me out on my own. For *not* finding me. I was like, where is she? She's supposed to be the one to make everything okay."

"I know. But I can't do that, can I?"

"No."

My heart ached to hear that, but it was a good ache. It made what I'd realized with Manuel even more true. The ache of holding him in my ten-year-old arms, rocking him back to sleep. Those nights of peanut-butter crackers at the table. Taking all the treasured objects he'd found outside, moving them to a safe place. That was all over now.

"I only ever wanted to make things better for you."

He nodded, his eyes glowing wet in the dim light. "And I haven't told you enough how grateful I was—how grateful I am. For the money, for putting up with my shit. For keeping my nose clean. Sorry. Gross." We both laughed a bit as he wiped his nose.

"It's okay," I said. "I'm gross, too."

"I had a lot of time to think," Theo continued. "And drink. And ask my friends to fucking pay for my vodka sodas. Anyway. My conclusion is you probably should have cut me off earlier. But we can't go back, so now I think the best way to say thank-you to you—to say sorry—is to actually get my shit together."

He didn't look ready to get his shit together. He looked haggard, in need of a shower and a haircut. But weren't we all. And this was just the start.

"I'm so happy to hear that," I said. An earlier version of me—perhaps even yesterday's version—would have stood up right then and there, found a notebook, and asked him what was next. But that wasn't my job anymore. "Anything I can do, you let me know."

"I will."

"And if I can't do it for you," I said, "I'll tell you. I won't just bottle it up. We need to talk to each other more."

"We do," he said.

We smiled at each other.

"Listen to you two. My babies," Mom said, reaching for the two of us with her good arm.

Theo draped himself over her. "We're so glad you're gonna be okay," he said, his face buried in her pillow. I leaned over next to him, patting her shoulder gently.

"I am," she said. "We're all gonna be fine."

But as the light switched on—a nurse had come to check in on her—her face revealed a vulnerability I hadn't seen since she'd arrived, since right after Dad died. She looked lost. Scared.

I sat back in my chair, my heart and brain fighting. One part of me wanted to keep testing my new philosophy. Do nothing. Just be there. I couldn't do everything for Theo, and I couldn't do everything for Mom. Maybe I had nothing to offer but comfort. But my other inner voices were still loud. *This was it*, they seemed to say. Comfort was merely *fine*. Comfort would be a lie.

"I don't know about that," I said. Mom's eyes met mine. "I mean, maybe we are okay, but we have some work to do." Theo looked at me, confused and wary, but I went on. "I think we need to keep talking about your accident."

"What about it, hon?" she asked, her tone weary.

I swallowed, steeling myself to say what I couldn't say the first time around. To say what I'd never been able to say. "You're an alcoholic."

She huffed, her brows lifting as if I had hit her. She seemed to look to Theo for support, but he just sat back in his chair, biting his lip. I was tempted to make an appeal to Theo, too, but I resisted. He could make his own judgments. The nurse who was taking Mom's blood pressure cleared her throat slightly, wrapped up her instrument, and left.

"I am going to say this," I said, keeping my eyes on Mom's. "And then, I'll leave it up to you. I'm trying—I'm going to try not to be up in your business."

"Ha!" Mom's shock briefly broke into an affectionate smile. "Yeah, right."

"You can dismiss me, or pretend to be outraged, or tell me you'll be fine, but I'm not going to budge. Not once have I ever dared to tell you to stop. But now I am." I took a deep breath. "Stop drinking. Save your life. If you want my help—or Theo's help—we're here."

"Okay, now you stop," she said, sharp, imperious, like I was ten again and she was tired of my whining. "You wait. Let me think."

She closed her eyes, breathing through her nostrils as if she were soldiering on under a wave of pain.

Mom looked at both of us in turn. "I hear what you're saying, I do," she said. "But those people and their programs, with their prayers and chanting . . . That's not who I am, you know that. I'm just living my life. And right now I'm tired, and you won't let me smoke my cigs, and my headache is back. Of course I wasn't gonna have more than one with my pain meds. I'll cut down, all right? I promise I'm gonna cut down."

My hands were shaking from adrenaline. "I don't think that's how it works. Either you acknowledge you have a problem and you want to get help, or I'm going to—I don't know what I'm going to do. But I do know I love you, and I'm not going to watch you die."

Next to me, Theo sighed. "I think you gotta go to AA, Ma."

We both glanced at him in surprise. I nodded once, in thanks. He returned it.

Mom frowned, her lips shivering, her eyes filling. The fear was back on her face. She couldn't seem to bring herself to look at either of us, so she looked at the ceiling, tears slowly rolling down her cheeks. Soon, however, her free hand moved on the bed, searching. We both took it.

"Well, if you really think so," she said in that un-Mom-like whisper.

Theo looked at me. "We do," he said. "It's not gonna be fun anymore, anyway. I'll be all scared for you. Robin's gonna be all worried all the time."

"What else is new?" Mom said with a weak chuckle.

I found myself laughing along with the two of them.

"Don't waste the Hamm's in the downstairs fridge, then," Mom said. "Give 'em to Nance or something. Don't pour 'em down the toilet."

"Sure, Ma," Theo said. "We'll get rid of it for you."

"If that's what it takes," she said, sniffing. She was beginning to look more like herself. "There's a few of those folks that stop in the River, I'm pretty sure. Nance knows which ones."

"It's supposed to be anonymous," I said, unable to hide a smile.

"Not in Brokenridge, sweetie." She winked at me. "I heard they have good coffee."

My controversial take . . .

You only really fall in love once, and I had my turn. Prove me wrong.

A few weeks later, Jake and I met for coffee in Pole City. After I had apologized again for pushing him away, we had agreed that we were in different phases in our lives. He was ready to lock in place, he said, and we both had thought I was, too. We had both hoped I could fit into his life, but for different reasons: him, because he wanted a partner; me, because I wasn't fully ready to bring him into mine. As much as I wanted to move on, I'd told Jake, I still had parts of myself I'd neglected, wounds that needed attention long before he came along. Before I could run fully into the next life with anyone, I had more growing to do in this one. More growing in another direction.

It took some time getting used to, but I had accepted it. I would never return to my place next to him in his comfortable bed, greeting Tiger with chin scratches. I could not be the girlfriend I'd wanted to be, traipsing across the countryside next to him and his friends. In fact, I didn't know if I wanted to be a girlfriend at all. I had been a loving partner once, and as much as I wanted to re-create that, I couldn't do it right away. I was still mourning its loss.

Since I'd retrieved all of my stuff from Jake's town house, I didn't have the heart to unpack. Mom had given my childhood room over to storage, and Theo was back, so I was sleeping on the couch, digging out toiletries and clothes when necessary, bickering with Mom over small things. In her newfound postsurgery sobriety, she was up at odd hours, wheeling herself around the house in her casts, making tea, smoking in the backyard, watching *Jeopardy!* and reruns of *Touched by an Angel* at high volumes. The DWI prevented her from driving on her own, so she was having to rely on my questionable stick-shift skills to get her around town in her old Chevy, her wheelchair folded and stashed in the trunk. If the Chevy wasn't available—today, for instance, Theo had taken it to class—we had to rely on the kindness of those blessed with vehicles. And for myself, I had to rely on the old Schwinn.

Now, I slowed my bike in front of a pink house with a porch lined with wind chimes. I could have sworn I'd passed this house fifteen minutes ago. I thought I was getting closer to the river, but I was starting to suspect I was lost. I glanced back at my makeup case, which I'd strapped with bungee cords on the rack over the back wheel.

The chimes hanging from the pink house tinkled in the breeze. The street was quiet. According to my GPS, I was still headed in the right direction. I kicked back up onto the pedals and pushed forward, feeling the wind across my skin, my hair.

Two weeks ago, around the time Mom finally had her surgery, I had given my notice at work. Coasting on the proceeds from the sale, I had entered a career buffer zone. What was on the other side of that buffer, I did not yet know. All I knew was that I didn't miss my job, didn't find myself wishing I could go back. I had applied to the multimedia special-effects makeup program in Portland, and I'd made it past the first round of applicants. Now, I needed to send them a diverse portfolio of characters and creatures. Problem was, I didn't have a diverse portfolio—all I had were Shakespearean ghosts. Today I was trying to fix that.

Suddenly, the street curved, sloping down, and there were the banks of the Mississippi. I grinned and whooped, attempting the no-hands trick for a shaky moment before riding the hill down toward the muddy river. I knew where to go from here.

When Levi had confessed his feelings at the hospital, I'd been looking for stability. For control. This new version of the past—and Levi in the middle of it, his heart on his sleeve—had scared me. I'd tried to tell him as much in a text. Levi being Levi had insisted we should talk. He was right. I needed clarity on his closed door, I needed assurance that he really knew himself as well as he thought he did. And I needed someone willing to be a monster.

Outside his apartment building, I locked my bike on a rack and rang the buzzer, my heart racing in my chest.

No answer on the buzzer.

Again I waited, wondering if perhaps he wasn't home, but the Honda was parked down the street. Maybe he had looked out his window, seen me there, and decided to ignore the doorbell.

"You're early."

I turned back to the street. Levi stood in cutoff jeans and nothing else, his eyes widening in surprise. In his hand was a plastic baggie, and at his feet was Harpo, finishing his business.

"Well, it seems we have a lot to talk about." Reaching behind me to pat the makeup case, I said, "And a lot to do."

"Right." Harpo jogged in circles around his shins, unleashed and happy. "Are you sure about this, Robin? That you want me to be your model . . . person?"

His question had two meanings. Underneath, it seemed he was wondering if I were sure I wanted to see him at all. If I were sure I wanted to face what he'd said. When I loved people, I did things for them. When Levi loved people, he turned them inside out.

"Theo wasn't available," I answered, which was as much of a confirmation as I could manage right now.

His eyes traveled to my clothes, Gabe's old purple afterprom T-shirt and a pair of bike shorts I'd scrounged at the church rummage sale. "You look *sporty*," he said.

Harpo ran over to greet me, tongue lolling and tail wagging. "I biked here."

"Your old Schwinn," he said, a smile flashing on his face as he scooped an unpleasant pile. "You want water? You want to go inside?"

I was still feeling the endorphins of the ride. It wasn't normal between us, but at least the panicked nausea wasn't returning, at least the flutter in my chest was not the urge to run away. "Yeah, sure."

Levi looked at the baggie in his hand and squinted back at me. "This is not how I pictured this."

I grinned. "Me neither."

"Mission accomplished," Levi was saying, patting sweat off his face with a kitchen towel. Before we could make our way inside, we'd had a brief interlude in which Harpo had jetted down the street in pursuit of a squirrel. We'd had to corner the dog in a neighbor's peony bush and herd him home house by house. I wiped my own sweat with the bottom of my T-shirt.

"Kinda reminds me . . ." Levi called from the kitchen. "Remember when we had to get Gabe away from those Amway salespeople at the fair? We had to infiltrate the conversation without making him suspicious. Draw him away with the promise of more beer. It was like a spy movie."

"You're comparing Gabe to your dog going after a squirrel?" I called back from the living room, where Levi had set up a chair and mirror.

"If the shoe fits," Levi said. "I'm just saying. We make a good team. Robin's got the strategy, Levi's got the brute strength and the balls to execute."

I snorted as I began to pull out my compartments, making sure nothing had slid out on the ride over. "You've got something," I called back. "I don't know if it's balls or just a lack of gray matter in the brain."

"Yeah." I heard him clear his throat. "Something's off."

I looked up at Levi through the opening between the rooms, where he looked back at me. I knew what that catch in his throat meant. I sighed. "Do you want to apologize again so you don't have to spend all afternoon beating yourself up?"

"An apology in person means more." He came in from the other room, face clean, towel around his neck.

I pointed at the chair, indicating for him to sit. "Fifteen texts in a row has some power."

"Well, I'm sorry again," he said beside me. "Robin, look at me."

I did. His eyes on mine seemed to spill something inside me. Something warm and refillable, so I'd never have to worry about it running out. "Thank you for your apology," I pushed out.

"You're welcome. You don't have to forgive me."

"I'm not sure that I do forgive you." As Levi settled in the chair, I looked for foundation. Something that would protect his face from all the green stuff I was about to apply but not interfere with the color. "I'm not sure there's anything to forgive, except maybe saying all that in front of my mom."

"I know." Levi shook his head in regret.

"Stop moving your head," I told him, resuming my coverage of his cheek.

He continued speaking in a subdued way, trying to keep still. "It was like all of a sudden my ancient lizard brain took over. Like, oh shit, these feelings are actually real enough that someone else noticed." He began to take on a scratchy, Kermit-like voice. "*Robin's single. Do a mating dance. Show her your colorful spiky things.*"

I found myself smiling. "God, you're weird. Channel that lizard energy into Swamp Thing."

Levi's face lit up. "Oh, is that what you're doing? You're pulling out the ol' Swamp Thing?"

"Hey, it got you third place."

"It got *you* third place."

"True." I put my finger under his chin. He lifted it.

"I do appreciate having you . . ." I flushed a bit as I leaned back, gesturing toward his bare torso. "As a canvas."

"It's the least I could do."

I leaned back in, this time with the first layer of green. "I wonder if Gabe could ever picture us doing this."

"I think he could. He wrote me a letter, too, remember?" At that, Levi lifted his hip and pulled out his phone. "Told me to go look after you. Make sure you weren't going to be a shut-in forever."

"Ha," I said. At the memory of my own letter, my heart beat with the same bittersweet surge I'd gotten when Gabe's name in my inbox blew up my life. My solo, sedentary life.

"I went back and read it, and what he said . . ." Levi paused for a moment, considering. "First of all, when I told you back at the garage sale I wanted more for you? That had nothing to do with my feelings."

"I think I understand."

"You think, or you do? Because you're my friend first." Levi spoke with gravity, as if he'd been holding this for too long. "And that's why I never, *never* said anything about how I felt. To Gabe, or to anyone. Because I respected both of you. I loved your relationship."

I smiled at his grave sincerity, which was almost undercut by the green face paint I'd begun to streak on his face. "No, I know. I thought about it, too. I don't think you were trying to make a move this whole time or anything. I never really did. I was just scared."

It had hit me in the middle of the night. Everything I'd done in the past few weeks—confronting my family, learning to let go and focus on myself, applying to the program in Portland, coming to terms with the fact that Jake wasn't my future, coming to terms with the fact that my future wasn't set at all—none of it could have happened without Levi, his insistence on honesty. His own, and mine. His outpouring of feelings didn't always come at the right time and wasn't always to his advantage, but it allowed him to embrace every moment so fully, to drop into other people's feelings with full abandon—and his own. I had something to learn from that, I now knew.

Levi pointed to his screen. "Can I read some of it to you?"

Gabe's letter, he meant. I crossed my arms, feeling nervous for some reason. "Shouldn't that stay between you and him?"

"I think you're going to want to hear it."

I did, but I didn't. "If it was so important, why didn't he just write it to me himself?"

"I don't know."

I readied myself to refuse again, but I was stopped by a sudden wave of longing, of curiosity. I'd been conjuring Gabe's voice, his presence, throughout this entire journey he'd sent me on a year ago. But here he was in his own words, swooping through the air of this old apartment like the smell of Nag Champa incense, landing like a chin on my shoulder, ready to push me forward again.

"Go on, then."

Levi glanced at the screen of his phone, and then at me. "Are you sure?"

"Go."

"First two paragraphs are about our friendship," Levi began. "Then he goes, *All the clichés about dying are true. Starting to think about regrets. Especially regarding our resident warrior wife/worrier wife Robbie . . .*"

I smiled to myself. Warrior wife. Worrier wife.

"*I wanted so much for us and so much for our town and everything I wanted was* out there, *just ready to be pwned . . .*" Levi paused. "That's a gaming term," he explained.

"I know," I said, motioning for him to continue.

He kept reading. "*. . . so I went after it every day, not really thinking about anything but how to get what I wanted. But I know Robbie had wants, too.*"

Sometimes he would stare at me while I watched TV. *What are you thinking about?* I never took the question seriously because I hadn't dared to. When someone like Gabe looked at you, it was hard to see beyond him.

"*She was as good at making everyone else's wants her wants, like, almost too good . . .*"

Sometimes he'd kidnap me when I was working weekend shifts at the restaurant. I'd hate it at first, demand to go back, but then we'd get pizza from Casey's and go sit on our car above Brokenridge Lake, listening to the birds call to each other at sunset.

"*When I'm gone she's going to have more room to want things for herself. I hate not being there to see what they are.*"

I hated it, too. Him not here. I would have traded anything of mine for one more hour, one more stubbly kiss on the cheek. What could I give? My TV. My Sudoku books. My car, now my bike. Mostly objects. But space. Time. Space that wasn't soaked in memory, the minutiae of our lives. Time that wasn't swallowed by grief. By worrying about Mom, by helping Theo. No, I suppose I'd never had that kind of time. Not while Gabe was here, and not after. But I hadn't wanted it. I hadn't even thought to want it. I hadn't even known it existed.

"*I wish I could follow her dreams like she followed mine*," Levi finished.

The makeup. That was the first thing I'd gone for on my own, aside from Jake. I briefly wondered what it would be like if Gabe had gotten the chance to follow through on this letter, to come along to Portland on this dream of mine. I could see him trying to do our laundry, trying to pack me lunches, getting distracted by some home-brewing project or a local campaign for more crosswalks.

I looked back at Levi, smiling at the thought. Another kind of grief climbed slowly through me, but this one did not have the burning urgency of fear of being without him, of uncertainty. "I'm a glue player."

Levi seemed to recognize the term but still looked confused.

I laughed to myself. "It's a soccer thing, apparently."

"It's a basketball thing, too. Steph Curry couldn't be Steph Curry without Andre Iguodala."

"Right, so it's like what you said. My thing has been making everyone else's lives easier, but maybe the program in Portland could be my own thing. I just wish I could have figured it out sooner."

"No shit. Hell, you could be working for A24 by now."

I laughed. "Can you forward your letter to me? If you don't mind. I like hearing his voice, sometimes."

"Me, too. Sent."

I picked my sponge back up and began to finish greening the other side of Levi's face. "I used to pull up my Bubbl profile for a laugh. All those little tidbits *I thought* he wrote."

Levi cringed. "Glad I could make you laugh."

I smiled at him. "You did." I thought of that first day I'd read the profile with Theo at the kitchen island, how each one had sent a shiver down my spine. "I was almost not going to go through with it, the whole dating thing. Until I read those."

"Wow."

"Yeah."

We were quiet as I readied him for the faux moss. If I were working in movies, I'd have real prosthetics—maybe even some I'd designed myself—but today liquid latex and cornflakes would have to do. As I applied dots of glue, I had an urge to reactivate Bubbl right then, to look back at the photograph Levi had chosen, the profile picture in which I was riding the very Schwinn I had ridden to find him today. I wanted to read what he'd written for the prompts that had given me such joy and confidence over the past year, to make sense of it in this new context. But I didn't have to bring up the stupid dating profile to feel that way, did I?

He was right here. Green and still and waiting.

"Can I ask you something?" I placed the first flake on his forehead.

"Shoot."

Another line of texture, along his jaw. I could smell the peppery shampoo in his hair. "If you had a thing for me all those years . . ."

"Yeah," he said, watching my hands as they moved across his chin.

I took a deep breath, preparing to conjure courage for what I was about to say, but I found I didn't need it. I was getting good at being honest. "Is there an expiration date?"

He looked up at me, his eyes flashing. "Are you—are you serious?"

Among all the things I'd let go recently—Jake, my job, my obsessive tendencies—I felt the absence of Levi the most. His energy, all the goofy, intense fixations I used to shy away from. "I've missed you."

"I guess that depends on what you want." I didn't know if his muted tone was a result of shock, or resistance, or if he was merely staying still to keep my work intact.

"What I want." I wasn't scared of this question anymore, but I didn't have a better answer. I applied more glue to his cheek. "I feel like a feral creature right now," I told him.

"No, I'm the creature," he said with a small smile. "You're finding yourself."

I straightened with my handful of cornflakes, words coming fast. "Yes, and whatever I'm feeling for you is mixed with so many other things. And I don't know what I'm going to do next. Or where I'm going to be. So if you don't want to get tangled up, I understand." I resumed my row of cornflakes. "But if you wanted to come around sometimes, I would like that."

We blinked at each other for a moment.

"Okay," he said. "I will."

Perhaps this offer wasn't appealing enough. Levi didn't strike me as a measured, patient person, but it was what I had. "Good," I said, still unsure of how he was receiving what I'd laid out or what his answer meant. But it was the best way I knew to love him—to fall in love with him—without losing myself.

I stopped what I was doing and took his hand from his lap, shaking it. "So we agree. The door is open."

He looked down at our hands, intertwined. "It is?"

I nodded as whatever had spilled earlier—something strong and hot and sweet—coursed through me. The look in his eyes was enough to know that he, too, was unsure of where we'd end up. But he wasn't unsure about me.

"Can I ask you a question?" He pulled me closer.

I found that though my heart was pounding, the rest of me was content, calm. "Shoot."

"Do you mind getting messy?"

"No," I said. I put my hands on his shoulders and lowered my face to his.

I'll know it's time to delete Bubbl when . . .
I'll just know.

I wandered the produce section of the Apple Market, feeling for the ripest tomatoes. We had sausage from the Sandersens' farm down the road at home. I didn't have four types of cheese, but three types would do. I grabbed basil from the rack. I was making a lasagna.

"Is that you, Mrs. Mayor?"

I turned. It was the same elderly woman from Mom's birthday, Gabe's construction-money donor. I decided to correct her this time, though I realized, to be fair, I didn't remember her name, either. "You can call me Robin," I said.

"I heard you were leaving us," the woman said, a tone of warning in her voice.

How did she hear? I suppose Mom could have spilled the beans to any number of Brokenridge gossips. Or the woman's information could simply be out of date, referring to my former plans to move to Pole City. It wasn't the first time someone had asked about my business, and it wouldn't be the last. But I found I didn't mind anymore. In fact, since I had been privy to so many revelations lately—and since I knew I was leaving, anyway—I had become somewhat of an oversharer. I sighed and put on a smile.

"Yeah," I told her. "My ex-boyfriend broke up with me because he thought I was having an emotional affair with my dead husband's best friend, and I had to move back into my mom's house, so."

"Oh, my." The woman clearly wasn't prepared for this answer.

"I was helping run the Green River for years," I went on. "But instead, I've decided to abandon the business to my college-dropout brother and my recovering-alcoholic mother—you remember Margie Lindstrom—and move hundreds of miles away to pursue a career in special-effects makeup."

Mom and Theo had sidled up during my little monologue, Mom's arms full of two-liter bottles of ginger ale, her new drink of choice.

"And we're very proud of her," Mom said, speaking too loudly, as she often did whenever she spoke to anyone of a certain age. "Aren't we, T?"

Theo removed a Tootsie Pop from his mouth and looked up from his phone. "Sure."

"Now, if you'll excuse us . . ." I started.

"You know what I say?" the elderly woman said, looking at the three of us, clutching the loaf of bread she was holding to her chest.

"What?" Theo said, looking stone-faced.

The woman's powder-blue eyes met mine. "I say, good for you, Robin."

"Really?" Now it was my turn to be taken aback. "Thank you."

"You got the rug pulled out from under you, but that doesn't mean you need to stay where you fall, huh?" She put a hand on my arm and winked. "You deserve a new life."

And she took her loaf of bread and carried on with her shopping.

I turned to Mom and Theo. "What is that woman's name? I can't remember . . ."

"I do see her around sometimes, but I couldn't say," Mom said, shaking her head, piling her bottles of soda into my cart.

The one person in Brokenridge Mom didn't know.

"Come to think of it, I think she's a widow like you and me, Robbie." I smiled as I watched her survey the lemons. "I think she mostly keeps her own company."

• • •

The next morning, we sat outside, the three of us, Theo with his iced coffee, me with my *Far Side* mug, Mom with her menthol and ginger ale. I was having second thoughts. More like third or fourth thoughts.

"Yard looks pretty," Mom said. I had let the native grasses creep up closer, and the stems were sprouting late blooms, some of them turning yellow, gold, rust red. "I like the natural look."

"Thanks," I said.

Maybe if I stuck around, Levi and I would have a real shot. We were still just friends, but we could keep falling for each other. Maybe if I stuck around, I could keep volunteering with the theater, though it'd be hard to get weekends away while I was running the restaurant, at least at first. Maybe Mom and I could figure out a way to work together, get the Green River back to its former glory. The whole county would come by for their special occasions, like they used to. We'd rub elbows at the chamber of commerce with the Sheas and the Rundles and the Kellehers and the Hassans. I could drive Mom to AA every day.

"Say the word," I said as I looked over at Mom, "and I'll stay."

"You're not staying," Theo droned, sipping his iced coffee.

I turned to Mom. "Are you sure you can do this on your own?"

"She won't be on her own," Theo said, looking up from his phone.

"I have Theo, I have my sponsor," Mom said. "And you being here is not gonna prevent me from drinking, you know that, right? I'm an alcoholic, sweets. Only I can stop myself." Pride and shame tussled in her voice. "Shoot, I'd find a way to drink whether you were on my tail or not." She burst out in her hacking laugh. "Did it under all your noses for years."

My breath caught in my throat. I liked our shared honesty, but I was still getting used to speaking candidly about her disease. The one topic about which I didn't want to discuss logistics. "You were not that sneaky," I finally said.

"Oh, I'm just yanking your chain," she said, blowing out smoke. "I would ask why you didn't stop me earlier, but I think I know."

"Because you're my mom," I said, exasperated. "I can't tell my mom what to do. Believe me, I tried."

The three of us chuckled. I reached for her hand.

In an hour, I would be on the road to the Amtrak station. There was a train all the way from Chicago to Seattle—the Empire Builder, it was called—and I'd be picking it up in Saint Paul. I had a few weeks to explore the area before my program started. Manuel was helping scour the local listings in Portland. A place with a running path nearby was nonnegotiable. Finally, we'd joked, I'd be able to run through the Pacific Northwest for real.

"If you have any problems calculating how much to order, you call me," I told Theo.

Theo leaned his head back in his chair. "The system app does that for me. You don't need to be a frickin' accounting genius to work an app."

"But we have a unique setup because—"

"I know, know. You told me."

"And you have my—"

"Shush. Yes, I have your PowerPoints."

And thankfully, he had plenty of time to review the Green River Manager Training document I'd made for him. He had decided he was going to take a year off college, letting go of his apartment, hopping between Jay's house and Mom's house—like he already did much of the time, anyway. He had become disenchanted with forensics, it turned out, and he was really only sticking with it because he had promised me he would. Now, he knew, he needed work experience of some kind. Of any kind. As I suspected, he was excited about creating the Green River's social-media presence, with Mom as the star. I told him I hoped he would find something he loved, and he assured me he would. We agreed: sometimes it just takes time.

A horn sounded from out front. I'd left my phone inside, I realized.

"All right, Robbie," Mom said, putting out her cigarette. "Your ride's here."

We all stood and made our way through the house. Near the front door, I pressed my fingers to my lips and brushed a photo from some distant Christmas when my dad was still alive. "Bye, Dad."

"She'll be back, Bart," Mom said beside me, resting her head on my shoulder.

"Hopefully not too soon," Theo said, picking up one of my suitcases.

I gave him a little shove as we dragged my luggage out the door.

"I mean it, Robbie." He yanked the suitcase forward. "Don't worry about us, okay? You gotta give that place a real chance."

"Look at you, giving little brotherly advice." I watched him haul my case down the steps. "I am going to worry about you, but maybe not as much as I used to."

"Come here, you angels." Mom pulled us both into her arms.

Soon, Theo extracted himself and went outside with my bags, and it was just me and Mom.

"Quit smoking, will you?" I whispered into her ear.

"Ha!" She let go and gave me a once-over, her gaze as sharp and bright as I'd ever seen it. "*One day at a time.*"

Levi closed the trunk, grinning over at me as I approached the Honda. "You ready?"

"No," I replied. I opened the passenger door. "But I will be."

The sun was setting over the prairie just near the border of North Dakota and Montana. I'd managed to snag a seat in the viewing car, with giant windows on all sides, so I could watch the landscape roll out in front of me. We'd be going through Glacier National Park and later along the Columbia River Gorge, where the wildflowers would soon come back, covering the fire-charred mountains. Watching the countryside from the train car made me feel simultaneously protected and at full alert, like if I didn't hold my breath marveling at its beauty I would miss something extraordinary. In Brokenridge, I could never miss anything. I knew the square mileage like the couch cushions knew the indent of my body. I could see everything coming from acres away. Even the worst thing that could possibly happen—the light fading from Gabe's eyes—had rolled toward me slowly from a distance, like a storm cloud over the beet fields.

When you love someone, you let them go. Right? That's what they say. But what if your love for everyone had bled through your entire life? How do you let go of life? You die. Maybe literally, in some cases, but not in mine. It was an old version of me who died along with my husband. I mourned her as much as I mourned him. She haunted me. Still does. Ask Pam Chomsky.

Levi and I talked on the phone during the ride, but sometimes we didn't. Sometimes I listened to the playlists he'd made, trying to figure out which of the Hidden Beaches' songs he'd written for me: he knew how much I loved puzzles, so I'd have to listen to the lyrics and guess, he'd told me. He would come through Portland on tour someday. Maybe I'd see him soon, or maybe I wouldn't, but I had a feeling I would. We were on the verge of growing something new, after all. But it wasn't the kind of love that demanded a plan, at least not right away. It had deep roots, a history, and with the memory of Gabe between us, history was never far from mind. Now that I was building my own life, I didn't have to wonder what he was thinking, or what he wanted for us, or what anyone wanted from me.

I leaned my head against the train window and felt the last of the sun. I knew what I wanted, and that was enough.

Acknowledgments

Thank you to Joelle Hobeika, my editor and advocate at Alloy for over a decade, who can read my mind as well as she reads everything. Thank you to Lucia Macro at HarperCollins, for loving and believing in this character and her world as much as I did; to Asanté Simons, for helping usher this book to the finish line; and to the entire William Morrow and HarperCollins team. Thanks also to Josh Bank and Sara Shandler, also at Alloy, who teach me how to better tell a story every time I work with them.

A few communities gifted me the time to write, the space to think, and invaluable, inspirational company: the Loghaven Artist Residency in Knoxville, Tennessee; the residency at the Kimmel Harding Nelson Center for the Arts in Nebraska City, Nebraska; and the Creative Writing MFA program at the University of Mississippi. To my UM mentors, colleagues, and fellow writers, including but not limited to Melissa Ginsburg, Kiese Laymon, Mary Hayes, Matt Bondurant, Tommy Franklin, Garth Greenwell, Amy Lam, Tyriek White, Mary Berman, Morgan McComb, and Sarah Heying: This is far from the book I had in mind, but it's the book that came out, and my writing is all the better from the time we spent together. Thank you. And to my beloved MFBlaze writing group, Ross, Elsa, and Matt: see you next month.

A grateful nod to the works of Joan Didion, Carole Radziwill, Becky Aikman, and Nora McInerny, and to the many perspectives on the *Widow's Voice* blog from Soaring Spirits International. Through researching I have learned there is no one way to grieve a spouse. This book owes everything to those who have shared their stories of widowhood, whether it resembles their experiences or not.

Enormous gratitude to Kay Holt, from whom I was honored to hear an account of new life after death full of care, grace, and honesty. Kay, this book would not exist in this form without you, and I hope Robin's story makes you proud. Thank you, too, to Aunt Deb and Uncle Bud, for connecting us and for your support of my writing through the years. Aunt Barb and Uncle Cameron, thank you for the use of Lindstrom as a namesake. The beauty I imagined on Robin's drives was always inspired by the Minnesota farmland that surrounds your home.

To Sally, Ian, Elise, Helene, Mandy, Emma, and everyone in my chosen family: thank you for cheering me on and reminding me the world exists outside of Microsoft Word. Wyatt, my big bro: you're a lyrics genius. Thank you for writing Levi's songs, for taking me ice fishing, and for always being my role model in how to love the land. Dylan, my little bro: thank you for your legal consultation regarding DWIs, for always being willing to talk in silly voices with me, and for being proud, even when I take a big risk like quitting a steady job to write.

Mom and Dad, I remember sitting in your backyard two years ago, telling you that unfortunately this is the only thing I can do with my life. Thank you for loving me as I stumbled around looking for this truth for so many years, and thank you for hearing me now.

Finally, Dane, my love, my new family. You held my hand on a bench in Lawrence and told me it was okay to leap. I'm so happy I landed next to you.